SHADOWS OF ANTIOCH

THE CRUSADERS CHRONICLES: BOOK 3

BRYAN R SAYE

Dedicated to my wife,
Jessica,
who always pushed me
farther than I thought I could go.

CONTENTS

Siege of Antioch

Labels on map:

Bohemond of Taranto

To the Iron Bridge

Malregard

N

Raymond of Toulouse

Mt. Staurin

St. Paul Gate

Sea Piper Killises?

Godfrey of Bouillon

Iron Gate

Dog Gate

The Citadel

Gate of the Duke

Silphus Peak (500 mt.)

Antioch

Mt. Silphus

Bridge of Boats

To Alexandretta

Orontes

Bridge Gate

St. George Gate

La Mahomerie

River

Tower of Tancred

To S. Simeon

PROLOGUE

PROLOGUE

AD 1115
Jerusalem

Roland woke before the sun, stretching and groaning as he sat up on the cloak he'd spread out over the low grass the night before. A crescent thumbnail of a moon hung in a cloudless predawn sky, though there was the faintest whisper of orange in the east. Dim shadows from a nearby copse of trees, barely darker than the surrounding gray, lay over the ashy remnants of last night's fire, their soft edges shivering in the light breeze.

Beside the pile of ash lay a single sack stuffed with nearly everything he owned: enough stale bread for a meager breakfast, a small knife as long as his index finger and as dull as his fingernail, a linen cap in desperate need of patching, a satchel with a handful of random bronze coins he may or may not be able to spend, and—wrapped in a worn and fraying swath of cloth—a gold-chained necklace with a single teardrop garnet as its pendant.

Propped beside the sack rested the round shield he'd made the day prior—the quartered white and beige fabric indistinguishable in the dim light. He couldn't help but smile, tired and run-down as he was. He was essentially a squire now, even if Sir Daniel had never officially said it, and he only hoped that his mother and father smiled down on him. Never mind that he didn't have a sword—or axe or dagger or anything more than the small knife; he *felt* like a squire.

It didn't take long to eat the bread and drain the sip of water remaining in his waterskin. He dusted off his cloak and flung it over his shoulders, then secured it with a short black pin and hefted his sack. The shield came next, the leather strap letting it hang from his shoulder, and he turned to give one more look at the patch of woods where he'd slept. After kicking away the ash from the fire, it was as if he'd never been there.

Roland reached the Zion Gate as the sun rose from its own slumber, casting a wave of golden light upon Jerusalem's high walls. He decided to wave to the two guards, Lawrence and Etienne, the same two guards he'd seen nearly every morning for the last several years. They furrowed their brows in confusion and didn't bother to wave back.

He didn't care.

Before going to Sir Daniel's home at the back of Saint James Cathedral, Roland took a quick detour to one of Jerusalem's many blacksmiths. There, Elbert greeted him with a warm smile as he filled his forge with coal and prepared for the day.

"Off to see your friend again, are you?" Elbert asked, nodding to the shield on Roland's back.

Roland absently touched one of the many hammers hanging from the wall of the smithy. "I am," he said. "Though I don't believe I should call him 'friend.'"

"Not many do," he said, dumping another spadeful of coal into the forge.

"Why is that?" Roland asked. "They speak so highly of him, and yet he lives alone. Why doesn't he have a squire already?"

Elbert shrugged. "Never wanted one."

"Why?"

"What makes you think I know?"

"It's odd. He seems a good enough man to me."

"I'm sure he is." The blacksmith threw some kindling atop the pile of coal. "But they don't call him 'tou Pouthená' for nothing."

"From nowhere," Roland said, translating the Greek. He frowned in confusion. "But he's from somewhere. He's from Constantinople. He told me."

"Maybe it's 'cause he came from nothing," Elbert suggested. "You know, the offer still stands. Your old man would've been pleased to see you as a smith's apprentice."

Roland frowned. "I don't want to be a smith's apprentice," he said. "I want…I don't know…I want to make a difference."

Elbert scoffed and lifted yesterday's unfinished sword. "And what do you think it is *I* do? You think these are for decoration?"

"That's not what I meant."

Elbert dropped the sword and grabbed an already lit torch hanging from a nearby mount. "I know, son," he said, touching the fire to the kindling. It went up in a flash of orange and red. "I know what it is you want. I'd just hate to see you in the ground because of it. Off you go. I'm sure your 'friend' is waiting."

Roland turned to leave, then stopped. He met Elbert's gaze, asking the next question with his eyes. His old friend smiled.

"I've got some bread in the back," he said. "And maybe a knob of cheese. Don't take all of it," he added as Roland dashed to the back of the smithy.

"Thank you," he said, stuffing his sack with food as he headed out onto the streets of Jerusalem.

Soon he stood in the shadow of Saint James Cathedral and stared over the low fence behind it. Sir Daniel's home was modest, especially for a knight, and Roland began to wonder why he hadn't purchased an estate like so many other knights and lords did.

The door creaked open, and Sir Daniel stepped outside. He met Roland's gaze, said nothing, then turned around and went back in. Roland rounded the fence and waited, staring absently at the closed door. He was about to knock when it scraped open, and Sir Daniel stepped outside with a bolt of linen under an arm.

"What am I making today?" Roland asked.

Sir Daniel set the linens down beside his own extinguished firepit and tossed Roland a small satchel. "A gambeson," he said. "Meager armor, but better than that shirt you're wearing."

Roland peered into the satchel and saw several needles and spools of thread. "Armor made from linen?"

"Aye," he said. "Dozen layers or so. Make it nice and thick."

"That's it? Linen?"

"Aye," he said again, picking up an armful of small logs for the fire. "Unless you've got some money for mail I wasn't aware of."

"Don't you?" Roland asked.

Sir Daniel dropped the logs into the firepit. "Sure, I do. That's why *I've* got mail."

Roland glanced at the roll of fabric. "And linen will protect me?"

"Like I said, better than that shirt you're wearing. Trick's not to get hit. Now build me a fire," he added, then disappeared back inside.

Roland had the fire going by the time Sir Daniel returned with a cast-iron tripod and pot.

"More glue?" Roland asked.

"*Güvec*," he muttered, setting up the tripod and hanging the pot.

Roland debated asking what a güvec was and decided against it, instead sitting beside the knight and letting a silence fall over them. Roland recalled Sir Daniel's final words the day before—*come back tomorrow, and I'll tell you how she dies*—and decided it best not to be the one to break the quiet. He took the needle from the satchel, turned it over in his hands, realized he didn't know what to do with it, then put it back.

"We traveled southeast from Dorylaeum," Sir Daniel suddenly said, and Roland knew he was talking about the next leg of the crusade. "We took the towns of Iconium and Heraclea. They put up only a token resistance. I suppose word of our victory at Dorylaeum put a bit of fear into them. After those two cities, Tancred, along with Godfrey's brother Baldwin, took a shorter path through Cilicia, while the rest of us trekked through the mountains. Weary, dry, miserable march that was. Lost a good deal of horses and some people to hunger, but somehow we came through. Amina, Novella, and me." A grin as he glanced back at his paddock. "And *Ankída*. Scrawny as that horse is, she's a sturdy mare. Outlasted many a better beast and still going strong. Gevorg and the others from the Armenian village stayed at Iconium. They saw no reason to cross the mountains, had no desire to reach Jerusalem."

"And Hendry?"

"Aye, Hendry made it through. He and his mount, Tencendur. The princes had a council at Baghras sometime in October. Antioch stood between us and Jerusalem, and we had a choice: skip the massive city and risk leaving an army at our back, or besiege it and risk our crusade stalling out in front of its walls. Only real option was the second, and I was sent with another two thousand men to take the Iron Bridge leading into Antioch to make way for the army."

ACT I

1

AD 1097
November
Twelve Miles North of Antioch

W e reached the Iron Bridge from the north, arriving at noon, with a cool easterly wind reminding us that winter rapidly approached, despite the heat of the midday sun shining down from a clear sky. I was surprised to find the bridge made of massive stone bricks rather than iron as its name implied, though the two high towers protecting it on either side of the Orontes River were black as a smith's anvil. Whether they were iron or not, I can't say. It seemed unlikely. Each tower arched over its end of the bridge like a city gate, though nothing looked to be barring our passage except a few hundred Saracens standing at the foot of the bridge near the first tower.

We stopped perhaps three hundred yards from them. Even this didn't quite feel safe. I'd seen a Saracen kill a man from a greater distance. Of course, the man had worn no armor while we were clad in mail from head to toe, carried red-cross-emblazoned kite shields, and wore conical or kettle-shaped helmets specifically built to deflect falling arrows. We'd learned many lessons since setting out from Constantinople six months ago.

There were two thousand of us, arranged into four shield walls, and I stood in the front row of the vanguard, spear in hand and shield resting against my thigh, though I could swing it into place should even the glint of an arrow appear in the distance. We were a small army, to be sure, at least when compared to the forty thousand who had survived the trip through the mountains and rested now back at Baghras.

Not all of those forty thousand were soldiers. Amina and Novella were among the civilians, and they remained safely in the care of Father Luke, along with his new aid, Piccolo, and Migliorozzo, his ostiary. It had been four months since the battle of Dorylaeum, and most of that time we'd spent on the move, trudging through craggy desert mountains and dry wasteland. The occasional encounter with pockets of Saracen resistance kept us sharp, and I was glad that my girls had the opportunity to rest and recover after so arduous a journey.

My girls. Father Luke married Amina and me shortly after Dorylaeum, and Novella had become something of a daughter to us. It was a new feeling, being the protector of a small family, one that brought a pang of remorse and shame. I'd cared for William, my brother, yet I'd also held him as he bled out in my arms. He died because of me, because of my pride and ambition, and that guilt now drove me to trek through foreign countries and enemy lands—it compelled me to join the very vanguard I stood in—all to reach Jerusalem. I could almost hear Bohemond's words as he'd carved the cross into my cheek.

"You shall carry it to Jerusalem, kneel before Christ's empty tomb within the Church of the Holy Sepulcher. Then, and only then, will your sins be forgiven."

I tried to push the thoughts of William from my mind. I

had a family now, a daughter who admired me and a wife who loved me. My gaze drifted to Amina's length of blue cloth wrapped around my arm, the same blue cloth I'd worn in every fight since Dorylaeum, and I felt a smile come unbidden to my face. It was a token, a promise that I would return from battle.

"What're ye smiling for?"

I glanced at Hendry, my knight and mentor, the closest thing I'd ever had to a father. His mane of bushy red hair bunched comically under his helmet. It looked like someone had tried to saddle a sheep and the wool had refused to cooperate. It only made my grin wider.

He shook his head at my smiling face. "Bloody fool," he muttered. "Smiling 'fore a battle. Have I taught ye nothing?"

"Don't die?"

"Ye had to learn that one from me?"

I thought for another moment. "I can fight from horseback now."

"Haw!" His hard demeanor broke, his smile wide as he looked at me. "Can ye, now? That's news to me."

"I can!" I tilted my spear forward, couching it under my arm like he'd shown me. The tip wavered a few feet out in front of me, but I curled my hand underneath and used my forearm and elbow to anchor it to my ribs. The wavering stopped, and I smirked. "See? You hold it like this," I said, nodding to the now-steady tip, "and stick that end in the other guy." I righted the spear. "Easy."

"A lance is a wee bit bigger than a spear, lad."

"It's the same thing."

"Oh, it is? One day ye'll find out." He glanced at the small throwing axe stuffed into my belt. "Why're ye carrying that again?"

"You won't let me throw this," I said, patting Skull Splitter. The larger axe—a gift from Hendry—hung from a carriage on my belt. It had earned its name from its first victim, a Saracen spy named Fahri who'd essentially fallen into the blade. I'd done little besides hold it.

"Only an idiot throws his weapon."

"Even though I saved your life throwing it?"

He scoffed, but it was obvious he suppressed a smile. "Aye, even an idiot can get lucky."

"Seems *you* were the lucky one," I said, then scooped the throwing axe out and turned it over in my hand. It was little more than a thin axe-head with a six-inch hilt, all forged from the same piece of steel. It was light, with a point on the back end of the blade and another at the top. The hilt was wrapped in twine for a better grip. I'd made it myself—with the help of a smith who traveled among us and the use of Asbat's tools, God rest his soul. We'd since sold the tools, so any future smithing work would be bought. I slipped the throwing axe back into my belt. "Maybe I'll get to use it today."

"Mebbe," he agreed. "And mebbe ye'll remember which end is the sharp one."

I flexed my left hand, felt the still-healing wound on my palm. Testing the throwing axe hadn't gone well. "It was one time."

"Do ye ken how many times *I've* stabbed meself?"

"Is it none?"

"Yer a canny lad."

I sighed, looked again at the Iron Bridge, at the Saracens guarding it. "Should we try talking this time?"

Hendry belted a laugh. "I'm sure that'll work."

"It's worth a shot."

"Aye, and so is riding a snail into battle," he said, "and I've a guess how *that* would end."

I shrugged. "Maybe they don't want to fight."

"And I dinnae rightly care what they want. Now hush. Here comes the father."

SHADOWS OF ANTIOCH | 15

Father Caldwell paced in front of our shield wall, somehow unperturbed to be so close to Saracens without any armor. Like Father Luke—who was something of a spiritual mentor to me—he wore the black robes of a priest. *Un*like Father Luke, he also wore a six-inch gold crucifix studded with jewels suspended from his neck by a gold chain as thick as my thumb.

"Soldiers of Christ," he shouted, his voice carrying over us. "You go to slay the Saracen horde, the enemies of God. Nay," he shouted this last word and raised a finger straight up, as if he were pointing to the heavens. "They are enemies of decent men everywhere!"

I could almost hear Hendry roll his eyes. Neither of us were overly fond of Caldwell.

"Go and chase them from our land! Land that was ours before they set their filthy feet upon it. Return to Christendom what is Christendom's!"

Cheers came up around me, yet I very much shared Hendry's exasperation with the priest. It seemed, however, that we had little choice but to endure his speeches. Caldwell had become something of a favorite of Lord Tancred's in recent weeks, likely due to his constant praises and promises of successful battles that were "the Lord's will," as he was fond of claiming. The fact that we'd won most of our fights had merely proven his point.

He raised an aspergillum, a small mace-like rod with a perforated ball on the end filled with holy water. He waved it toward us, and droplets of water rained on our armor and stained the front of our shields.

"I bless you," he shouted, and I winced as a drop hit me in the eye. "I bless you for battle! I call forth victory upon you! No snare shall stop you as you slay the heathen hordes! End the enemies of mankind!"

He made his way down the front of the shield wall, and

Hendry leaned into me. "Mebbe he should wash us *after* the battle."

I snickered, though the laugh died in my throat as we saw movement on the bridge. The Saracens seemed tired of watching us and were moving into position to open fire. Likely, they didn't see the three shield walls lined up to our rear, but that didn't make me feel any safer standing in the front.

"Shields!"

The command came from somewhere down the front line, likely from Sir Jurian, one of Tancred's knights, who often led the vanguard. I hefted my shield from the ground, hooked my arm through the small leather loop on the back of it, and grasped the handle, bouncing it a few times to get it comfortable in my grip. I recalled the first time I'd held a shield—roughly made and much smaller than this one—how it had trembled in my hand, how absurdly heavy it had felt. After months of training and fighting, of desert marching and hard living, this kite shield felt as if it belonged in my grip, like it was an extension of my own arm.

"Spears!"

I lifted the butt of my spear from the ground and rested the shaft against the upper rim of my shield, the tip steady in front of me. More spears fell into place over my head from the second and third row, and everyone else raised their spears straight up, not threatening any enemy but creating a screen to deflect incoming arrows. We quickly became a mobile fortress bristling with steel-tipped death and guarded by hardened linden and oak.

"Forward!"

As one we moved, feet stomping together, mail rattling, spears dipping and rising with each step, everything in unison. A whistle in the distance, and the first hints of arrows rose into the clear sky. Having survived Dorylaeum and seen the mayhem that twenty thousand mounted Saracen archers can do, how every volley blotted out the sun and darkened the battlefield, this salvo of a few hundred arrows seemed like nothing but a wisp of black clouds.

"Shields up!"

We kept moving, but those of us in the front row hunkered behind our shields as we walked. The second row raised theirs, covering us and them together, and every row behind them followed suit, raising a roof of shields above us. A few moments later came the clattering of arrows as they cracked off the faces of our shields and ricocheted harmlessly away. Some found small gaps in our defense, pinging off helmets and thudding angrily into the ground. A few met with mail, scraping down tightly riveted steel rings and plunging into the dirt, stumbling the knights and squires they struck yet leaving no lasting wound. A small handful hit just right, piercing mail, shredding skin, obliterating organs, and crushing bone. So few found targets that individual wails of pain could be heard instead of the general cacophony common among such pitched battles.

Somehow, this was worse.

Volley after volley came, each doing little to slow us down even if together they thinned our numbers by the smallest margin. I peeked through the small gap between my shield and Hendry's and saw the Saracens backing up with each shot. Soon the packed dirt and gravel of the road gave way to the stone bricks of the bridge, and our iron-shod boots clanked with each step. We passed under the first tower, its black walls dotted with dozens of narrow windows, and I sensed what was about to come.

"Edges, turn! Turn!" Sir Jurian called.

The command came a moment too late as arrows shot from the narrow openings on each side to join the forward volleys and drop the men on our flanks. Stones thrown from the arch above us thudded angrily into our shields before rolling away. More stones fell into our path and jostled our formation, one cracking into the helmet of a crusader hard enough that he crumpled to the ground. I heard the clanking of shields falling together as those on the outer edge pivoted and protected our shield wall from the sides.

We passed halfway over the bridge, away from the first tower, and the rain of stones ceased. I knew another shield wall marched behind us. They would clear the few Saracens inside the tower and atop the arch. It would be a chaotic, tight-quarters skirmish, and I was suddenly glad to be in the vanguard.

The arrows from the main body of Saracens had ceased to arc up and rain down upon us and instead came in flat as we neared them. They hit my shield face with the force of a heavy kick, and our forward movement slowed as their arrows pummeled us. One skittered off the new mail on my legs—"chausses," they were called—and crunched under someone's boot behind me.

A brief lull, and I glanced through the gap in our shields and watched the nearest of the Saracens slip their bows away and draw curved scimitars and small, square shields. They'd halted underneath the second tower, and it seemed that despite our numbers, they were not yet willing to surrender the fastest road to Antioch without a fight. No doubt they'd heard of the cities we'd taken, of how Heraclea and Iconium had fallen, how Tancred and Baldwin had run wild through Cilicia. If they could hold us at this bridge—regardless of how slim their chances—they could potentially delay the upcoming siege of Antioch.

I was close enough now to see the whites of their eyes, which should have been wide with fear at the sight of a wall of armor and spears slowly marching their way. Instead, the Saracens gritted their teeth in courageous determination, steadied their weapons in their hands, and formed a tight line in front of their archers. Enemies they were—at least for today—but I'd always had a healthy respect for their bravery.

"Charge!"

I stayed in step with Hendry on my right and Elric on my left, and we lurched forward as one, running the final few steps and jerking our spears forward. Feeling resistance in my arm, I knew I'd hit something—either shield or Saracen. It mattered not for this initial thrust as I planted my feet, shoved again, and felt the man behind me push his shield into my back and add to my force. Wailing filled the air, no longer the isolated individual cries of lone crusaders but, instead, the rising chorus of pain that—even though I knew it was coming—pierced my ears and brought a quiver to my heart.

It never gets easier. Standing in the shield wall, taking a life, watching the man on the end of your spear realize he's breathing his last breaths as he uselessly writhes in pain and flails in panic caused by impending death. You push him off as you search for another target, your spear and those of the crusaders around you shuttling back and forth like the oars of some malevolent ship cutting its way through an ocean of blood and flesh. Step, thrust, step, thrust until soon you're stepping over still-squirming bodies, the men behind you hacking down with swords and axes and ending their suffering as you steadily plod forward.

This had become the norm since Dorylaeum: their arrows unable to penetrate our overpowering shield wall, their scimitars too short to reach through our fence of spears. Aside from random skirmishes and quick ambushes, they'd suffered nothing but defeat.

And today would be no different.

2

The battle was won, and we owned the bridge, yet the day was far from over. Saracen bodies littered the stone, locked in their death throes, lifeless eyes staring at the still clear sky. Crusader corpses lay intermingled with the Saracens, though we'd lost few compared to the hundreds we'd killed. Men lifted the corpses of our enemies and hurled them over the side of the bridge to fall into the Orontes below. Mangled and bloodied bodies piled up on the shores of the river, redirecting its flow and leaving pink stains on the water's surface. Squires—men like me—carried deceased crusaders to the plains on the northern side of the Iron Bridge and began the arduous process of burying the dead. This would be yet another in a long line of graveyards that now marked the path from here back to Nicaea.

Taking a break from digging graves, I now stood back on the bridge. I'd removed my helmet and set it on the stone parapet of the bridge, and now my gaze lingered on the custom piece of armor. Originally meant for a Saracen named Temür, it had been crafted and gifted to me by Asbat, Amina's now-deceased father. It was conical—as most of ours were—

with a raised ridge that ran from the nape of the neck, over the crown of the head, and into a nose bar that had been molded in the shape of a horse's head—one horse's head, specifically.

The head had been designed after Temür's horse, Safanad, which I'd slain in the heat of battle. He'd loved his horse almost as much as I loved Amina, and he'd never gotten over me killing it. Vengeance filled his heart, and he'd threatened me with scaphism, an ancient practice of feeding a man honey and milk, then pinning him between two boats and letting him slowly become covered in his own filth until all manner of disgusting creatures ate their way inside him. A horrific way to die, one that I'd escaped through the aid of Hendry and Sir Wymond. But even then, Temür had sought me out during the battle of Dorylaeum only days later. Hendry had once more come to my aid, and together we'd fought him off. He'd fled with an arrow in his arm and a sword in his back.

I absently wondered where he was now, if he was watching the crusade, waiting for a time to strike at me again. Or, hopefully, he'd died from his wounds and been left to rot in a field somewhere. Temür was a vicious opponent, mostly unhinged and filled with revenge-fueled hate for me.

I desperately hoped to never see him again.

"A well fought battle."

Rainald stood beside me at the waist-high parapet of the bridge, apparently needing a break from the grave-digging for the moment, as well. He'd been a near-constant companion since our first meeting on the outskirts of Constantinople. He'd helped Migliorozzo train me in the shield wall, accompanied us on our quest into the Anatolian wilderness in search of Saracen raiders, and even joined a hundred of us braving Saracen arrows as we stormed an occupied hill during the battle of Dorylaeum.

"Aye, something like that," I muttered. I looked down at the mess we'd made of the Orontes and watched the red streams join the flowing gray waters. Another body bobbed to the surface, caught on some underwater stone or bramble, and jostled about for a moment before breaking free and drifting out of sight.

"You seem to have come out relatively unscathed for someone in the vanguard."

I had a single bandage just below my elbow. An erratic scimitar had somehow bounced within our shield wall and cracked against my forearm. It hadn't penetrated the mail, yet the blow had been hard enough to break the skin underneath and leave an open sore that bled into my aketon. A quick bandage job, to be sure, but enough to staunch the bleeding. Already I'd re-donned my armor.

"Aye," I said again, then fell silent.

"What ails you, friend?"

I glanced at Rainald. Blood crusted his own kettle helmet, and his surcoat was nearly shredded, barely hanging from his shoulders by a few stubborn fibers. He'd been among the men who'd cleared the first tower. They'd seen far more losses than those of us in the shield wall.

"I don't rightly know," I said, though I imagined it had something to do with the bodies floating steadily away and the sound of shovels piercing dirt as squires interred our own casualties.

My friend, ever mindful, must have picked up on my musings. "Surely you didn't think we would walk into Jerusalem," he said. "And surely you didn't think that we would be welcomed as liberators."

"Just thought it would be easier by now."

"You've barely a scratch," he pointed out. "You've taken to the role of crusader like a fly to manure."

I rested a hand on Skull Splitter. Even though the axe saw no action today, it had previously wetted its blade on dozens— or more—Saracen warriors. "You know what I mean."

A silence, then he said, "I do. Taking a life is never easy, even if that life is the life of the enemy."

Pointing out the difficulty of a thing does little to make the doing of it any easier. I opened my mouth to tell Rainald as much when a very familiar voice echoed over the bridge.

"Haw!" Hendry cried, and both Rainald and I turned to see my knight kicking at the massive oak door that barred his entrance into the bridge's second tower. "Haw!" Another kick. "Come out, ye jessies!"

Rainald and I hurried over, and Hendry shot us a glance.

"Good, lad." He nodded to Skull Splitter. "Hack this door open."

"What's going on?"

"There's some Saracen jessies inside too feart to come out."

I looked up at the stone arch of the tower, followed it to the other side of the bridge. A pair of knights stood at another door, also kicking uselessly at the heavy oak. "Maybe because you're going to kill them."

"Aye," Hendry said. "That's the plan."

"And you're wondering why they won't come out?"

He scoffed. "I dinnae say I was wondering, lad. I ken *why* they're feart." He kicked again. "Now get yer axe, and do some work."

I didn't move. "Maybe we let them go?"

Hendry belted a laugh and nodded to the south, toward Antioch. "Aye, let's send 'em back to Antioch to join the garrison. Canny lad, ye are."

"Let them go the other way," I said, pointing to the north.

"Why're ye so set on letting 'em go anywhere?"

I gestured around the stone bridge—the now-black stone bridge, stained so from spilled blood. "Didn't we end enough life today?"

He seemed to think on that. "I dinnae ken," he said, then kicked the door again. "Mebbe just a few more. Are ye gaun to

SHADOWS OF ANTIOCH | 25

hack this door, or do I need to take that wee axe from ye and do it meself?"

I drew Skull Splitter and stepped to the door, then paused. "What if they surrender?"

Hendry said nothing, only looked at me with a frown.

"If they surrender their weapons and armor, will you let them go?"

His frown deepened. "Fine, lad," he said. His voice had changed, if only slightly, yet I'd been around Hendry nearly every minute for six months. I recognized compassion when I heard it, even if it was layered with sarcasm and grit. "They leave their weapons and armor. I'll let 'em go in their skivvies and nothing else."

"Thank you."

He waved away my sentiment. "Aye, lad. Just get on with it."

I leaned into the door. *"Silahlarınızı bırakın!"*

"Where'd ye learn that?"

"Amina's been teaching me." I listened but heard no reply. *"Silahlarınızı bırakın!"* I shouted again. *"Çık!"*

"What are you saying?" Rainald asked.

By now, several other knights had joined us, likely at the sound of one of their own shouting in Turkish. "I'm telling them to drop their weapons and come out. I'm—"

"Teslim oluyoruz!"

I pressed my ear against the door again.

"Teslim oluyoruz!" they shouted again.

"They surrender." I looked at Hendry. "And you'll let them go?"

"Aye, lad," he said. He gave a hard look to the other knights standing around him. *"We'll* let 'em go. But in their skivvies. No bow, no weapons, no armor." He pointed north, away from Antioch. "And *that* way."

"I don't know how to say skivvies in Turkish," I said with a grin.

"Figure it out."

"Aye," I said, then leaned once more toward the door. *"Çık. Zırh yok."*

A pause. *"Tamam! Tamam!"*

"Kılıç yok," I added, reminding them to drop their weapons along with any armor.

"Tamam! Kılıç yok. Zırh yok. Tamam!"

I waved Hendry and the others back. Our small group had grown to over a dozen knights now. "They're coming. Back up."

Everyone stepped back with their hands on their weapons. I stood in the front, Skull Splitter still in a loose grip, and slung my shield from my back and into my offhand. *"Tamam,"* I called. *"Çık."*

A thud came from the other side of the door as whatever had blocked it was likely shoved aside, then the heavy door creaked and groaned and slid slowly open. The knights around me tensed, and we watched in unison as four Saracens stepped through the doorway. They wore tunics and nothing else, their legs showing below the bottom of their tunics, bare feet padding gently on the stone as they stepped onto the bridge. Their hands were open before them, palms facing us, and they started trembling once they saw all of us lined up outside the door.

I gestured to the north. *"Git,"* I said. *"Bu şekilde."*

They looked north, saw the scattered crusaders still on the bridge, the hundreds more on the road, and the still-growing graveyard beyond. *"Bu şekilde?"* one of them repeated.

I nodded and pointed again. *"Bu şekilde."*

They looked south, and every knight around me took a step forward.

"Bu şekilde," I said again, stepping forward and pointing north once more.

"*O tarafa gidersek ölürüz,*" he said.

"What's he blethering aboot, lad?" Hendry asked.

"They're afraid to go that way."

"Aye, they should be."

I shot him a glare, though it did nothing to change his own hard demeanor. "You said you'd let them go."

"I said I'd let 'em go north."

I slipped Skull Splitter back into its carriage and slung my shield to my back. "*Bu şekilde,*" I said, putting a hand on the shoulder of the one who spoke and physically turning him north. "*Bu şekilde*…and…" I trailed off, unsure how to say the rest. "*Bu şekilde…yo…yoksa ölürsün.*" I gestured to the men around me.

They exchanged glances with one another, then nodded and turned north. They walked with heads down, stepping over the gore that covered the bridge, eyes lingering on their brethren still being hurled unceremoniously over the side. Crusaders paused as they passed, staring unflinchingly at the Saracens and their slow retreat across the bridge. Hands moved to sword hilts, but no one stopped the four men as they made their way across the bridge.

"Ye ken they're probably still dead," Hendry said.

"Probably," I agreed. "But we didn't kill them."

3

L etting the Saracens go ended up being a wasted venture, since I saw them the following morning in fetters marching behind Bohemond and his two thousand men-at-arms as they came to reinforce our numbers on the bridge.

By the time he arrived, we'd fully cleared the corpses; the black stains lingering on the stone were the only sign there'd been a battle. Bohemond visited our completed graveyard, where Caldwell assured him that the twenty-nine men-at-arms whose crusade ended here had received the proper Christian burial rites and thus died as martyrs for their faith. Bohemond then selected a few hundred men to remain at the bridge, and the rest of us prepared for the ride to Antioch ahead of the main army, which would be coming the following day.

We'd hobbled our horses nearby before assaulting the bridge, and Hendry and I retrieved Tencendur and *Ankída* from Thomas, the boy with a lisp who seemed to have somehow become Hendry's personal stable hand over the past months. Tancred had given us the horses—and Thomas, in a way— before the battle of Dorylaeum several months ago, and we were lucky they still lived; many crusaders had lost their mounts during the crossing of the mountains. More than once I'd assumed *Ankída* would fall and not rise again, but—scrawny as she was—she trekked on, matching pace with the purest bred steeds and bearing my weight with relative ease, despite my ever-increasing arms and armor.

We rode south, three and a half thousand strong, all on horseback and with Bohemond at our head, his standard held high. We followed in organized columns of mounted soldiers, spear tips shivering above each of us, helmets glinting in the sun, and surcoats, most with Bohemond's blue and red, flapping in the breeze. Small hamlets and abandoned mills and farmsteads dotted both sides of the road, but we saw no people. Though we posed no real threat to them—our target was Antioch—they'd likely fled at sight of us.

Surprisingly, no Saracen warriors met us on the road. I suspected those who'd survived the battle at the Iron Bridge had fled back to Antioch, relaying our somewhat limited numbers and strength. Perhaps Yaghi Siyan, the Seljuq ruler of Antioch, hoped we would pass his city by. Or, more likely, he'd heard of the tens of thousands of crusaders coming in our wake and knew that the upcoming siege was inevitable, regardless of whatever battle he may win against those of us in the vanguard.

Our company followed the meandering Orontes as it wound steadily south and west. The twin mountains Staurin and Silpius gently rose in the distance. Scouts were dispatched toward them to survey the path to the city—Antioch was nestled into the western slopes of these mountains—and we continued to ride along the road that followed the river.

The day wore on, and eventually our path bent sharply south, angling for the western side of the twin mountains. Here we passed an empty church, though I doubted anyone had fled it at our approach. It looked long abandoned. An Armenian-style pointed dome rose from its center, though this was pock-marked with gaps and fissures.

Our scouts returned, reporting no sign of Saracen war parties or even a single scout, and we continued on. By midday we reached Antioch. A fortress along the lines of Constantinople, it made Nicaea look like a peasant village as it spread west down the slopes of the twin mountains like spilled grain. A six-mile-long wall at least thirty feet high encircled it, like stones containing a massive firepit. High square towers stood up from the walls at irregular intervals, and movement atop each one implied Saracen guards, likely armed with bows that could reach us from a great distance.

The western wall extended to within easy bowshot of the Orontes and even butted right up to the river in the southwest of the city. In the east, the walls climbed the slopes of the mountains, and a massive citadel of stone near Silpius's peak was fully encircled by a second high wall and numerous towers. A small, craggy path led east from the wall just north of the citadel, winding its way between the two mountains. It was essentially impassible by all but the most skilled navigators. Here lay the city's only eastern facing gate, the one gate we were unable to besiege during the eight months we would remain encamped outside those high walls.

Antioch had five additional gates, the Saint Paul Gate to the north, the Saint George to the south, and three more along the western front. One of these western gates—it would come to be known as the Bridge Gate—had been built where the river met the wall in the southwest. It opened directly onto the Orontes at a wide stone bridge, thereby covering the only road leading from the city to the ports of Alexandretta and Saint Simeon.

I gaped at Antioch as we traveled toward it, no small part of me realizing that this massive city stood between me and Jerusalem, between me and the absolution of my sins.

William's dying face once more passed before my gaze, and as I shook it away, I wondered if I had the heart and courage to survive whatever lay ahead. I didn't know fully what we faced —none of us did. Perhaps I would have abandoned my absolution and chosen to live with my sins if I had.

And maybe Amina would still be alive.

Bohemond made camp in the north to begin the siege of Antioch. We stayed some distance from the walls—perhaps eight hundred yards, perhaps a bit more—yet even at that distance I saw the shadowy silhouettes of archers standing at the parapets, watching us as we prepared to besiege their city. The occasional arrow would arc into the sky, nearly invisible in the glare of the setting sun, then thud into the grass far enough away to be almost silent.

Our camp was up and ready by evening, and we slept in shifts with eyes constantly on the road to the north and the city to the south, fires burning to light the darkness. A long and eventless night passed, and the rest of the crusader army arrived the following morning.

Tancred, leading the remainder of Bohemond's forces, arrived first. He attached himself to our camp, bolstering our number to nearly five thousand. Next came a veritable parade of princes and lords, all from northern France and all setting up between us and the nearest gate. Robert of Normandy, Robert of Flanders, Hugh of Vermandois, and Stephen of Blois marched in one by one, each leading a force of thousands that took the better part of the morning to go around our camp. A vanguard led the way, knights in full regalia with banners flapping in the wind, as much as a show of force for the garrison of Antioch as to keep their own men organized.

After the knights of the vanguard came the rest of the men-at-arms, equipped well enough for battle yet most lacking horses and heavy armor. Even some knights marched among these men-at-arms. I sat atop *Ankída* as I watched, a small pang of guilt at my fortune and their affliction. My horse had survived, and using Asbat's tools, I'd been able to repair my mail after Dorylaeum and had even acquired chausses and a pair of helmets—both as backups as I still wore Temür's helmet. I'd learned to install iron plates into my boots to guard my feet in a shield wall, and my supply of weapons now included three spears and one lance, a Saracen bow I didn't yet know how to use, and the throwing axe I had built myself, much to Hendry's displeasure. I was among the best equipped of those present, and I was a mere squire. Luck had been kind to me on the long journey to Antioch.

After the northern French came the Provençals under Raymond of Toulouse. They bypassed both Bohemond's camp and their northern brethren to blockade the next gate, which we would eventually begin calling the Dog Gate, though I cannot tell you why. Along with the knights and lords and men-at-arms came the group I'd been waiting for: the civilians. Shopkeepers and blacksmiths and tailors pulled wagons behind Raymond's contingent of men, and I watched in anxious excitement for the rumble of Asbat's wagon, knowing Amina and Novella—my girls—would be sitting at the front of it.

Only a few days had passed since I'd seen them, yet every time I left for battle was the same. Amina fighting back tears as she watched me go and knowing I may not return. Her eyes lingering on mine as she tied the small length of blue cloth around my right arm and made me promise that I'd return it. The cloth was cut from the hem of her cloak, and she always fastened it on my arm with her father's horseshoe-shaped iron brooch.

I wore it still, smiling wide as I watched her approach. She sat perched on the wagon seat, her hands guiding the ever-faithful oxen, Grendel and Beowulf. Novella sat by her side, an equally large smile on her little face. She leaped from the wagon—much to Amina's consternation—and charged toward me. To my surprise, a small hen fluttered from the wagon behind her, following with its idiotic bobbing head and bouncing body. I dismounted and scooped Novella up in my arms, holding her tight as the hen pecked at my boots.

"She's going to hurt herself, Danya," Amina said sternly, though the smile on her face betrayed her.

"She's fine," I said, then looked into Novella's beaming eyes. "You're fine, right, *mia paperotta*? Strong enough to jump down?"

She nodded furiously. "*Forte*," she said, flexing her little arms. "*Forte*. Like you, Danya!"

"*Forte*," I repeated, then set her down.

Amina had climbed down from the wagon by now, and I'd barely let go of Novella when she fell into my arms. For a very long while, we stood in silence, embracing as if we'd not seen one another in years. Novella wrapped her arms around our knees, and I felt a peck at my foot. I looked down to see the hen trying to eat my boots.

"What's this?" I asked.

"She's Myrtle!" Novella squealed. "'Mina said I could keep her!"

I raised an eyebrow, and Amina shrugged. "You like eggs, don't you?"

"Sure," I said, pulling them close again. "Sure."

Within Bohemond's sprawling camp, the men-at-arms fell into familiar clusters. Hendry established his lean-to—still refusing to use a real tent—while I built my own shelter, which sprang up from the side of Asbat's wagon and was large enough to house Amina, Novella, and me. And Myrtle, of course, who I soon learned slept with Novella, which in turn meant she slept with me. I also learned that, with winter approaching, I'd likely not see any eggs until spring. That plus the fact that Myrtle awoke with the dawn and for some reason thought she was a rooster was why the hen quickly became my least favorite member of our small group.

Father Luke and his two ostiaries, Migliorozzo and Piccolo, along with Sir Wymond, Rainald, and Elric, who had become Sir Wymond's second squire with the death of Sir Daw at Dorylaeum, also pitched their tents nearby. Lastly came John Mark and Thomas, Hendry's lisping stable boy. They claimed they'd chosen the location out of kinship to Hendry and me, though I suspected it had more to do with Amina's well-earned reputation as a good cook.

During the trek through the mountains, most of the crusaders had gotten their sustenance from crusty barley loaves, hardtack, and almost-stale horse bread, which was made with gritty ingredients including split-peas, oats, and even acorns. Amina, on the other hand, had somehow been able to turn roughly ground wheat into mostly soft *yufka*, Turkish flatbread seasoned with foraged herbs and spices. On rare occasions, she also found the time to cook güveç, a stew with vegetables and lamb—or, more often, chicken, since lamb was something of a luxury. She simmered it in a heavy cast-iron pot that I at one point argued we leave behind. The stew and flatbread eaten together had quickly changed my mind, and the pot remained with us as we built our camp at Antioch. I thought then of how Myrtle would taste in the stew.

During the first two weeks of the siege, you'd be forgiven for believing we rested at the city rather than besieged it. The garrison did little but watch as we set up in its shadow, and even local as-yet-unconquered Saracen cities left us alone. The lords of the crusade took this time to send foraging parties into the forests and fields that surrounded Antioch.

Tancred had previously built relations with the Christian Armenians in the region of Cilicia to the north, so I was sent to the city of Adana with a party of three hundred men-at-arms, a journey that proved uneventful except for Rainald's sprained ankle, which happened as he loaded supplies onto a cart. He complained much of the five-day return trip, griping about his sore foot with seemingly every step his horse took. Still, we remained in a joyous mood. It was as if we'd forgotten we rode through enemy territory at the head of a caravan of a hundred carts laden with food and wine. We were a prime target, and yet we'd been left alone.

We often ate the best cuts of slaughtered cattle roasted long over a fire until the juices dripped and the smell grew unbearable. Fruits, vegetables, wine, grains, meats, and spices of all kinds found their way into our hands. Nightly feasts characterized these two weeks, the only reminder that we besieged a fortified enemy city being the constant gaze of its inhabitants from the high walls.

Amina and Novella adapted well to this time. Now that our months of travel had ended, Amina built up a brick oven so she could cook larger quantities of her *yufka*. The quality improved, as well, with access to finer grains. Soon our small section of the camp became known as The Bakery, and Novella handed out rations with a smiling face—Myrtle always bobbing around at her feet—and an unnaturally joyful demeanor for a five-year-old coping with her first siege and the recent loss of her mother. She'd still not told me what had happened to her father or if she ever knew him. I'd decided against prying.

Novella's Greek had improved enough to communicate, and I'd picked up a great deal of Italian, thanks in no small part to Piccolo. He'd recovered from his ordeal at Dorylaeum, though having no thumb on either hand meant he could no longer carry a weapon. It mattered little, since he'd sworn to become a priest should he survive that harrowing night we'd spent tied to a stake in a frigid river. We'd both lived, and he'd kept his promise and now shadowed Father Luke.

And so two weeks passed in relative peace. But October turned to November, and this grace period came to a stuttering halt. The nearby city of Harim—controlled still by Saracens— began daily harassment, sending sortie after sortie of horse archers to harry us so that no one could venture from the camps without a small party of men-at-arms.

The garrison of Antioch seemed emboldened by this, dispatching their own raiders from the gates to the south, which we had not yet been able to blockade. They fired at us from across the Orontes, and Godfrey—who'd camped his soldiers farthest south and nearest the river—took the worst of it. Eventually, we built a ramshackle bridge out of boats, allowing us to respond, though we still buried new crusaders every day.

Garrison archers even ventured onto the slopes of Mount Staurin—the northern of the twin mountains and nearest to Bohemond's camp—and from there were able to reach us. These combined attacks severely hampered our once plentiful foraging, forcing us to be more intentional with our rations.

Around this same time, allied ships arrived at the nearby port of Saint Simeon, carrying craftsmen and construction supplies for the crusade. Bohemond, ever insistent on asserting his power over the other lords, managed to secure the supplies for the erection of a somewhat ramshackle fort, which we built between our forces in the north and the Saint Paul Gate. The fort—called Malregard—managed to at least stymie the garrison archers. We were still left with the daily sorties from Antioch and the Saracens' constant harassment from Harim. Nothing could yet be done about the garrison, though Bohemond—perhaps attempting to justify his usurpation of the supplies—volunteered to lead an assault party of his own toward Harim.

And so it came to late November, and I once more sat astride *Ankída*, cloak flapping behind me, lance upright in my arm, Skull Splitter and Thief's Prick on my belt, and my sturdy, cross-emblazoned kite shield resting along my back as I awaited yet another battle.

4

W e didn't know where Harim was—at least, not exactly —so a vanguard of a hundred mounted knights and squires had been sent east in search of either the city or the Saracen raiders who populated it. The vanguard would attack, then feign a retreat, hopefully leading the Saracens here, where three hundred more of us waited in the rocky desert with sand blowing all around us. We sat in the shadows of a high craggy cliff with the hopes of remaining out of sight until we received word from the vanguard. The sun inched its way behind the brown peak to my left, and I watched the movement of the crag's shadow as it crawled farther across the desert floor. More mesas and buttes rose from the dreary countryside, random pillars of stone that broke up the monotonous desert landscape.

Our own movement had been reduced to the bare minimum—with the dry sand and often violent winds, we would leave a dust trail that could be seen for miles around. We'd been sitting on horseback for hours, and even Bohemond fidgeted at the head of our small army. His standard-bearer sat beside him, and flapping in the wind was Bohemond's large, rectangular banner, quartered blue and red and frayed at the edges from time and use. Hendry and I were at the southern flank under the command of Tancred, the same place we'd been since morning. Sir Wymond, Rainald, and Elric were also among us somewhere.

I sighed, long and loud and bordering on childish.

"What, lad?" Hendry asked.

"I didn't say anything."

"Ye didnae need to. Yer moaning like a bairn."

"We've been sitting here all day." I shifted in the saddle. "My backside hurts."

He frowned at me. "Get doon and stretch. I dinnae want ye falling from yer horse again."

"One time."

"Haw! More like every time."

I shifted my feet in my stirrups. "I'm not going to fall."

"We'll see."

"We're not even going to fight today." I leaned back, felt my back pop. "It's been hours. They're not going to find them."

"The vanguard'll find 'em, and ye'll have yer fight 'fore the sun's doon. I'd bet me beard on it."

"But your beard is glorious."

He smirked. "Aye, 'tis. One day mebbe ye can grow yer own."

"I can grow a beard," I protested, touching the stubble on my chin. I was eighteen, a man, and if all I had now was stubble, that was likely all I'd ever have. "Kind of," I added, then grinned. "Amina likes it."

He belted a laugh. "I'm sure she does, lad. How're yer lasses doing?"

"They're good," I said. "*Sono bravi.*"

"That the wee lassie's tongue?" he asked.

"Italian," I said.

"Hmph. And yer lass's teaching ye the Saracen one?"

"Turkish."

"Aye, that." He looked at me sideways, then said nothing else.

"What?"

"Yer keener than ye look."

That was as close to a compliment as Hendry gave. The correct response was to take it in silence, which I did, and together we went back to quietly watching the horizon. Time dragged on, and the shade of the cliff stretched farther and farther away as the sun continued to set and the temperature dropped. A soft wind blew along the desert floor and hugged the stone walls. It was edged with the chill of approaching winter, and I pulled my cloak tighter about my shoulders.

The faint purple of evening had lined the eastern horizon when we finally saw movement: distant, swirling clouds of dust blowing from around the cliff face. Bohemond sat upright in his saddle, and every man among us did the same. I flexed stiff fingers and shifted atop *Ankída* in a rather weak effort to loosen up before we faced whatever rounded the cliff.

First came a lone rider wearing the same red and blue we all did. He galloped hard toward Bohemond. The two conversed, and before they finished their brief conversation, the rest of the vanguard came spilling into view. They rode angrily, any formation they may have had broken in their feigned retreat. Dust rolled behind them like a wave, shrouding anything—or anyone—that might be following them.

"Here we go, lad," Hendry muttered. "Yer aboot to get yer fight."

I drew a breath to steady myself. As bored as I was, I preferred that to a horseback charge, especially a blind one into a cloud of dust.

"Ride!" Bohemond shouted from the front. He turned to face us, raising his lance high above his head. His standard-bearer waved the banner, the quartered red and blue snapping and fluttering in the wind as Bohemond thrust his own lance once more alongside it. "Ride!"

That turbulent evening is still vivid in my memory. My first cavalry charge, the first time I unhorsed a man with a lance. The vigor and power flowing through my veins, a mixture of anxiety and fear and excitement—the volatile concoction that causes some men to loose their bowels and others to rise up in strength and courage. I belong among the latter; when put under pressure, I strike back in a violent explosion. Too violent, as time has shown. Looking back now with the knowledge of the losses I would suffer in the coming months, I often wish I was more cowardly. Had I been too afraid to go on, too afraid to trek across arid desert, wade through bloody war, and fight foreign enemies in a foreign land, then perhaps I would still have her.

But if I had been too afraid to fight, I would never have had her in the first place. I do not know which is worse.

Yet I've strayed too far. In that moment, none of this was on my mind, only the grip of my legs on the mass of muscle that was *Ankída* beneath me. My feet pressed into the stirrups as I held on with all I had, desperate not to fall from the saddle. We broke into a gallop, the tumultuous stampeding of hundreds of horses drowning out all other sounds and thoughts as we formed a wedge with Bohemond at our head. He was a tragic man, a fallen man, a greedy man, but by God, what a warrior he was! Like a hero from a story, a man on fire, unafraid and unswerving in his audacity and ardor as he charged into battle. There was none other like him when it came to martial prowess.

We pounded across the flank of our retreating vanguard and entered into the brown haze left in their wake. For a brief moment, I saw nothing but darkness and dust, then as one we emerged from the cloud.

SHADOWS OF ANTIOCH | 43

And directly into mounted Saracens.

They still had their bows drawn, arrows nocked and ready to continue their storm of steel-tipped death. Bohemond led the thrust into the side of their loose formation with the force of a hammer striking an anvil. Only this anvil shattered with our blow. Lances cracked and snapped as they flung men from saddles, and once dangerous arrows fluttered harmlessly away. Cries of pain and fear and shock rent the air. I followed Hendry, riding just behind him and to his right. I couched my lance, forearm steadying it, bicep gripping it against my ribs with all my strength. Hendry's warning rang in my head.

"A lance is a wee bit bigger than a spear, lad."

I chose a target, aimed, then closed my eyes and thrust. The force of the impact vibrated up the shaft of the lance and into my arm and shoulder, nearly throwing me from *Ankida*'s back. The lance slid in my grip, burning the flesh of my palm as it moved, but I held firm. My eyes jolted open as I jerked back—only my feet hard in the stirrups kept me atop *Ankida*— and I watched the Saracen career off his horse. He trailed a crimson cord of blood as he spun in the air, his mount tumbled over, and both rider and beast disappeared into the mayhem of dust and hammering hooves.

We smashed our way through their formation, jostling horse to horse, knee to knee, rider to rider, with only a few of our men falling in our wild charge, then we burst out the other side to clear and fresh air. Half our riders had already discarded their lances. Some had snapped upon impact, though others were dropped willingly in favor of sword or axe or mace.

Bohemond led us in a tight turn as we reformed our wedge and aimed once more for the now panicked and retreating Saracens. I followed, guiding *Ankida* with my legs, shield and lance still gripped tight. Hendry glanced over his shoulder, saw me still mounted, and flashed a fierce grin.

"Stay with me, lad!" he cried over the thunder of our horses.

I started to shout a reply, but we were already moving into place for our second charge. Once more we dove into dust and darkness, and I lost sight of anything beyond Hendry and the horses to my left and right. Dust and wind whipped at my face, stinging my eyes.

Cries in the near distance, and suddenly a Saracen came into view. I aimed and thrust my lance. It caught the rider between the shoulder blades as he tried to retreat. The force of the strike folded him over the saddle, and the lance stayed in his back for the briefest of moments. I felt the resistance all the way down my arm as the lance bent, creaking and groaning before snapping with the sound of thunder and flying from my grip. The Saracen bellowed in pain as he was flung from his horse, then disappeared into the dust as I galloped by him, jerking Skull Splitter from its carriage.

Ankida crashed into a rider. She twisted to the side, and we jarred to a sudden halt as the rest of the cavalry thundered by. Before either of us could react, another rider emerged from the cloud of dust and slammed into us. Both were Saracens, and both saw how quickly I'd been singled out from the once cohesive cavalry charge. I saw only the three of us in our small pocket of brown dust, though I could hear and feel the presence of hundreds of others still riding hard all around me.

Their scimitars screamed into the air. I caught the first blow on my shield and bent backward in the saddle as the second strike cut the air in front of me. *Ankida* backstepped on her own, and a pair of follow-up attacks fell short, one nearly taking *Ankida*'s ear. I leaned forward and struck, the heavy axehead of Skull Splitter pushing aside the desperate parry of the nearest Saracen. His hand and sword spiraled into the air together as a blow from the second rider cracked into my shield. I leaned into the second Saracen, pushing him off balance before following up with another overhead strike that buried Skull Splitter into his collarbone. He bellowed in pain, then fell dead from the saddle as I pulled my axe free with a sickening squelch.

The haze was slowly lifting, revealing a truly horrendous display, as chaotic and gory a battlefield as I'd ever seen. Riderless horses stamped aimlessly around, fading in and out of sight as they passed through pockets of gloomy dust. They foamed at the mouth, bled from lance-induced gashes running down their sides, and whinnied in fear or pain or both. Horseless riders shouted their deaths from the blood-soaked dirt, some clawing at the ground as they tried to drag themselves away from the battle. Others lay where they'd fallen, crushed from the stampeding horses or missing arms or legs; bodies had even been split in half by the power of our charge. A horse galloped by, dragging its rider by a stirrup as his dead body bounced along the sand behind it. Despite the many battles I'd seen up to that point, I still felt a wave of nausea come over me.

The flicker of a red and blue banner caught my eye before disappearing into the haze. In its wake came Bohemond himself, thrown from his saddle and hurtling to the dirt below. He landed amid a cluster of still-mounted Saracens, an arrow already lodged in his thigh and blood running from his nose. He sprang back to his feet, but he had no lance, only a shield and an undrawn sword and dagger on his hip. The Saracens fell on him with shocking speed. Likely they knew who they'd unhorsed and sought to deal a crushing blow to the crusade.

I kicked *Ankída* toward him, hooking Skull Splitter under an arm as I yanked my throwing axe from my belt and threw. It whistled in the air, caught a Saracen between the shoulder blades, and knocked him from his saddle. The others paused at my sudden attack, and Bohemond dragged one down into the sand and crushed his face with the rim of his shield. I crashed into the skirmish, Skull Splitter rising and falling and hammering a scimitar from the grip of a Saracen. He wheeled about but not fast enough, and I buried my axe into his chest.

A blow landed on my back; it didn't pierce mail, but it knocked the wind from my lungs. I gasped and turned to swing my axe but found it still stuck in the dying Saracen's chest. I tried to raise my shield, yet was too slow and could only watch as the Saracen swung his sword for the killing strike. But Bohemond was there, once again pulling the man from his saddle with a single arm, this time cutting his throat with a small dagger on the way down.

Ankída reared as a trio of arrows thudded into the ground at her forelegs, and Skull Splitter finally ripped free as I tumbled backward, barely missing *Ankída*'s bucking hooves as she kicked at nothing before running off into the haze.

"Irritating little splinter," I muttered from the floor of the battlefield.

Yet I had no time to ponder her departure as a rough hand caught the back of my surcoat and pulled me to my feet.

"Need you up," Bohemond snapped, and I saw at least six more mounted Saracens closing around us. He'd dropped the small dagger and drawn his sword. He glanced at my axe. "Know how to use that thing?"

"Well enough."

"Good."

He didn't wait for them to strike, instead lashing out with a speed I didn't think possible from a man his size. He was at least a foot taller than me, yet even so his sword snaked out like a striking viper and slashed the thigh of the nearest enemy, the follow through tearing a chunk of flesh from the horse he sat upon. The attack slung dual arcs of blood—one from man, one from beast—both of which splattered along the rumps of the nearby horses. The animal reared and threw its rider from its back.

I raised my shield and stepped between the stamping feet

of a pair of horses as a scimitar beat down into its hardened oak surface. Skull Splitter rose and fell, and yet another Saracen would end the day short a limb. He howled in pain as his weapon tumbled to the ground. I ignored him, ducked another blow, swung at nothing and hit it, then stepped once more between shuffling horses.

A scimitar clanged into my helmet before ricocheting off, though the blow was hard enough to rip the chin strap and send the helmet twirling into the dust. Blood ran over my eyes, and my ears rang like a struck gong as I backpedaled, shield held desperately above me as blows rained down on it. One of the scimitars snaked around the edge of the shield and slashed the mail at my arm, sending broken rings scattering into the dusty air. I felt the burn before I saw the blood, and my fingers went limp as the shield slipped from my grip.

The neck of a horse thumped into my exposed head, sending me to my hands and knees. Hooves pounded the sand around me, I jerked upright, shield no longer above my head, and gave a desperate swing of my axe. It landed in flesh, something howled in pain, then the axe was ripped from my hands as whatever I'd struck pulled away.

Thief's Prick—my trusty seax—found its way into my hand. I jammed it into the first thing I saw—the calf of a Saracen rider—and ripped it sideways, tearing through cloth armor and flesh and drawing a yelp of surprise and pain. He struck down at me, though his blow was hasty and ill-aimed, and I easily sidestepped it as I slashed along the backside of his hand. He dropped his weapon, and I leaped and stabbed, grabbing his saddle with my free hand and driving Thief's Prick into his chest. The blade grated along ribs as it buried itself to the hilt. He wheezed, met my eyes, then fell sideways from the saddle.

I tried to pull myself onto his horse, but the beast seemed to be done fighting and bucked me off before joining *Ankída* wherever she'd run off to. The remaining riders still jostled around us, closing the space we had to fight and pushing Bohemond against me. Our backs met as more Saracens appeared from the hazy dust like specters from hell, first two, then four, then a dozen more as if somehow the entire enemy army knew Bohemond stood exposed and dismounted with only me at his side.

"At least we took a few of them with us," Bohemond grunted. His bleeding face looked worse, and his helmet was also gone, though he still had his shield.

He'd barely finished the sentence when the roar of charging horses fell over us. Surcoats of blue and red appeared from the dust, worn by riders wielding swords and axes and maces, and crusaders tore through the surrounding Saracens. Men were hurled from their saddles, horses toppled over from the charge, and those not struck turned tail and fled into the brown cloud.

And with that the battle was over. Dust continued to fall, hooves thudded distantly as our saviors chased away our enemies, and all around us came the cries of yet another crusader victory, intermingled with the desperate pleas for help from fallen warriors.

5

B ohemond looked callously down at a wounded Saracen who struggled to drag himself along the blood-soaked dirt with a single good arm. The other was missing below the elbow, and every inch he crawled left a trail of dark blood behind him. Bohemond thrust his sword into the Saracen's back, eliciting a weak groan of pain, then silence fell over us.

"Thank you," he said, nodding casually at me as he scanned the bodies for more survivors. "I don't think I would have survived without…" he trailed off as he finally raised his face to look at me. He saw the cross-shaped scar on my left cheek—the scar he'd given me—and smiled. "God's bones. It's you." He laughed, the sound loud and echoing and completely out of place in the aftermath of such a battle. "You're the boy who stole my sword. The thief."

I frowned. It had been a long time since anyone had called me that. "Aye, Lord." I wanted to add that I wasn't a boy or a thief—not anymore—but decided against it. "Daniel."

"Yes, Daniel." He was grinning widely now. "I remember you. Did I not relieve you from my service after Nicaea?"

"You did, Lord.

"And yet here you are."

"You bid me serve Lord Tancred."

"Did I?" His brow furrowed as he thought. "If you say so. In any case, I'm glad I did. You proved..." he trailed off, searched for the next word. "Helpful. You were quite helpful just now."

I felt as if I'd been more than just helpful, though I bowed my head in respect. "Thank you, Lord."

He waved at the bodies all around us. "I fear these Saracen thugs might have gotten me if you hadn't shown up."

A shadow passed over us, and I turned to see Hendry atop Tencendur with *Ankída* in tow. "I see ye found me squire, Lord."

Others followed—Sir Wymond, Rainald, and Elric among them—and soon there was something of a crowd around us. Likely they'd come in search of Bohemond.

"I did," Bohemond said. "I'd forgotten he belonged to you."

"Aye, Lord, and quite the burden he is. I found the lad's horse and thought him dead." He smiled down at me. "I shoulda kent he'd just fallen off. Again."

I bristled at that, ready to defend myself, but Bohemond spoke up first. "Well, the *lad* wasn't the only one to be unhorsed," he said. "And perhaps it isn't quite his fault; he rather foolishly charged into overwhelming odds to come to my aid."

Hendry barked a laugh. "That's me lad. Brave, but a wee bit foolish. Gaun to get him killed one o' these days."

"It hasn't yet," I said.

Hendry grinned. "Aye, and yer welcome for that."

I wiped a bit of blood from my eyes. My head was beginning to ache, and my left hand dripped blood from the gash in my forearm. I wanted this conversation to end so I could patch myself up.

If Bohemond's wounds affected him, he didn't show it. "I suppose I should be thankful for his foolishness," he said. "We could always use more brave men. And besides, we can fix foolishness."

Now Sir Wymond laughed. "That's what I said, Lord, and we've been trying for six months."

Bohemond chuckled along with him, but when he finally looked down at me, I could see an intensity in his gaze. "Nevertheless, you came to my aid without hesitation, and for that I owe you much. I'll not forget it, even if it was driven by foolishness." He flashed a smile, and I could see once more why so many men followed him. "Though even the best knight needs a dose of foolishness every once in a while. Especially when his lord is in need of saving." He looked to the gathering crowd. "I don't suppose someone has my horse."

"I have him here, Lord," Sir Wymond said, then led a massive destrier forward.

Bohemond took the reins and swung himself into the saddle, paying no mind to the blood still running from his face or the arrow sticking from his thigh. "I've an army to see to. You should rest, thief. I'm sure I'll see you again."

And he was gone, taking with him most of the entourage and leaving only Hendry, who looked me over and smirked.

"Ye look like quite the minger, lad."

"I don't know what that means."

"I'm betting ye can guess."

I gave myself a once over. Dirt and dust and blood caked my surcoat, the mail underneath damaged and in need of repair. Drying blood plastered my hair to the side of my face, and sticky blood clung to my fingers.

"Messy?"

"Something like that. Let's get ye fixed up."

After a quick bandage made from the torn cloak of a Saracen, we set about to building yet another graveyard to mark our presence, though—to my shock—this one held only three knights. After, we slept in the desert with the wailing of wounded and dying Saracens as our nighttime song. Eighty-two living Saracens sat in fetters nearby, stripped down to loin cloths, their almost-naked bodies battered and bruised and shivering in the cold. A hundred more lay dead in a pile of corpses, dead eyes staring at nothing, arms and legs and torsos intermingled in a mangled mess of flesh. Anything of value had long since been stripped away from the battlefield, and a hundred or more new horses had been added to our number.

Morning brought a chilling wind, and we ate a breakfast of hard bread, giving none to our captives, then began the march back toward Antioch. A single priest whom I didn't know stayed behind with seven crusaders too injured to either ride or walk. We'd brought no carts to bear them back. Bohemond promised to send men to their aid, but one look at the seven sorry men told me they wouldn't survive the day and whatever aid Bohemond sent would only find more corpses to bury.

At least he'd left them a priest.

"Who did this to you?"

Amina held my forearm delicately, looking at the scrap of bloodstained cloak that Hendry had hastily wrapped around the laceration. We'd just arrived back at the camp, and I'd had little chance to properly see to my wounds, especially when so many others had been hurt far worse. It was early afternoon, a low fire burned, and the smell of Amina's güvec filled our small section of the camp, which was populated with its usual crowd.

"I didn't exactly ask his name after he hacked at me," I said. Novella offered me a warm *yufka*. I took it with my free hand and dipped it into the simmering broth of the soup still hanging over the fire. *"Grazie, paperotta."*

She grinned, then moved to pass out more of the soft flatbread to the others, Myrtle following in her shadow. Sir Wymond, Rainald, Elric, and John Mark sat around the fire with Hendry, and all five happily accepted the bread. Father Luke, Migliorozzo, and Piccolo stood not far off. Piccolo— whom Novella called her *zio* Picco—smiled widely as he took the bread from her, holding it dexterously between his first two fingers. He'd quickly become accustomed to living a life without thumbs.

"I meant this horrid bandage," Amina said. I could feel the scabbed flesh pulling against the cloth as she tried to inspect the wound underneath. "Who did *this* to you?"

"Haw!" Hendry hollered. "Now, that's not fair. We didnae exactly have a physician's storeroom in the desert, lassie."

She smirked at him. "Clearly," she said, then looked again at my bandage. "I'll need to pull this off." She met my eyes with a knowing look.

"I know," I muttered. "It's going to hurt. Just do it slow and —GAH!"

She ripped the makeshift bandage from my arm, tearing it and the scab free at the same time, and blood seeped out of the cut that ran from my wrist to my elbow. Sir Wymond and Hendry belted a laugh almost in unison.

"A little warning next time," I whined.

"Oh, please, Danya. You can fight in battles but cannot handle tearing off a little scab?"

I held out my bleeding arm. "A little scab? Look at it!"

She shrugged and waved a dismissive hand. "You're fine."

Father Luke gave a laugh of his own, then sat beside Hendry. "Better you than me, my dear," he said to Amina. "Though Daniel does seem to fuss a bit more when you tend his wounds."

"She's less delicate than you, Father."

"I'm delicate enough," she said, then waved to the others casually eating around the fire. "And why didn't they get as hurt as you?"

"He fell off his horse again," Sir Wymond said through a mouthful of *yufka*.

Amina frowned. "Again?"

"I saved Bohemond! Why does no one talk about—hey!" I yelped as Amina took my head into her hands. She bent me back and inspected the gash along my hairline.

"I know, I know," she said. "A little warning next time." She released my head. "Now enough complaining. Off with your shirt. Let's take a look at the rest."

I winced as she helped me out of my shirt, the movement reminding my body of its many aches. My back and ribs throbbed from the battle and ensuing night spent on the hard desert floor. Novella stared at me, concern etched onto her little face as she saw the cuts and bruises that dotted my flesh and the blood beginning to drip from the freshly peeled scab.

"I'm okay, *paperotta*," I said, and she forced something of a smile.

"Mi prometti?"

I frowned. "I don't know that one."

"Promise me?" she asked with her thick Italian accent.

"Of course." I flexed an arm and grinned. *"Forte."*

"Forte," she whispered back.

Amina pressed a wet rag against my bleeding arm, and I instinctively jerked back. *"Forte,* Danya," she said with a smirk as she grabbed my wrist to hold my arm still.

A horn blew, echoing loud and long over the camp, and we turned in unison to see Bohemond marching the eighty-two prisoners toward the walls of Antioch. I noticed an additional four Saracens walking with these newly captured men, and recognized them as the four men whose freedom I'd negotiated on the Iron Bridge. Caldwell—that overly ambitious and boisterous priest—walked alongside Bohemond.

"What's going on?" Amina asked.

Hendry frowned and met Sir Wymond's eyes. Both gave an almost imperceptible nod, then stood together. "Come on, lad," Hendry said. "Bohemond'll want ye there for it."

Amina quickly finished the bandage as I stood. "For what?"

"Ye'll have to see."

Elric, Rainald, and John Mark joined us as we hurried to catch up with the growing procession. I glanced back at Amina and gestured for her to stay. She gave a gentle nod.

We reached Bohemond as he stopped just short of bowshot near the Saint Paul Gate. Despite knowing we were out of range, I still felt a pang of anxiety at the sight of Saracen archers atop the walls. The prisoners were led to the front, Bohemond stood at their head, and a single knight each held a captured Saracen still before him. With swift kicks, the prisoners were forced down to their knees.

Then a near silence fell over us.

The late afternoon sun shone from the west, casting long shadows across the matted grass where the knights stood and the Saracens knelt. Nothing moved but the wind, and a thick tension hung in the air as everyone but me seemed to know what was about to happen. Bodies moved along the walls as a crowd gathered over the gate, and I barely heard the gentlest shuffling of feet as men and women formed a crowd behind us. It seemed everyone at Antioch—both within its walls and without—watched in anticipation. Amina, thankfully, had remained behind with Novella.

I should have known what was coming. Bohemond was a merciless man, a brutal and single-minded leader. I'd been at Nicaea when, after the battle with Kilij Arslan, he'd employed our only working stone-thrower to hurl the severed heads of our enemies over the walls as an act of intimidation.

How effective it was, I'll never know.

Instead, I flinched in surprise as Bohemond's sword scraped free from its scabbard, the sound louder than it should be and echoing through the stillness, ringing out over the silence with authority. I knew that sword; I'd carried it once. I'd watched a wretched thief named Bojan kill my brother with it, then I'd slain Bojan myself with the very same sword. It supposedly cost half a village to make, and I distinctly remember my awe the first time I saw it. I felt a similar awe now as the glare from the afternoon sun threw marigold rays of light from its glistening edge.

Bohemond stood in front of the first prisoner, and the nearest knight grabbed a handful of the prisoner's hair. He jerked his head down, and Bohemond's arm moved as quickly as I'd seen it during the battle. In a single swift motion, he cut the head from the prisoner.

A fountain of blood burst forth as the now-limp body tumbled forward into the grass. Blood pumped from the corpse's neck, pooling around the body as the head hung in the hands of the knight, suspended by the hair he still clutched, more blood dripping gently down onto the lifeless body.

I felt my stomach in my throat. Not from the gore, which I had seen more times and worse, but the coldness of it. These men were unarmed, nearly naked, imprisoned. The battle was over, nothing could be gained from their deaths aside from a bit of intimidation against the inhabitants of Antioch. Yet was that worth slaying them? Was that worth murdering them?

The first arrows flew a few moments after the beheading, yet they landed more than a dozen paces short. Roars of protest rained down on us from the men atop the wall, who were understandably heated to see their brethren slain with such disregard. This did nothing to halt Bohemond, and he stepped to the next prisoner and repeated the process. He moved slowly, methodically, deliberately, pausing after each murder to gaze up at the walls of Antioch.

It took almost two hours for him to kill them all. My eyes lingered especially on the four men whose surrender I'd secured at the Iron Bridge, actions which today proved useless as Bohemond executed them.

6

Our small fire burned and crackled and did little to push back the cold of winter. Mid-November had given way to late December, and sharp winds blew in nightly from the east. The fire flickered in the drafty air, and even the hot cast-iron pot hanging above it rocked on its rickety tripod. We huddled around the fire doing little but watch the walls of Antioch and listen to the stew simmer.

After clearing out Harim and building Malregard—the ramshackle fort near the Saint Paul Gate in the north—we'd experienced little action in our section of the camp. We trained daily, and frequent skirmishes still occurred to the south and west, though Godfrey and Raymond and the other Franks took the brunt of those.

Often Hendry and I would accompany a light foraging party, but with Harim no longer a threat, we met few Saracens. Even so, we more often than not came back empty-handed. We'd long since plucked the land clean, and anything we'd missed had died in the cold. The princes rationed the meat we found, but even this was rare. The time of free foraging had ended and every provision was something of a struggle, so we watched in dreary silence as Luke stirred his infamous cabbage stew seasoned with God-knew-what.

He took out the spoon, smelled the stew, nodded his approval, then dropped the spoon back in.

"What'd'ye put in it today, Father?" Hendry asked.

"Cabbage and onions and leeks," he said cheerily enough.

"And?"

The aging priest smiled at him. "Water."

Hendry sighed and pulled his cloak tighter around his shoulders. None of us had expected such a cold winter—especially as early as December—though Hendry seemed especially agitated. "Why dinnae ye just feed us fodder?"

"Because the horses need it."

This drew a short laugh from Migli, who sat beside Luke with his mail in his hands. He clipped a ring into place and held it up to examine it in the fading late. Sir Wymond, Rainald, and Elric sat nearby, all with their own mail in their hands. There was little else to do besides train and check—and recheck—our gear. Thomas lounged among us, lazily plucking the strings of a lute that had definitely seen better days. He thumbed out a gentle rhythm that none of us recognized.

"You seem agitated," Sir Wymond said to Hendry.

He scoffed. "Oh, do I? It's a wee bit cold, and the father's feeding us hot water for supper."

"It's stew," Luke said.

"It's water, Father," Hendry insisted. "Cabbage-flavored water."

"I take it you miss Scotia, then?" Migli asked.

"Haw!" he shouted. "Every day."

"Eat anything like cabbage stew back home?" I asked, earning myself a chastising glare from Luke. "Not that your stew isn't delicious," I added.

"They have cabbage everywhere, lad," Hendry said, "but me lassie made the best brose."

"What'th brothe?" Thomas lisped, still plucking away at his lute.

"Bit o' oats and barley, mebbe beans if ye got 'em. Boil it thicker than porridge. Add some butter if yer feeling right." He chuckled. "Goes doon a bit better than Father Luke's stew."

"Perhaps I should stop cooking," Luke said with a weary grin. "Though I imagine you would complain of hunger then."

"But I could *really* go for a bit o' smoked haddock," Hendry went on, ignoring the priest. "With a nice ale. Mebbe some grouse. Couple o' bannocks to sop up the juices. Aye, that sounds aboot right."

"Bannocks?" Elric asked.

Hendry was too deep in his memories to notice who'd asked the question. "Simple bread. Bit thicker'n that," he said, then nodded to Novella, who held a small stack of *yufka*. She flashed Hendry a big smile, and Myrtle clucked from her seemingly permanent position at Novella's feet. "Me lassie was a proper cook. She'd grind the oats herself, mix in flour and water and more'n a little butter and salt. On good days we had jam or honey…" he trailed off and smiled, his eyes going distant for the briefest of moments. "Aye," he finally said. "Aye, I could go for some bannocks."

It was only the second time I'd ever seen Hendry reminisce about his home. The first had been the day Bronwen, his horse, had died. *My* horse, after he'd given her to me. In any case, his wife had given Bronwen to him before he'd set out with Bohemond, so seeing the animal drown had affected him enough to stop and think of home.

Food, it seemed, did the same.

"What about you, boy?" Sir Wymond asked, and it took me a minute to realize he spoke to me. "You miss Constantinople?"

"Not really," I said, deciding not to complain about being called me "boy." "I didn't exactly have the best life there."

Sir Wymond snorted a laugh. "Worse than this?" he asked, waving at the disorder around us.

The camp spread beyond sight in every direction, the ground trampled into a muddied mess by the thousands of men and their waste. Smoke lingered forever over us from hundreds of small fires just like ours. It smelled of musk and crap and old food and stale bread. Disease ran rampant through our ranks, and it seemed that every day we buried a crusader who'd suffered no physical wounds.

"Worse than this," I acknowledged. "I slept in a little hovel of rotting wood walls and a dirty rush floor. The roof leaked, the food was scarce and worse than Father Luke's stew."

"I'll just eat it myself," Luke muttered.

"I scrounged and stole what I could," I went on. "I wasn't liked, barely tolerated." I glanced at Amina, and she flashed me a smile from behind her makeshift brick oven. She'd met me only once when I lived in Constantinople, though I'd told her a great deal of my time there. "Aye, this is much better."

The next morning, Hendry and I were summoned to meet Lord Bohemond. We hadn't seen him since he'd executed the prisoners after the battle in the deserts of Harim. We'd been commanded to wear no mail and bring no weapons, something that brought more discomfort than I expected, even though we were still within the camp. I'd grown so accustomed to traipsing around armed and armored that leaving everything behind left me feeling naked, so it was with this in my mind that we walked into Bohemond's section of the encampment.

What can I say about Bohemond's quarters that I have not already? His tent was like a small building, a fort all its own, an estate in the middle of our ramshackle encampment. A pair of guards stood out front, hostlers tended to his personal paddock nearby, and dozens of storage sheds—each under guard—crowded the small clearing around his tent. It was truly as elaborate a camp as was possible under the circumstances.

Inside waited Bohemond, leaning against the same massive chair from which he'd carved the cross into my face. He wore no armor, only his surcoat and his sword at his waist. Carpets draped the floor, and chests and armoires and armor stands hugged the perimeter. Tancred stood at his side, arms crossed and face as unreadable as ever. Neither of these men had liked me not so long ago, and I'd done little to improve their opinion of me in my first months with the crusade. Since Dorylaeum, however, I felt I'd become a valuable asset to both princes, even if Bohemond seemed to have forgotten who I was until the battle near Harim. Ralph of Caen, Tancred's chronicler, sat at a table in the back of the tent, ink and quill in hand, ready to record whatever was discussed in his hearing.

Bohemond gave me a cursory look, then turned his attention to Hendry. "Sir Hendry," he began, "I shall make this quick: I have missed your presence among my knights. I wish for you to re-enter my service."

Hendry bowed his head. "As you wish, Lord."

"My nephew has informed me that you've served him with distinction, and he has already given his blessing for your return to my service. Seeing as my standard-bearer did not survive Harim, I would see you holding my banner in the next battle."

"'Tis an honor, Lord," Hendry said with another slight bow. "And me lad?"

Bohemond smiled. "Yes, your lad. What to do with him? Would you serve me, as well, thief?" he asked, his iron gaze landing on me.

"He's not a thief anymore, Lord," Hendry put in before I could reply. "Hasnae nicked a thing."

"I suppose not," he said, keeping his eyes on me. "What do *you* say?"

I wanted to bristle under his questioning—and accusing—stare, but I'd given ample reason for his distrust. Instead, I merely said, "I'm no thief, Lord."

"Perhaps. Yet I recall the last oath you gave me." He eyed the scar on my cheek. "The oath that earned you that scar. The oath you disobeyed for the love of a woman. Does she still live?"

"Yes, Lord."

"And she is among us?"

"Yes, Lord."

"I wonder…Would you disobey me again to protect her?"

I thought of lying but knew he'd see through me. In addition to his martial prowess—which seemed unmatched—he was a shrewd leader. Lying would gain me nothing. Besides, I no longer truly cared what he thought of me. I'd continue to fight for him—or Tancred or Godfrey, for that matter—until we reached Jerusalem, but I wouldn't sacrifice Amina for it.

"Probably, Lord. If her life were danger and there was something I could do about it, I cannot say I'd leave her to her fate."

To my surprise, Bohemond smiled and glanced at Tancred. "As you said he would say."

"He's more honest now than he once was, Uncle," Tancred replied, and I thought I heard a hint of respect in his voice. I'd earned that respect fighting at his side at Dorylaeum. "It is not altogether a bad thing."

"I suppose not. But what am I supposed to do with him now?"

Both princes studied me, and I felt especially small that morning. I didn't regret my answer, didn't regret most of my recent actions, yet that didn't make me feel any better standing under their hard gaze. I may not have cared what they thought of me, but that didn't make them any less intimidating.

Then, once more to my surprise, Tancred spoke up in my defense.

"He's risked his life," he said. "Risked it without thought. I've watched him enter battle without reservation and face down overwhelming odds. Indeed, I stood at his side as we fought near Dorylaeum. He's a brave boy, a bit foolish and led mostly by his emotions, but he'll not shirk his duties."

"So long as his woman is safe," Bohemond pointed out. "Still, I saw the same in the deserts of Harim. He fought with courage and killed without hesitation. The Saracens deserved no mercy, and he showed them none. It seems that you're willing to die, yet unwilling to let your woman suffer the same."

"That is a succinct way of putting it, Lord," I said.

"Is it?" He scrutinized me for another moment, then drew a breath, seemed to think as he held it, and let it out in a long exhale. "Very well," he finally said. "I desire Sir Hendry in my services, and it seems you come as a pair. At this point, I will not object. You may regret that decision in the coming days."

"Why's that, Lord?" Hendry asked.

"I'm sure you've noticed our supplies are dwindling. With the raiders of Harim dispersed, Armenian traders and merchants are approaching from the north. I'm told they plan to establish a market nearby, yet their prices will be exorbitant." He smirked, and I thought I saw a touch of malice. "As much as I would like to simply *take* what we need, we cannot upset the merchants. We'll need them eventually. Nevertheless, I would not pay their fees if I could avoid it, and it seems we have already exhausted all the local foraging opportunities. I've spoken with Robert of Flanders. He and I will each build a force of two hundred knights. Among us will be several thousand men-at-arms. Infantry, men on foot."

Tancred scoffed. "Fodder," he muttered.

"True enough," Bohemond agreed. "We've not selected the best among us for this journey, yet they will come, nonetheless. Someone must carry our spoils back."

"Spoils?" Hendry asked.

"Yes, spoils. We go in search of new foraging grounds."

"And if we meet Saracens, Lord?"

He smiled. "Then we will kill them."

7

W e struck out east under clear skies with only thin wisps
of clouds dancing along the blue canopy. Robert rode
with his knights and squires at the front of our small convoy,
and Bohemond led us at the rear. Four hundred of us in total,
between the two lords. In the middle walked several thousand
crusaders, though at this point I feel that title needs some clarity. Not all crusaders were knights or squires; some were armed
mercenaries, others Danes or Normans who'd been fighting
since their youth, and others still servants of lords who'd
trained and equipped themselves sufficiently for battle. These
men were relatively well armed and armored. They wore mail,
and most had swords or battle-axes or war hammers in addition to spears. Many had no horses, and it was this that truly
distinguished them from the knights and squires.

However, the men who traveled with us were none of
these. They were pilgrims, first and foremost, many wearing
cloth armor and no helmets. The best among them had mail
and spear and shield, the poorest only tunic, buckler, and
dagger. Yet since we'd devastated the forces of Harim, the
only opposition we met came from within Antioch, so the

decision was made to leave our allies at the city as well equipped as we could. This would be a foraging run and nothing more, and we needed only men who would carry the spoils, not stand in a shield wall, though some could if it came to that.

We passed south of the Iron Bridge. A guard of several hundred men-at-arms had been left to hold it, and crusader banners now flapped in high winds atop the black towers. The same wind bit at my face and cut through my surcoat and mail. It pulled at Amina's blue fabric cinched securely on my arm, whipping the blue length of cloth furiously as we rode east. I tugged my cloak tighter about my body, sheltering both Amina's token and myself from the wind.

We rode around the twin mountains of Antioch, continued east until midday, then cut south with those same mountains looming now a league to our west. Even from this distance, I saw hints of Antioch's citadel near the top of Mount Silpius, a gray blur on the brown landscape. Yaghi Siyan likely sat in the citadel at this very moment, fretting about how to relieve his city of its besiegers.

The day dragged on, and we eventually passed through small settlements nestled in the desert, no more than six or seven buildings each, always built around one or more wells dug into the hard ground. They were populated by a mixture of Armenians, Greeks, and Turks, both Muslims and Christians. I saw no animosity among them—or toward us—and we stopped at each and traded. We bartered peacefully enough yet always left with a better bargain than was probably fair due to the unspoken threat our small force represented.

The largest of these settlements contained a dozen buildings, including a small church built at its center. It reminded me of Novella's village before Temür and his Saracens had burned it to the ground. A smith's forge spouted smoke, a distant tannery reeked of drying hides, and a graveyard with fourteen tombstones even sprawled into the grass behind the church.

Caldwell—who had accompanied us at the behest of Bohemond and was the only noncombatant among us—spoke briefly with the local priest, and we soon "relieved" him of the burden of storing a cask of homemade wine and a wheel of hard cheese. A cart was also commandeered, and we added it to the growing train of spoils—or, to put it as Caldwell did, our "caravan of well-earned provisions."

We continued south, going from settlement to settlement and increasing our caravan, until a distant haze that was the city of Al Bara rose on the horizon. Most among us had heard of the city, and those who hadn't—myself included—were told about it as we traveled. Not a massive city by any stretch, it nevertheless was well known throughout the region for its olive oil and wine and was often used as a home base for pilgrims seeking to visit the many Christian shrines in the area. As a result, it saw a great number of travelers and merchants.

Yet evening fast approached, so we built camp a few miles north of the city. Bohemond dispatched scouts while we slept, and in the morning we discovered no Saracens in the surrounding desert and no local garrison at Al Bara. This latter piece of news came as something of a surprise, given that Aleppo was only fifty or so miles away.

The city had low walls in some areas and no walls in others. We left much of our force in the desert on the city's outskirts, and Bohemond and Robert followed Caldwell into the city. Hendry and I accompanied Bohemond, and a knight named Sir Pate and his unnamed squire followed Robert. It became quickly apparent that this was not the priest's first visit to Al Bara as he led the six of us directly to the church at its center.

The church had a small pyramid-style tomb attached to it and a garden of pomegranate trees growing behind it. The city's priest was a short, elderly man named Father John, apparently in honor of Saint John Chrysostom, who was said to have visited the area. He hobbled out from the church's portico to greet us, a walking staff clicking on the terra-cotta walkway. His long, gray-and-black beard stretched nearly to his waist, and he gripped its ends with his free hand.

He appeared kindly enough, but the sight of Bohemond and Robert with their banners held high in the morning sun seemed to unnerve him. And rightly so, since it seemed likely we'd be adding a healthy portion of Al Bara's goods to our "well-earned provisions." True, we would leave behind gold and silver, but we would also likely be setting our own prices.

Still, he was a gracious host, and after we hobbled our horses in a nearby stable, he happily led us through the garden. To my surprise, pomegranates hung fat and ready from sagging branches despite the cold. When John noticed my shock, he stopped and cupped one of the ripe fruits.

"Pomegranates are excellent winter fruits," he said, his voice thick with his Armenian accent. He released the fruit and tugged at his beard, twisting the end into a point before continuing through the garden. He seemed to stop at every other tree, whispering in Armenian to each one, almost as if he was saying goodbye to his fruit, which he knew we would be taking.

Buying. The fruit we would be buying.

"Pomegranates hold a special place in both our faiths," he went on.

"Both our faiths?" I asked, and that earned me a look from Caldwell. Asking questions, it seemed, was not the domain of a squire.

"Ours and that of the Saracens," John answered, paying no heed to Caldwell. "Islam."

At this, Bohemond scoffed. "It is just a fruit," he said, plucking one from its branch. He smelled it, then laughed to himself. "Unless it was the fruit Eve cursed us with in the garden."

This earned a laugh from Robert, though John knit his brow in thought. "Perhaps it is…" He trailed off, then shook his head as if to clear the thought. "In any case, the Book of Moses talks of the Israelite spies carrying back pomegranates from the Promised Land as a sign of the land's fertility and abundance. Even their priestly robes and holy objects had pomegranates on them."

"Why would they want pomegranates on their robes?" I asked.

Bohemond frowned at me this time, and I realized I might be overstepping my welcome. John, thankfully, didn't care. "Pomegranates supposedly promote life. They cleanse us physically and bring good health and energy. The Muslims even believe pomegranates grow in their paradise." He pulled one down. "They're taught that one seed of every pomegranate is from Jannah. It is important, then, that they eat every seed. Their prophet, Mohammed, once said—"

"We are not here for a lesson on what the heathens think," Caldwell cut in.

If the outburst bothered John, he didn't let it show. "Very well," he said, stroking his beard once more. "What *are* you here for, then?"

"Provisions," Bohemond answered. "Food and drink."

He nodded in understanding. "To prolong your siege."

"Indeed," agreed Robert, speaking for the first time. "Winter has been harsher than expected, and we have exhausted all the local foraging grounds."

"You mean you have taken all you can from the surrounding villages?"

The prince frowned. "We have paid for what we can."

"And what you cannot?"

Bohemond scoffed loudly. "What could not or would not be sold was taken by force. What does it matter?"

"I believe it is written somewhere that you shall not steal," John said.

"We are on a mission from God," Caldwell said, though even I thought his voice lacked true conviction. I believe Caldwell would have had no objections to taking what he wanted by force, regardless of our mission.

"Charity should not cease just because you are called to task," John countered.

Bohemond smirked, though Caldwell bristled under John's tone. "We seek to reclaim the holy seat of our faith," Caldwell replied, his voice rising in mock indignation. "If our Christian brothers will not share their alms, then it is they who are not being charitable. It is not theft to take what is rightfully owed us."

Even Hendry flinched at that. Neither he nor I ever pretended that we did the right thing in pillaging or that it was God's will that we do it. Yet war dictates certain things, and we mere soldiers are pragmatic men to a fault. Without supplies we would never take Antioch, let alone reach Jerusalem, and so pillage we must. But to say we were *owed* the goods we pillaged?

"As you say," John acquiesced, though he clearly did not agree. But Caldwell was backed up by six armed men, and that can make an argument quite persuasive. "Al Bara has many goods for sale. We have a bustling market, and..." he trailed off and glanced once more at his pomegranate trees. I thought I saw a hint of sadness in his eyes. "And the church will happily provide what you need in exchange for your *charity*. I ask only that you leave one tree with its fruit."

Caldwell looked as if he wanted to argue, but thankfully Robert spoke first.

"We accept," he said, "and we thank you for your hospitality."

And with that, our small army descended on the city. At first, the merchants of Al Bara seemed to delight in our presence. That is, until the haggling began, and our men walked away with far more than what their coins were worth. For myself, I mostly followed Bohemond and Hendry as they oversaw the purchasing and loading of the wagons and carts. We acquired more than fifty oxen and donkeys to pull the heaviest ones, and even discovered two dozen casks of wine in the back of the church that John was willing to part with.

I found a moment alone with the Armenian priest and thanked him once more for his hospitality, as forced as it was. He offered me a single pomegranate from the tree that we'd been instructed to spare, and I took it hesitantly.

"Why do you give me this?" I asked.

"Because I fear the ones your lords have loaded onto their wagons will not reach men such as yourself."

"Men such as myself?"

"Those who cannot afford the *charity* of their Christian brethren." He winked. "Enjoy the fruit."

8

W e spent another day traveling southeast in the desert, moving from settlement to settlement and adding to our already burdensome caravan. Lines of wagons and carts rumbled alongside us in the fading light. Each kicked up a pillar of dust that left a brown cloud trailing for miles. The convoy was filled with bundled wheat and straw, live chickens in crudely built cages, fodder for the horses and other beasts of burden, dried meats and salt, and even one heavy cart laden with precut horseshoes. Another twenty wagons overflowed with barrels of ale and beer and wine. A herd of cattle—at least three hundred cows and half as many sheep—followed closely behind the wagons, driven along by the several thousand infantry who walked along on foot.

After two full days in the desert wilderness, we were back-tracking now, returning to Antioch the same way we'd come. Hendry and I traveled with Bohemond in the lead of our now-massive company, and Robert and his men followed in the rear, likely a mile or more east of us. We'd met no resistance, and the weather had been as pleasant as possible for late December, which merely meant there had been only cold wind and no rain. Though now, looking up, I saw a bank of black clouds so sharply defined it was like a curtain flung across an otherwise perfectly clear sky. If we didn't sleep in the freezing rain tonight, we'd surely wake up in it.

With that in mind, we stopped under the rapidly darkening sky. Bohemond and Robert built separate camps in the east and west, and the infantry established a third between us. The lords rewarded our successful foraging by opening a few casks of the wine. It was, rather selfishly, distributed to the four hundred knights and squires, leaving none for the several thousand infantry—the ones who'd marched on foot through the desert, herding the cattle and guiding the wagons the entire time. For them, two dozen barrels of beer and ale were tapped. They didn't seem to notice the discrepancy, and instead drunk themselves into as much of a stupor as that little bit of alcohol could provide.

Morning came with a hangover—my first in months—and still it had not rained, though the curtain of black clouds now encompassed the entire sky. Distant flickers of lightning lit the northern horizon, and only a thin sliver of light was visible in the east. It seemed the rising sun had found the only gap in the clouds and shone all the more fiercely.

Or maybe that was the hangover.

We broke camp slowly, as I was obviously not the only one sluggish from our night of celebration. My mail felt especially heavy, and *Ankída* seemed to sway between my legs. A few moments in the saddle fixed that, though the ache in my head remained. Even Hendry moaned as he mounted Tencendur.

"Oof, lad," he said, gripping the pommel and shielding his eyes from the tiny bit of light glaring angrily at us. As Bohemond's new standard-bearer, he held the banner in his left hand. It sagged in the windless morning, not helped by Hendry's light grip. "Got a bit blootered last night, didnae we?"

"Not sure what blootered is," I said, "but I don't think I like it."

"Aye," was all he muttered in response.

Hendry and I sat in silence—along with the rest of Bohemond's knights—and watched as the growing thunderclouds finally overtook the angry morning sun, and the infantry between the camps began to organize the wagons and cattle. I could only just make out Robert's mounted knights on the eastern horizon.

A few drops of rain finally began to fall, coming slow and heavy in big, fat drops that thumped onto my helmet like miniature war drums.

"I dinnae like that," Hendry said, putting words to my own thoughts.

I removed my helmet and set it on my lap. Soon the cold rain soaked my hair and plastered it to my face, but it was better than the drumming, so I let it be.

"What's that?" I asked, lazily nodding toward the east. A patch of brown had joined the gray and black of the thunderclouds. It looked like the clouds themselves had gotten dirty, smothered in the dust from the desert floor.

"I dinnae ken..." Hendry trailed off, and I realized it the same moment he did.

"Saracens."

"Aye, lad. Saracens."

The sudden arrival of armed enemies is always enough to clear a hangover, and we both felt the lingering effects of our night of drinking vanish behind the realization that battle was likely approaching. And fast.

"Saracens!" a cry arose. It echoed through the camp, and soon we saw Bohemond riding hard toward the infantry.

"That's us, lad," Hendry said. He renewed his grip on the banner, and I slipped my helmet back on—unintentionally dumping a bowl's worth of rainwater onto my head—then we kicked our horses to join him. Bohemond's banner drew the rest of our forces with us, and soon we'd all joined our lord as he halted at the edge of the infantry's camp and stared intently to the east.

The brown cloud continued to rise, though it was still farther away than Robert and his men, yet it spread even as we watched, both to the north and south, and it quickly became apparent the Saracens sought to surround us. The infantry began to move, some rushing toward us and others grabbing arms and moving to defend our spoils. I glanced at Bohemond and saw his stoic expression, his face devoid of emotion and fear. It was the face of a warrior, a prince, a lord. The Saracens continued their move to surround us, yet there was not even a hint of panic in his steely gaze as he thought of his next action.

"Shield walls," he suddenly shouted, kicking his horse into motion. Hendry rode at his side, Bohemond's banner flapping in the cold, wet rain. "Shield walls!"

The infantry responded, those with shields forming lines around our wagons while those without stood behind them and fought to control the cattle, a task made nearly impossible in the growing storm and confusion. They dashed about in a frantic, panicked mess of movement, but even so there were enough battle-hardened men that indeed a shield wall formed. It was shallow—three or four men deep at its thickest—yet it just might hold long enough for us to push back the Saracens, however Bohemond planned on doing that.

"Defend our spoils," he cried, riding up and down the shield wall with Hendry at his side, their horses throwing great clumps of muddied desert floor. His voice echoed magnificently over the men, instilling in them courage and valor. "This is our food! Our livelihood! Defend it with your life!" Then he was back among us mounted knights and squires. "We ride west," he said, the gusto gone from his voice and replaced with

SHADOWS OF ANTIOCH | 79

a tension that was shocking. "Quickly! Before they surround us."

With not another word, we did exactly that, and two hundred of us thundered across the desert. The storm intensified as we rode, and thick sheets of rain smacked into our faces. I watched the frantic infantry continuing to form their wall, slipping in the muck as they watched us ride away. We pounded by them, our horses churning the soaked dirt into trampled mud. Hendry rode beside Bohemond, the quartered blue and red standard continuing to whip angrily in the growing wind and thick rain, and I followed close behind.

I saw my first glimpse of the Saracens as they galloped several hundred yards to our south, barely visible through the veil of rain. The heavy downpour had begun to beat down the rising dust, and they were nothing but gray specters gliding across the waterlogged wasteland, a blur of movement in the desert. The Saracens rode parallel to us, and I knew they were trying to cut off any retreat. I glanced north and saw a similar force much farther off. Together, there were at least a thousand of them. It was a daunting number against our two hundred, and I knew this would be not a battle but a slaughter if we failed to outrun them.

"Lances!" Bohemond cried. "Lances ready!"

I jerked my massive lance from the saddle and fought it into place. It rolled in my wet palm, made worse by *Ankída*'s bounding gallop and the icy rain and wind in my face. I tightened my grip and just managed to couch it under my arm. It bobbed out in front me, swaying side to side as it cut through the rain. I wrestled my shield into my off hand, the reins held tight between two of my fingers, though I doubted *Ankída* needed any guidance. She'd keep up wtih the men to my left and right with or without my help.

Hopefully.

The Saracens' lighter and faster horses continued to outrun

our heavier steeds, and their lead grew. Soon they would cut us off and meet with the rest of their army riding in the north, and we'd face their combined strength. Our charge would likely not be able to punch through at that point, especially weakened by the muddy ground and torrential downpour. Even if it did, it would come with heavy losses, yet I had no idea what else we could do but continue forward, hoping to crash through their line before it fully formed.

But Bohemond was a prince for a reason.

"On me!" he cried, then veered to the left, cutting sharply toward the southern Saracens and putting as much distance as possible from the others in the north. Our wedge angled, and *Ankída* huffed as I tugged on the reins. Some knights or squires tumbled from their saddles as their mounts tripped on the turn, riders and horses going down together in an explosion of mud and water. The rest of us continued on, and we chewed up the few hundred yards between us and the Saracens in a flash.

They reacted quickly, not breaking their pace as they fired a volley directly into us. The rain did little to slow their arrows, and hundreds of them shot by like diving falcons in the tempest. Yet we'd learned hard lessons through countless battles and now rode with wide gaps in our formation. Most of the arrows battered the rain around us, hitting our gaps and doing little else. I heard a single, almost distant cry of pain as one man was struck and killed. I glanced back to see his horse continuing its mad charge without rider or weapon.

We hit the Saracens like a hammer. Archers flew from horses, lances snapped with resounding staccato cracks, misfired arrows vanished into the storm, and beasts and men careened off one another as we sliced into their still-galloping formation.

Some had turned to take flight from our charge, and my rain-soaked hand struggled to hold the lance as it struck the rump of a fleeing horse, the tip ripping through flesh and rebounding back up. I heard the animal scream in pain, watched it buck its rider from the saddle and kick the horse behind it in the muzzle, then I was gone, bursting out the other side of their formation and into mostly free space as the rain continued to batter us.

My first instinct was to gallop to safety, yet Bohemond knew that the rest of the Saracens would only harry us all the way to Antioch. We'd unhorsed many in our initial charge—perhaps a hundred, perhaps fewer—but that meant a thousand or more were still at our flanks, still able to pursue.

So we rounded for another attack, this time riding back east to hit the disorganized rear of the same Saracens as they stumbled over the casualties we'd just produced. Riders fought their way around each other, horses charging in every direction as they tried to recover from the shock of our charge. Some had finally turned, giving up their mad ride to surround us, and now struggled with the rest of the Saracens as they sought to regain some kind of cohesion. If any of them saw us, none gave a warning.

We hit them with much the same effect as before, coming through the curtain of rain like an unseen ship in the night. We hit them like lightning from the storm that still raged all around us. Saracens rocked from saddles and died before they hit the ground, their mangled bodies further trampled underfoot as we hammered and punched our way through them once more.

With such little resistance, it was over quickly, and the Saracens who remained in our wake—though still outnumbering us at least four to one—turned back the way they'd come and fled, leaving behind the mutilated wreckage of hundreds of dead and dying men and horses.

We halted and watched and cheered as they fled, but it would be a temporary retreat, of that we were sure. They would regroup, realize they still had the upper hand, and likely attempt once more to surround us. Even if they didn't, I could already see their northern flank—the second half of their attempted encirclement—riding hard across the desert floor toward us.

We were not free yet.

And closer still came mounted men from the east. Through the gray haze they rode, and soon I saw Robert's banner as a flood of knights joined us and relief washed over me. The two lords met at the front, and we formed something of a semi-circle behind them.

What to do? Charge once more into the Saracens and hope to break them as we had the others? Turn around and attempt to outrun them? Return to the infantry and make a stand?

"To me!" Bohemond cried.

"To me!" echoed Robert.

And I had my answer.

"*Deus vult!*" they screamed together.

Nearly four hundred knights and squires answered back—*Deus vult!*—and as one we broke into a gallop, Bohemond and Robert at our head pointing us toward the Saracen riders in the north. Our banners whipped and snapped in the rain and wind, lances bobbed and dipped, steel tips slick like flint in the wet and dreary morning.

The Saracens had expected we'd continue our retreat, not angle to intercept them. They tried to wheel about, to perform their standard retreat and fire technique, yet the mud and rain proved as fatal an enemy as we were. Their turn was slow and clumsy, rider bumping into rider as they attempted to get into position before quickly realizing their mistake and firing a sporadic volley.

An arrow bounced from my shield, and another struck my helmet. The successive blows bent me backward on my saddle, feet and legs screaming in pain as I tried to stay atop *Ankída*. My lance drifted skyward, and I forced it down, using its weight to pull me back upright just as we crashed once again into the Saracens.

The tip came down into the head of the nearest rider. It ground down the steel helmet and ripped through the mail at his shoulder, shattering his collarbone and bludgeoning him from his saddle. The blow vibrated up my shoulder, and my teeth rattled in my head, yet I held strong, angling the lance back in front of me and catching another Saracen in the thigh. This time it sliced through the rider and into his horse, grating along the animal's ribs and burying itself nearly a foot inside the beast. Rider and mount made such a noise that I will never forget, screeching in unison at the sudden pain and shock, then the horse went limp and collapsed immediately. My lance caught on ribs and snapped as *Ankída* continued her forward charge, leaving me with splintered wood and nothing else.

I dropped it and drew Skull Splitter, but already we were free of the Saracens and into open space. I prepared to wheel about, but Bohemond and Robert continued forward, charging north and away from the battle.

It was finally time to retreat.

9

We sat in the rain and waited, rows of knights and squires watching the south with vigilant eyes. Bohemond and Robert were at our front—as always—and I sat atop *Ankída* beside Hendry. The rain had amplified from bad to worse, then from worse to horrendous. Great rivers of mud the color of molten bronze ran across the desert floor. It washed away the dirt and blood from our surcoats, but left us a sopping, shivering mess.

Lightning danced in the sky, illuminating the charcoal clouds from within and pulsing like a beating heart. The occasional lancing fork of cobalt light struck the ground, searing my eyes and lingering in my vision long after the momentary flash faded. Booming thunder rolled across the barren desert, rumbling like an angry god before fading into the gray.

Caldwell was among us, somehow. I didn't recall seeing him during the battle—if our desperate retreat could be called that—yet he sat with the princes nonetheless. His priest's robe looked as drenched as the rest of us. Rainwater ran down the massive crucifix still hanging about his neck, dripping onto the saddle beneath him. His hair clung to his face despite the cloak pulled up over his head, and he sat slumped over his horse, clearly in as sour a mood as was possible, though for that I couldn't blame him.

Hours had passed since our retreat, and still we saw no sign of the Saracens. According to Robert, his frontal assault had pushed back the initial charge. Yet in the distance he'd seen the rest of the enemy forces held in reserve. Banners identified them as Duqaq, king of Damascus. He'd brought an army of thousands, most on foot, though a great number were mounted, as we'd already seen. But even their infantry had been armed with spear and sword and shield, wearing thick mail and ready for a prolonged battle. Robert had decided that —as the saying went—discretion was the better of valor and had turned tail and fled west, where he'd joined us for the final retreat. Three hundred and eight of us had survived, a staggeringly high number considering we'd only had four hundred mounted men to begin with.

But we were not waiting only for signs of the Saracens; we were waiting with the hope that our own infantry had been left unharmed after our cavalry charges had scattered the Saracen horse archers. Yet after Robert's report of the full size of Duqaq's army, our hopes were slim.

"Should we send men back?" I heard Robert ask.

Bohemond scoffed as a reply. "To what end?"

"To see if any survived."

"If men had lived, we would have seen them by now."

Robert waved a hand at the veil of rain. "Would we?"

"Perhaps not," Bohemond acknowledged. "But what can you hope to do if we find them? Do you think Duqaq will have fled the field? No, Robert. Our men are dead."

Robert persisted. "And what of the provisions we spent two days collecting?" His tone remained neutral, measured, while Bohemond—now that the battle was over—let emotion into his voice.

That emotion was anger.

"Our spoils are gone," he snapped. "And I will not risk the lives of my men to recover whatever remains of them."

"Without food, our men will die under the walls of Antioch."

"No, they will not. The Armenian markets will have to suffice."

"You know as well as I that only a few of us will be able to pay their sure-to-be exorbitant prices."

I thought of the Al Bara priest's comment and how he'd claimed men like me would not be able to afford the charity of our Christian brethren. Yet I wasn't poor, at least not in the same manner as a great many of the pilgrims who'd accompanied us. If they were forced to rely on the Armenian markets, then they might indeed starve.

With that sobering thought, we resumed once more our quiet sentry. While we waited, I opened *Ankída*'s side bags and checked on the pomegranate the priest had given me. I was saving it for Amina and Novella to share, and I realized now that it was likely the only spoil we'd return to Antioch with.

"I'll go myself," Robert finally said. He spun his horse, faced the men. "I am returning to the battlefield," he called, eyes going across the knights and squires sitting stoically in the rain. "I go in search of survivors, in hopes of recapturing some of our provisions. I'll not force any man to join me, yet I welcome your company."

At first no one moved, and I noticed several of the men glancing toward Bohemond. These all wore his surcoats, and as knights and squires in his service they were waiting to see their lord's reaction. He said nothing, and so did they. Then, slowly, men from Robert's side came forward. First one, then two, then a dozen. Soon, roughly fifty men had moved their horses forward and now stood at their lord's side.

Bohemond studied the small party, eyes narrowed in cold,

calculated thought. "I cannot send you alone," he finally said, though more than likely he wanted to be able to lay a claim to any spoils that might be recovered. He looked back to his own knights and squires. "Ten men. And the father," he added, nodding to Caldwell.

The priest turned his wet, brooding face to look at Bohemond. Water ran down his high cheek bones and into his thick beard. "Me?"

"Yes, you," he said. "There are likely Christian men in need of a proper burial."

Caldwell's expression shifted from brooding to annoyed. "And I'm to bury thousands of men? While the Saracens remain not far off?" He paused to scoff. "And in *this* weather?"

Bohemond nearly smirked. As much as Tancred liked the priest, Bohemond seemed to get an odd pleasure out of torturing him. It was likely why he'd insisted on the priest's presence on this expedition in the first place. "I'm sorry the weather has turned unpleasant, Father, but these men died as martyrs. You would not condemn such men to purgatory, would you?"

Caldwell scowled but said nothing.

"And besides," he went on, "my men can dig, if it comes to that. Speaking of which," he said, turning once more to his men. "Ten volunteers."

Men hesitated, but slowly a few joined the ranks of Robert's. I recalled the ending of a battle not so long ago under the walls of Nicaea. It had been my first, and I'd spent the aftermath digging graves while priests scurried around blessing men and reading last rites. It had felt right then, and it felt right now.

"I'm going to go," I said quietly, only loud enough for Hendry to hear me. He shot me a glance. "I'll be fine."

He thought for a moment, then shrugged. "Dinnae die."

"I'll try not to." I kicked *Ankida* forward. "I'll go," I said, this time loud enough to be heard. Bohemond glanced at me, then exchanged a look with Hendry, who only shrugged again.

"Very well," Bohemond said, then turned back to Robert. "I wish you luck," he added, though his tone implied something quite different. "Do not let anything happen to my men."

The rain didn't pity our situation and stepped up its assault, shrouding our vision beyond a few dozen yards. The wind blew it about in thick sheets, buffeting our faces one moment, then gusting from behind and nearly pushing us from our mounts the next.

We traveled slowly and always with a pair of us riding a hundred yards in front as scouts. One would return to the main body of our small army every few minutes to swap out with a fresh rider, leaving a single scout alone in the desert and rain for a short time. This was repeated until eventually it was my turn.

I didn't know the man I rode with. He served Robert, his name was *also* Robert, and his horse was a small rouncy. That was the extent of my knowledge of him before he cursed the rain and rode back to be relieved, leaving me alone on an island of water and mud.

And so it was that I saw the remnants of the battle first.

A heavy gust of wind blew in from behind, pushing aside the rain and clearing the path ahead for a heartbeat. Hundreds of bodies sprawled on the desert floor, most already half-buried under filthy puddles of mud and blood. Arms and legs stuck from their temporary graves, fists clutching weapons or shields or nothing but air. Wagons lay overturned, the oxen or donkeys that had pulled them dead alongside them, mouths open, tongues lolling out, and vacant eyes staring straight as their insides spilled onto the desert floor. Spears sprouted from the ground like quills from the back of a filthy porcupine, quivering in the wind and rain.

Then the wind shifted, and I saw nothing but a curtain of water.

"Why'd you stop?" a muffled voice asked beside me.

I turned and saw Pate, the knight who'd accompanied Robert in Al Bara.

"We're here," I said. He shook his head to tell me he couldn't hear me over the storm, and I opened my mouth to shout when the wind shifted once more, and he saw the same scene I had.

"God's bones…"

"Aye," I muttered. "God's bones, indeed."

The Saracens had not been gone long. The blood of the dead and dying was warm, and wounded men still crawled across the dank wasteland in their own blood and filth. Most of these barely living would be dead in a few hours as their wounds took their toll. Some missed limbs, others eyes, and most had at least a pair of arrows sticking up from their dying bodies that shivered and trembled as they hauled themselves through the mud.

Fortunately, the Saracens had not taken all our spoils, only most of them. Unfortunately, whatever they couldn't take they'd ruined, spilling carts and wagons over into the mire and slaughtering the oxen and donkeys that had pulled them. The blood and guts of these butchered animals smothered the supplies; bundles of wheat, dried and cured meats, and baskets of fruits and vegetables. All now ruined beyond use. Barrels of beer and ale had been smashed and now lay empty beside puddles of brown sludge. A cart that had carried chickens now held the dead bodies of murdered birds.

Robert led a dozen men through the carnage, hoping to find something salvageable or living. He returned later with nothing. The rest of us dug, a truly useless gesture in the rain. After an hour of no progress—or, rather, an hour of using our axes and swords and hands to dig out the same sticky blood-soaked mud that the rain pushed immediately back into our shallow hole—we gave up and piled the bodies together. Caldwell prayed over them all at once, speaking in a hushed and hurried voice with his cloak still drawn up over him.

And so we left our fallen where they lay, with the words of an indifferent priest prayed over them and the hopes that God would take mercy upon their souls.

INTERLUDE I

AD 1115
Jerusalem

S ir Daniel went quiet and stirred the güvec as Roland
continued to cut his gambeson. He'd already cut three
layers from the fabric, and judging by the sun approaching its
apex in the sky, he knew he'd probably not finish the cutting
today, let alone the stitching.

"I still remember the mound of bodies," Sir Daniel said,
his voice almost a whisper. His eyes went distant as he stared
into the soup, and Roland thought he saw the hint of a tear
glistening in the corner of his eye. "I'd seen only one other like
it, and that had been near Civetot, before we took Nicaea. A
mountain of sun-bleached bones, picked clean by the ravens
and vultures and left by the Saracens after they'd annihilated
the People's Crusade. This was different. This…"

He drew a breath, swallowed, cleared his throat. Roland
waited patiently, linens on his lap, shears held tight in his hand.

"These men…" Sir Daniel started again, then paused as
his voice cracked. "These men had been alive a couple of

hours ago. I could see their faces, see their eyes…" he trailed off once more, and silence filled the small space around the gently crackling fire. Roland watched the smoke drift up and surround the small pot of güvec, then lifted the shears and continued to quietly cut the linen. He thought perhaps Sir Daniel was finally done, that he had reached the point where he could dwell on it no longer.

But the old knight had more to say.

"I cannot fully explain what that sight did to me," he went on. "It put me down a path that I'd give anything not to have walked. I'd been through battles and would suffer countless more, yet something about those mutilated bodies left a scar on my mind that I would not be rid of for some time. Perhaps because most of them were pilgrims, not warriors, or perhaps because it had not been a battle, but a slaughter. These men stood no chance against Duqaq's army, and they'd been mercilessly and ruthlessly killed."

Another silence, and this time Roland spoke into it. "The Saracens are brutal, heartless heathens," he said, hoping to lift Sir Daniel's spirits.

Instead he scoffed in disapproval. "Aye, the Saracens were our enemies, true enough. They stood in the way of us and Jerusalem. They were brutal, yes, but so were we. I'll let the priests talk on who's a heathen. And heartless?" He shrugged. "I've seen atrocities on both sides. Bohemond had executed nearly a hundred half-naked prisoners not a month before. We'd catapulted the heads of their dead into Nicaea. We were about to do much worse inside the walls of Antioch. We killed them, and they killed us. But I don't resent them."

Roland set the shears down. "How could you not?"

"They were protecting their home, same as we were trying to reclaim it. We were invaders to their minds, and I can't say I blame them for anything they've done. It likely wasn't *these* Saracens that took Byzantine land. It was their fathers, or *their* fathers. They had as much right to defend themselves as we did to invade."

"But they killed pilgrims," he said. "They—"

"I'm not telling you my story so you can think it was good against evil," Sir Daniel cut in. "We crusaders did our share of cruelty. Maybe more. Men raped and killed on both sides. Some of the blood on my own hands is innocent blood. No, lad. This wasn't good against evil, just force against force. Who's stronger was all that mattered, and this time it was them."

"But…" Roland frowned. "Then what was different? If you hadn't resented them before, why did you then?"

Sir Daniel frowned. "Because it was my fault. *I* fled with Bohemond, with Robert, with the other horsemen. *I* left those men to the Saracens. *I* abandoned my brethren, and they died for it."

"What could you have done?" Roland asked. "You say Duqaq had thousands of men. What difference would a few hundred horsemen have done against such odds? What could you have done?"

"I could've died with them," he said.

Roland's mouth hung open. "You could've died with them," he repeated. "I…Why would you?"

"Because there are worse things than dying, lad, and I was about to do them."

ACT II

10

AD 1098
January
Antioch

J anuary looked to be an uneventful month.

As Bohemond had predicted, the Armenian markets had arrived in full by the beginning of January. And as *everyone* predicted, the prices were so inflated that even the lords of the crusade struggled to keep their men fed. However, after the disaster that had been our foraging run near Al Bara, we had little choice but to pay their exorbitant fees. Some of the lords gathered together and did what they could, pooling their resources and purchasing supplies. Bohemond, Raymond of Toulouse, Godfrey, and the other extraordinarily wealthy princes were able to supply their men out of their own funds. They did this not out of the goodness of their hearts but out of a desire to keep us alive. Without men-at-arms to wield swords, shields, and spears, they would quickly become lords of noth-ing. Being the squire of Hendry—who remained Bohemond's standard-bearer—I was comparatively well fed, as were Amina and Novella.

Others, however, were not so lucky. Men sold all they had to eat, eventually becoming so desperate as to part with their weapons, armor, and—lastly—horses. Even the most noble of knights was soon reduced to riding donkeys or walking. Poverty-stricken pilgrims begged at the edges of the market, hoping to be fed on Christian charity, which was in as short supply as the food itself. Starvation and disease ravaged the men, and those suffering were quickly shuffled beyond the camp and forced to fend for themselves in order to contain their maladies. Our graveyard—built in the far north near a church we'd passed on the way in—swelled to five times its size in the matter of a month. Trenches filled with the waste of both human and animal covered the plains not far from our camp.

Some crusaders became thieves in order to live, which meant others became watchmen in order to prevent theft. Examples were made of those caught, men were executed or forced into hard labor, and a series of pillories were built atop a low hill for all to see, even the garrison of Antioch, who likely took joy in our hardships. Caldwell, along with many of the other priests, preached for repentance in order that God may continue to bless our crusade as he had in the months before.

I didn't bother to point out that the months before had been warmer and filled with food.

Several knights and lesser earls and dukes, those who had retinues of their own, set out on foraging runs with the hopes of finding some kind of sustenance to keep themselves fed. Many of these weren't sanctioned by the lords of the crusade, though they turned a blind eye. That is, until a small force of three hundred men led by a man named Ludwig was wiped out by Antioch's garrison. The garrison must have witnessed his departure, because not long after they sent their own force through the Iron Gate in the west and ambushed Ludwig, killing him and all his men.

It wasn't long after this that Peter the Hermit, the man who'd led the People's Crusade almost a year prior, chose to abandon our cause. He left in the company of a knight named William the Carpenter. While few mourned the loss, Tancred himself set off after them, returning them to the camp within a week. Peter, being a religious man himself, was sent to the priests for "correction." William, however, was a ranking knight in the service of Bohemond, so he spent an entire night lying on the ground in his lord's tent like a piece of rubbish. In the morning came his "trial," and many called for leniency, likely feeling sympathy for the man's decision to flee, given that it was compelled by the same hunger and fear that nearly all of us experienced. Bohemond either felt this same sympathy, or—more likely—didn't want to lose yet another knight, since he eventually acquiesced to the wishes of the others and offered William a place back among his soldiers.

Another man of import also set out from the camp. Taticius—Emperor Comnenus's half-Greek, half-Arab general who'd accompanied us since Nicaea—claimed he was leaving to meet the emperor and bring reinforcements. He took with him a thousand or more engineers, though he left his supplies in the camp as a sign that he would return. Time would show him a liar, and we saw neither Taticius's return nor the arrival of any reinforcements sent by the emperor.

In all, the winter dragged on, and more men died to the elements than the enemy. It was this that drove Tancred and Bohemond to organize another supply run into Cilicia, the region that Tancred himself had mostly subdued on our travels to Antioch. Hendry—being more miserable than I'd ever seen him—quickly volunteered, which meant I'd be traveling, as well. Given the dangers of leaving Amina and Novella alone in camp—disease, starvation, the lust of men-at-arms who'd not been with a woman in months—we decided to bring them along.

And so it was that mid-January arrived, men died in droves under the walls of Antioch, and I found myself sitting in a tavern in the city of Adana, warm, well fed, surrounded by friends, and nursing my second ale.

Hendry, on the other hand, nursed nothing.

"Long may yer chimney reek," he called out as he tossed back his third ale. I was probably the only one who understood him—and that was saying a lot, since I didn't quite—but that didn't stop rounds of "here, here" from echoing through the meager tavern. Before the words had even faded, the barmaid had replaced Hendry's drink, earning herself a pat on the backside and a wink from the nearly drunk Scot for her efforts. She returned the wink with a coy smile.

"You should slow down, Sir Hendry," Amina said, though even she was smiling. I'd seen Hendry drunk before and knew that he'd be loud and especially talkative for a time, then pass out within the next couple of hours. He was essentially harmless, and so I did little to try and slow him down. Besides, we'd be completely unable to understand him in an hour or so.

"Aye, mebbe," he muttered, setting his drink down. Then he winked at Novella and raised it again. "But yer a long time dead."

Novella giggled as Hendry downed the ale. Myrtle clucked and fluttered on her lap. Novella had convinced me to bring the chicken along for fear of it being eaten while were away. Despite me wanting to eat the chicken myself, I had a hard time telling Novella no.

Amina sighed and looked at me. "I don't know what that means," she said.

I shrugged. "I only *mostly* know what he says."

Thankfully, Hendry was in the explaining mood, another

side effect of the alcohol. "It means being dead's forever, lassie. But being alive isnae, so I'm gaun to be alive."

She smirked. "And tomorrow? When you awake to a sun too bright and your wits too dull?"

"Haw! Me wits're never dull!"

"And the sun?" she asked.

"Never too bright!"

"Then I shall hear no whining in the morning," she said. She spoke in the same tone she used on Novella when she became too rambunctious, which was frequent.

He frowned and looked as indignant as I'd ever seen him. "I willnae whine!"

"Aye," she said, doing her best Hendry impression. "Aye, you will, lad!"

This received a burst of laughter from the men around us. Sir Wymond, Elric, Rainald, and John Mark all sat with drinks of their own, though, like me, they were still on their second rather than their fourth. Thomas the lisping stable boy had come along, too, though he was still in the markets in search of a new lute to purchase with the gold coin Hendry had given him. I couldn't help but admire his dogged determination despite the pattering of rain on the tavern's windows.

Another two hundred knights and squires were spread throughout the city and ravaging taverns and shops in much the same manner as we were. Adana felt like a paradise compared to the long, cold days staring up at Antioch's walls with the constant threat of steel-tipped arrows, bowel-loosening disease, and starvation, though tomorrow—after a final run through the city's markets—the five-day journey back to Antioch would begin.

Thanks to Hendry, I suspected we'd be getting a late start.

"Yer not a bad one, lassie," Hendry said, then beckoned to the barmaid to bring another ale. Amina caught her attention and waved her off. Hendry didn't notice. "Not a bad one at all," he said again. "As me ma used to say, 'Good gear comes in wee bundles.'"

No one responded, and Hendry sighed at the table full of inquisitive looks. He locked eyes with John Mark, as if it had been him alone who didn't understand whatever it was Hendry's ma was trying to tell us.

"She's a *wee* lassie," Henry explained emphatically, putting his thumb and pointer finger nearly together and squinting at Amina through the small gap. "A wee peedie thing!"

John Mark glanced at me, brow furrowed in confusion.

"Wee means small," I translated. "So does peedie."

Hendry huffed at the both of us. "'Course peedie's small! What else would it be, lad!?" He turned to Novella and nudged her on the shoulder—a bit too hard, as she nearly fell from her chair. This drew a giggle from her and Hendry both. He helped her straighten up, then leaned in close as if he were going to whisper a great secret before nearly shouting, "A nod's as good as a wink to a blind horse, eh, lassie?"

"Who's nodding at a blind horse?" John Mark asked, but this only made Hendry belt another laugh as Novella covered her mouth and giggled.

"So Amina is good gear?" I asked, forgetting about the blind horse and trying to return to his ma's great bit of wisdom that had started this entire thread of conversation.

"Aye, now yer getting it," he said. "She's good gear come in a wee bundle."

I thought on that for a moment, glanced at Amina with a smile, and nodded. "She is good gear."

"Great gear," Hendry put in.

"Gear?" she asked with mock indignation. "I'm gear now?"

"*Great* gear!" Hendry shouted again, then turned back to the barmaid. "Where's me drink?"

The barmaid saw Hendry, then shared a glance with Amina, who only shrugged in defeat.

"Why's she looking at *ye?*" Hendry asked. "I'm a grown mannie, I am!"

Amina was saved from answering when the tavern door squealed open and Thomas came bursting in. He held the biggest lute I'd ever seen and wore an even bigger smile.

"Look at thith thing!" he shouted, then ran across the tavern to join us, nearly stumbling with the huge lute in his hands. He set it down on his lap, leaning awkwardly back since the instrument's long neck came up passed his shoulder.

"Where did you find that?" Amina asked.

Thomas's grin spread even further. "A Turkith vendor," he replied gleefully. "Ever theen a lute *thith* big?"

"That's not a lute," she said, and Thomas frowned. "It's called a *divan bağlama.*"

"What's a *divan bağlama?*" I asked.

Thomas held it up. "It'th a big lute."

I looked at Amina for clarification, and she shrugged. "It's a big lute," she admitted.

"Play us a tune," John Mark said.

Thomas plucked a few of the strings, grinned at the vibrant tone that filled the tavern, then plucked a few more. After another minute of playing with the instrument, something of a beat finally took shape, fast and joyful. The men of the tavern fell silent one by one as Thomas played louder and louder, and soon the only sound was that of the *divan bağlama.* He didn't sing, and I found myself wondering what it would sound like with his heavy lisp.

Amina met my eyes, and I thought for a moment she was going to sing. She often sang in the camp while she cooked, and I enjoyed listening to her as much as I enjoyed the food that came after. Instead, she grinned, grabbed my hand, and pulled me from my seat. My hands found her waist, hers landed on my shoulders, and our feet beat on the faded wood of the tavern floor. Her steps were graceful and fluid, practiced and elegant, while mine thumped, clumsy and heavy, yet neither of us cared. Boots began stomping in time with Thomas's thrumming. The room spun, and we danced until sweat beaded on my head.

Elric ended up alongside us, a woman I'd never seen in his arms. Hendry grabbed the barmaid and joined in, but drunk as he was, he was even clumsier than me, though that didn't stop him from clomping about the tavern with a wide grin. The barmaid had a smile to match his, and both laughed as they danced. Novella leaped between Amina and me, and we held her tight and continued our twirling around the tavern.

This is one of those memories that I still dream of. A night spent in a tavern with friends, my woman in my arms, the giggling of Novella louder even than Thomas's new toy. Amina's smile brighter than the burning candles scattered about the dust-filled room. Later, in the darkness of an inn built atop the tavern, I would hold my wife as she slept, the sound of the trickling rain mixing with her comfortable snoring to create a winsome lullaby as I lay awake with her hair in my face and the curve of her body in my arms. That moment of pure peace—of contentment, of comfort, of divine happiness—is not easily captured. It's vaporous, smoky, like morning fog that fades at the first sign of the sun. It is a fragile thing and, once found, is easily lost and almost never recognized until far later when age and time have taken their toll. Not until many years later do we look back and see it for what it was: pure, blessed magic.

Father Luke once read me the words of Solomon, supposedly the wisest man to have lived. I think of them now as I recall this memory, this night in Adana that was likely the last great night of my life.

For everything there is a season,
and a time for every matter under heaven:

a time to be born, and a time to die;
a time to plant, and a time to pluck up what is planted;
a time to kill, and a time to heal;
a time to break down, and a time to build up;
a time to weep, and a time to laugh;
a time to mourn, and a time to dance;
a time to cast away stones, and a time to gather stones together;
a time to embrace, and a time to refrain from embracing;
a time to seek, and a time to lose;
a time to keep, and a time to cast away;
a time to rend, and a time to sew;
a time to keep silence, and a time to speak;
a time to love, and a time to hate;
a time for war, and a time for peace.

Indeed, there is a time for everything. That night, it was a time for embracing, for dancing, for laughing. A new time was coming, however. A time to weep, to mourn, to lose.

A time for war.

The sun rose over Adana, burning away the morning fog and dark clouds and leaving a day that was as clear as it was cold. The rain had stopped sometime in the night, but the dirt and cobblestone paths between the booths and shops in the market had yet to dry. We trudged through mud and muck and found vendors and merchants unaffected by the dreary conditions as they happily hawked their wares.

I followed Amina as she stopped at a booth littered with small flowers and sacks of ground grains. *Ankída* dutifully trailed me with Novella sitting in the saddle. Myrtle slept on *Ankída*'s rump, and, to my surprise, the horse didn't seem to mind. The majority of our party of crusaders had already begun the trip back to Antioch. As Hendry's squire, I'd been chosen to stay behind and wait for him to sleep off his hang-over—still in the company of a certain barmaid—though I likely wasn't the only squire waiting on his knight. There were many of us who would have to rush to catch up with the main body on the road to Antioch.

"What are we looking for again?" I asked Amina.

She smelled an herb I didn't recognize, though to be fair there were precious few herbs I *would* recognize. "*Kekik*," she said.

"And what is kekik?"

"You probably call it thyme." She stepped away from the booth with a frown. Clearly whatever she'd been smelling wasn't kekik. "Or maybe oregano."

I didn't bother to tell her that I knew neither of those herbs, then tugged on *Ankída's* reins and continued to follow her from booth to booth. I found a leatherworker while she shopped and bought a strip of leather long enough to make a carriage on my belt for my throwing axe. I purchased a new cloak for Novella that was lined with fox fur and much nicer—and more expensive—than anything I'd ever worn. Amina frowned, and Myrtle squawked when I slung it over Novella's shoulders, but her squeal of happiness quickly softened Amina's expression. Myrtle clucked indignantly, then moved from *Ankída's* rump to Novella's lap.

The morning dragged on, and Amina was met with more futility in her search for kekik. We passed windows with pots and jars and cooking supplies, a blacksmith who offered to sharpen Skull Splitter and replace the worn antler hilt on Thief's Prick, and a butcher who offered me an insultingly low amount of money for Myrtle. Still, I thought about it. A baker—who was far more savvy than the butcher or blacksmith—let Novella taste a bun before talking me into purchasing a dozen. A cobbler watched the baker, then easily convinced me that

Novella needed a new pair of boots. After twice witnessing what was clearly my weak spot, a jeweler showed her a cruciform brass brooch for her new cloak that made her smile and look pleadingly at me, so of course I bought that, as well.

Our trip to the market ended without success. At least, without success for Amina; Novella had clearly made out quite well. We returned to the inn atop the tavern to find the barmaid long since gone and Hendry snoring soundly underneath a worn blanket. He groaned and rolled away after our gentle prodding, so Amina unceremoniously jerked open a pair of shutters that let a dust-filled shaft of light stream in as if the sun itself had risen inside the room. It landed directly on his face, at which point he pulled the blanket up over his head like a toddler refusing to wake.

"Sir Hendry," Amina said, once more reverting to the voice she used on Novella. "Sir Hendry, is the sun too bright?"

"Aye, lass. 'Tis…" His voice scratched as if he'd swallowed a pint of acid the night before, which I suppose he sort of did.

"We have to go," she insisted.

"Aye, I'm sure we do…" he muttered, his voice tapering off at the end as he surrendered once more to sleep.

"We need to catch up to the others."

"Aye…" was all he got out that time, and gentle snoring followed.

Amina frowned and nodded to Novella, who leaped onto the sleeping knight.

"Haw!" he cried, and the lump under the covers contorted into the fetal position.

"*Zio!* Look at my boots," she called, pulling down his covers and shoving her new boots into his groggy face. "See?"

He burped, then pushed himself to sitting with Novella now on his lap. "Aye, lassie," he muttered. "New boots." He frowned and squinted at the sun. "Ye look like a real bonnie lass."

"And I have buns!" She offered him the sack of buns—still hot—and he almost smiled at the scent.

Then he spotted her new cloak and knit his brow in confusion. "That new, too, lassie?"

Novella nodded emphatically, then held out her brass brooch. "And look!"

"That's a proper brooch," he said, then glanced at me. "Fox fur?"

I shrugged. "I always wanted a nice cloak," I said.

"But *ye* still dinnae have one," he pointed out. "Fox fur, boots, a new brooch. We came for food, lad. How much am I paying ye?"

"I've been saving," I said.

"Aye, I see. Good thing Bohemond's feeding ye."

Amina laughed. "Danya cannot say no to Novella. He is a soft, soft man."

"I am not," I protested weakly.

"No?" She leaned over and kissed me. "I wasn't complaining."

"That's enough o' that," Hendry muttered. "Now come get yer lassie off me so I can find me britches."

11

I walked with *Ankída*'s lead in one hand and Amina gripping the other. Novella sat once more in the saddle with Myrtle on her lap, and Hendry rode nearby on Tencendur. He constantly shielded his eyes from the glare of the sun and swayed a bit in the saddle, but he made no complaints. He bore his hangover in steadfast silence, though I doubted he even remembered his promise to Amina to not complain.

We followed the tracks left by the rest of our party as they headed east. The ruts from hundreds of wagons, oxen, donkeys, and horses—along with two hundred mounted men-at-arms—were easily visible in the packed dirt. A gently flowing creek meandered beside us and occasionally crossed our path as midday turned to afternoon. During a short break to let *Ankída* drink and refill our own skins, Novella rushed glee-fully into the water—much to Amina's irritation, Myrtle's surprise, and my amusement—only to return with a sopping wet tunic and a wide grin. She shivered as she climbed back into the saddle, bundled tight in her new cloak and with lips already turning blue in the cold January wind. Myrtle, who had been pecking at my boots as if she wanted to eat the leather, fluttered back to Novella's lap.

Scattered across the rolling hills around us were stray homesteads with wide fences built around pastures turned brown by the winter. Sheep and goats and a few horses roamed within their boundaries as hostlers or shepherds paused to watch us with wary eyes. We passed by larger hamlets, complete with lodgings, shops, and numerous paddocks and farms. Amina forced us to stop briefly at each of these in further failed pursuits of kekik.

We eventually came to a long-abandoned church of stacked, moss-covered stones and rotting logs of ancient oaks. The thatched roof was in dire need of repair, and a gaping hole on the southern wall probably once held a door. A nearby water mill leaned onto an outcropping of stone as if supported by it. It looked a century older than the already antiquated church, though the wheel seemed to still function, creaking and groaning with effort as it steadily turned in the gentle current of the creek. Water trickled down the decomposing planks and bubbled lazily back into the slow current.

A single sheep stood in front of the water mill. The fence that was supposed to contain it had fallen down, its remnants barely visible in the weeds and tall brown grass. The sheep raised its head to look at us, seemed to mull over what to do at our sudden appearance, then turned and began a hasty retreat to the north.

Well, hasty for a sheep.

For a moment, we merely watched, then Hendry sighed and pulled a lead from somewhere inside Tencendur's saddle. "S'pose I'll grab her," he said, then trotted along after the sheep. Soon they both disappeared over a gentle hill.

"Should we follow?" Amina asked.

I shrugged. "There's only the one. I doubt he needs help." I turned back to the water mill and church. "I don't think anyone lives here anymore."

Amina studied the outcropping of stone beside the water mill. "There might be kekik there," she said, almost to herself.

I followed her gaze. "In the stone?"

"In the ground around it," she clarified, then added, "We have to wait for Hendry anyway."

She was right, so I helped Novella climb down from *Ankída* —Myrtle fluttering down beside her—and wrapped the reins around the only post of the fallen fence that remained upright, though I doubted it would hold if *Ankída* truly wanted to run. We had to pass through the mill to reach the stone beyond, and I was surprised to see the millstone still turning. The circular runner ground over the bed stone, despite the lack of wheat for it to pulverize, an echoing grating sound filling the otherwise empty mill.

Shuffling footprints covered the powdered floor, and several clean circles stood stark on the stone where barrels of wheat or grain or flour had once sat. A single overturned and empty barrel rested in the corner. Even the bed stone had been picked clean, and what little remained had been crushed into a disgusting paste by the runner as it continued its circuitous path.

"I wonder where the miller went," Amina said.

I shrugged, crossed the mill, and stepped back outside through a second door. Amina followed, and we discovered a long-dead garden built along the back wall. Browned fragments of once-carefully cultivated vines that were decidedly absent any fruit climbed the stone on wooden frames. A handful of holes in the ground indicated that carrots or turnips had once been grown here, and a single uprooted and ravaged fig tree lay in the dirt, now nothing more than a corpse of branches and long-dead leaves. A low stone wall surrounded the garden.

Shrubbery hugged the wall and climbed its rocky face to create a waist-high barrier of green. Not far from the fence sat the church, though now we could see a cemetery behind it. Gravestones of varying sizes rose haphazardly before a gently rising hill. There were markers carved into crosses, simple square tombstones, and massive, man-size marble displays. At the top of the hill stretched a forest of oak and fir and pine.

"Nothing here," she said, giving the dead garden a once over. Amina moved to examine the dry and brittle grass around the stone outcropping, found it similarly bare, then stood, frowned, and turned toward the church. "Maybe there?"

"In the cemetery?"

She shrugged. "Maybe. It grows around stone."

"Why do you need this kekik so badly?"

"It's for your güvec," she said with a playful smirk. "You want bland güvec?"

"No," I mumbled, then followed her over the low stone wall and into the cemetery. Patches of green contrasted with the dirt and dying grass, though even I could tell Amina's search was a vain pursuit. She walked along the stone base of the church, ran her hands along the low wall, and circled each of the gravestones.

I leaned against the church's back wall as she searched with Novella and Myrtle her constant shadows. A rotting door hung open from rusted hinges, revealing the heavily shadowed interior of the church. A massive, wooden cross with a life-size carving of the crucified Christ stood at the front, a low wooden altar at its base sitting among scraps of cloth and the crumbled remains of a pulpit. Pits from a woodsman's axe scarred what might have been a single, lopsided pew but was now only a pile of pillaged firewood. A slice of bright afternoon light shone on the floor near the front of the church through the open door.

"I don't think we're going to find anything," Amina said. "Kekik is a hardy herb and usually grows in winter. It seems—"

The distinct *thwap* of an arrow interrupted her, followed immediately by a thud as it buried itself into the hanging door of the church, rattling the ancient wood, then vibrating like a plucked string. I didn't wait to see where it came from—didn't care—and instead rushed forward, grabbed Amina and Novella, and shoved them into the darkened church with Myrtle bobbing quickly after them.

"Danya!" Amina started to shout, but I didn't hear the rest as I wrenched the door shut—nearly ripping it from its rusted hinges—and turned in the direction the arrow had come. Four men wearing mail and armed with bows waited on the crest of the low hill just beyond the cemetery. They held their weapons ready, yet their arrows remained nocked and only casually pointed in my direction. None were mounted—an odd thing for Saracens—and another man stood in front of them, a curved scimitar hanging from his belt.

My own mail was tucked safely into *Ankída*'s saddlebags at the front of the mill, along with my shield and helmet. Only my weapons hung from my belt.

"I see you, *at hırsızı!*" the front man called, and it was then I noticed he was short an arm. The mail sleeve at his left hung limp and empty, and stark white hair fell down to his shoulders as he removed his helmet.

"Temür," I muttered.

He walked casually down the low hill, the archers following close behind him. "I see you've found a woman, *at hırsızı*," he said.

"What do you want?"

"And was that the little girl from that dung-filled village where we first met?"

"You mean where I killed your horse?"

He grinned, though the malice was barely concealed behind the mock smile. "Clever as always, *at hırsızı*."

"What do you want?" I asked again.

His grin changed, and unrestrained joy leaped forward to replace the malice. I was reminded immediately of his lack of sanity, of his ever-changing mood. "The same as ever," he nearly sang. "I want you dying, pinned between two boats, covered in your own filth while all of Allah's most insidious creatures eat you alive."

I glanced at the church door, hoping that Amina hadn't heard that. I'd told her of Temür—it seemed only right given he'd killed her father—though I'd left out many of the details of the time I'd spent in captivity, of how Temür had threatened me with a torture called scaphism.

"That's not going to happen," I said, then made a show of looking behind him at the archers. "Why don't you have a horse? Afraid I'll kill it again?"

"Perhaps I should kill *your* horse? The one you left out front?"

"You touch *Ankída*, and you'll be short two arms."

He scoffed. "I ventured all the way from Dorylaeum," he said, "across mountains and wasteland, all with one arm. I abandoned Kilij Arslan's army and fell in with Yaghi Siyan of Antioch. I left behind my village, my people, my possessions. I've sacrificed much to reach you, boy; I've given all to avenge Safanad. Do not think your mere words can sway me now."

"You've failed to kill me twice already," I pointed out, drumming up as much mock confidence as I could. "How many times does it take?"

"Just once more, I think. Don't forget that it was your redheaded savior who rescued you before. And given that I have several more men seeing to him as we speak, I think it unlikely he'll come rushing to your aid today. In fact, I do not think you will meet him again."

"He can be persistent," I said, hoping I spoke true.

"We shall see."

"Why the game?" I asked. "Why the warning shot? Why not just kill me outright?"

Another grin. "The boats still await you. You will die eventually, just as Artaxerxes killed Mithridates, though I shall try to make you suffer longer." He turned his gaze to the church's door. "And besides, now that I see you have an adorable little family, I will want you alive when I flay the flesh from their bodies."

Never had I felt a threat impact me in such a way. It brought a rage that I'd never known possible. I hated Temür then, more than I'd even hated my own father as he'd left me —*the boy*—on the steps of that orphanage.

"You really shouldn't have said that," I said.

"And you shouldn't have killed Safanad." He raised a hand, and four arrows came at once.

Having no shield, I dropped instinctively to the ground and came face-to-face with Grigor Avagyan. At least, I came face-to-face with his name etched into the elevation of the nearest tombstone. Judging by the size of the stone, he'd been a wealthy man, and I was thankful for that, since I just managed to hide behind the monument commemorating his earthly life as arrows bounced off the massive stone.

I rose immediately, throwing axe already in hand, and hurled it at Temür. He sidestepped, and the axe spiraled through the air and caught the nearest archer in the thigh. He dropped his bow and fell with such a horrendous howl of pain that I thought the axe-head might have crushed something other than the flesh of his leg.

I sprinted across the cemetery, aiming away from Temür and toward the nearest of the archers. All three had already nocked arrows by the time Skull Splitter and Thief's Prick made their way into my hands. I threw the heavy axe, distracting one archer but doing no damage. An arrow whistled by, clipping my shirt but missing flesh. Another thumped into the ground at my feet as I closed the distance to the third archer. He recovered from my clumsy axe throw and frantically shot his arrow. His panicked rush sent the arrow sailing high, and he dropped his bow and reached for his scimitar. But I was already there, burying Thief's Prick into his stomach and ripping it upward until it grated on ribs before twisting hard and jerking the seax free. He clutched uselessly at his stomach as his blood and innards leaked out.

I heard Temür shouting behind me, commanding his archers to shoot me.

"*Onu vur! Onu vur!*"

I grabbed the dying Saracen before he could fall and spun us both around just as the other two archers fired. One arrow sailed inches wide as the other crunched into the back of the man I'd gutted, drawing a low groan of pain. It screamed out the other side with enough force to spray my shirt with red blood and shining rings from his mail. The man in my arms mewled, coughing up more blood thanks to his multiple wounds, and I shoved him aside and scooped my axe off the dead grass.

The two remaining archers had split, one staying on the hill and nocking another arrow as the other ran down the gentle slope toward the church. I charged, but Temür moved to block me, and I gave a hasty swipe with Skull Splitter. The heavy weight of my axe pushed his light scimitar aside, though he held his ground, and his steel-edged sword whipped back up, slicing the air in front of me. I stabbed low with Thief's Prick; it clipped off his mail as he sidestepped, then I jerked forward and felt his nose crunch under the crown of my head.

"Gah!" he screamed, stumbling back with blood running down his face. I pivoted around his desperate swipe, kicked him hard enough to send him stumbling backward, then ran toward the church. The archer was there, wrenching open the door, and I could hear Novella screaming inside. I threw

SHADOWS OF ANTIOCH | 119

Thief's Prick, and it spun end over end so that the hilt clanged off the back of the archer's head. He stumbled, unhurt but dazed as I closed the distance between us.

An arrow struck my side, grazing my ribs and scoring a shallow cut. The blow staggered me, and I met the other archer at the church in a loping, falling gait. We both crashed into the door, slamming it shut hard enough for the old wood to groan in protest. Novella shrieked from inside, Myrtle clucked comically, and I felt a spasm of pain in my thigh as the Saracen rammed a thin dagger into me. I stumbled back, yet kept a grip on his shirt and dragged us both to the ground. We hit the dirt hard. The dagger jerked in his grip and twisted in my leg. I ignored the pain and tried to bring Skull Splitter up, but the heavy axe was nearly impossible to wield as I lay on the ground. Instead, I dropped it and grabbed at the blade in my thigh. His hand clamped overtop mine, and we screamed and spat into each other's faces as we both fumbled for the dagger still lodged in me, blood running slick between our hands as pain lanced up and down my leg.

The mill door slammed open, and Amina staggered into the garden with Novella in her hands and Myrtle clucking after them. Amina tripped over the Saracen atop me, inadvertently kicking him aside and letting me get control of the dagger. I ripped it free, teeth gritted in pain, and jammed it into his side, twisting and wrenching it back and forth, eliciting a howl of pain that echoed through the cemetery.

Hendry stumbled from the church next, wielding his sword and backpedaling as he fought off a man with a scimitar. Both stumbled over me, as well, and I lunged after the Saracen battling Hendry and swiped my stolen dagger across his back. He yipped at the glancing blow, but the distraction was enough for Hendry to finish the job.

Amina still held Novella, both now cowering against the back wall of the church. Temür and the only remaining archer stood across the cemetery, and I could see the debate raging across Temür's face as blood from his broken nose ran into his beard. He glanced from Hendry to me, then took a step back. As he did, the archer fired another arrow. It flew wide of me, though I heard a yelp of pain and turned to see Amina bleeding from a wound in her shoulder as the arrow glanced off her and thudded into the church.

And I saw red.

Hendry would later tell me that I was letting off a string of Scottish curses I'd learned from him. I recalled no such thing, though I do remember scooping up my axe and sprinting across the cemetery, no longer feeling any pain in my thigh. The archer struggled to get an arrow nocked, but Skull Splitter heaved through the horn bow, splitting it in two and taking several of his fingers with it. He fell back and started to scream, but Skull Splitter thumped across his open mouth, throwing a shower of teeth and bone and blood and sending him spinning to the ground.

A whimper came from across the cemetery, and I saw that one of the archers still lived. It was the man that had taken my throwing axe to the leg as the fight had begun, and he dragged himself across the dirt, leaving a trail of crimson blood from the wound. I stomped after him, unaware of anything else, my heart thrumming in my head, a red haze over my vision, and Skull Splitter came crashing down, clipping his ribs and sinking into the dirt beside him. His cries rose and pierced the clear, afternoon sky as my axe rose and fell again, this time landing directly between his shoulder blades. He lurched and tried to pull himself away, but another blow in the same spot stilled him, yet the axe rose once more, ready to—

"Danya!"

I froze, Skull Splitter high in the air, blood dripping down onto me from the axe's wetted edge, and turned to see a horrified Amina clutching Novella's face into her chest, hiding her from the grisly scene. Her arm was red with blood, but only a little, and, as the haze that had covered my vision faded, I saw that her injury was minor at best. Hendry stood beside her, sword sagging in his hand, eyes locked on the Saracen's battered body at my feet.

"Danya, enough," Amina said.

My heart thumped a little less loudly in my ears, and I began to hear the sound of Novella's terrified cries.

12

T emür had disappeared into the forest during my outburst, though even then I knew it wasn't the last time I'd see him. Amina's wound was as superficial as it seemed and took almost no time to clean. We washed it in the river and wrapped it in a bandage torn from one of the dead Saracens' cloaks. As for myself, the gash in my leg had been made worse by the scuffle on the ground with the man who'd wielded the dagger in the first place and worse still by my stomping across the cemetery like a fool. Amina cleaned it while Novella silently passed her the thread to stitch the laceration closed.

Amina insisted on giving the dead a proper Christian burial despite their apparent lack of Christian faith or a priest to perform last rites. An hour was wasted digging shallow graves on the outskirts of the cemetery. She knelt at the new mounds of dirt with Novella once again at her side. For a long moment, no one said anything.

"*Pater Noster, qui es in caelis, sanctificetur nomen tuum,*" she began, and I recognized the words as the Lord's Prayer. Novella joined in, and both their voices fell over the dead. "*Adveniat regnum tuum. Fiat voluntas tua, sicut in caelo et in terra.*"

Amina paused, glancing up at me, and I remained silent. Novella kept her gaze distinctly on the dirt. *"Panem nostrum quotidianum da nobis hodie, et dimitte nobis debita nostra sicut et nos dimittimus debitoribus nostris. Et ne nos inducas in tentationem, sed libera nos a malo."*

"Amen," I said, though my voice was too quiet to be heard by anyone but me.

We found *Ankída* out front where we'd left her, still munching at the dead grass as if nothing had happened. Despite my protests, Amina forced me into the saddle so I could rest my wounded leg, which by now had begun to throb in pain regardless of how still I kept it. I made room for Novella to sit with me. Instead, she climbed atop Tencendur with Hendry, who'd somehow survived the attack without a single wound. Hungover or not, he remained the most stalwart knight I would ever meet.

We hastened now to join the others, no longer stopping to look for kekik, either at random spots of green grass or the many local markets we continued to pass by. It was evening when we finally reached them, and they'd already established camp for the night on the slopes of a gentle rise that over-looked leagues of flat plains. We built a low fire and ate stale bread and onion stew in silence. Novella hadn't said a word since the cemetery, and now she laid her head down and fell soundly asleep on Amina's lap. Myrtle was nestled up against them as if she were a cat and not a hen.

"I'm sorry," I muttered. Hendry had joined Sir Wymond and the others, leaving me alone with Amina.

Amina ran a hand through Novella's hair. "She's already been through so much, Danya."

"I know."

"I understand it's impossible to keep her from *all* blood-shed. We're at war, and she'll see what she sees. But she shouldn't see it from you. Not like that."

"She's already seen it," I said, recalling the night her village had burned to the ground. "The first day I met her, I held her in my arms while I fought off four Saracens. I comforted her as her mother bled out in front of us. She's seen blood shed, and she's seen *me* shed it."

"Not like that."

"What's the difference?"

She frowned and said nothing. She didn't need to. I knew what I'd done was wrong, but I found myself pushing back. To some extent, I regretted what I'd done, regretted the way I'd killed a wounded man. But I thought once more of the pile of slain crusaders drenched in the rain and mud and blood in the deserts south of Al Bara, of the absolute slaughter that Duqaq had dealt out. Even worse, I saw the arrow glancing off Amina's shoulder, recognized that it only missed because the man who wielded the bow had been aiming at me.

I knew that she lived not because I protected her but because of luck.

I needed to be stronger.

"Men die in war," I said curtly. "We don't get to choose how."

She was clearly not satisfied with that response. Why should she be? It was a poor response. "So you had no choice?"

"He tried to kill you."

"But he didn't."

"He could have."

"But he didn't," she said again.

"Because of me," I nearly shouted. Novella stirred, and I lowered my voice. "Because of the blood I shed. Both of you are alive because of these," I said, holding up hands that still had crusted blood and dirt in their crevices and under the fingernails. "What am I supposed to do?"

"He was defeated, Danya. You killed an unarmed and wounded man."

"He tried to kill you," I said again.

"And you stopped him. The fight was over. You're supposed to have mercy."

"He deserved no mercy, and I showed him none," I said, unknowingly echoing Bohemond.

"Do *we* deserve mercy? You should show them mercy because Christ showed it to you first."

I scoffed. "That's not...I...you can't just..." I trailed off, sighed, then scoffed again because I could think of nothing else to say. Once more, she was right. If I didn't believe in Christ's mercy, then my journey to Jerusalem was in vain. I only traveled to receive mercy from my own sins; the least I could do was show mercy of my own. "You sound like Father Luke," I finally muttered.

She gave a weak smile. "Is that a bad thing?"

"Sometimes."

13

The rider came with the rising of the sun. His quartered blue and red surcoat had been shredded, his mail tattered, and blood ran from a blunt strike to his head that seemed to have also relieved him of his helmet. A hasty bandage still clung to his thigh with the broken shaft of an arrow poking through the bloodied cloth. His horse—having ridden hard through the night—collapsed from exhaustion upon arriving at the camp, and the rider tumbled to the ground. He rose, stumbled again, then Sir Wymond arrived and rushed him to see Bohemond.

It was the eighth of February, and the lords of the crusade were gathered in council within two hours of the rider's arrival. Hendry and I joined in as Bohemond's bodyguards, and I watched men arrive at our makeshift meeting space. It was little more than a massive pavilion sheltering an overturned oak log with a crude map laid atop it and stumps to act as chairs surrounding it.

I recognized many of the lords. Tancred, of course, sat beside Bohemond, and Hugh of Vermandois, brother to King Philip of France, lounged with the same air of unearned confidence he always had. Robert of Flanders was in a hushed discussion with Stephen of Blois, an older man, perhaps fifty, though not frail or without vigor. I'd not seen Stephen in combat or leading troops in any real capacity, but Bohemond and Tancred held him in high esteem, so I did, as well. Godfrey of Bouillon was present, calmly sitting and watching the others attentively. Raymond of Toulouse—likely the eldest among the lords, and the one who least hid his dislike of Bohemond—coughed regularly into a bloodied cloth he clutched in his left hand. Perhaps another dozen lords were present, yet they spoke little—if at all—and so I cannot recall their names. Other knights and squires stood with their lords just as we stood with ours, filling out nearly every space available underneath our pavilion and extending beyond. At least a hundred of us had gathered.

Idle chatter flowed among the men, both lords and bodyguards, and it seemed the council lacked any sense of urgency, which did much to relieve my own anxieties at seeing the manner of the rider's arrival. None of the lords seemed overly concerned, and I hoped that this meant good news had been brought rather than the ill tidings I'd originally assumed.

I was wrong.

After a prayer from Caldwell in which he sought God's guidance and wisdom to lead the men—and, as always, the strength to slaughter any Saracen threats—the council began in earnest, and Bohemond delivered the news with his usual blunt simplicity.

"Twelve thousand men are camped at Harim," he said.

The idle chatter went out like a snuffed candle, and sudden silence—heavy enough to feel—fell over the council. My own anxiety returned with vigor, and I felt my heart pounding in my head. That was no small number.

"Twelve thousand Saracen warriors," Bohemond went on,

speaking as if he were sharing a bit of trivial news that didn't concern him, "under the leadership of Ridwan of Aleppo."

The men around the overturned oak log exchanged nervous glances with one another. No one seemed to know what to say, likely thanks in part to Bohemond's deadpan delivery. Finally, Godfrey broke the awkward silence.

"How can we be sure?" he asked. Godfrey was a humble man, and a man I would come to respect in the following years.

"My scout is not a liar," Bohemond said. "And he knows how to count."

Godfrey frowned, but—as usual—took no offense at Bohemond's curt reply. "I mean how can we be sure it is Ridwan's army. How do we know they ride from Aleppo?"

"They likely aren't all from Aleppo. Banners from all over Anatolia were displayed with confidence, though Ridwan's was most prominent. He leads them; I have no doubt."

"It would seem that Antioch's call for aid has finally been answered," Stephen muttered.

"And answered well," Bohemond agreed. "Ridwan's army is large enough to lift Antioch's siege."

Scattered exclamations sounded among the men as they each shouted their disbelief.

"Lift the siege?"

"Twelve thousand!?"

"Surely not."

"My lords!" Robert called out, raising his voice over the commotion. "My lords, please! We gain nothing with this chatter, and we gain nothing in doubting Bohemond's scouts. More men will be sent to learn what they can, but we cannot waste what little time we have by waiting. Harim is not far from here. The question we face is what to do *now*."

"Robert is right," Godfrey agreed. "We must act with haste. But how? What can we do against such numbers?"

"Surely we ride to meet them," Hugh said, stating it as if there was no other option.

"Ride out with what?" Tancred asked. "I count a mere one hundred horses remaining in my service. One hundred!"

"You are lucky, then," Godfrey muttered. "I can offer no more than sixty mounted knights. The rest would march on foot."

Other lords mumbled their agreement and offered similarly slight numbers. With *Ankída*'s continued vitality and Bohemond's charity, I hadn't realized how fortunate I'd been. Hendry and I both still had our horses and seemed to be among a rare few.

Hugh pounded the log, silencing the other lords. "We cannot sit and wait," he insisted. "They would crush us between their army and the walls of Antioch."

"Hugh is right," Robert agreed, though he said the words tentatively as if they pained him.

"Yet it remains true that none of us can produce any sizable force of mounted cavalry," Stephen said. "We can bluster and argue until we are red in the face, but we cannot face Ridwan's army with twenty or sixty or even a hundred mounted knights."

"And we cannot muster twelve thousand infantry," Godfrey said. "At least, not without risking Antioch's garrison sallying against those that remain."

"What do you suggest?" Raymond asked. He hadn't raised his voice, yet merely speaking drew a bout of deep chest coughs that silenced any further comment from him for some time. The knight behind him offered him a cup of wine, which he took and sipped between his wheezing hacks.

Stephen looked as if he wanted to answer but eventually only sighed and shrugged. "I don't know. We are trapped."

"It seems we cannot win the fight with Ridwan," Tancred

said. "Yet we cannot abandon our siege. There *must* be something we can do."

It was then I realized that Bohemond had been silent since delivering the initial news. Having served him thus far—and sat with him in more than one council of war—I knew he already had a plan. I glanced his way and saw him watching the conversation with mock interest, waiting for his moment.

Robert leaned over the map, eyes focused. "We could bolster the garrison at the Iron Bridge," he said, laying a finger on the map. "Force Ridwan to fight his way through."

"Which he will," Tancred said. "Eventually. It will slow him, true, but we cannot stop twelve thousand men at the bridge. And even if we could, it may cost *us* twelve thousand."

"And then we face the same problem," Stephen agreed. "Sending twelve thousand men to the Iron Bridge would weaken our siege to the point of breaking."

"I can take men from the Gate of the Duke," Godfrey offered. He pointed to the western gate that his own men besieged. "Not twelve thousand, but perhaps enough to slow Ridwan at the bridge."

"That would leave exposed the roads to Alexandretta and Saint Simeon," Robert replied. "We could lose contact with the ports."

"I did not say I liked the idea," Godfrey said, "but it is better than letting Ridwan ride unopposed over the Iron Bridge to slaughter us under Antioch's walls."

"Instead he slaughters you at the bridge, *then* slaughters us under Antioch's walls." Robert shook his head. "No. It is too risky. We cannot take many men from the walls, especially those guarding gates and roads. We may end up losing two battles at once."

"What about Raymond's men?" Hugh asked, gesturing to a spot on the map between Godfrey's and Bohemond's camps. "He guards no road."

Raymond had passed the wine back to his knight. "And I have as few cavalry as the rest of you," he said. "You would have me march my men against an army twice its size?"

"You have the most men-at-arms," Hugh said. "Surely it should be you who meets Ridwan in battle!"

"I'll not see my men slaughtered for nothing," he said, raising his voice as much as he could without breaking into another fit of coughing. "Meeting Ridwan with infantry is a terrible idea."

"All we have are terrible ideas!" Hugh shouted back. "Surely we must choose the best of them!"

"Then take your own men to their deaths," Raymond replied. "All twenty of them!"

Bickering ensued, so much so that I could not distinguish one lord from another. Accusations flew of cowardice, of greed, of fear, of impiety. Raymond's coughs broke up the din of noise, punching into the overlapping conversations like thunder in a rainstorm.

It was then that Bohemond finally rose. He stood and spoke, firm and loud, his strong voice carrying over the racket. "We cannot face Ridwan without cavalry." Men trailed off mid-sentence, the bickering faded, and all eyes once more turned to Bohemond. "We cannot face Ridwan without cavalry," he repeated. "Marching at him with any number of infantry is suicide."

"It could delay him," Hugh insisted.

"We do not want to delay him. We want to defeat him."

"Then what do you suggest?" Godfrey asked.

"Only my nephew was with me when we first eliminated the threat of Harim," Bohemond said, seemingly ignoring Godfrey's question. He glanced down at Tancred. "We were outnumbered two to one, yet we struck them with such force that I lost only three men. We slaughtered hundreds, I took eighty-two prisoners, and I buried only *three* men and lost not a single horse."

I didn't bother pointing out that we'd left seven more men injured in the desert, men I'd never seen return. Even so, this meant only ten fell in the battle, a small number by any measure.

"What is your point?" Stephen asked.

Bohemond looked to Robert, once more ignoring the question. "You were with me when we faced Duqaq," he said.

"And we were defeated."

"Were we?"

Robert scoffed. "We lost thousands of men. All our supplies. I cannot recall a more resounding defeat since we set out from Constantinople."

"And yet, we rode through their men like a child through tall grass. It was our infantry who were no match for them."

"It was a defeat, Lord Bohemond."

"Because of our timing," he countered. "We were four hundred men against nearly ten thousand. Had *we* been the ones to surprise *them*, I believe we could have routed their entire army."

"With four hundred men?" Hugh asked. "Absurd."

Bohemond turned to him. "Have you been on the receiving end of a well-coordinated cavalry charge, Prince Hugh?"

Hugh scoffed, but said nothing.

"Let me assure you, it is devastating. Men are folded in half, riders are thrown from their steeds. Lances shatter like massive oaks and blood runs thick in a moment's time. The earth is churned into a mire, and bodies stack upon one another. The Saracens have seen this twice now. They know what our knights can do, what our knights *have* done, and they fear it."

"We still have no horses," Robert said. "I can field barely

fifty. Your own man admits he has less than one hundred," he added, waving to Tancred. "Godfrey has even fewer." He glanced around him at the many lords gathered at the oak. "I doubt any of us could employ more than a hundred. What will one hundred knights do against twelve thousand?"

"Pool them together," he said, using the same blunt voice he'd delivered the initial news with.

Hugh threw his hands in the air. "And I suppose you wish to lead them?"

Bohemond grinned. "You're welcome to lead the assault."

"I'm welcome to take all our horses and see them slaughtered under Ridwan's army? Brilliant idea. Lords," he added, looking at the others, "let me have your horses and knights to ride them. I'm sure you won't be needing them."

"If you give them to me," Bohemond said, ignoring the comment, "then I will not see them slaughtered. Robert and I have already seen firsthand what we are capable of. Give us command of all the mounted knights, and we will route Ridwan's army tomorrow after he crosses the Iron Bridge."

"You wish to *let* him cross the Iron Bridge?" Godfrey asked. "I do."

Godfrey frowned, yet whatever doubts he may have been feeling, he hid them behind his unwavering calm demeanor. "This is madness," he finally said, his voice low and stern. "Yet you have suggested what I thought was madness in the past, and it delivered us Nicaea."

He referenced Bohemond's idea of portaging warships through the hilly country of Bithynia to blockade Nicaea from the lakeside and force an end to the siege. It had indeed seemed like madness then, yet it had worked.

Mostly.

"I vote we give Bohemond and Robert whatever mounted knights we can spare," Godfrey said, looking to Robert and receiving a nod of agreement. "The rest of us will stay behind with the infantry and ensure the siege remains intact."

Raymond raised a hand clutching a blood-dabbled cloth as a sign of agreement.

Hugh sighed, shook his head in frustration. "Very well," he said. "Let Bohemond be responsible for the death of the remainder of our horses."

"I shall come along," Stephen said. "If my men are to die, I would die with them."

Bohemond dipped his head in a show of respect, a rare gesture from the normally arrogant lord. "Very well." He scanned the rest of them, waiting for any further objections. After receiving nothing but silence, he said, "Send your men to my camp. We leave at nightfall."

14

Amina buttoned the front of my aketon, the same aketon she'd made for me after the siege of Nicaea. It was thin, since it had been made to go under mail, and she'd already repaired it countless times. She ran a finger over a particularly nasty gash in the linen and the scar left by the stitching she'd done to repair it. Perhaps she thought of the real scar underneath, the one on my chest just below my ribs given to me by the steel tip of a Saracen arrow at Heraclea. The wound had bled for hours, and I still recalled her face as she pulled the arrow from my flesh. Even now, she seemed to struggle to pull her eyes and hands away from the stitching so she could secure the trio of buttons that held the aketon in place.

Once the aketon was snug, she helped me step into my newer chausses, the mail leggings I'd bought at Iconium. She worked in silence, cinching them tight onto my legs and fastening them to the aketon at my waist. The mail hung down to my ankles, and she slipped on my boots that were shod with iron to protect my feet in the shield wall. Novella watched in silence with Myrtle clutched in her arms like a comfort object.

Next came my mail hauberk, made by Amina's late father,

Asbat. He'd originally made it for Temür, though he'd given it to me with the unspoken promise that I'd use it to protect his daughter. I'd had it altered to fit my growing physique more tightly in Baghras. Newer rings stood out on the armor, distinctly brighter than the surrounding mail, more scars of more battles. She seemed to inspect each one before slipping on my mail coif, tugging at the fringes to get it to lay across my shoulders where she tied it in place to create a seamless piece of mail from my head to my ankles.

Bohemond's quartered surcoat of red and blue was draped over the mail, and I raised my arms as she cinched my belt over the surcoat. Skull Splitter and Thief's Prick fell into their familiar places on my hip, and my throwing axe hung from the new carriage I'd sewn. Amina helped me slip into a pair of new leather gloves. Finally came the helmet—also made by her late father for Temür. Cheek guards hung from the buttressed rim of the helmet, and a raised ridge ran from the nape of the neck, over the crown of the head, and into a nose bar that had been molded into a horse's head. This horse had been modeled after Temür's, an *Al Khamsa* named Safanad that I'd killed in battle.

Lastly, Amina tied the thin piece of blue cloth around my right arm and clasped it with the same iron brooch she'd used a dozen times before. Her fingers lingered for another moment, playing with the token and straightening the brooch, then she cupped my face and our eyes met for the first time since I'd asked her to help me with my armor.

"Bring it back," she said, her voice breaking slightly. She knew this battle was different, even if I hadn't told her that we'd be outnumbered at least ten to one. Amina sensed the discord in the camp, sensed the dread looming over everything since the council of the princes. It seemed as if a darkened cloud had fallen over the crusade, and our very success teetered on the edge of a blade.

"I will," I said, though I lacked my usual conviction.

Novella stood in Amina's shadow, clutching her leg while Myrtle pecked at the ground beside them. Her face was the same jumble of emotions it always was when I left for battle: fear, worry, anger, concern. Now, however, there was a distance between us. She wanted to hug me goodbye, to tell me to be *forte* as she always did, but she hadn't spoken to me since the fight in the cemetery, since I'd hacked a wounded Saracen to death in front of her.

"I'll be back, *mia paperotta*," I finally said.

She said nothing, only kept staring at me with her troubled eyes.

I knelt, and she shifted just that much farther behind Amina's legs. I waited a moment, hoping she'd come forward, even if she still said nothing. But she remained hidden as best she could, clearly worried about me yet too afraid to speak.

"I'm sorry," I whispered, then stood back up.

"She still loves you, Danya," Amina said.

I scoffed lightly. I'd never been a father before—was barely one now—and didn't know how to handle a situation like this. I'd tried apologizing, talking with her, playing with her. I'd even shown affection to Myrtle, who was easily Novella's best friend. None of it had worked to close the fissure between us.

"I'm sure."

"We both do." Amina stood on her tiptoes and kissed my scarred cheek. "Come back," she whispered. "Come back to us."

Within an hour the sun had fallen, and within another hour seven hundred of us—all mounted and ready for battle—moved out under cover of darkness so as not to alert Antioch's garrison. We'd still not blockaded all the gates, and we didn't want to risk word getting to Ridwan's army that we moved to ambush him. Surprise was the key element of our strategy, the other elements being luck and audacity. I have learned in my years that these three working in concert can overcome many seemingly insurmountable obstacles.

We traveled north and east, in the general direction of the Iron Bridge, though with no intention of crossing it. Bohemond, Robert, and Stephen rode at the head of our jumbled formation, halting us once we reached the sprawling plains in front of the Iron Bridge. The Orontes flowed across our north before curling down toward Antioch, only visible by the light of the moon shining down from a clear nighttime sky. The gentle foothills to our south led into the twin mountains, Silpius and Staurin, and I saw nothing but a thick forest of oak and pine to the east. These plains, perhaps three miles square with natural borders on nearly all sides, would serve as our battlefield.

Stephen and Robert each took command of several hundred horsemen, while only a hundred and fifty of us formed up behind Bohemond. We spent the night in silence, awaiting word from our few scouts who had been sent to find the enemy.

I'd never been more anxious before a battle than I was that night, and it had little to do with the overwhelming odds we faced. I trusted Bohemond. I knew that if he led the charge, then he at least believed we had a chance, and while he was not a good man, he was a great leader of men. If he believed, then so would I.

No, it wasn't the odds that brought the unease; it was the way I'd said goodbye to Novella. Or, rather, *not* said goodbye. She'd been worried for my safety yet unable to overcome her newfound fear of me to say so. I'd scared her that day at the cemetery, and I was beginning to wonder if I could ever undo the damage, if I could ever make her trust me again. Thus far,

I'd been the man standing strong—*l'uomo in piedi forte*, as she would say—between her and violence. I was the warrior who'd kept her safe, her protector.

Now, it seemed, I was the monster she needed protection from.

"What is it, lad?" Hendry asked.

I glanced at my knight. "I didn't say anything."

He smirked. "Aye, but yer wearing yer thoughts on yer face. What's bothering ye?"

I thought about staying silent, but Hendry looked genuinely concerned. It was an expression I wasn't used to seeing on him. "Novella," I muttered.

Hendry misunderstood and looked at the blue token on my arm. "Ye'll survive, lad," he said. "Ye'll bring that bit o' blue cloth back to yer lassies. Bohemond's got a plan, and when he's got a plan, there's little to stop him."

"I know," I said and thought of leaving it at that. But Hendry raised an eyebrow, knowing there was more. "I kind of lost control," I said. "When Temür ambushed us."

He nodded. "Aye, ye did, lad. More'n a wee bit too."

"Novella still won't talk to me."

"Ahhh," he sighed, finally understanding my mood. He said nothing else for a long while, brow furrowed in thought as he seemed to be mulling over his response. It was another expression I'd rarely seen him wear—that of deep thought. "If it makes ye feel any better," he finally said, "I dinnae ken what *I'd* do if I found the man that took me lassie from me. Killing him once wouldnae be enough."

"But is that the right reaction?"

He scoffed. "Dinnae much care if it's right, lad. Man that killed me lassie deserves the worse kind o' hell. I'd be fine giving it to him."

He was right, and even I felt that my anger at the Saracens who'd nearly killed Amina was justified. But anger and action are two different things, and I couldn't unsee the horror on Amina's face, couldn't unhear the terror in Novella's cries. "Novella used to look at me like I was her hero."

"Ye still are. Ye saved her once, and ye were just protecting her."

"Was I?"

"Aye, at first. What happened after…" he trailed off and shrugged.

"She used to think I was her guardian angel," I muttered. "Now she thinks I'm a monster." I scoffed. "A devil, almost."

Then Hendry, returning to his usual form, said, "She's not wrong."

I frowned. "That doesn't make me feel any better."

"It wasnae s'posed to. We're both monsters, lad. No one can see what we've seen and do what we've done without being a bit o' one. Least, not and live to blether aboot it. Ye'd be dead by now if ye didnae have that monster in ye. It's what keeps ye alive, what made ye me squire in the first place. Ye fight like the de'il himself, and that's why yer still breathing."

He wasn't wrong. I'd said as much to Amina—more than once—but that *also* didn't make me feel any better. "So it's just who I am?"

"Sometimes, aye. Ye need that de'il in ye to live. Ye need the monster. Ye just have to learn *when* to let 'em oot."

I looked east, toward the Iron Bridge, and thought on the army that was likely camped not too far away. "I suppose I'll need to let the devil out tomorrow."

He followed my gaze, and Tencendur nickered as if he sensed the approaching army. "Aye, lad. We've not seen an army this size, least not since Dorylaeum, and that was a close one even with the numbers being equal." He sighed. "They've got us at least ten to one, likely a lot more. Yer gaun to need the de'il by morn."

Our vigil lasted all night, but in the bleak light of dawn, the scouts finally returned. They spoke with the lords, and I didn't need to hear what was said to know that they'd found Ridwan. Stephen and Robert took their men west. Bohemond rounded the rest of us up and led us just over the crest of a low hill to the south of the plains where we were out of sight of the Iron Bridge—abandoned now, in an effort to let Ridwan through as quickly as possible. For a long while, we sat atop our horses in silence. Bohemond's probing gaze fell on us as the sun continued its slow rise in the east, its dull light brightening as it climbed over the horizon. Soon a blue sky as clear as a freshwater spring spread over us, and one single wisp of white clouds drifted by in the north, its oblong shadow gliding across the foothills now at Bohemond's back. To the east shone the barest hints of the forest, and I could just make out the high peaks of Antioch's twin mountains to the south.

Bohemond cantered to the front of our lines. "Robert's men have confirmed my number," he said, his voice firm but not rising to the level of a shout. It didn't need to, with our forces so small around him. "Twelve thousand men from Aleppo and the surrounding area, marching under the command of Ridwan. They will be here within the hour. I'm told less than four thousand of them are mounted, but the rest are armed and armored. They come with spear and javelin and their curved sword. They come with bow and arrow, with mail and helmet and shield. They come ready to make war on us, to bring us battle under Antioch's high walls. They will find us sooner than they expect, and they will find us ready."

He heeled his steed and trotted along our formation. "I stood with you at Nicaea," he went on. "When Kilij Arslan tried to trap us between its walls and his army. He was no match for us then, just as he was no match for us at Dorylaeum, where he ambushed us with an army of twenty thousand horse archers." Here he paused and made eye contact with Sir Pate, a man once belonging to Robert and now under the service of Bohemond. "*Twenty thousand*," he said again. "And still we sent him running. Have we seen him since?"

"No," Pate replied quietly.

"What?!"

"No," he almost shouted.

"No," Bohemond agreed, then trotted on. "No, we have not. We destroyed his army, slaughtered his men, and sent him limping home, licking his wounds. Now Ridwan of Aleppo," he said the name with a sneer, "comes to try his hand against us. And yes, they outnumber us. They know they do; we know they do. For each of our horses, they have five. For each of our warriors, they have *seventeen*." He scanned us as he said this number. "Seventeen," he repeated. He grinned fiercely and drew his sword. "Yet they do not have enough men. They do not have enough horses. They do not have enough javelins or arrows or spears or swords to repel us, us warriors of God." He struck his shield, his blade ringing off the white face painted with the red cross of Christ. "They will find us an army like they've never known. We shall crush them as we crushed Kilij Arslan, and they will return to their city beaten, broken, and bloodied. *Deus vult!*"

"*Deus vult!*" the cry echoed. "*Deus vult!*" we shouted. Lances pounded the grass, and swords cracked against shields. Hendry jerked Bohemond's banner up and waved it in the air where the wind caught it and whipped the quartered blue and red, snapping it back and forth. I ripped Skull Splitter free, beat it against the iron rim of my own shield.

As I have said, Bohemond was not a good man, but he was a great leader of men.

After a short while, he raised a hand to quiet us. Weapons were sheathed and lances held upright, and eventually we fell silent.

"They will come soon," he said. "Robert and Stephen will meet them in battle, and we will wait. They will strike

Ridwan's vanguard, and we will watch. All may seem lost, men will die—very many of them—and still we will do nothing. Then, finally, when the time is right, we will strike like angels from heaven." He paused, grinned that fierce grin again, the one edged with mania. "No," he corrected. "We will strike like demons from hell. We will push their army back to where they came from." He scanned us one final time. "For now, men, we wait."

His speech now over, he trotted to Hendry and dismounted. "Leave the banner," he said, "and the horses."

Hendry obeyed, I followed, and soon the three of us stood at the top of the low rise. The plains stretched once more before me, the brown grass now visible in the light of the sun. Due to our small numbers, I could only just see the trampled mess we'd made during the night in the plains below, and then only because I knew where to look. The black tips of the Iron Bridge's towers were barely visible in the distance, and I saw no sign of Robert or Stephen to the west.

Knowing that our silhouette atop a hill would be visible for miles, we pulled our cloaks over us and lay in the icy dew-moistened brown grass of winter. Bohemond watched the plains, and Hendry and I followed his gaze, three sets of eyes locked on the stillness below. No one spoke. No one moved. An hour crept by as the sun continued its upward journey, its heat doing little against late-winter's chill.

A scouting party came first, thirty or so men on horseback cantering from the Iron Bridge and across the plains. Their inspection of the plains felt cursory; likely they thought the size of their force would deter anything like the ambush we'd planned. Even so, they spread out and scanned the brown grass, riding nearly up to the base of the hill we lay upon. Yet hundreds of feet still separated us, and if they saw us, they made no move to report it. Instead, they continued west until they were once more out of sight.

Next came the rising cloud of dust that always accompanied a moving army, especially one as large as Ridwan's. It spread over the Iron Bridge like a brown fog, spilling into the plains as if pushed by a malevolent wind. Dim silhouettes grew out of the fog, figures of men blurred by dust and distance, nothing but black lines marching into the plains.

As the miles between us shrank, I saw the glints of spears, of swords, of armor. I saw shields smaller than our larger kite shields. Row upon row of infantry marched through the plains, moving west toward Antioch, making no move to face us in the south. Horsemen rode beside the infantry, a hundred or more on either side. They trotted in time with the infantry, matching their cadence, spread out to watch their flanks. These men carried bows and spears—critically, they had no shields—and wore lighter armor more suited for their agile tactics.

This was the vanguard, at least three thousand men strong. Already they outnumbered us, and still we'd not seen the majority of their forces. Notably, most of the mounted Saracens were still to come, attached to the main body of the army or its rearguard.

They made their way across the plains, not hurried yet making good time. They were rested, that much was clear, and they knew their purpose: to drive us Christian devils from Antioch. Likely they expected to encounter some kind of resistance at the Iron Bridge. I can only guess what our absence there made them think—perhaps that we'd redoubled our efforts to face them at Antioch, or even that we'd fled the city in fear— but they showed neither haste nor excessive caution as they marched. Scouts continued to ride to and fro, perusing the plains, yet largely ignoring the foothills behind us where our one hundred and fifty mounted men waited.

The vanguard had nearly reached the middle of the three-mile-wide plains when the main army began to cross the Iron Bridge. Here came the majority of the Saracens, fifteen hundred mounted archers flanking either side of the central body of several thousand infantry. Again came shields and spears and bows. Men marched in neat and orderly rows and columns. Flags whipped in the wind, emblems I didn't recognize showing the different factions that had come together under the command of Ridwan. They trampled the earth, their footsteps so numerous I imagined I felt them rumbling in the ground beneath me. I didn't, of course, but that didn't stop my own heart from fluttering in fear. I trusted Bohemond, even in that moment, yet seeing almost ten thousand men marching with the sole intent of killing you can bring a touch of fear into a man.

I saw the faintest glimmer of the rearguard crossing the Iron Bridge when the first scouts returned from the west. They rode hard, clearly having seen either Robert or Stephen, and within minutes of their arrival the vanguard was in motion. Horse archers separated from the infantry, spreading out like wings ready to envelope whatever threat may come. The infantry moved into a tighter formation, shields that had been carried were slung, spears that had been held lazily were gripped firmly with resolve.

Then came Robert, his banner—twin golden lions on a red background—whipping behind him as he rode at the head of several hundred mounted cavalrymen. Lances jutted forward, their steel tips extending far beyond the front of their horses. They cantered at a steady pace—not charging yet not merely trotting—closing the distance between them and the vanguard while maintaining their own tight formation. The mounted Saracens spread farther, and arrows started to whistle into the air, but Robert kicked his horse into a sharp gallop. His cavalrymen outran most of the arrows, their ranks spreading to let those that landed among them hit nothing but dead grass and dirt. I counted three knights thrown from their horses as Robert outpaced his own men,

and slowly they formed a wedge behind him and his standard-bearer.

He slammed into the front rank of infantry with a crash
that we heard even from the distance. Men were thrown aside
as the heavy destriers pounded through, piercing the first two
rows with ease. Lances cut down Saracens, cries of pain and
fear and anguish met our ears, and still Robert forced his way
through the lightly armored infantry, stabbing and slicing and
kicking even as his charge became a trickle and he reached the
center of the three-thousand-man strong formation. There, it
stalled—as we suspected it would with three hundred men
assaulting three thousand—but a mounted knight is a terrible
thing, whether he is charging or not. Lances were abandoned
as they broke or became stuck in dead men, and the knights
hacked down at their enemies with swords and axes, with
maces and hammers, punching them with the iron rims of
their shields, kicking with iron-shod boots. The mounted
archers proved useless, unable to reach the knights and unable
to shoot for fear of killing their own.

The battle raged, and the infantry began to panic. Those
caught in the center could do nothing but die while the fringes
started to abandon the fight and flee back toward the main
army, who had by now picked up their pace, almost running to
reach the battle. They were easily outstripped by their own
flanks of mounted archers, who had reached the battle within
minutes yet found themselves as useless as the mounted men of
the vanguard. Even so, they moved to surround the battle, to
make escape impossible, and I fidgeted beneath my cloak. As
fearsome as that initial charge had been, as valiantly as Robert
still took the fight to the Saracens, the impetus was lost and
soon the main army would arrive. A mounted knight is a
terrible thing, but so is a horde of thousands of Saracens. And
with several thousand mounted archers surrounding them,

there would be nowhere for Robert to retreat once that horde began to take control of the fight.

Yet Robert had no plans for retreat. Not yet. For out of the west, which the Saracens seemed to have forgotten about in their haste to respond to Robert, came Stephen, riding into the flanks of the mounted archers who'd surrounded the fray. His banner depicted a hunter with a bow, and he charged forward, Saracens tumbling from saddles, men dying before they hit the ground. Some scattered in response; others remained too engrossed with the fighting already going on to notice they were being slaughtered to their rear. Stephen had ridden as a column, not a wedge, and his charge was almost a hundred knights wide. Before the mounted archers could finish organizing for a retreat—or for anything—almost half of them were down in the grass, hundreds of men dead without having inflicted a single blow.

Stephen's men continued their charge, cutting through Saracens to join Robert in the battle, and soon five hundred mounted knights were wreaking havoc among the infantry. They killed hundreds, hundreds more had fled, and the archers —those who remained—were once again useless, forced to canter around the plains like bees surrounding a destroyed hive while the honey is robbed from within.

Yet now came the main army closing around the fight, enveloping the knights already intermingled with the vanguard. The rearguard had also finished crossing the Iron Bridge and rushed to join in, as well. They were quickly falling into a disorganized mess, masses of men rushing to aid their comrades while hundreds more fled the opposite direction.

Stephen's banner had reached Robert's now, and their combination seemed to enliven the men, yet even as I watched, knights fell. What had been over five hundred cavalry had fallen to half that. The main Saracen army had finally reached the fight, pushing their way into the conflict, their swords and spears joining those of their dying allies.

"My lord…" Hendry murmured.

Bohemond said nothing, his gaze hard as he watched the battle unfolding beneath him. Stephen's banner went down, though what became of Stephen himself was impossible to see. Our knights began to retreat as the sheer weight of Saracens forced them back. Even the rearguard was entering the battle, and the Saracen army—once a massive force of three distinct divisions—began to push together in their desperation to fight off Robert and Stephen.

"My lord…"

Again, he said nothing. Robert's banner was falling back now, surrounded by a circle of knights fighting their way to fresh air and freedom. The horse archers, sensing their time finally upon them, started firing, and hundreds of arrows darkened the sky as they shot into the clash of men and steel and horses. Saracens died alongside knights and squires, yet I doubted they cared. This was their chance to eliminate our most powerful asset—the mounted knight—and they were going to take it. There was little chance they'd let either Robert or Stephen escape.

"My lord…"

"Mount up," Bohemond finally said, standing quickly and throwing his cloak aside. We followed, jumping to our feet and discarding our own cloaks. "And don't forget my banner."

15

W e moved quickly, sprinting down the hill and mounting our waiting horses. Bohemond turned to the men—who had formed something of a crescent at the base of the hill—and scanned them one final time. Yet he'd already given his speech, already given his call to action. All he did now was raise his lance and scream, "*Deus vult!*"

The men echoed the cry, then we pounded up the hill, crested the top, and charged down again. For the rest of the men, this would be the first time they'd see the army, the first time they'd lay eyes on the massive numbers engulfing our small forces in the plains below. Even for myself, seeing it again snatched the breath from my lungs. Thousands of Saracens had crowded into the center of the plains, the vanguard, main body, and rearguard now a single, motley group. They engulfed the remaining knights like the angry Mediterranean Sea beating upon a small yet stubborn ship, Robert's standard somehow still shivering above the mayhem like a single mast. The path of Robert and Stephen's cavalry charge stood out in the Saracen army like the wake of a ship, a bloody gash from the east carved through what had once been the vanguard and extending deep into the main body.

A group of perhaps two thousand mounted archers waited in the west in an effort to prevent escape. Another several hundred horsemen spread throughout the plains, circling the battle and doing little other than watch. The closest of these Saracens pranced about in front of us, and he saw nothing as we rode through him. I watched as Bohemond caught him between the shoulder blades and flung him from his saddle like a bale of hay. His shout finally drew the attention of the other nearby horsemen, yet even they could do nothing as we cut them down.

Bohemond led us in a wide column, similar to the way Stephen had entered the battle. Our horses ate up the ground as we barreled through the Saracen stragglers, killing a dozen or more men before we'd even neared the army. Scattered arrows sprinkled the ground around us, uncoordinated and hastily shot as their owners tried desperately to respond to our sudden arrival. Most missed their targets, a few landed in shields or careened off helmets. Not a single one of us fell.

"Wedge!" Bohemond called, his voice thundering over the pounding of the horses and the shouts of the enemies who still died around us. Likely no one beyond those closest heard him, yet as we moved the others began to follow. "Wedge!"

Our line condensed, and we formed a wedge with Hendry and me on either side of our lord at the front. The mounted archers were finally falling into something of a formation to our left and right, yet we ignored them now as we charged the main army. The enemy infantry wielded a combination of spears and scimitars and daggers. Their armor was as varied as their weapon choice, some with shields and helmets and mail, others with nothing but fabric gambesons and leather caps. It wasn't until we were nearly on them that they saw us, shouts of surprise echoing over the muddied plains as their flank—if any part of that mass of men could be called a flank—turned to try and meet us. I saw the fear in their eyes, the tremor in their hands, the sweat on their faces.

I chose a man and aimed.

I thrust as we hit them, just as I'd been trained, and my lance skidded past his own spear as he struggled to haul it into place. It cracked into his shoulder, twisting him and throwing him to the ground where he disappeared into the sudden chaos. Then we were crashing through, bodies hurled aside or ripped asunder, men trampled underneath our beating hooves, their unsteady spears glancing harmlessly off our own shields and armor as the power of our assault ground through their ranks. More impacts thundered up my lance, rattled my arm, throbbed in my shoulder, yet I held firm as my weapon did its dirty work, gashing men open with the combined force of *Ankida*'s charge and my own thrusting. I saw one Saracen lose his head entirely as Bohemond caught him in the neck. Hendry punched another in the chest, the force of our charge pushing him into the men behind him, tearing through their already disintegrating formation, until finally the tip sheered through his ribs and out his shoulder and once more Hendry was jamming it forward at a new target as the Saracen fell beneath us.

They clawed at us, trying desperately to pull us from horseback, yet we didn't stop shoving forward, ramming and kicking them aside as we bowled through them. One Saracen caught my surcoat hard enough to tilt me in the saddle. I jabbed down with my shield, felt its iron rim crunch into his helmet, jabbed again, and his weight was gone as he fell into the crush of men around me. I rocked back upright just as my lance sliced into the mail of another Saracen. He shrieked from the blow, his own cry quickly cut off as the impact crushed his lungs and killed him almost instantly. The force of the strike pushed me back, and the lance slid in my hand. I renewed my grip, felt my leather glove twist from the force. The lance bent, the already-dead body still pinned on the end, then it snapped with a crack like thunder, shattering midway through the shaft and throwing splinters the size of my forearm raining down among the Saracens. I stabbed someone in the face with the tattered remains of my lance, dropped it, then drew Skull Splitter.

Our forward movement had slowed, the impetus of our initial charge already fading. Saracens crowded around us, hands still reaching up to pull us down. My heavy-bladed axe rose and fell, and an arm spiraled into the air. I kicked with iron-shod boots, punched out with my shield, and hacked again and again with Skull Splitter. *Ankída* bit the hand of someone trying to grab her bridle, and I took his arm at the elbow.

Pain in my thigh, and I looked down to see someone had pierced my mail with a short dagger. Skull Splitter cleaved into his collarbone, and he fell quickly, leaving the dagger embedded in my leg. I kicked my leg, and the weapon fell free just as another hand pawed at my surcoat. As I turned to face the threat, a sword cracked into my shield on the other side. I swung indiscriminately, both shield and axe moving together, the iron rim cracking into a helmet while the heavy-bladed Skull Splitter tore through mail and opened the flesh underneath. Another Saracen stabbed me in the leg, his blade turning on my mail chausses and scoring a thin cut in *Ankída*'s side. She bucked and kicked, caught the Saracen in his face, turning his helmet sideways, then I cracked Skull Splitter aside his head. His helmet rang like a dreadful bell, his one visible eye rolled back, and he joined the hundreds of others beneath the crashing hooves of our horses.

The Saracens kept coming. Dozens of them, hundreds of them, surrounding us as our charge stuttered out completely and the mass of Saracen bodies continued to press in. Swords and spears thudded into my shield and turned on my mail as I continued to swing, my arm aching with effort, my hand cramping as it clutched the shaft of Skull Splitter with stubborn determination. The shield in my left arm sagged lower as blow after blow struck it, the weight of the heavy oak seeming to grow with each hit. Bohemond's banner was nowhere to be seen, though Hendry still fought at my side. I watched him kick a man in the nose, his sword following up and opening his throat. But even as the man fell, three more Saracens took his place, and Hendry swayed in his saddle, desperately fighting off the enemy.

We were losing. We'd killed many more than we'd lost—many, many more—but how did we truly believe that seven hundred mounted men could defeat an army of twelve thousand? True, the cavalry charge is devastating, but so are twelve thousand swords and spears in the hands of twelve thousand Saracen warriors. Even as I continued to fight, my mind turned to Amina, to Novella, worried now what Ridwan would do to them once he reached Antioch, once he'd finished us off and crushed the remainder of the crusader army under the city's walls. If we couldn't stop him with nearly all our cavalry, then the men still maintaining the siege stood no chance.

"Robert!" came a cry from the west. "For Flanders! For God! *Deus vult!*"

I turned, saw the red banner with twin golden lions pushing toward us. Its fringes were torn and tattered, and a smear of blood stained the lower of the two lions, yet even so hundreds of men were gathered underneath it. Robert rode at their head, his sword rising and falling, the men around him like angels come to rescue us, and soon the crush of the Saracens around me lessened and I could maneuver. Renewed strength filled my limbs, and I fought on, Skull Splitter striking the conical helmet of a Saracen, the blow crushing the steel and sending the man crumpling to the mud from which he would never rise again. Blood ran down my arm from a wound I didn't remember receiving, but still I fought. I chopped with Skull Splitter as if I were cutting wood, punched with the pointed, iron-strengthened bottom of my shield, and kicked furiously as *Ankída* tried to push her way forward.

Our numbers had more than doubled now, and I saw Stephen still alive at Robert's side. The two lords joined Bohemond, and the rest of us followed, our momentum rising as we cut and thrust through the Saracens. I found myself behind Hendry, both of us hacking and stabbing, kicking and thrusting, and enemies fell beneath us. Our horses began moving once more, shoving forward, trampling Saracens. I could feel the fear rising in the enemies around us, and that feeling brought a surge of confidence.

"Gah!"

I looked at Hendry, saw a sword buried into his thigh. He took the hand from its owner with his own sword, yet another followed, hacking into the mail at his side. Hendry rocked in the saddle, and I kicked *Ankída* closer to him and drove Skull Splitter into the back of a Saracen.

A spear rose from the mayhem, I hacked it aside and struck at its owner, but he ducked and the blow went wide. He dipped under *Ankída*'s snout, popped up on the other side, and I jammed my shield down. The iron rim glanced off his helmet and cracked into his collarbone. The impact spun him, the spear twirling in the air like a reed in the wind, and he thrust wildly.

The next moment is embedded into my mind, seared there like the light of a fire in a dark night, like the flash of lightning in a dreadful storm, like the rising sun on a clear morning. The Saracen's wild thrust caught Hendry beneath his raised sword arm, the steel tip piercing him at his armpit where the mail was thinnest. He stopped spinning as his spear took hold, and he thrust upward again. I heard Hendry's collarbone snap, saw the spear jut out beside Hendry's head and strike his helmet from underneath, knocking it clean off and freeing his mane of red hair. Then the Saracen, realizing what he'd done, whipped the spear down and pulled the now-limp Hendry from the saddle.

"No!"

I dismounted, surrounded almost entirely by our own men, no longer thinking about anything but getting to Hendry. The Saracen—alone among us—jerked the spear free and turned to face me a second too late as Skull Splitter easily took his head. I kicked his body aside, let my allies trample it as they continued their charge, and knelt beside Hendry. He was somehow still breathing.

"Hendry…"

Blood ran from his side like a river, a growing puddle of crimson spreading around us, soaking through my chausses and wetting my knees. He looked at his wound, grimaced in pain, looked back at me, then released his grip on his shield. With his only good arm, he reached across his body and grabbed his sword by the blade. Shaking, he lifted it toward me.

"No," I muttered, voice cracking as I fought back tears. "It's yours…y-you'll wield it again…"

He grinned at that, and we both knew it wasn't true. Already his face was pale, and I watched as the last bits of color drained. Even his hair and beard—his glorious beard— seemed to lose their redness. He was dying; we both knew that.

"Take…her…ye goon…" he mumbled, then fell silent as more blood filled his mouth. He pushed the sword into my chest. I gripped the hilt just as his arm went limp and fell back into the mud. His eyes fluttered shut, and he let out a final, wheezing exhale.

And died.

I've heard it said that your life flashes before your eyes in the moments before your death. I've been near death a dozen times, and still I've not seen these flashes. However, as I watched Hendry breathe his last, I thought of what my life had been before him and what I had become after him. He'd saved me from death, from poverty, from wretchedness, and now he had died in a field thousands of miles from his own home, and there was nothing I could do to stop it.

He'd saved me—countless times—and yet I couldn't save him.

I don't know how long I knelt there in the middle of the battle, though I suspect it could only have been moments. I heard the knights still fighting around me, heard the shuffling of their horses as they tried to regain their momentum. Saracens cried in pain, horses whinnied in anger, knights shouted their battle cries, blood ran in the mud and muck around me, and I knelt—alone—beside the only father I'd ever known.

"*Requiem æternam dona ei, Domine,*" I muttered.

A knight pounded by, his horse stamping the ground beside me and drawing me from my trance. The charge was gaining more energy, and the push of the knights continued steadily by me. Mud and dirt and blood flew in great clumps in their wake as they passed, yet I was left behind, at ground level now and no longer elevated above the chaos on *Ankída*, who I could no longer see.

And the Saracens, those not maimed or killed by the cavalry, saw that. They saw an exposed crusader kneeling over a dead knight and knew that they would have their chance at revenge—however slight—for their own losses.

Yet I wasn't done. Revenge would be mine, not theirs.

I stood slowly, slipped Skull Splitter into its carriage on my waist, and tightened my grip on Hendry's sword. "Mon then,"

I muttered, voice scratching and low in my throat as I turned toward them. "Mon…"

And they did.

The first Saracen came with an overhead strike I'd seen a hundred times before. I raised my shield, stepped into the blow, and thrust Hendry's sword into his stomach. I didn't wait to watch him die, instead whipping the blade back out—it was immensely lighter than Skull Splitter—to catch another Saracen across his helmet-less face, the blow throwing blood and teeth and bone and sending the man spinning to the ground.

I felt a crack on my back, knew my mail held, and spun toward the assailant. Hendry's sword lashed out and smacked into a Saracen's forearm. He yelped, I jammed my shield into his stomach, then brought the sword up into his chest as he bent over in pain. Two more Saracens charged, and I backpedaled out of range of a pair of strikes, watched as they practically leaped to close the distance, then stepped forward, raised my shield, and thrust. The sword caught the nearest man in the shoulder as a strike thudded into the face of my shield. I stepped forward again, headbutted the first man, then swung wildly behind me, felt the blade turn on mail as pain lanced up my side. Two more strikes came in near-unison, one clumsily thumping my ribs with the flat of a blade and another cracking into my helmet and sending it careening into the havoc around me.

My ears rang as I nearly fell. On instinct, I raised my shield. A scimitar cracked into it, and I ducked, felt another scimitar whistle through the air above me, then lunged forward, hammering a man in the chest with my shoulder before stepping back and thrusting. Hendry's sword pierced mail, glanced between ribs, and buried itself into his chest. I jerked it out, stumbled backward as another blade swung down where I'd just been.

Something pierced my lower back, and I turned to see a Saracen wielding a spear. He thrust again, I sidestepped, and he stabbed another Saracen in the thigh. Both yelled in surprise, and I hacked at the shaft of the spear with Hendry's sword, felt the blow vibrate up my arm as a reminder that I wasn't wielding Skull Splitter. The Saracen dropped his spear and pulled out a sword, but I was already moving again. I turned his hasty blow aside with my shield and stabbed him in the stomach.

More pain, this time in my thigh, and I fell to a knee, my shield jerking up in time to catch a second strike. Yet I had no more strength, and a third blow turned my shield aside, while a fourth slapped into the mail at my chest, knocking the air from my lungs but doing little real damage. Even so, I collapsed, sword and shield held out to my sides. A Saracen stepped over me, and I tried to raise the sword, but he stomped down on my wrist.

Then he was gone, and my world was filled once more with the thundering of hooves and the whooping and howling of knights and horses. Bohemond was back, he and Robert and Stephen and hundreds of others, and they tore once more through the men around me, this time riding in the opposite direction. After a handful of heartbeats that were filled with cries of pain and surprise and death, the world fell eerily silent, and I simply lay there, staring up at a perfectly clear sky, my breath rasping in my throat, my wounds throbbing as warm blood seemed to flow all around me.

After a long while, I pushed myself to sitting. The cavalry had cleaved through the entire army, then turned back and charged again. It was this second charge, it seemed, that had finally broken the forces of Ridwan. Men fled indiscriminately, tossing aside weapons and shields as they ran to the west, back in the direction they'd marched from just hours prior. Even the mounted archers had begun to flee, rushing back toward the

Iron Bridge and abandoning their fellow infantry in much the same way we'd abandoned our own when we'd faced Duqaq two months ago.

We'd won.

Later, chroniclers would suggest that God had miraculously multiplied our numbers to two thousand or given us angels to fight alongside us, yet I was there and will tell you confidently that this wasn't the case. There had been no heavenly intervention, but rather that devastating combination of audacity, luck, and surprise had won the day. Surely Ridwan had not expected five hundred men to charge headlong into him, and surely he had not expected more to arrive at his flank.

As I've said, the cavalry charge is a terrible thing. The force of it gashing into the flank of an army is powerful, even when it's as small as a hundred and fifty men. Yet it does more than kill; it demoralizes. Watching mounted knights tear through the men to your left and right as if they were old wineskins will put an intense fear into even the bravest of men. It was this fear that quickly spread throughout the Saracen army. They had no backup, no rearguard to come to their aid as they should have had. Bohemond had waited until the very last moment, when all of Ridwan's forces were pushed together in the center of the plains, when the fear could run through every part of their army and no one could rescue them from it.

Every man was running for his own life now, their thoughts on nothing but getting out of the way of the next charge. Unlike us crusaders, Ridwan's forces were joined together by coercion or gold, by fear of their leader or hatred of us, none of which will strengthen a man's heart when the blood begins to spill.

Our cavalry continued to harass the fleeing army all the way to the Iron Bridge, and I would later learn they'd chased them as far as Harim in the west, capturing men and supplies and, more importantly, thousands of horses. The Saracens torched their own fort at Harim for fear of us, then fled all the way back to Aleppo. The threat from Ridwan was gone—for good, it would seem. We'd won the day, turned the tide of our crusade, and defeated an army that outnumbered us seventeen to one.

Yet I'd lost Hendry, my mentor, my knight, my best friend.

It hadn't been an even trade.

16

I t took almost an hour to find *Ankida*. I felt such a surge of relief to discover her alive that I cried. She stood on the shores of the Orontes, drinking the clear water as if it were her reward for the work she'd done. I mounted up and surveyed the horrific aftermath of the battle in search of Tencendur, Hendry's horse. Thousands of bodies littered the plains, most dead but many still moaning in pain. Some stared expressionless at gaping wounds, others clutched uselessly at their guts as they tried to keep their innards from spilling. One man sat in the mud, filth smearing his vacant face as he held his severed forearm in his good hand, congealed blood still oozing from the stump.

While the rest of the crusaders continued to chase Ridwan's army, looters seemed to materialize from the woods and surrounding hills. Some were remnants of the very army we'd just defeated, men who'd fled only to return as our cavalry crossed the Iron Bridge. They paid little mind as they searched the dead bodies of their one-time allies, coming away with whatever they could carry, and fleeing once more. I was too weary to do anything about it, not that I *could* do anything, since there were probably a hundred Saracen looters, and I saw only three others wearing the same surcoat I did, and two of these were sitting dejectedly in the mud as the third seemed to be caring for their wounds. Peasants came, as well, from some of the local villages that were scattered around Antioch. These men were more wary, eyeing both me and the Saracen pillagers with caution as they pilfered what they could.

It was early afternoon when I finally found Tencendur. The mighty destrier had been spitted by a pair of Saracen spears and lay dead a quarter mile from where Hendry had fallen. I salvaged what I could from Tencendur's saddle, then rode *Ankída* back to Hendry, her hooves stepping deftly around the mass of bodies that seemed to go in every direction. The shockingly clear sky brought a stark clarity to the atrocity that had occurred, the sheer amount of death and destruction that we—seven hundred men—had wrought against an army of twelve thousand.

My knight lay just as I left him, his mangled right arm splayed out to his side and his left draped across his chest. His eyes, still open, looked up at the sky, and it seemed to me he had the remnants of a grin on his ghostly white face. He hadn't been looted, and I decided then to bury him in his armor. I thought of putting his sword back into his scabbard, yet his last words had been for me to take it, so instead I removed his scabbard from his belt and secured it to my own. I closed his eyes and wrapped him in his own torn and blood-stained cloak, but even pulled tight it didn't cover his massive body. After a cursory search, I found three more cloaks that were mostly clean and wrapped him in those, tying them tight with a pair of belts I'd also taken from nearby corpses.

Then I sat in the mud. I expected to start crying again but realized I hadn't stopped since I'd found *Ankída*. The relief I'd felt at discovering her alive was quickly overshadowed by the despair at seeing Hendry's shrouded corpse. I bowed my head and continued to weep, found my hand had drifted out and was resting on Hendry's chest. He was already cold, and that brought a wave of anger along with the sadness. I scanned the corpses around me, saw the Saracens who'd taken Hendry's life, and found myself regretting that they were all dead and unable to suffer any further torment for what they'd done. They'd been defending themselves, defending their land, and we were the invaders, but none of that mattered. Hendry was dead, and one of them had wielded the spear that had killed him, so I sat in the mud and blood and filth and simmered in useless, undirected anger.

A shadow fell over me sometime later. I looked up to see Bohemond. More knights surrounded him, each of them holding the lead to at least four horses. His armor was bloodied and torn, his surcoat split down the middle of the quartered red and blue so he wore it almost like an open vest. He had no helmet, and dried blood stained his dark hair. From his saddle hung six severed Saracen heads, tired there by their hair, their dead eyes filled with fear and their mouths open in lifeless screams.

"Sir Hendry?" he asked, his eyes on the shrouded figure at my side. I only nodded, and Bohemond drew a long breath. It was the closest I'd ever seen him come to expressing grief. "He was a good man," he finally said. "A tragic loss. Truly."

Succinctly put, as always.

"Many soldiers of Christ gave their lives to continue our crusade," he said. "Today's sacrifice will not be in vain, I promise you. We are digging graves in the east. Take your time, mourn your friend, then bring him there for a proper burial. Father Caldwell will be present."

I watched him ride slowly away, the severed heads bobbing against his horse. The other knights had similar trophies hanging from their own saddles, and I knew almost immediately what Bohemond had planned for them.

I turned back to Hendry's corpse, the anger still simmering just beneath the surface, then I heard his voice in my head.

"I dinnae ken what I'd do if I found the man that took me lassie from me. Killing him once wouldnae be enough."

Killing him once wouldn't be enough.

I rose, almost without thinking, and pulled Skull Splitter from my belt. Killing them once wasn't enough, so I would do it again. I would gather my own trophies just as Bohemond and the others had. I chose a Saracen, my eyes locked into his neck, and I raised Skull Splitter. Shockingly, Amina's face passed before me, and the axe shivered in the air. I saw her knowing gaze, the reproach in her eyes. I knew I shouldn't do it; she would say so, and it would be true. I saw Novella, eyes wide in fear, silent scream on her lips as I hacked at the man who'd nearly killed Amina less than a month ago.

Then I saw Hendry, spear jutting through him, jerking him from the saddle, slamming him to the ground, and ending his life, and my axe fell.

An hour later, I stood over a new mound of dirt that was Hendry's final resting place. Caldwell mumbled words I paid no attention to, and six severed Saracen heads hung from *Ankída's* saddle behind me. Rainald knelt nearby, his own knight—Sir Wymond—buried not far away. We'd both lost our mentors, yet no heads hung from Rainald's saddle.

We reached Antioch before the sun fell, though it sat low in the west, hugging the horizon in preparation for its nighttime slumber. Riders had been sent ahead, and so hundreds—no, *thousands*—of sharpened stakes had already been set into the ground before Antioch's walls. They remained out of arrow range, but still close enough for the Saracens on the high parapets to see us as we mounted the severed heads on the stakes. Each head crunched through the wood, bones cracking open as the point struck through the crowns of their skulls.

I returned to the camp that night. Novella slept soundly,

and Amina watched as I finally cleaned myself of the blood and filth of battle. Some of the blood was mine, some Hendry's, but most was that of the enemy. She saw Hendry's sword on my waist, and neither of us said anything about it. She wanted to comfort me; that much was clear by her own troubled expression. I gave her no chance. Instead, I pulled the stained blue strip of cloth from my arm, handed it to her without a word, found my bedroll, and fell instantly asleep.

INTERLUDE II

AD 1115
Jerusalem

Roland looked down at his bowl of güvec. Steam wafted off in thin tendrils, and he could smell the carrots and lamb and a spice he didn't recognize. Kekik, he realized. He was smelling the kekik. He stirred the small bowl with the wooden spoon Sir Daniel had given him, then gave a hesitant glance at the knight, who silently stirred his own stew.

Roland had been enthralled by the description of the battle, how seven hundred mounted knights had defeated an army of twelve thousand. Yet now, with Sir Hendry's death, he felt the same weight of defeat that Sir Daniel must have. He'd long suspected that Sir Hendry hadn't survived the journey to Jerusalem, though a part of him had hoped he'd merely returned home to Scotia. Instead, Sir Daniel had buried him somewhere in Anatolia at yet another crusader graveyard. Roland found his eyes lingering on the sword at Sir Daniel's hip.

Sir Daniel glanced up from his stew and saw Roland's gaze.

"It was Hendry's," he said. He set the uneaten güvec down and unhooked the scabbard from his belt. He laid it across his lap, resting a hand on the brown leather scabbard, though he didn't draw the blade. The upswept cross guard—polished to a silvery sheen—flickered yellow light from the midday sun. "She's mine now."

"I…I'm sorry," Roland muttered, though he knew the words were pointless and many years too late.

"Thank you, lad," Sir Daniel said, and Roland could see the despair on his face. The sword was all that remained of Hendry, which meant it was more than just a sword. "We got good at digging graves," he went on, fastening the sword back to his belt and picking up his stew. "And the priests got their practice at reading last rites. Wasn't the last graveyard we built, not by a long shot. A hundred and thirty-six crusaders met their end on those bloodied plains, and we took a lot more Saracens with us. A lot." He fell silent again and went back to stirring the güvec as if he needed to move and the stew was the only thing available.

"It was a victory," Roland said, more to fill the silence than to say anything worthwhile.

Sir Daniel nodded absently. "Aye, it was. A miraculous one, at that. We saved the crusade, saved the siege, pillaged hundreds of horses. We reversed the slaughter that Duqaq had handed out to us. We left thousands of Saracens dead in the mud. But Hendry…" He gritted his teeth, and Roland saw a flash of raw anger pass over Sir Daniel's face. His jaw trembled as he seemed to try to control it.

Roland stayed silent this time as he finished off the güvec. Once done, he set the bowl aside and picked up his linens and shears. He still had at least six more to cut. He might be done by evening, at least with the cutting. He still doubted the strength of the armor, that it could stop a sword, yet he also remembered Sir Daniel's first armor had been a gambeson, and he'd survived more than one battle with it.

"Six heads each," Sir Daniel suddenly said. Roland met the old knight's gaze. "Those of us who survived took six heads each, placed them on sharpened pikes. A thousand heads, probably more, gaping up at the garrison. Another fear tactic, I'm told. The cost of siege warfare." He scoffed. "But if I'm honest, I didn't care about that. I wanted to punish them for Hendry's death, as if mutilating Saracen corpses would help ease my pain. As if the Saracens inside Antioch's walls had anything to do with it. As if killing them would bring back my friend."

Roland thought of his own father. He'd died to the pestilence and not a sword, yet he still felt he understood Sir Daniel's despair. Roland would do anything to bring his father back. If given the choice, he might even mutilate corpses.

"Amina...she wanted to talk about it, to comfort me." He shrugged, and for a moment Roland could see him as he'd been seventeen years ago: young, scared, and ashamed. "But what was she going to say? I'm sorry for your loss?" He paused, wiped a tear from his eye. "Eventually she brought me to Father Luke. Not that I wanted to talk to him, either, but a man can only deny his wife for so long."

17

AD 1098
March
Antioch

I stopped walking and stared across rolling hills that were just beginning to turn green as spring settled over us. A church rested atop one of these hills, standing out sharply against the mostly clear sky behind it. I recalled this church from our march toward Antioch months ago, long abandoned before we'd ever arrived. Brown brick walls caught fading orange light from a setting sun and cast faint shadows on the grass. An Armenian-style pointed dome rose prominently from the center of the church, gaps and fissures pockmarking the dome from weather or war or both. An ancient, west-facing door of dark wood—likely oak or pine—hung open as its lone entrance, and a massive glassless window lined with wooden supports looked south toward Antioch.

"Come on," Amina said, looping a hand under my arm and tugging me toward the church.

As much as I wanted to turn around and return to Antioch, I put up little resistance to her gentle guiding.

"You'll feel better," she insisted, but I knew she was wrong.

I hadn't told her the details of what I'd done after the battle with Ridwan, of the Saracen heads I'd hacked from their dead bodies. But it wasn't long before she saw the uncountable rotting mementos we'd placed on sharpened pillars under the walls of Antioch, and—with my distinct change in demeanor after Hendry's death—it hadn't taken her much thought to figure out I'd participated. She'd been understandably horrified. Hendry's death changed me; she knew that; I knew that. Six months ago, I'd never have committed such an atrocity, but now I felt such a thirst for revenge that I knew I could do worse still. To emphasize my anger, I'd even named Hendry's sword *Vindicta*.

Vengeance.

Though it was *my* sword now. It hung from my belt at that very moment, bouncing against my thigh, a steady comfort with each step I took.

Amina had done what good women do: she'd tried to talk to me, to help me heal, to love my wounds away. And I did what cowardly men do: I shut her out, insisted I didn't need healing, told her there were no wounds. She'd seen through my bravado and lies and begged me to seek out Luke for confession. "The Sacrament of Reconciliation," she'd called it. But how was I supposed to reconcile what had happened? Hendry had died, and I'd doled out my revenge. Confession would do nothing to reconcile that. The Saracen heads would remain on the spikes, Hendry would still be in the ground, and I'd still have a burning within in me to shed more blood as recompense.

None of that mattered, though. I loved Amina, so I'd go to Luke, confess my sins—despite the hate and anger inside me, I knew my actions had been wrong—and receive forgiveness, even if I knew I'd feel no better after. For her, I would've done almost anything, and I say "almost" because I would soon prove that there were things I wouldn't do.

We finally reached the church with the sun dangerously close to disappearing below the hills. A single, wide oak shot up beside the building, and the low sun threw an elongated shadow that sheltered three black-robed priests sitting in the grass. More priests worked a small garden of tomatoes, leeks, and cabbages that grew against the northern-facing wall. None seemed to pay us any mind until Amina dragged me over to the oak. At her request, I left my weapons with the priests sitting there, then followed her into the church.

A vague square of soft orange sunlight shone in from the massive south-facing window, and nearly a dozen smaller shafts of dust-filled golden light filtered down from the broken dome. Two priests knelt in this flood of illumination with water-filled buckets and thick brushes. They scrubbed at the sandy floor, pausing just long enough to look up at us as we entered before quickly resuming their work. They seemed frustrated, and rightfully so, since their chore seemed to be in vain. I assumed they'd been given such a banal task as a result of some infraction on their part. Perhaps they'd just come from confession themselves and this was their penance, to pointlessly clean the floor of a church that would likely be just as dirty tomorrow, thanks to the gaps in the ceiling and a massive southern-facing window that had no cover.

At the eastern end of the church, under an apse of simple brownstone arches, Rainald knelt with bowed head and folded hands. The church's marble altar lay in front of him, covered in a green cloth, and his sword and shield rested on the ground beside the altar. In my own anxiety and discomfort at my upcoming confession, I'd forgotten Rainald would be here. He'd left hours before us, insisting on maintaining an all-night vigil before the altar in preparation for his knighting ceremony the following day. I smiled faintly at my friend, his head still bowed in pious prayer. If any of us deserved knighthood, it was him. Rainald was a good man, the very best of us squires, and with the death of Sir Wymond, he had no knight. It only made sense to elevate him to fill his former master's position.

Yet I had no knight, either, though I doubted very much that either Tancred or Bohemond respected me enough to bestow upon me any title. Likely, they'd just continue as they had since Hendry's death and leave me to my own devices. I was squire to no one, it seemed.

I turned away from my friend to find the confessional nestled in a darkened corner of the church. It was little more than a wooden booth with a matching pair of doors at its front—one for the confessor, one for the confessant—and a small candle burning outside to let potential penitents know that a priest waited inside to hear their sins. I stared at the candle and the closed doors of the confessional and felt my heart rise to my throat. Luke was inside, waiting for me. I'd spoken with him many times in the months we'd known each other about nearly everything. Our first meeting came on the night I'd been hired to kill him, something I still felt shame for despite his insistence that he'd forgiven me. After all, I hadn't hurt him. I'd only stolen from him, though I'd since paid him back for everything I took. He'd become a mentor and, dare I say, a friend. Even so, something about the sanctity of the confessional booth caused an unnatural amount of discomfort in me.

"Oh my," Amina murmured from beside me, breaking me out of my reverie. She meandered toward the massive window and gazed out over the rolling hills back toward Antioch. The city rose like an angry fist in the very great distance, hazy and obscure in the dim light and faint shadows. The rough brick edges of the church's window—and the vertical wooden supports on either side—framed the landscape, along with Antioch in the distance, as if someone had hung a painting on the wall. Amina stepped into this painting, set afire by the burning light of the setting sun, her shadow thrown onto the stone floor as she gazed out over the picturesque countryside.

"Look, Danya," she said, glancing over her shoulder to me. I moved beside her to take in the sight. Antioch hugged the twin mountains of Silpius and Staurin—nothing but hills at this distance—and its citadel stood strong and tall at Silpius's peak. High walls meandered down the slopes, circled the city to the Orontes, and then proceeded up again, leaving the river that appeared to be little more than a blue line along the greenery. Thousands of tents and temporary structures filled the plains around the mountains; our camp, surrounding the city, pushing in slowly in an attempt to capture it. A low, brown fog sat over the camp, the result of hundreds of cook fires and makeshift forges, of the stench of waste and filth that accompanied us wherever we went. It looked as if a blight had fallen on the green hills and stretching plains, quarantined between the sapphire hue of the Orontes and the gray stone walls of Antioch.

It was a sight I'd seen a dozen times before, though now from this unique vantage point, the sheer weight of our numbers staggered me. We were a plague come to their land, one Antioch would surely succumb to, even if it would continue to cost crusader lives.

"Father is probably waiting for you," Amina said softly.

I didn't respond; I wished nothing more than to stand here with her a moment longer, though whether that was out of a desire for her company or a dread of the confessional, I cannot say. Either way, she gave me a gentle nudge, and I silently crossed the church, glancing once more at her silhouetted figure, bracketed by the stone walls of the church as the fading light of the sun bathed her small frame.

With a frown, I slipped inside the small wooden booth. The door creaked shut behind me, and shadows descended as I sat on the worn white bench that had been repurposed from a shattered crusader shield. A fading smear of red from the cross that had once decorated its face showed at the edge. The very air felt stale, as if it hadn't left the confessional since its construction. A thin, nearly opaque screen separated me from Luke, and he was little more than a dark outline against the darker shadows of his side of the booth.

"Bless me, Father, for I have sinned," I said, then hastily made the sign of the cross and mumbled, "In the name of the Father, and the Son, and the Holy Spirit. My last confession was…" I trailed off. I'd given a confession at Baghras, though I didn't remember what I'd confessed. How long ago was that? "Months," I finally said.

Luke's shadow nodded from the other side of the screen. "And what are your sins?" he asked.

Here we go. "I've killed men," I said quickly. "A lot of them."

"This happens in battle. The task of a soldier is not an easy one."

"And I…" I trailed off again, unsure how to continue. Do I just tell him that I hacked heads off dead Saracens? That I hung them from my saddle and stuck them callously onto sharpened posts? "Hendry died," I finally said, starting with something he already knew. "I got angry. Violent." Another pause. "And I…beheaded corpses." I fell silent for a moment, then quickly added, "And I'm afraid I'll do it again, and that I'm wasting my time in here."

"In where?" he asked.

"In this box. Talking to you. Confessing my sins. How can I be sorry for something I still want to do? How can I confess and be absolved of a sin that I want so badly to repeat?"

"You want to behead more corpses?"

"No," I muttered, "but I want to punish them."

"The Saracens?"

"Yes."

"For killing Hendry?"

"Yes."

A pause. "Did you not already kill the men who slew him?"

"There is a city full of them just over the hill, Father."

I heard him draw a deep breath and let it out slowly through his nose. For a long moment, neither of us spoke, and I stooped over, head down, eyes staring at the uneven boards that made up the floor of the confessional as I heard my own words echo again in my head. I heard the venom in them, the hate, the vengefulness.

"I told you," I muttered after he still said nothing. "How can I be absolved of a sin I feel such an urge to repeat?"

"The desire isn't sinful but rather can lead us to sin," he said. "Saint James tells us that each of us is tempted when we are lured and enticed by our own desires. Desire then gives birth to sin and sin to death." He paused again and seemed to search for words. "War is evil, though it is often a necessary evil. All men who are called to wield the sword must face this evil with every drop of blood they shed. They must watch their path to ensure they remain on the straight one, and they must approach the Lord with penitent hearts each time they stray."

"What if I still desire to stray?"

"Then embrace the sacraments even more. Confess. Take the Eucharist. Approach the Lord closer and closer, more and more often. He never tires of welcoming back His wayward children."

Easily said, but the idea of coming to this confessional any more frequently than I already did—which wasn't often— sounded more like torture than forgiveness. I thought of saying as much, but instead muttered, "As you say, Father."

"Once forgiven, you will do the penance laid out before you?"

"Of course."

He shifted on his side of the screen. "When Jesus was taken in the Garden of Gethsemane, Saint Peter attacked the guards with his sword. Our Lord commanded him to put aside his weapon. You, like Saint Peter, are brash. You are quick to act, slow to think, and hasty with violence. Yet you know your weakness, as did Saint Peter. And so, for your penance, you must leave Sir Hendry's sword free of further bloodshed. You must stow it away and never use it again."

I scoffed. "You would stop a warrior from using his weapon?"

"I would stop *you* from using *Hendry's* weapon," he clarified. "I'm sure you have others."

"That's not…" I trailed off. Not fair, I wanted to say. Not a just penance. But I knew those were lies. "Why?"

"Perhaps you will learn restraint while the blade is away."

"And if I don't?"

"Then the Lord will meet you again with open arms offering the same forgiveness He offers you today," he said. "Now give your act of contrition."

I didn't want to. I wanted to deny him and leave. Damn him and damn his forgiveness. I'd get it myself when I reached Jerusalem, when I knelt before Christ's empty tomb. I was undertaking the ultimate penance already, wasn't I? A crusade to liberate the Holy City? Bohemond himself—not to mention the pope—had promised forgiveness of sins in return for this mission.

My heart thumped in my chest. I placed a hand on the door, ready to leave. But I couldn't. I knew that. What I'd done had been horrific, and part of me hated myself for doing it. Yet I also hated the men I'd done it to.

Who did I hate more?

"My God," I said slowly, swallowing down the lump in my throat as I began my act of contrition. "I am heartily sorry for having offended Thee, and I detest all my sins, because I dread the loss of heaven and the pains of hell, but most of all because they offend Thee, my God, Who art all good and deserving of all my love. I firmly resolve, with the help of Thy grace, to confess my sins, to do penance, and to amend my life."

"God, the Father of mercies," Luke began, "through the death and resurrection of His Son, has reconciled the world to Himself and sent the Holy Spirit among us for the forgiveness of sins; through the ministry of the Church may God give you pardon and peace, and I absolve you from your sins. In the Name of the Father, and of the Son, and of the Holy Spirit."

"Amen," I muttered, once more making the sign of the cross, yet feeling no better than when I had entered.

Neither Rainald nor Amina had moved as I left the confessional. I glanced once at my friend, a small part of me irritated now rather than inspired by his piety, then took Amina's hand. We returned to the camp under cover of night, and she watched in thankful silence as I tucked *Vindicta* away in a chest.

I only wish I'd left it there.

18

The next morning, in a field of green not far from the very same church, one hundred of us stood in a tight formation in freshly cleaned armor and surcoats of quartered blue and red, Bohemond's colors. Skull Splitter hung from my belt, and Thief's Prick rested at the small of my back in a sheath. I held no shield. Elric stood to my left, and Sir Pate to my right.

Rainald knelt in the grass with his back to us a hundred paces away. He wore a clean white vesture with a fine red robe draped over it. A sky of the clearest blue shone over us, and only a single, malevolent cloud could be seen to the very far south. A warm wind out of the west reminded us that spring had arrived in full, a welcome replacement to the cold and stinging rain.

Tancred held Rainald's sword and shield, and Bohemond stood over the young squire while Father Caldwell prattled on beside him, intoning the various duties Rainald was about to inherent once he accepted his new role as a knight in the crusader army.

"To protect the poor," Caldwell wailed dramatically, gesticulating our way as if any of us listened. "To guard the maiden. To slay the heathen. To defend Christ's church."

He went on and on, and all the while Rainald knelt in the grass at Bohemond's feet. Finally, after what felt like an hour, he gave a mass—which was far shorter than his previous speech—then finally fell silent and gestured to Tancred, who stepped forward with the sword and shield. Caldwell spoke quietly over the weapons, blessing them for service to Christ, then the sword was passed to Bohemond and Tancred slung the shield onto his own back.

Bohemond drew the weapon, slowly and carefully, the scratching of the blade as it left the scabbard echoing out over the silent hills. He examined it, gave a nod of approval, then rested it on Rainald's right shoulder.

"Do you renew your allegiance to me, Bohemond of Taranto?" he said, his authoritative voice carrying easily over us with seemingly less effort than Caldwell had needed.

"I do," Rainald intoned.

"Do you swear to follow the duties as laid out by the Church?"

"I do."

"And do you swear to obey me in all my orders, to lay down your life if required, and to maintain this oath until your dying breath?"

"I do."

Withdrawing the sword, Bohemond struck Rainald across the cheek with the back of his left hand. "May this be the last blow you receive without just recompense. Stand, *Sir* Rainald, and receive your weapon."

Rainald stood, and Bohemond returned the sword to the sheath and passed it back to Tancred, who then buckled the weapon round Rainald's waist.

"You are a knight," Bohemond said, "a warrior, a guardian

of the realm and of Christ's church. Act in accordance with these duties."

A week later, *Ankída's* hooves—along with those of nearly a hundred other horses—steadily clacked on the cobblestone path leading to the port of Saint Simeon. Five times as many infantry marched ahead of us, all of us dressed in the surcoats of either Bohemond or Raymond of Toulouse. Scouts rode to and from our formation, keeping wary eyes on the hills for any Saracen ambushes.

Yet no battle came, and I suspected it had a great deal to do with our victory over Ridwan. It seemed that he and Duqaq of Damascus had decided to leave Antioch to its fate. No harassment or raiding parties of any kind—except the odd skirmish from Antioch's garrison—had come in the weeks since our victory. And since the icy rains of winter had been replaced with the easy winds and gentle warmth of spring, foraging had become more abundant, trade was easier, and life during the siege of Antioch seemed to be improving along with the weather.

Even now, as the sun dipped below a low rise in front us, the shade brought a gentle breeze rather than the chilling cold I'd become accustomed to. The clear sky was already dimming in the east, and even with the pleasant weather I could sense the groaning of the men around us. They wanted to stop and make camp, yet Bohemond was anxious to reach Saint Simeon, so we continued on. We were maybe a mile out from the city, and ships awaited us there, already docked in the port and filled with supplies commissioned by the lords of the crusade: lumber, hardware, weapons, armor, food, and even craftsmen. These supplies would allow us to build up an abandoned mosque near the Bridge Gate—the gate just south of

Godfrey's encamped forces—making it into a fort similar to Bohemond's Malregard in the north. With the Bridge Gate then blockaded, we'd have only the Saint George gate in the south left before a near-total encirclement of Antioch was achieved. The Iron Gate in the west would be the only gate remaining, and the natural barriers of cliffs and mountains would be enough to prevent any real supplies from reaching Antioch through there.

"A bloody pillar?" Elric asked, and even though I hadn't been paying attention to the conversation, I could hear the surprise in his voice.

"Indeed," Luke replied. "Some say for as long as forty-two years."

He scoffed. "A bloody pillar," he said again. "Why?"

"Saint Simeon believed it brought him closer to God."

He made a show of looking up. "How high was the pillar?"

Luke frowned again. The poor priest seemed to be trying to give us a bit of history on the naming of the port we traveled to; now he found himself defending the actions of a monk who had died six hundred years ago.

"Not physically closer," he said.

"How does living on a pillar bring you closer to God?" I asked.

"He was seeking an ascetic lifestyle, one devoid of earthly goods and wealth."

"Couldn't he have just lived in a monastery?"

"He tried that. Even the monks were shocked with his austerity and the extraordinary lengths he went to in order to achieve the ascetic life he sought. He was judged...unsuited to community life and asked to leave the monastery."

Elric barked a laugh. "A monk too serious for a monastery? Sounds like a joy."

"Life is not only about joy," Migli said.

"Right," he agreed, "it's about drinking and women too."

"It's about suffering," Piccolo corrected. *"Sofferenza."*

"Suffering and endurance," Migli added. "Saint Paul teaches us that. 'We rejoice in our suffering, knowing that suffering produces endurance, and endurance produces character, and character produces hope, and hope does not disappoint us.'"

Luke smiled at Migli's recollection of scripture. "Paul's letter to the Romans," he acknowledged.

"But why suffering at the top of a pillar?" I asked.

"He was not seeking suffering," Luke clarified, "but avoiding earthly distraction. There is a difference."

"But a pillar," I insisted. "Doesn't it seem…odd?"

"Perhaps, but he did not go straight to the pillar after leaving the monastery. He lived in a hut for some time first."

Elric barked another laugh. "A hut?"

Luke gave an exasperated sigh. "Why is that funny?"

He smirked. "Poor guy couldn't catch a break. He gets kicked out of a monastery, then lives in a hut."

"He *chose* that life. He *chose* to live in austerity, and for one and a half years he *chose* to live alone and fast. It's said he once passed the whole of Lent without food or water."

"Sixty days!?" Elric exclaimed.

Luke frowned, but Migli cracked a smile. "Forty days," Migli corrected. "Lent is forty days."

Elric was no less impressed. "I barely go forty minutes without eating."

"That's called gluttony," I jested, though Luke's frown only deepened.

"Forty days without food or water is truly a miracle," Luke said.

"What's the point of that kind of a miracle?" Rainald—*Sir* Rainald—asked, giving his first input into the conversation. Unlike the rest of us, Rainald asked the question out of genuine curiosity, a desire to learn more about this man's ascetic life choices.

"To demonstrate faith. To prove your devotion. To mimic the very life of Christ as He fasted in the desert."

Rainald nodded and seemed to mull over the answer.

"But Simeon wasn't in a desert," Elric put in, still smirking. "He was in a hut."

"*Saint* Simeon." Luke shot him an admonishing look, one that Elric promptly ignored. "He moved to the desert after his time in the hut, and so he continued to live the life of our Lord. But even then, too many came to him for advice and instruction."

"So he moved to the pillar?" I asked.

"So he moved to the pillar," Luke repeated, "which he found among some ruins in Telanissa. He built a platform on top, and local boys would bring him food and water."

"For forty-two years?"

"Some said so, yes, though we cannot be sure. I have heard thirty-seven years, as well."

"And now he's got a port named after him," Elric said.

"And now he is with our Lord," Luke corrected, "which is surely of more value than the naming of a port."

"Not if that port's got the supplies we need."

We were met at the city's gates by a boisterous Italian named Bruno. He led us to the port, though most of our men splintered off to peruse the markets or taverns or less savory locales as the sun neared the western horizon. Elric and I stayed with Rainald, who in turn stayed with Bohemond. Luke, Migli, and Piccolo—having no need for ale, supplies, or women—came along as we traveled to the port.

We passed a low hill, atop which rested a monastery complex with a stone wall surrounding it. A sharp-angled church built of gray stones dominated the center of the complex, and dozens of smaller buildings—living quarters and granaries and even a stable—filled the grass within the wall.

"Saint Simeon's monastery," Luke pointed out.

Elric chuckled. "Forty-two years on a pillar..."

Bruno, riding at the front with Bohemond, spun in his saddle. "*Fifty*-two years!" he bellowed happily. "Saint Simeon the Younger spent fifty-two years atop his pillar!"

"The Younger?" I asked. "Wait, there was an elder? There were *two*?"

"*Certamente*," Bruno called back.

I glanced at Piccolo. "Certainly," he translated.

"There were two Simeons," Bruno went on, curbing his horse to ride alongside us, "but many stylites."

Bohemond watched him, then frowned in annoyance. Clearly, he expected the guide to remain with him. Thankfully, he knew the way to the ports and continued to lead us, content to let Bruno prattle on among us rather than ride with him.

"What's a stylite?" I asked.

"A pillar-dweller."

"You mean more than two people dwelt on a pillar?"

"*Certamente*," he said again. "Many more."

"Why?"

"To get closer to God," Piccolo put in.

Bruno slapped his thigh. "*Senz'altro*. The stylites know something we do not, *amici*."

I grinned and shared a glance with Elric. "That the higher up we go, the closer we are to heaven?"

"*Macché*," Bruno said with a laugh, then looked at a Piccolo with a grin. "Your *amico* is a bit of a fool, I think."

"He's figured you out already, Daniel," Migli put in.

"He forgot the 'and brave' part," I offered. "I'm foolish and brave, remember."

Migli started to say something, then flinched as Bruno shouted suddenly.

"*Caspita!*" Bruno yelped, eyes glued to Piccolo's hands. Both of them were short a thumb; one he'd lost in battle some time

190 | BRYAN R SAYE

ago, and the other had been taken by Temür to 'balance him out.' "You have no thumbs!"

Elric stifled a laugh, while Piccolo frowned. "You're quite observant," he said.

"*Mi dispiace*," he muttered. "I meant no disrespect. But..." he pulled a face and winced. "How does a man lose *two* thumbs?"

"By being unlucky," he answered.

Elric quickly added, "Or by following Daniel."

"That's not fair," I said.

"I broke my arm," he pointed out, holding up his right arm and rolling back the sleeve to reveal a gnarled scar.

"That wasn't my fault!"

"Who suggested we run up that hill at Dorylaeum?"

I scoffed. "We held the hill, didn't we? It's not my fault you can't stay behind your shield."

Elric grinned. "Fair enough."

"I do not blame Daniel," Piccolo said. "I am thankful to be alive. God delivered us that day."

Elric scoffed. "I thought it was Sir Wymond and the others who came rushing in with swords and horses."

"They were instruments," Piccolo pointed out, then quickly added, "though well-timed ones."

After a night spent inspecting the ships and supplies, we left early the next morning with a train of nearly a hundred wagons pulled along by oxen and donkey, all of which had been purchased by Raymond and Bohemond. It took nearly two hours just for our train to finish leaving the city gates, all of which I spent sitting atop *Ankída* beside Rainald and Elric and watching the slow, dragging process. I saw barrels of wine and beer, crates of dried and cured meat, piles and piles of fodder for the horses, and—perhaps most importantly—nearly two dozen wagons designated to carry nothing but the lumber, nails, and tools to transform the abandoned mosque into our fort. A hundred or more craftsmen also rode small horses or donkeys in between the wagons.

I recalled the time we'd spent escorting the portaged warships from Civetot to the Askanian Lake in our effort to encircle Nicaea and end the siege. The massive carts had turned the eighteen miles into a journey of almost four days through rain-soaked hills and mud. A battle waited for us at the end of that journey, one that cost us half the ships and hundreds of men. We'd salvaged what we could and, after a short but fierce skirmish at the port of Nicaea, ended the siege.

Raymond's men led this particular caravan, while we stayed in the back with Bohemond. The infantry had spread out among the wagons, and we marched slowly—so, so slowly —northeast toward Antioch. Day one brought us through a wide valley with gently rising hills on either side. Ten riders were sent to survey each hill. They found nothing, and eventually the valley spilled back out into sprawling plains where a shallow brook—some offshoot of the Orontes—crossed our path. The wagons slogged through the water without incident, and we made camp once all had crossed. A guard was set, an uneventful night passed, and in the morning our trek continued.

We traversed more plains that seemed to never end, passed the sporadic cypress or oak standing lonely in the grass, all with the meandering Orontes ever following on our right. It wasn't until early afternoon that we saw the walls of Antioch looming in the very great distance and a dense forest of pine encroaching from the north. Gentle, rolling hills stretched to the south, and it was atop one of these that I finally saw the mosque we were to build into a fort. From beyond these southern hills came the Orontes once more, sparkling in the late afternoon sun as it cut across the plains.

The wagons had drifted apart, allowing the space between them to grow as we traveled, and I could barely see the wagons at the front of our caravan as they neared the river. Scattered infantry littered the plains, none grouped or marching in any kind of formation. Seeing our destination, it seemed, had welcomed laziness into our convoy, and even Bohemond made no move to correct it. He and Raymond showed no signs that they feared the Saracens.

They were wrong.

19

They came from the rolling hills to the south. At least, that was our best guess as we discussed the battle the next day. None of our men who saw the Saracens' immediate approach would still be alive by the day's end, and no one camped under Antioch's walls noticed the garrison leaving the city until after the battle had already begun.

For us in the rear of the caravan, it began with shouting in the very great distance, toward Antioch, then the rush of our own infantry as they fled back toward us. What had once been scattered men-at-arms walking lazily toward the camp became a clustered mass of retreating men. They were joined by craftsmen who leaped down from their wagons and dropped their reins, leaving their oxen or donkeys to fend for themselves.

Yet I still could not see the enemy.

Then a man, still nearly a quarter mile away, fell with an arrow sticking from his back, and it seemed that his death opened the floodgates. More men lurched to the ground, struck with arrows that shivered in the afternoon sun. Some tumbled head over feet as their momentum carried them spilling into the grassy plains like overturned barrels of grain. Finally, mounted men appeared from the southern hills, nothing but small shadows in the distance. They poured down among the wagons, infantry, and craftsmen, throwing darts and javelins, firing arrows from their horn bows, howling and yelping war cries, and men began to die by the dozens.

"Dear God..." mumbled Luke. He shared a glance with Piccolo and Migli, the three of them unsure what to do. Piccolo had been a warrior not too long ago—and a good one, at that—yet without his thumbs, he couldn't fight. He had no weapons and wore only a dull brown robe instead of mail. Migli would have to protect them both, and he seemed to recognize this as his hand drifted to his hilt.

"To me!" Bohemond shouted, and around him gathered perhaps thirty of us mounted men-at-arms. The rest of the cavalry were in the front with Raymond, and I absently wondered if they'd been caught unawares just like the infantry that were still falling in the plains ahead of us. "To me!" Bohemond called again.

More Saracens flooded into the plains—hundreds of them —and unleashed their storm of arrows. It was clear we were once more outnumbered, and this time they had the element of surprise. There would be no audacious cavalry charge to win the day.

At first, Bohemond did nothing but watch. He seemed to be counting the enemy, realizing we could not assault them, could not turn back several hundred men with only thirty of our own. Yet we couldn't simply let them kill our infantry and —perhaps more importantly—seize our supplies. Something had to be done.

"What do we do?" Luke asked, sharing my own thoughts.

Bohemond ignored him. He scanned the rest of us. His eyes landed on me, then he glanced at *Ankída*.

"Is that a rouncy?" he asked.

I nodded. *Ankída* was likely the only rouncy among us, a smaller horse than the destriers that the others sat upon. "She is, Lord," I said.

He looked again at the Saracens, still some distance away. They were slaughtering the infantry, slaughtering the craftsmen. I followed his gaze, felt the hair on my neck stand up. I discovered that I wanted a battle and only wished I still wore *Vindicta* so I could shed Saracen blood with Hendry's sword. I glanced resentfully at Luke; Skull Splitter would have to do. My hand inched toward the axe, everything in me longing to ride out to meet the Saracens despite the overwhelming odds.

"Is she fast?" Bohemond asked, interrupting my thoughts. I didn't answer quickly enough, and he asked again, impatiently. "Is your horse fast?"

"Very," I answered honestly. She wasn't as powerful as the others, or as stout or strong, but she was faster. Much faster, and she'd proven time and again that she could even outpace many Saracen horses, *Al Khamsa* or not.

"Go to the woods," Bohemond said. "Circle around the slaughter. Get to Antioch. Bring more men."

"Lord?"

"We cannot win this," he said, voice rising in anger, "and we cannot abandon the supplies." He said nothing of the men. "Get Tancred, Godfrey, Robert. Even that weak-willed Hugh. Bring anyone! Go! Now!"

He didn't wait for my reply and instead gathered the rest of the cavalry and rode away from the dying men-at-arms, just as he'd done when we'd faced Duqaq. The infantry were once more on their own. Luke, Migli, and Piccolo delayed for a moment, then seemed to realize the same thing the rest of us already knew: nothing could be done to save them. They galloped after Bohemond and the knights.

I kicked *Ankída*, jerked her reins to the north, and sped across the plains while the Saracens continued their rampage through the caravan. An arrow thudded into the grass in front of me, another quickly followed, and a trio of Saracens veered away from the main battle—if it could be called that—to give chase.

Ankída climbed the gentle rise before the forest, and soon we galloped between trees, low branches slapping at my face and pinging from my helmet. The screams of the dying echoed from the plains behind me as another arrow cracked into a trunk near enough that I could make out the gray fletching. I lost sight of Antioch's walls among the oaks and pines, and the canopy of leaves blocked the sun, forcing me to guess as I reined *Ankída* around, cutting to what I hoped was the northeast.

Three arrows whipped by almost in unison, one clipping off my shoulder hard enough to rock me in the saddle. My mail protected me, though I would have a bruise in the morning, and I hauled myself back up and continued pounding ahead, letting *Ankída* weave her way through the trees. She splashed through a small creek, leaped a felled oak, then burst once more into the daylight, revealing that we had indeed been riding in the right direction. Antioch loomed in front of me, and I breathed a sigh of relief at the familiar sight: the rising smoke from hundreds of cook fires, thousands of tents sprawled out under the walls, and banners whipping in the afternoon wind.

On the road to the south lay the first wagons of our caravan, the distant outline of the decaying mosque rising from the hills beyond. Some of the drivers were slumped over, reins hanging loose in their hands, arrows sticking from their chests and back, while others had abandoned their wagons only to die in the grass instead. The oxen and donkeys that pulled them seemed oblivious to the battle going on behind them and instead waited patiently in their yokes. A trail of bodies led west, back to where I'd just come from, and arrows littered the plains.

The Orontes cut across the grass a hundred yards in front of me, the ripples glittering in the afternoon sun, and I saw both the bridge of boats that we'd built during our first weeks at Antioch and the stone bridge a quarter mile south of it that led over the river and to the Bridge Gate. It seemed half of Antioch's garrison stood on the walls above the gate, and they watched their men continue their slaughter.

An arrow whistled nearby, reminding me of my pursuers, and a glance over my shoulder showed they were gaining. *Ankída* was fast; it seemed these three were faster. There was no way I'd reach the bridge of boats before they overtook me, and even if I did, I'd be unable to cross that unstable scaffolding without being shot. Instead, I spun *Ankída* and faced them, a move that seemed to catch the three of them off-balance. They curbed their horses a dozen paces away, and all aimed and fired at the same time. I pulled my shield into place and kicked *Ankída* into a gallop, charging at them as a pair of arrows ricocheted off my shield. The third sailed harmlessly by as I ripped Skull Splitter free. The first strike cut across the grip of the nearest Saracen's bow. Fingers spun into the air, he dropped the shattered weapon, and my follow-up caught him in the jaw, threw teeth, blood, and bone, and sent him tumbling from his horse.

The others secured their bows and drew their vicious, curving scimitars. I caught one on my shield, then leaned out of the way of the other and hacked with Skull Splitter. I scored only a glancing blow on the second man's shoulder. He yelped in pain but maintained his bearing well enough to counter, his own sword cutting across my chest, tearing through my surcoat and throwing a handful of rings from my mail. His strike didn't break flesh, and I punched him in the chest with the rim of my shield. He tottered backward, the high back of his saddle the only thing keeping him mounted, and Skull Splitter buried itself into his exposed midsection. I wrenched the axe free, and he howled in pain and dropped his sword, clutching at his stomach as he tried to keep his innards from spilling.

A blade hammered the mail at my back, folding me over the pommel of my saddle and knocking the wind from me. I kicked *Ankída,* and she jerked away just as another strike beat at the now-empty space behind me. I sucked in a desperate mouthful of air, gasping and gulping and feeling vomit tickle the back of my throat. The Saracen followed, and I barely raised my shield in time to catch his next blow, but I was still staggering from the first strike, and he easily knocked it aside. *Ankída* backpedaled on her own, pulling me out of range of yet another attack, but he quickly closed the distance. Again I raised my shield, and again he knocked it away, but I'd finally gotten some air back into my lungs and was able to raise Skull Splitter in a hasty parry. His blow shoved my weapons aside, and I leaned out of the way of his follow-up strike, then raised my shield yet again. He grabbed it with his off hand and tore it free, then tossed it to the ground and swung hard at my now exposed side. I jerked Thief's Prick from my belt and gave a hasty parry, then brought Skull Splitter driving down. It glanced off his conical helmet, thumping awkwardly into his collarbone. The axe-head turned on his mail, but the blow was enough to distract him as I leaned forward and buried Thief's Prick into his chest. The fierce tip pierced mail and sliced between ribs, and warm, dark blood flowed instantly over my hand. His arms went slack, his sword tumbled from his limp hand, and he glared daggers at me as he slowly fell from the saddle.

I wiped the blood from Thief's Prick on what remained of my surcoat and sheathed the seax, then bent low and scooped up my shield. To the southwest, hundreds of Saracens were regrouping after finishing off our infantry. Wagons had been tipped and oxen killed, but none of the supplies had been outright destroyed. They were salvageable, should we win the day. I saw no sign of Bohemond, nor had I seen Raymond and the vanguard, though I spotted a small crowd of crusaders across the bridge of boats. They'd seen my brief skirmish and now gazed at the gathering Saracens.

"Saracens!" I shouted, riding along the shore of the Orontes. "Saracens in the plains! They attacked the caravan! Get Tancred! Get Godfrey! Get help!"

Men were scrambling now, rushing throughout the camp, donning armor, grabbing weapons, and soon they streamed across the bridge of boats as quickly as the rickety contraption allowed, each small ship rocking in the current as the ropes lashing them together groaned in protest. Bringing horses across this precarious bridge would take a great deal of time and effort, so men came on foot, some still buckling belts or slipping on helmets. Godfrey's banner joined the growing crowd as men formed a shield wall on my side of the river with me sitting atop *Ankida* at their head as if I commanded them. Soon Godfrey himself crossed.

"What's happening?" he shouted up at me after spotting my position and assuming I held some modicum of authority. It felt odd looking down at the lord.

"Saracens attacked the caravan, Lord," I said, pointing south with my axe. They'd fully regrouped now and—having spotted us forming on the river's shore—were riding hard toward us.

"Where is Bohemond? Raymond?"

"I don't know, Lord. Bohemond was in the south. He rode to safety and sent me to get help."

"And Raymond?"

"He led the caravan. I've not seen him since the ambush began, Lord."

Men still crossed the bridge of boats, and they fell instinctively into the shield wall. To the south, the Saracens pulled up short and drew their bows.

"Shields!" Godfrey bellowed just as the Saracens opened fire. "Shields!"

I kicked *Ankída* into a desperate gallop, turning away from the shield wall and riding out of range as hundreds of arrows filled the sky. I heard the smacking of shields coming together behind me, followed quickly by the staccato crack of arrows slamming into hardened oak and linden. The Saracens continued their barrage, yet Godfrey's men remained stalwart, their shields raised high as they took the assault with steadfastness that came from months of defending against this very thing. I circled around to the edge of the woods, unable to do anything now but watch.

The arrows continued, though even I knew that the Saracen riders couldn't have more than a few volleys left. They'd come from the city to ambush our caravan, not engage in a prolonged battle. Soon, they would have to decide between retreating back inside their walls or engaging us in full.

That decision was quickly made for them as a rumbling echo fell over the plains and the Bridge Gate creaked open. More Saracen warriors—on foot, like Godfrey's men—flooded through the gate and across the stone bridge. Yaghi Siyan, it seemed, was tired of our siege. He sought a battle to end it.

And a battle he received, because no sooner had the gate opened than the thunder of hooves sounded in the distance, and Bohemond and Raymond together galloped around the tumbledown mosque and ripped into the rear of the Saracens. The crusaders' charge shattered what little formation the Saracens had and sent riders scattering like ants from a smashed anthill. Godfrey seized the initiative and broke the shield wall. His men rushed forward with a mighty roar, charging alongside the Orontes to join the ensuing battle.

Crusaders still crossed over the bridge of boats and swelled

Godfrey's shield wall into the thousands. Antioch continued to release troops, and the two forces charged each other with fanatic tenacity. It seemed the entire garrison was pouring across the stone bridge leading from the gate. What had begun as an ambush—an attempt by the Saracens to stop our caravan and hinder our supplies—was quickly turning into a large-scale pitched battle.

I kicked *Ankída* and rushed to join the fight, seeking out Bohemond, who, along with Raymond, still harried the mounted Saracen archers who had laid waste to our own infantry not an hour ago. The horse archers fought to put space between themselves and the cavalry, yet that was a difficult thing when mounted and armored men were already among you, even if there were only sixty of them. The Saracens had exhausted their arrows and eliminated their most serious threat. Instead of using their normal tactic of retreat and fire, they were forced to fight hand to hand against superior armor.

The mounted melee descended into mayhem, and it was into this mayhem I came. Skull Splitter unhorsed an unsuspecting Saracen, cracking into his back and knocking him from the saddle. I whipped the axe out, a ribbon of blood arcing into the air as he fell, then rammed *Ankída* into another Saracen. Our horses crashed together, jarring both of us in our saddles. He held on, yet I ended him before he could react, then sought Bohemond's banner, powering through the skirmish until I found myself beside both Rainald and Elric.

"There you are," Rainald hollered. His blade was bloody, and he'd lost his helmet, his short dark hair wet with sweat and blood. "I was worried you'd fallen off again."

Elric brayed in laughter but said nothing else as there came a massive crash in the plains. Godfrey's men had finally reached the battle, colliding with the Saracens still rushing from the open gate. They met like two opposing waves in the sea, any semblance of order gone as men stabbed and kicked and clawed and punched one another. The Bridge Gate thundered closed as the battle began in earnest. Yaghi Siyan was telling his men a simple truth: they must either win the day or die trying.

"I guess we're fighting, then," Rainald said.

"What else were we doing?" Elric asked.

As they spoke, Godfrey's right flank began to fan out, forming a crescent in the plains and forcing the mounted Saracens to fight in the confined space between them and us. No longer did they outnumber us, and we charged headlong back into the battle, knowing now that they had nowhere to go except through us or through Godfrey's men, the latter wielding heavy shields and long spears and wearing thick mail. Even their path over the bridge was blocked by the mass of their own infantry. Too many had been sent into the fray, and at least a hundred of them were crammed together on the stone bridge, pressing against one another as they tried to make their way into the fight. Sporadic arrows came from the walls, though these fell almost harmlessly among Godfrey's men in the rear who still had their shields raised high. The archers didn't fire upon us for fear of hitting their own allies.

I chose an enemy, and *Ankida* seemed to sense my mind. Without any goading, she broke into a gallop and closed the distance in a handful of steps. He spotted me and readied himself to attack, yet I could see the fear in his eyes. His once successful ambush had turned into more than he'd prepared for. He'd donned only a light mail vest and had forgone a shield, just as the rest of the mounted Saracens had, and none of them wanted to continue this fight.

Our encounter went as I expected; I caught his blow easily on my shield, then swung underneath the iron rim and felt Skull Splitter punch through his thin mail and earn more Saracen blood. He wheezed, I shoved him aside, and he tumbled backward from his saddle. I sought out another, and soon it became a killing field. The mounted Saracens found themselves beset by angry cavalry on one side and a formidable shield wall on the other.

Yaghi Siyan had badly misjudged the capabilities of his forces—especially since they hadn't prepared for such a battle —and he'd underestimated what months of crusading had done to us. The siege of Nicaea, the battle of Dorylaeum, the trekking through the mountains. Harim. Duqaq. Ridwan. All of it had refined us like hardened steel, stripping away the weakest among us and leaving only a core of ferocious men-at-arms, soldiers who had faced everything the Saracens could throw at us and won nearly every time. We were veterans, each of us worth a dozen lesser warriors. Yes, even me, a young man of eighteen who'd picked up his first weapon less than a year ago. The fires of battle had forged me into a terrifying weapon, and in those plains before the Bridge Gate, I released that weapon upon the Saracens.

My arm ached as I fought; only a mixture of resolute determination and my compelling desire to avenge Hendry kept my hand gripping Skull Splitter. My axe rose and fell, blood running down the oak shaft, soaking my leather gloves, drenching the mail at my wrist and forearm, yet still I pressed on. We all did, steadily pushing the Saracens back toward the bridge, and with what sounded like the hesitant rumbling of defeat, the gate finally began to open again. The Saracens continued to push one another, this time pressing back into the city instead of into the fight. Godfrey had found similar success, and the ground was littered with Saracen bodies. I saw swords and axes rising and falling, spears shuttling forward and back, bloodied banners trembling in the wind. Saracens were cut down as they fled, some shoved over the bridge to be taken by the rushing waters of the Orontes.

Bohemond was suddenly beside me, and I saw a feral look

in his eyes as he spied the open gate. Antioch was within reach. He hacked his way onto the bridge, and I followed, the two of us killing as we forced our way through the mash of bodies. He kicked a man over the stone railing, stabbed another between the shoulder blades, and hacked mercilessly into the back of a fleeing man. I was ever at his side, Skull Splitter scoring hit after hit, downing Saracens with ruthless efficiency.

But the gate was already descending once more, and a panic swept through those Saracens who would not make it through. They pushed each other now, shoving their own allies over the bridge in an effort to reach safety, but the gate shut with an ominous thud that seemed to echo across the battle-field. An odd silence followed that irrevocable sound, and Saracens turned to face us, eyes wide with fear, weapons held instantly into the air as a sign of surrender. Bohemond howled in frustration, screaming directly at the gate with such ferocity that even *Ankída* took a cautious step back. For another terri-fying moment, nothing and no one seemed to move.

Bohemond looked down at the nearest Saracen, saw his sword held aloft in surrender, then stabbed him callously in the chest. He kicked him off his blade as terror swept through the Saracens remaining on the bridge. With another unrestrained bellow of fury, he hacked through the surrendering troops. I hesitated for a moment, but that was all it took. Men-at-arms descended on the surrendering Saracens around me, and soon only crusaders remained alive on the bridge.

20

T he arrows came shortly after Antioch realized we were accepting no surrenders. We fled the bridge, *Ankída* nimbly stepping around the hundreds of corpses as she cantered to safety. Godfrey led his men in a more calculated retreat, shields remaining raised and pressed together as they steadily marched away from the city. Once finally out of arrow range, I turned back and truly took in the sight for the first time.

The grassy plains had been trampled into a muddied, bloodied, and corpse-riddled disaster. Bodies—both man and horse—stretched along the shores of the Orontes and across the plains in front of the stone bridge and then followed the path all the way back toward the caravan. Great rivulets of thick, red blood filled the ruts that the wagons had made in the dirt, and crimson smeared the once-gray bridge. The startlingly clear sky shone in stark contrast to the devastation spread along the grass.

"Heathens!" Bohemond bellowed, taking my attention from the wasteland. He'd sheathed his sword and now threw his only remaining weapon against the walls of Antioch:

curses. "Hell-spawned, hog-hearted heathens! Lice-covered louts! Incestuous, ill-bred idolaters!" He drew a deep breath, face tense, savage eyes calming only slightly, and I absently admired his skill with words. "I'll kill every man in that cursed city." He spat, then looked at those of us around him. The sight of us seemed to relax him, and he cracked a good-natured but defiant smile. "Gods bones! We were so close."

"It was a still a miraculous victory, Lord," Elric put in.

"Miraculous?" He belted a laugh. "Today's victory was achieved by the determination of you men." He swept a glance over us. "Your boldness won the day. Your blood and sweat. No miracle from God." His eyes met mine, and he paused. "Thank you, Daniel," he said, and I realized it was one of the only times he'd used my name. "Thank you for getting help."

I could find no words and gave a solemn nod.

He sighed and glanced almost casually back at Antioch. "Bastards," he muttered.

"Where's Sir Rainald?" Elric asked suddenly, and we scanned the mounted men around us. Rainald was nowhere to be seen.

Panic gripped my heart. "Has anyone seen him?" I asked, sweeping my gaze around. "Anyone?"

The knights and squires exchanged awkward glances. I suspected each of them had lost a friend, as well, and they cared no more for Rainald than I did for them.

"Men die in battle," Bohemond said bluntly. "Especially those who fight as hard as Sir Rainald does." He saw the distress in my face, and his expression lightened by a fraction. "You may search the corpses," he added, "but I will need your aid before long. The priests will find him, if he was slain." He looked at the others. "Tend to the seriously wounded. The rest of you begin collecting our supplies. Today's losses will be for nothing if we cannot construct the fort."

Elric and I searched as close to Antioch's walls as we dared, turning over the bodies of crusader and Saracen alike, always breathing a sigh of relief to find a random face instead of our friend's. It was gruesome work, though I'd done worse and not that long ago. The thought of losing Rainald was too much to bear—especially after I'd already lost Hendry.

In the end, we found neither the corpse of my friend nor a single living person, though hundreds of bodies still lay near the walls, far too close for us to inspect. The Orontes had claimed at least another hundred men, and though most of those had been Saracens, Elric and I agreed to peruse the river downstream when we were able.

The rest of the evening hours were spent collecting the supplies we'd taken from Saint Simeon. We laid them inside the abandoned mosque sitting near the forest, where they would be used the following day to begin building it into a proper fort.

Others came forward from the camp—mainly women, children, and priests—to collect the fallen crusaders and begin the digging of yet another graveyard. Luke, Migli, and Piccolo had survived the ordeal and were among the other priests, scurrying around the graveyard and praying over men as they were buried and forced to rest forever underneath the battle-strewn fields of Antioch. The Saracen garrison—there were decidedly fewer of them than ever before—stood atop their walls and watched our grim work. By twilight, the plains were cleared of the crusaders we could reach without risk of arrow fire, and only the Saracen dead remained.

I was about to venture with Elric to the Orontes and begin looking once more through corpses when a brilliant fire burst to life above the Bridge Gate. It lit the parapets in bright orange light, and I saw Saracens standing watch near the flames as a horn blew and dozens of figures joined them atop the walls. These newcomers were clearly prisoners, the blood smearing their faces and bare chests visible even from the battered fields surrounding the city. They stood naked, held at the edge of the wall by their Saracen captors.

"Men of the west!" a voice called down from the wall. Yaghi Siyan stood beside the prisoners, clearly visible in the orange firelight that flickered behind him. "Men of the west, come see your *crusaders*," he bellowed, sneering this last word. "Come!"

Men-at-arms began to gather, Bohemond among them, still bloody and in his armor. Siyan continued to call out his challenge, the prisoners swaying from exhaustion and their wounds. I hoped silently that Rainald was among them, and that Siyan was about to negotiate their release, though with Bohemond's brutal treatment of our own captured Saracens, we had no prisoners of our own to exchange.

"Come, crusaders!" he yelled again, the fire growing beside him and illuminating the rightfully angry Saracens and downtrodden crusader prisoners atop the wall. "Come!"

Godfrey and Raymond and many other lords and princes joined us, and soon hundreds—or perhaps thousands, I couldn't be sure—stood with me and stared up at the walls of Antioch.

"I have fifty of your fellow Christians," Siyan yelled down at us. "And even one of your knights." He turned toward the prisoners, and his guards dragged a single man forward. Even from the distance, I knew it was Rainald. "Behold," Siyan went on. "Behold Rainald Porchet, servant of Bohemond! Servant of Tancred. Servant of God, so he says."

I reached for Skull Splitter, though there was obviously nothing I could do. Even so, I gripped the haft of the weapon, squeezing it tight as an outlet for my rising anger. Rainald was like a brother to me, and in that moment I thought of William, how I'd been unable to save him, had actually been the cause of his death. I'd let Bojan kill him, watched helpless as it had happened, and once more I could do nothing as another madman had control over someone I held dear.

"What do you want, heathen?" Bohemond shouted up, tactful as ever.

Siyan smiled fiercely in the hellish light of the dancing fire. "I want you to leave," he called down, "and take the rest of your army with you."

Bohemond scowled. "You'll need more than fifty prisoners to negotiate that."

As callous as he was, he was right. We'd come too far, and to expect us to leave in order to save fifty men—even if Rainald was among them—was a ridiculous demand.

"Perhaps your knight feels differently?" Siyan said.

He gestured to the guards, and Rainald was pushed so far forward that his naked torso bent over the low parapet atop the wall. Siyan drew his sword, extravagantly raising it high enough for all to see, then he placed it along the back of Rainald's neck. I stepped forward, jaw clenched, heart racing.

"We have to do something," I said, though even as the words came out, I knew they were pointless.

"Do what, boy?" Bohemond said, his tone hard. "Abandon the siege? Surrender the crusade?" He scoffed. "Sir Rainald swore his oath, same as you, same as me. If we die, we die as martyrs. You would not turn back if it were me atop those walls, and I would not want you to. I'll not flee for the lives of fifty men."

Once again, he was right, though that didn't make his cold demeanor any more palatable. My best friend was likely about to die, and there seemed nothing I could do.

"I think he wants to live," Siyan yelled. He looked at Rainald. "Do you want to live, Christian?"

Rainald said nothing, only gritted his teeth and scowled at Siyan.

"Do you want to live?" he asked again. "Renounce your

faith. Renounce your God. Renounce your crusade. Do this, and you shall live. Do this, and I will heap riches and rewards on you that will make your fellow crusaders burn with jealousy as they languish below in their pitiful squalor."

Do it, Rainald, I thought. *Do it. Renounce God and live. Please. I would rather you lived as a Muslim than died as a Christian.*

"Do this," Siyan went on, "and I will find a place for you among my princes. I will raise you up as a lord of Antioch. I will put men under your command and women under your bedsheets. I will—"

"Never," Rainald said, and my heart dropped as his hoarse voice echoed softly over the plains, little more than a whisper on the evening winds. "Never," he said again, turning this time to glare up at Siyan. "Never!"

Siyan's cocky smile vanished as if slapped away. I expected him to counter, to try and sway Rainald again. That hope vanished like morning mist as he swiftly raised his sword and severed Rainald's head in a single strike. Hanging over the parapet as he was, Rainald's head careened down the wall, bouncing once against the hard stone and leaving a bloodied imprint before falling into the Orontes below where it would be forever lost to time. A trail of blood spurted from his naked corpse and sprayed the cold stone of the bridge.

A roar went up among us as lords, princes, knights, squires, priests, paupers, and commoners all cried their protest. I remained silent, a deep grief seizing my heart, pulling me down, anchoring me to the earth in such a way that felt I could not stand. I sank to my knees, heart rising to my throat, burning anger scalding my veins. Guilt and bitterness and desire for vengeance roiled together in a repulsive mixture of hate that would sit with me for far too long.

Yet Rainald had died as he'd wanted: a martyr. He'd hoped for nothing less as he'd set out for Jerusalem, knowing he stood little chance of reaching the city himself. He'd surely prayed that his sacrifice would be enough to help the crusade succeed. He'd died so men like me could reach the Holy City. So men like me—broken, selfish, despicable men like me—could kneel before Christ's empty tomb at the Church of the Holy Sepulcher and receive our absolution.

The already high fire flared brighter as hay and kindling and lumber were brought forward. A moment later, the fierce, raw screams of the remaining prisoners fell over the fields like a tempest as they were burned alive. That horrible sound of torture I can only compare to lightning, piercing and sharp and searing into your mind in such a way that it lingers long after the sound has faded, scarring your vision with its fierce presence so that, years later, you still awake with their terror-filled cries in your head.

More than torturing crusaders, more than eliminating prisoners, what Siyan did was reveal his hand. He had no intention of peacefully surrendering the city, even after his resounding defeat in battle only hours before. By executing his prisoners—and in a way barbaric enough to rival anything Bohemond had done—he was telling the men of his city one thing: fight or be killed. No peace could exist between us, no amicable exchange of Antioch. Once we entered the city, blood would be shed—liberally.

There was nothing stopping that now.

21

Amina was waiting expectantly for me when I finally stepped from the darkness and into the dim light cast by her low-burning fire. The wood had burned down to little more than embers that glowed with the barest hints of orange, doggedly holding on to the last vestiges of heat they could offer before succumbing to the night with the rest of us. She sat cross-legged beside it with Novella curled up alongside her, her head resting on Amina's lap, her small frame rising and falling in the gentle breathing of sleep. A neatly organized pile of supplies had been set aside at the very edges of the fading circle of light: bandages, thread, needle, honey, oil, and even a small pail of water, all carefully laid out so my wife could methodically and efficiently clean my wounds as she'd done dozens of times in the past.

She stiffened at my approach, likely in reaction to the pain she saw in my eyes. She knit her brow and frowned sadly, and I knew she longed for me to tell her how I felt though she knew that I would not. I shared little of how I felt during our time at Antioch.

I set my shield down, resting it against the chest that held

Hendry's sword. A wave of sudden sadness washed over me, and I blinked blurry eyes until they were clear again, then unbuckled my belt and laid it beside the shield. Amina stood, gently set Novella's head onto a small hay-filled pillow, and moved to stand across from me. She met my gaze with shared sorrow in her eyes. Whether she knew of Rainald's death or not, his loss scarred my face, hidden beneath a layer of blood and mud but still visible to someone who knew my soul so well.

I swallowed a lump, opened my mouth, then shut it again without saying a word. She reached up and wiped away a stubborn tear that had escaped down my cheek. After a moment of silence when her eyes never left my own, she untied the length of blue cloth that had somehow managed to stay pinned around my bicep. She tucked it into her own belt before beginning the tedious process of removing my clothes and armor until I stood before her in only my breeches. Her fingers traced the scars and fresh cuts across my chest and back, stories of past battles mixed among new tales to tell, and waves of goose bumps prickled to life on my flesh.

Soon came the tender pressure of damp cloth, followed by water running down my bare skin and the gentle kiss of the cool night air as she washed away the battle. Dirt and grime filled the once-clear bucket until the water inside turned the color of old blood. Next came oil and honey, soothing balms over red and torn flesh. Finally, she pushed me down to my knees and sat behind me, hands probing a deep and wide gash between my shoulder blades. Her caring touch slowed my still-racing heart, despite the pinch of the needle as she worked to stitch my body back together.

More tears welled without warning in my eyes as she worked, falling soundlessly down my cheeks. I'd lost another friend, watched Rainald's head bounce down the city's walls before disappearing into the Orontes, and yet here I sat in the tender arms of a loving woman. I lived—battered and bruised as I was—while Rainald had died.

I heard once more the echoing screams of the other prisoners—their piercing, unrestrained shrieks of pain and terror as Siyan burned them alive—and realized that at least Rainald hadn't suffered as they had. The thought brought no comfort, and I pinched my eyes shut, ceasing the flow of tears and bringing about a self-imposed darkness. Misery and hate swelled inside me like a volatile brew, and I felt drunk with the emotions. I was filled with a deep desire to curl into a ball and weep for my losses, yet at the same time I craved the opportunity to march into Antioch and kill Siyan along with every Saracen inside those walls.

Amina's shadow moved as she worked, backlit by the fading fire and nothing more than a faint outline on the dirt in front of me. I craved her closeness, craved the easy intimacy we'd experienced for so long, yet I couldn't bring myself to break the silence. I was heartbroken, bitter, vindictive, and vengeful all at once, and I desperately wanted to turn around and fall into her, to let her pull me close, to cry into her arms and let my emotions spill out as I confessed how utterly lost and alone I felt.

Yet I couldn't do it. Pain and loss seemed to have frozen me, and I merely gazed down at our shadows flickering on the ground. I watched her shadow work, felt the tug of the stitches in my back, even that pain a comfort since the touch of her fingers accompanied it.

"We don't have to go," she said suddenly, the more courageous one of us finally breaking the silence.

I wanted to look over my shoulder, to meet her gaze, but I couldn't even do that. Slowly and with great effort, I asked, "Go where?"

"Jerusalem."

"No?" My voice was low, barely a whisper.

I saw her shadow look at me. I could almost feel the pleading in her eyes, even if I couldn't see them. "We can go anywhere. Back to Baghras. Or Adana. Even back to Nicaea."

"And do what?" These words came a bit easier, and I found that I needed to hear the sound of her voice so badly that I would have talked about anything.

Her dimming shadow shrugged. "You could farm?"

I scoffed. "You see me as a farmer?"

"It's not so hard. Novella is already so good with Myrtle."

That drew a soft laugh that came out stifled and awkward, and a real smile cracked my lips for the first time in weeks. It was a struggle to maintain it. "She is," I said. "But I don't think I could be a farmer. Too much dung."

"It's easier to clean off than blood," she said, though she seemed to instantly regret that, because she quickly added, "What about a tailor?"

"A tailor?"

"You made your first gambeson," she pointed out. "And I can knit and sew. We could open a little shop, sell clothes and cloaks."

"I could line one with fur," I offered, "like I always wanted."

"You could," she said, and the way she said it sounded as if she were entertaining the silly ideas of a child.

"A tailor," I said, then gave a sad grin that I was glad she couldn't see. I blinked away a new round of tears. Both of us knew this was nothing but a fantasy. Still, not wanting it to end, I asked, "What else could we do?"

"You could be a smith," she said, her voice perking up, and I realized then that she likely needed to hear my voice as much as I did hers. "I watched my father enough to know the basics."

"Make swords instead of wield them?"

"You can make horseshoes. Or plows or sickles or spades. It doesn't have to be weapons."

I glanced at the chest that still held Hendry's sword. "But I know weapons," I said. "I know them well." *Hendry taught me,* I wanted to add, yet I wasn't quite ready to sidetrack this conversation, and any mention of Hendry would do just that.

"Then make swords."

"We sold all your father's supplies," I pointed out.

"It doesn't matter what you do. So long as it's you, me, and Novella. You can do whatever you want. You could be a jeweler, a stonemason, a carpenter, even a—"

I stiffened suddenly. Amina jerked in surprise, tearing some of the threads from the cut she was stitching. Fresh blood run down my back as her tense hands pressed a wet cloth against me to stop the sudden bleeding. My father had been a carpenter; Amina knew that. He'd abandoned me and my brother on the steps of an orphanage in Constantinople, forced us to live a life of crime until Bojan took us in. Now Bojan and William were both dead, and I hoped that my father had shared their end. It seemed likely that he had, that he'd drunk himself into a stupor and died in an alley all alone, though fate had been cruel lately. Hendry had died when he shouldn't have; perhaps my father had lived when he deserved death.

"Not a carpenter," I said firmly.

There was a long pause where all I felt was the press of her hands into my back, the warm blood soaking the cloth, the sting of where she'd torn the stitches free.

"Sorry," she finally whispered. "I just…I want us to be a family. Somewhere safe. Somewhere away from…" she trailed off, and her shadow waved vaguely around her. "Away from all this."

A tense quiet descended on us, and I stared once more at our shadows. I knew what she wanted. I wanted it too. Peace, a home, a life without war and death constantly looming over us. A life where I needn't bury the only father I ever knew, where I needn't watch as friends are slain in front of me. A life without the screams of dying men as they're burned alive.

But I wanted to reach Jerusalem more. I *had* to reach Jerusalem. If I didn't kneel at the foot Christ's empty tomb, I'd be doomed to live a life without absolution, a life forever burdened with William's death. Choosing a life of peace meant forsaking any chance of forgiveness for William's death.

Abandoning Jerusalem was abandoning my brother, and I couldn't do that.

"I can't," I said. "I can't leave."

"Why?"

"You know, Amina."

She sighed, her hands going limp on my back. "William would understand," she said. "He'd—"

"Would he?" I cut her off. "Would he understand? He barely understood who I was."

"He wouldn't want you to get yourself killed."

I felt a new pinch as she started fresh stitches. "I'm apparently the only one who can't die. Hendry's dead, now Rainald."

She stopped stitching for a moment before continuing. "Rainald's dead?"

I nodded into the darkness.

"I'm sorry," she said, and despite the triteness of those words, I knew she meant it.

"He died so the crusade could go on," I said. "So we could reach Jerusalem. So *I* could reach Jerusalem."

She stitched in silence for a handful of heartbeats, all of which I felt thumping inside my aching head. "I just...I don't want to lose you."

"You won't."

"Then why do I feel like I am?"

I said nothing. What could I say? She was right. I'd pushed her away, sheltered her from my grief as if I were doing her a favor, when she wanted nothing more than for me to open myself up. She wanted to heal my wounds—those of the flesh *and* of the soul—and I wouldn't let her.

"You're changing," she went on. "You've *changed*. And I'm afraid by the time we reach Jerusalem, we won't be able to undo it."

"Brave but foolish" they called me. Sir Wymond, Bohemond, even Hendry. Brave but foolish. It was the hallmark of my behavior in my youth, almost a badge of honor. The foolishness I'd proven many times over, but my bravery was only ever with a weapon in my hand. A truly brave man would have acted differently in that moment. He would have spoken truth, would have confessed what a sad and broken man he really was. He would have asked for help, especially from the person he loved most in the world, and he would have let her heal him.

Brave men do the right thing even when it is difficult, and I was not a brave man.

"I can't leave," I said again. "I can't."

22

T he next morning was gray and dark, as if God had overheard Amina and me talking the night before and wanted to reflect His disapproval of my actions. Rain threatened but never came, though distant thunder rumbled across our camp. Fog drifted down the Orontes like a ship at sea, then crawled up over the plains. With no sun to burn it away, it lingered over our camp like a damp cloth until midday.

And it was at midday that the news arrived.

Saracens had stolen out during the night. They'd risked their lives not to flee the city or to try their hands once more at battle, but to sneak from the Bridge Gate and bury their dead. The thousands of Saracen bodies that had littered the grass were gone, and in their place mounds had formed—hundreds of them. A Saracen graveyard had appeared in the plains surrounding the very mosque we planned to build into a fort. It was Father Caldwell who spread the news, riding through the camp like a town crier reporting a vicious attack underway.

"This cannot be allowed," Caldwell bellowed from atop his horse, shouting to no one in particular. "They've tricked us!

They've stolen their own dead from under our very noses while we slept!"

"Who cares?" Elric yelled, and Caldwell turned on him as if he'd blasphemed God.

We sat around a small fire as our lunch—a goose that John Mark had killed during a scouting run—bubbled over a spit. Only Amina and Novella were absent, having decided to venture down to the river to retrieve water. I suspected Amina's emotions still ran raw from last night, and she merely sought a bit of solitude. Novella, of course, would not leave her side.

"*You* should, good squire!" Caldwell shouted back, curbing his horse toward us. His shadow bathed us even in the dim, overcast light, and I'm sure he felt an overwhelming sense of authority as he looked down at us. "If we allow them such freedom of movement, surely their boldness will swell, and the siege will drag on."

Elric scoffed and waved a hand.

Migli spun the goose on the spit, a few drops of grease sizzling into the fire below. "I don't imagine burying hundreds of their dead would boost their confidence," he said.

"Seeing that many corpses would do just the opposite," John Mark added.

"Would thcare the thit out of me," Thomas put in. He held his massive lute—his *divan bağlama*—and plucked casually at the strings.

"But the audacity," Caldwell persisted. "The sheer daring of the garrison to risk death and venture beyond their walls. Surely they don't fear you as they should."

"Oh, they fear us, Father," I said. I ran Skull Splitter across the whetstone I'd lain before me, then looked up at him. "Trust me on that."

Elric grunted his approval. "We put plenty of fear into them yesterday."

"What do you want us to do about it, anyway?" Migli asked. "What's done is done."

Caldwell flashed an unrestrained smile. "You can dig them up."

At first, no one responded. Luke finally looked up from some piece of parchment he was reading. He seemed mildly disappointed yet unsurprised. He and Caldwell were far from friends, despite their shared profession.

"*Che schifo...*" Piccolo finally muttered. "Disgusting."

"Agreed," John Mark said. He'd been reaching out to scrape some flesh from the goose, but instead sat back and pulled a face. "God, now I can't eat."

Elric shrugged and sliced himself a hunk of meat, then ate it, still steaming, directly from the knife.

"Why would we dig up bodies?" John Mark asked. "What do you want to do with hundreds of Saracen corpses?"

Yet even I could have answered that. This was a siege, and that meant the struggle was as much mental as it was physical. We'd already beheaded nearly a hundred men in front of the city's walls and later planted a thousand or more heads on spikes—the latter of which still remained, though the crows had long reduced them to gaping skulls devoid of flesh. Siyan himself had just demonstrated the lengths he would go to in order to put even an ounce of fear into us.

"Show them they cannot move freely outside their city like they once could," Caldwell said. "Show them we own the Bridge Gate."

"We do," Migli said. "At least, we will once the fort's built."

"Maybe," I muttered. I couldn't get the image of Rainald's head bouncing down the city wall from my mind. I wanted to hurt them. "Couldn't hurt to put a bit *more* fear into them."

Caldwell gave an approving smile. Luke, however, gazed at me with mild shock. Even John Mark shot me a sideways glance.

224 | BRYAN R SAYE

"Fear," Caldwell howled. "Yes! Let the heathens know they cannot face us. That God is on our side! That it is only a matter of time before their city is ours, before we march through their streets and send them to the hell they deserve."

My hand twitched unconsciously at Skull Splitter's haft at the mention of shedding Saracen blood.

Luke shook his head in disappointment. "There are better ways."

"Agreed," Caldwell said. "With more men the graves can be dug up faster."

"That's not what I meant."

"I know what you meant, but not all of us are afraid to do what must be done."

"This is a thing that *must* be done?"

The two priests glared at one another, one atop a horse, his robe lined with silk, a massive golden crucifix hanging about his neck and a ruby ring on his pinky, and the other adorned in plain black robes with no jewelry of any kind.

"Would *you* dig up the bodies, I wonder," Luke added.

"I would do no such thing," Caldwell said. "I am a priest. Consecrated. Set apart. Holy. But the men…" he trailed off and shrugged. "*They* will do what must be done."

"Sure, leave it to us," Elric said. "Always up to men-at-arms to do the dirty work."

"You do not expect me to wield a sword," Caldwell pointed out, "just as I do not expect you to offer mass. Your battle is one of flesh and blood. Mine is of a spiritual kind."

Piccolo scoffed, but said nothing.

"You suggest this terrible task," John Mark said, "and yet you expect us to do it and not you."

"If doing God's work does not inspire you," Caldwell added, "then you should know that many of the corpses were buried with their armor and weapons."

Elric patted his sword. "I'll not trade my steel for theirs," he said.

"Nor me," John Mark added.

I didn't care about the mail or weapons. Like them, I had my own, and they were quite well made. Skull Splitter, Thief's Prick—both would last a lifetime if cared for and perhaps longer. And I'd seen the mail the Saracens had been wearing. Light and flexible and built for battle from a horse's back. I had no desire to wear it myself. Yet I found myself wanting to go anyway. Wanting to dig them up and scatter their remains across the plains or do whatever else Caldwell—or more likely Bohemond—had in mind to intimidate the garrison.

"None of you are brave enough to do God's work?" Caldwell asked.

"None of these men are foolish enough to desecrate a cemetery," Luke countered. "Even a Saracen one."

Caldwell looked at us for the span of several heartbeats. "Then you—"

"I'll do it," I said suddenly, and Luke snapped his head toward me. "I'll do what needs doing."

I stood, and John Mark jerked to his feet beside me. "Daniel!"

"I'm going," I said.

"Because this priest says so?" he asked, waving a dismissive hand at Caldwell.

"If it helps end the siege—"

"It won't!"

"—then I'll do my part."

He scoffed. "Your part cannot be digging up corpses."

I grabbed my belt and made to follow Caldwell. "My part is to do whatever needs doing."

Without another word, I stepped around John Mark and began the long walk to the mosque.

The fog had lifted by the time I reached the mosque, though the sky continued with its empty threat of rain as gray and black storm clouds lingered overhead. The mosque sat short and squat on the far side of the road to Saint Simeon, its single dome caved in and a massive oak growing through the opening. A courtyard of gray stone spread from the front of the mosque, and a pair of broken statues lay at its entrance. From the mosque's back corner rose a dull minaret that had perhaps been red once upon a time. A thin crack ran its length before ending at its broken and jagged top, and a mound of bricks and other debris that had likely been the rest of the minaret lay scattered next to it.

The mosque felt dangerously close to the Bridge Gate, though the arrows littering the road and grass a hundred paces from the mosque showed that it was at least out of bow range. Raymond of Toulouse had moved his command tent to the peak of a low hill south of the mosque, and five additional tents big enough to fit at least twenty men each suggested he'd brought a small army to defend the workers as they rebuilt the shattered mosque into something resembling a fort. The smoke from several small fires rose from among those tents, and I suspected men-at-arms were still preparing their food.

I felt the skin prickle at the back of my neck as I crossed the stone and dirt road to approach the mosque. I'd left in such a rush that I'd brought no armor, no helmet, no shield, and only Skull Splitter and Thief's Prick hung from my belt. Many of the wagons from yesterday's caravan still lay on their sides where they'd fallen in the road, though their contents had been stripped as the French Provençals had piled them neatly beside the mosque.

Already a dozen men were hard at work on the fort's construction. It had been named *La Mahomerie*, which was supposedly what the French called Christ's mother, though I'd never heard them say it. Bruno—that boisterous Italian who'd accompanied us from Saint Simeon—ran circles around the men, hollering orders that were often in Italian and indiscernible to the Provençals, who seemed to be largely ignoring him as they sorted lumber, stacked stones, or hammered boards into place.

Yet I hadn't come to survey the mosque or help with construction, but instead to see the hundreds of freshly dug graves spreading throughout the hills and plains surrounding the mosque. More crusaders—unarmored, like me—were already digging up the graves, and a heap of decomposing corpses grew nearby, arms and legs mashed together, naked bodies crushed under an ever-growing weight as more and more remains were thrown onto the mound.

A smaller and more neatly ordered pile sat beside the one of flesh. Swords and shields were stacked there with mail in dire need of repair and the distinctively curved horn bows of the Saracens. Cloaks, shirts, boots, belts, hats, and pants. Anything that could be salvaged, anything that could be sold, much of it still covered in crusted black blood.

The garrison stared at the grave robbers from atop Antioch's walls, likely simmering in anger as they watched us desecrate their brethren. Once more I felt woefully unarmored, especially so close to the enemy. Were I them, no order from any lord would stop me from lifting the gate myself and storming once more into battle.

"Here to help?"

A craftsman dragged a length of lumber by me, leaving a trench in the trampled dirt. I said nothing and stepped toward the makeshift cemetery. The nearest graves had already been disinterred, some still with crusaders inside them working hard to strip their occupants of any earthly goods. Heads bobbed in open graves as spadefuls of moist dirt were flung into the air. I stepped around the pillaged graves, glancing down to see some still had bodies inside, stripped naked and left to rot. I flinched as I passed a dead man with open eyes gaping up at the murky sky. His pallid skin bore clear spade marks in addition to the gaping wound in his chest that had ended his life. Likely, the crusader hadn't been careful about unearthing him. Why would he be? The point of this entire endeavor was to mutilate them, to humiliate them. Of course, he'd dug vigorously, unafraid to hack away chunks of flesh along with the dirt.

The scene felt eerily similar to the aftermath of the battle of Nicaea, where we'd fought off Kilij Arslan's forces and secured the siege. I'd stood in the shield wall beside a man named Theudo, and many hundreds of crusaders had died. Then, however, we'd dug fresh graves to fill with our fallen; we hadn't exhumed corpses to desecrate with the hopes of frightening an already frightened garrison.

A spadeful of dirt hit my calf and buried a boot, and I kicked it off as a reflex.

"Oy!"

I turned to the voice, saw a man standing in a grave. His eyes were level with my waist, and he rested an elbow on the ground as he glared up at me.

"Oy," he said again, wiping dirt from his face. "You 'ere to dig, then dig. Don't just walk in me way, throwing dirt back into me 'ole."

I took a pair of steps back. The ground gave way, and I fell, landing in an open—and thankfully vacant—grave. I hit the packed dirt hard and the freshly stitched laceration on my back tore open. Warm blood trickled from the wound and dampened my tunic. The man topside laughed before going back to digging.

For a long while, I simply sat in the grave. What was I doing there? Why had I left my friends and come to this Saracen graveyard? Digging graves wasn't anything I'd have considered only a few weeks ago, yet the thought of Hendry's death, of Rainald's head careening down Antioch's walls...it all brought a swell of anger and a rising need for vengeance.

Amina was right. I was changing, *had* changed. I was out of control, wild, like a man lost at sea with no rudder. Only I was no longer even on the ship; I'd been shoved overboard—or, more honestly, had leapt overboard—and now was nothing more than flotsam jostled about by the current. Fittingly, the current had taken me into an empty grave not unlike the one I'd put Hendry in only a few weeks ago.

I couldn't do it. This had been a terrible idea, one of my worst, and I'd had many. I climbed free of the grave and dusted the dirt from my clothes. The man who had been digging now knelt beside the open grave, the body of a slain Saracen lying in the grass with him. He pawed at the corpse, barely offering me a glance as he callously pillaged.

Shouting from far away, little more than a whisper on the light wind. I looked to the noise, saw a lone figure stumbling over the bridge of boats a half mile to the north. The shout came again, echoing indiscernibly across the distance, yet I didn't need to hear the words to know it was her.

Amina ran across the plains, and I stepped lightly over graves. Workers and looters paused to look on in confusion as she ran up the low rise leading to the road where I could finally hear her voice.

"Danya!" she shouted. "Danya!"

A few of the workers turned to me as I stepped dumbfounded into the mosque's courtyard.

I ignored them. "Amina!" I called back.

She turned to my voice, and I could see she'd been crying. Frantically, she sprinted toward me. "Danya! Don't do it!"

We came together atop the gray stone of the courtyard, the workers still looking on with the same confusion. Bruno hollered in Italian, then everything faded as I held her tight, pulling her into me with all my strength. I pushed her wild hair from her face and gazed into her eyes.

"Don't do it," she stammered. "Don't—"

"I didn't. I couldn't." I cupped her cheek in my hands. "I'm sorry. I'm so sorry. We can leave. We can go wherever you want."

She nodded furiously, a broad smile on her face as fresh sobs shook her. I pulled her close and kissed her, felt her tears on my face and lips.

"We can go today," I went on. "Right now. I just want to be with you. We can leave, and I'll—"

A horn shrieked in the distance, followed by the low groan of the Bridge Gate creaking open. The sound of pounding hooves rolled suddenly over us, and I turned to see dozens of mounted Saracens riding from the hills and plowing through the crusaders still looting the graves. They'd come from the Saint George Gate in the south, the only gate left unguarded.

"Danya…" Amina whispered, her voice cracking as she gripped my hand.

With a collective war cry, another hundred or more foot soldiers streamed through the now-open gate and across the stone bridge spanning the Orontes. It seemed they'd felt as I had, that nothing could stop them from avenging their fallen brothers, from stopping us merciless crusaders from desecrating the graves of men they likely viewed as martyrs.

The workers dropped their tools and retreated back toward Raymond's small encampment. Already men rushed through the tents, struggling to pull on armor while carrying shields and weapons.

"Danya…" Amina murmured again.

The mounted Saracens chased the looters through the graveyard, hacking at the unarmored men and filling the after-noon air with blood. Crusaders screamed and died, some falling into the very graves they'd spent the better part of the afternoon looting. Then, riding among the Saracens, I saw him: Temür. He rode with deftness and skill despite his one arm, guiding his horse with his legs as he chopped at the back of a crusader and threw a ribbon of crimson blood. Antioch must have been in dire straits to send a one-armed man into battle, even one as skilled as Temür.

"Danya!"

I tore my eyes from him and looked to Amina.

"What do we do?!"

"I don't..." I trailed off and scanned my surroundings. "I don't know."

Raymond's soldiers still hadn't put together a shield wall, even as the mounted Saracens butchered their way through the looters and looped around the backside of the mosque. Clearly they meant to cut off the workers' retreat, which in turn meant Amina and I had nowhere to run. Fleeing across the grass to the bridge of boats was suicide. Despite Godfrey's men already coming across our makeshift bridge, Antioch's garrison had already moved to block that route and now stood between us and safety.

Riders all around, a mosque beside us, and Antioch's garrison in front of us.

We were trapped.

Normally I would stand and fight. Indeed, everything in me wanted to. I looked again toward Temür, watched him drop yet another crusader, and felt a fiery desire to cut my way through the enemy until I reached him. Yet I had no armor, no shield. And besides, what would I do with Amina? Surely she'd be killed or taken captive into the city. No, this fight would have to go on without me.

"We run," I said.

"Where?" she asked, her voice laced with fear.

I turned to the mosque. "Inside."

And so we ran, feet pounding on the gray stone, sweat

beading into my tunic, Amina huffing beside me with our hands clasped between us. Hooves cracked onto the stone around us as the riders pounded into the courtyard. Swords rose and fell, blood misted the air, and men screamed and died. An arrow whistled overhead, and a horse bolted in front of us. I shoved Amina down and ducked as a blade cut the air, the momentum of the horse taking its rider quickly past us where he found a new target. Staying low, I pushed her forward, guiding us toward the open door of the mosque.

"I see you, *at hırsızı!*"

I risked a glance over my shoulder and saw Temür riding into the courtyard to join the chaos.

"I see you!" he screamed, ignoring the workers scattering around him. "I see you!"

"Danya!" Amina shouted.

A horse reared in front of us, its hooves kicking blindly at the air. I jerked Amina back, shoved her unceremoniously again onto the stone, and whipped Skull Splitter from my belt. The horse crashed back to all fours as its rider brought his curved sword down. I sidestepped and hacked at his hand, the heavy axe crushing bone and severing fingers, then grabbed Amina and pushed her once more toward the mosque just as the door slammed shut and locked us out.

"God's bones!" I shouted, then guided her along the wall. "This way!"

Amina hesitated, and an arrow clattered off the stone between us.

"Go!" I pressed her forward, though to where I no longer knew. "Go! Run!"

She stumbled ahead, racing across the mosque as another arrow cracked into the wall and buried itself between two brown stones.

Behind us, Godfrey's men collided with Antioch's garrison in a repeat of yesterday's battle. Raymond's knights were finally nearing us, yet all their presence did was push the mounted Saracens more tightly against the mosque. Workers shoved and screamed as the riders continued their massacre. One man fell dead in front of us, and a pair of Saracens took his place. I pressed Amina into the wall, standing between her and the riders. They scowled in unison, happy to have found another Christian to kill.

A stray arrow clipped the muzzle of one horse. It whinnied and reared, and I dashed around it to bury Skull Splitter into the rump of the other, sending the animal into a crazed spin. I ducked as the Saracen took a wild swing at me before he stumbled awkwardly from the saddle. The first horse crashed back down, and I drove Skull Splitter into its rider's leg. Bone snapped as the heavy axe bit through the man and into the horse underneath. Both cried in pain, and the horse bolted, taking with it the injured rider. The dismounted Saracen rose to his feet, but I was already moving, hacking Skull Splitter into his collarbone.

I took Amina's hand, warm Saracen blood now between our fingers, and started to run again toward Raymond's shield wall.

"Boy knight!" Temür cried. "Don't run from me, boy knight!"

I ignored him and pressed on, yet pain erupted in my back as something bit into me, hitting me with enough force to send me spinning to the ground.

"Danya!" Amina screamed, stopping her retreat and dropping to her knees beside me. She pawed at my injury, came back with a small dagger.

"No!" I pushed her away. "No! Keep running!"

She should have listened. She should have left me there to die in that courtyard. But then, I should never have been in that courtyard in the first place. I should never have answered Father Caldwell's call to desecrate graves. I should have gone with her to Acmonia after burying her father at Dorylaeum, or stopped in Heraclea or Iconium or Adana when we'd had the chance. I should have left the crusade with her and Novella when she'd asked only one day earlier. I should have found a farm to raise cows or sheep, a place where I could've cared for Amina, Novella, and that foolish chicken, Myrtle.

I should have done many things, then she'd still be alive.

Amina pulled me back to my feet, feet that instantly went weak once my weight was on them. I fell into her, and she held me up, wrapping her arms around me.

"You're okay," she said. "You're—"

Her face changed with a suddenness that shocked me. Her arms tensed around me, her eyes widened in fear, and I felt her hands grasp the shirt at my back, then she was spinning us, turning me so I came face-to-face with Temür with Amina between us.

He grinned that feral, crazed grin of his, eyes wide in insane rage. Amina jerked against me, and I felt something barely pierce my chest. She gasped, and a moment later we were falling, the sharp pain of whatever had stabbed me disappearing and replaced instead with the warmth of fresh blood. I landed hard on my back with her on top of me, her breath hot against my face.

Temür stepped over us, his bloodied sword raised, then lurched back as a spear glanced off the mail at his shoulder. Feet pounded the stone around us, and Temür backpedaled, though I could see he desperately wanted to stay and finish the job. He hesitated, then glared once more at me.

"Curse you!" he shouted, then turned and ran.

Raymond's men stepped by Amina and me as we lay on the cold stone, and a few moments later they were gone, pressing the garrison back toward the city and securing the mosque.

I started to rise when I heard Amina gasp for air. She

wheezed violently, and it was then I finally saw the wound that had sent us both to the ground. Frothing blood poured from a gaping hole in her chest, and she gasped again, coughing and dribbling blood from the corners of her mouth.

"Oh God…"

She looked at me with sheer panic in her eyes, the same panic rising in me like a vicious tide, crushing my chest as if in a vice. My breath was snatched from my lungs as if I'd been struck and not her.

"No," I whispered, rolling her onto her back as I stared down at the wound and ignored the searing pain in my own side. "No no no…" I pawed at her chest with awkward hands as I uselessly tried to staunch the blood.

She wheezed again, mouth opening and closing yet getting no air. I felt much the same, unable to breathe, unable to think as I slowly realized what had happened.

"Why?" I asked weakly. "Why did you turn us?"

She brought her shaking gaze down, saw the blood, then met my eyes once more. Despair took the place of panic, and I could tell she knew she was dying. She reached out, and her bloodied hand touched my cheek.

"Why?" I asked again.

Shockingly, she smiled as her eyes met mine for the last time. She tried to speak, but instead gave a weak, rasping cough and began to shiver in my arms.

"Y-you're going to be fine…" I stammered. "You'll see. Father Luke will patch you up. We'll take Novella. We'll leave. We'll go back to Adana, buy a farm. I'll raise cows and Novella will take care of Myrtle and you'll bake bread and we'll be a family and…and…"

I trailed off as she stopped shivering. Her eyes glazed over, and she stared blankly at the sky above, a final soft exhale escaping her lips as the last person who mattered in my life died.

"I can't do it, Amina," I said, fresh sobs racking my body. "I can't do it without you."

Yet I'd done this. Me. Temür's sword may have dealt the blow, but I'd killed her. My ignorance, my vengefulness, my hatred. What did I have left now? I hadn't kept my brother safe, I'd watched Hendry die, Rainald has given his life for the crusade, and now I'd killed Amina—my dove, my *peristéri*.

"Don't leave me," I said, voice barely a sigh. "I need you. I...I can't..." Tears took the place of words, and I pulled her back into me, her lifeless head pressed against my chest. "I can't do it alone."

But I had to.

I had no one left.

No one.

23

"The souls of the righteous are in the hand of God," Luke intoned, his voice calm and serene as it carried over the small group of us gathered at yet another gravesite. This one had sprouted from the shadows of the same church I'd given Luke my confession in barely a week ago. "And no torment will ever touch them," the old priest went on. "In the eyes of the foolish, they seemed to have died, and their departure was thought to be an affliction and their going from us to be their destruction; but they are at peace."

I'd heard Luke say these same words dozens of times before. The first had been days before the battle of Dorylaeum. The Saracens had attacked, and I'd helped Amina bury a stranger, a woman neither of us had ever met. She'd had no family, and we were the last people to see her face before it was covered with a makeshift burial shroud and spadefuls of dirt. Luke had said the words again a few days later as we'd buried Asbat, Amina's father. I remember thinking them profound and deep, a solace to those who wept and a comfort for those who mourned. They'd even come to my mind—the best I could remember them—on the day Novella's mother had been slain in front of us.

Now, however, I listened to them numb and indifferent. Amina was gone, and I didn't care that she was in the hand of God, didn't care that she was at peace. She could no longer be in my hand, and that thought brought another wave of anger as I knelt at her grave and stared down at the mound of dirt that would forever be her resting place.

Forever.

The dreary sky had changed little in the last six hours, and even now it didn't storm, though gray sheets of rain could be seen in the very great distance. Forks of lightning beat the faraway hills to the north, and thunder rumbled slowly over us. Men I knew surrounded me. Men I'd fought alongside and lived life with. I had spent the last several months continually in their company.

Luke stood at the top of the grave, head bowed in prayer. Piccolo held a sobbing Novella as he murmured words of comfort to her in Italian. He'd offered me none, likely thinking his words would be as meaningless to me as Luke's had been. He'd have been right. John Mark briefly rested a hand on my shoulder in an attempt to console me, though I knew his mind was on his own Eleonora. He was here for her, fought this crusade for her, and she waited for him safely back home. Elric said nothing, Thomas lisped his condolences, and Bruno—who for some reason felt a need to attend the funeral—stood stoically among us. He'd been the first to arrive after Amina had breathed her last, the first to kneel beside me as I held her body and wept.

They stayed longer than I would have guessed; no one left until the sun had long ago crept below the horizon and night had descended on us. One by one they trailed off until only Luke was left. He stayed another hour—perhaps more, perhaps less, I didn't know. I'd begun to lose track of time. He whispered another gentle prayer, said a few more words I didn't hear, then he, too, returned to the crusader camp.

Alone and in the midnight dark, I looked down at the blue scrap of cloth I clutched in my hand. I'd taken it from Amina's dead body. It had still been tucked into her belt from the night before. Her blood stained its fringes. I pressed the cloth against my chest and finally moved, lying forward onto the moist dirt of Amina's grave. I embraced it, dug my fingers into it, rested my cheek against it, and—after a long time—fell asleep atop her grave.

I awoke sometime later to a gray morning. The overcast clouds remained, and though it still hadn't rained, a thick layer of fog had settled once more over the dewy grass. Dirt had crusted on my cheek. I felt empty, as if my mind was a blank canvas.

Except it wasn't. One thing occupied it. Or rather, one person.

Temür.

He'd slept safely within Antioch's walls last night, while I'd wept over the grave of a loved one. He needed to die. And for that to happen, Antioch had to fall, even if I had to scale the walls myself and tear it down from the inside.

I rose slowly, legs cramped and stiff, back creaking like an old door, and made my way slowly to the camp. Luke's infamous cabbage stew hung above a small fire, around which sat every man who'd been with me the night before. Even Bruno joined them. Every gaze lifted as I walked into the camp. They looked at my disheveled clothes and dirty face and said nothing.

I knelt before my storage chest and opened the lid. Inside lay my mail, my chausses, my helmet. I saw my surcoat of blue and red, my worn cloak, my mail coif. I moved it all aside and found what I'd come for: *Vindicta*. Hendry's sword. *My* sword. I laid a hand on the brown scabbard, traced the upswept cross guard with a fingertip, and looked at the disc pommel and its bronze center. I gripped the golden-brown leather-wrapped hilt and drew it.

The blade hadn't seen battle since Hendry's death, and Luke had made me swear not to wield it. It was supposed to remain free of bloodshed, stowed away and never used again. But it only seemed right that it be the weapon that ended Temür's life. Standing, I secured the scabbard's chain to my belt and slammed *Vindicta* back home.

She was mine now, and she would drink all the blood she could.

INTERLUDE III

AD 1115
Jerusalem

Though Roland had known Amina would die, he hadn't been prepared to hear it. He couldn't imagine what retelling the story had felt like to Sir Daniel, though he noticed the old knight clutching the hilt of his sword as he spoke. Roland said nothing of it and set his shears down. He'd finished his twelfth layer now, which meant he'd have to learn how to sew before he could continue. With nothing to say or do, he stared at the ground and waited for Sir Daniel to continue.

Sir Daniel seemed to finally notice his iron grip on the sword. Deliberately, slowly, he released it and stood to his feet. "Come, lad," he said and walked through his fence without another word.

Roland leaped to his feet and chased after Sir Daniel as the knight stalked through the city. He led them through the Jerusalem markets, not bothering to acknowledge any of the venders as they shouted their wares. Instead, he squeezed through anxious shoppers and followed the curving path around the Temple Mount until the Church of the Paralytic came into view.

Sir Daniel entered the church, and Roland followed. He heard the familiar rippling of water as they stepped under the brownstone arch and into the narrow corridor. They passed the bench where Roland had first sat and listened to Sir Daniel's story. The apse at the end of the corridor had three tapestries hung around it. One depicted Christ's crucifixion, another His ascension to heaven, and the third showed the crusaders' sacking of Jerusalem in vivid detail. Sir Daniel stopped in the center of the apse and starred at the image of the crucified Christ. For a long while, neither spoke.

"God, I was so angry," Sir Daniel finally said. "So full of hate."

Roland swallowed, thought about saying nothing. "You had reason to be," he mumbled instead.

Sir Daniel gave a lighthearted scoff. "Everyone's got a reason to be, lad, but that doesn't make it right."

"But anger's so hard to control."

"And? What of it? Just because a thing's hard doesn't mean you can't do it. Often the hard thing's the one you *should* be doing." He turned to Roland and met his eyes with a gravity he'd not shown before. "If you remember nothing else I tell you, remember this, lad: being decent isn't the same thing as being moral. Weak men are often decent men. They do no harm because they *can't*, not because they choose not to. Only a strong man—a *dangerous* man—can be a moral one. The man who knows anger and hate, yet still loves; the man who *can* do harm, but chooses *not* to. *That's* a good man."

"So…so how do you control it?"

Sir Daniel turned back to the tapestry. "Why do you think I come here?"

ACT III

DANIEL'S KNIGHTING

24

AD 1098
May
Antioch

I knelt once again in the church north of Antioch, the same one I'd visited to give my confession to Luke after Hendry's death, the same one we'd come to for Amina's burial. This time I wasn't there for confession. I cared to receive forgiveness as much as I cared to forgive. Yet, just as Rainald had knelt in an all-night vigil the night before his knighting, so I did, as well.

Rainald had likely spent his time in fervent prayer, asking for counsel and wisdom—just as Solomon had in his vision from God—while I merely sat and stewed, longing for vengeance rather than guidance. Rainald had sought the title of knight so he could defend the poor and continue to fight in the crusade. He'd succeeded, at least until his death only a few days later. I'd craved knighthood since laying eyes on Hendry —first for the authority he wielded, then for my own pride. Now, I desired the title only so I could be among the first over

Antioch's walls when the time finally came to storm the city and shed Saracen blood.

Vindicta rested upon a new shield gifted to me by Bohemond that morning. Both leaned against the side of the altar, and I wore the same style of fine white vesture and red robe that Rainald had. I glanced toward the gaping window that framed a view of the rolling hills between the church and Antioch. The city's high walls rose in the very great distance, little more than a black silhouette against the setting sun, a smear of shadow protruding into the twilight sky. The sight brought a fresh wave of emotions as I thought of Amina standing by that window a month ago. Anger flooded over me, not sorrow or grief or mourning, but raw, hot, unrestrained anger. I'd buried my misery in the dirt with Amina and had room only for fury and hate.

In addition to another ten prospective knights kneeling in silent prayer, a single priest huffed around the darkening church, the scrape of his broom joining the gentle shuffling of his feet as he swept the dirt from one end of the stone floor to another. Some made it outside, ready to be blown back in by even the gentlest of breezes, but most of the dust simply took flight, drifting into the thin shafts of ochre light filtering down through the punctured roof of the pointed dome above.

Another hour of cleaning, and even he left, leaving me to ponder my thoughts in silence. I chose not to, and eventually fell asleep still upon my knees, head drooping down to my chest. I dreamed of Amina—as I always did now. We knelt together at the cistern in Constantinople, my senseless brother rocking in my arms, genuine concern painted on her face as she watched me try to comfort him. She hummed a gentle hymn underneath the shade of a sycamore just beyond Nicaea's walls and told me what it meant to have real Christian love. I lay exhausted in the middle of the battle of Dorylaeum as she gave me water and fed me berries and made me swear to let her help despite the danger. I felt her warmth against me as we lay in the attic of a tavern in Adana, the gentle rhythm of her sleep a soothing balm to my restless soul. I saw her standing at the window of the very church I slept in, watched as she looked over her shoulder and smiled at me with the sun bathing her in golden light as if she were an angel descended from heaven.

Then came the warmth of her blood in my hands, the sound of her gasping for breath as life fled her, the tremble of her lips and the flutter of her eyelids as she fought to hold on to the last few moments she had. A flicker of light and a fresh mound of dirt, and it was with this final image alive in my mind that I awoke to a dawn sun streaming through the open window and that same simmering hatred pulsing in my veins.

I stood, grasped my sword and shield, and stomped off to meet Bohemond in the fields beyond the church.

I wasn't the only one being knighted that day. Eleven of us waited in the grass, and though I knew Elric was somewhere down the line, I dared not turn my head to see him. We knelt in front of a formation of knights—all mounted—as Luke led us in mass. Scriptures were read, and we heard the story of Samson, how he'd slain a thousand Philistines with the jawbone of a donkey. I thought the tale of Samson's strength had been chosen to inspire, but instead Luke lectured us on Samson's lack of restraint, his battle fever that only sometimes served the Lord and more often served his own pride. Samson struggled to control himself and often chose the easier, more violent solution.

I felt especially targeted by Luke's homily.

Eventually we ate the bread and drank the wine that was Christ's body and blood, though by now all eleven of us were more focused on our swords and shields being brought forward by our respective sponsors. Though I was not officially his squire, a knight named Ásvaldr held mine. Better known as "Bad Crown," Ásvaldr had been a member of the Varangian Guard from Constantinople. Rather than wield a sword like most of us, he, instead, had a massive two-handed axe strapped to his back and a smaller, oval-shaped shield slung at a shoulder. Some of his long, black hair was tied at the nape of his neck, the rest flowing over his shoulders and mingling with a braided beard speckled with gray. He looked distinctly different from most of the other knights, and the Danish lilt to his speech often made him difficult to understand.

Once Luke completed his sermon of reproach, Bohemond made his way down our kneeling line, repeating the same words he'd said to Rainald not so long ago.

"Do you swear allegiance to me, Bohemond of Taranto?"

"I do," the would-be knight would say.

"Do you swear to follow the duties as laid out by the church?"

"I do."

"And do you swear to obey me in all my orders, to lay down your life if required, and to maintain this oath until your dying breath?"

"I do."

Then Bohemond would strike them across the cheek and add, "May this be the last blow you receive without just recompense."

Some words of personal testimony were then said, an individual exhortation shared that always ended with a command to remain steadfast and courageous and to fight with vigor and honor. I watched ten squires receive their knighthood, ten men who'd spent their lives serving knights and lords and working for this very moment.

I watched them, and as they each were slapped by Lord

Bohemond I thought of how little I belonged. I'd first wielded a weapon less than a year ago—and poorly at that. I'd lived life as a street urchin in Constantinople, scrounging for a living and protecting—or, rather, failing to protect—my handicapped brother. I was a nobody, from essentially nowhere, and yet now Bohemond stood in front of me, and I had no more time to dwell on my worth or lack thereof. I lowered my head, prepared my canned replies to his scripted questions, but for a long moment, he said nothing. Eventually, I looked up and found him smiling down at me.

"Daniel the thief," he finally said, and my heart sank. Had he brought me here only to embarrass me?

"Yes, Lord," I replied, voice quaking.

He glanced back at Ásvaldr who stood dutifully in Bohemond's shadow with my sword and shield. "This is the only man willing to hold your weapons. The only one of my knights willing to vouch for you."

I glanced to Ásvaldr, saw nothing in his stoic gaze, and swallowed a rising lump.

"A shame," Bohemond went on. "You come from poverty, do you not? Some Byzantine slum covered in filth?"

"Constantinople, Lord."

He waved his hand dismissively. "Yes, yes, a great city. But you dwelt not in high buildings or grand estates, but rather in a gutter like a rat? Is this true?"

My heart pounded in my chest as sweat broke out on my face. I could feel the eyes of the new knights beside me, could feel the stares of the hundreds of older ones from behind. "Yes, Lord," I murmured.

"You were a thief?"

I nodded.

"You swore an oath to me, and you broke it. You even stole my sword," he said, patting the scabbard on his belt, "and tried to kill poor Father Luke. That's what earned you that scar," he added, reaching out and grabbing my chin with a gloved hand. He turned my face and gazed at the rugged cross of disfigured flesh on my right cheek.

A murmur went through the men as he released my chin.

"Yes, Lord," I said. "A worthy punishment for my sins."

He scoffed. Then, to everyone's surprise, he knelt so we were face-to-face. "Your penance still lies ahead at Jerusalem, where you shall kneel before Christ's empty tomb."

"And I will, Lord."

"I know you will," he said, then leaned in even closer, "because you fight with *heart*, Daniel. You fight with courage, with reckless abandon, with valor. Despite your foolishness and your arrogance and your stubbornness, you are a *warrior*. And a warrior deserves a title, even if he comes from nowhere."

He stood and, without warning, cuffed me across the face hard enough that my ears rang and my head snapped to the side. Fresh blood ran from my scarred cheek.

"May this be the last blow you receive without just recompense," he said. "Sir Daniel tou Pouthená."

25

"That's supposed to be our new fort?" Elric asked.

I stared at the remnants of the monastery several miles south of the Gate of Saint George—the southernmost gate of Antioch—and shared my friend's lack of confidence. The monastery looked to have been quite the complex once upon a time, though now all that remained was a small village of ravaged structures surrounding an overgrown and cracked stone courtyard that stretched a dozen yards across.

Arrows stuck out from between stones and the rubble of leveled buildings, their fletching waving in the gentle morning breeze like wheat in a field. Green vines and inhospitable thistles smothered a pair of low stone walls that might have been a serviceable dormitory sometime in the distant past. The courtyard was surrounded by disheveled heaps of shattered bricks, decaying wood, cracked brownstones, chipped swords and shields and other ruined artifacts of past battles, and even one pile of furniture that seemed to have been periodically and haphazardly harvested for firewood. A tattered white scrap of cloth clung to a single post that might have once been part of an encompassing fence and waved in the wind as if the monastery complex tried to signal its surrender.

"At least the church is still standing," I pointed out.

Elric snorted a laugh. "Such that it is."

Amid the carnage and destruction sat a low chapel, stubbornly refusing to fall despite the wasteland around it. The courtyard-adjacent entrance had no door, and soot-colored stains in the gray stones surrounding the opening hinted that fire had been the cause. High-arched and gaping windows pockmarked the walls, the glittering colored glass at their base suggesting a time when the chapel had been beautifully adorned with stained glass that told the story of salvation.

"Nothing for it," I said. "Tancred'll be here before sundown. If we haven't at least unloaded by then, he'll have our backsides."

Three hundred men-at-arms and ten mounted knights—counting Elric and me—escorted six wagons, each pulled by a pair of oxen or trio of starving donkeys. The wagons overflowed with lumber, nails, stone, and any other scraps we hadn't used in our building up of the mosque near the Bridge Gate. With the completion of this new fort—if whatever we ended up building could really be called a fort—we would have a nearly complete blockade of the city's gates. The Iron Gate still remained unguarded in the east, but to reach it one must walk a narrow and arduous path through the mountains, so the decision had been made to leave it unguarded.

The wagons stopped in the church's courtyard, and men-at-arms began unloading while we joined Ásvaldr and the other knights to watch lazily from horseback. Bruno had come along, as well, having earned himself a reputation among the lords for his part in the construction of Raymond's fort at the mosque, a fort that had already withstood a pair of failed Saracen raids.

Our scouts arrived later that morning, and I was glad to see

John Mark at their head. He rode up beside me with a smile, sitting upon Falhófnir, the same horse that Bohemond had gifted him months ago before we'd even reached Nicaea. Somehow it still lived, despite how many of our horses hadn't survived.

"Greetings, Daniel," he said, then gave a smile. "Or should I say *Sir* Daniel."

"What have you found?" I asked, not acknowledging a jest that had already run its course.

He frowned but said nothing of my curtness. "A caravan. Approaching from the south."

"Merchants?"

"Probably. There were a dozen or so men and even more carts and wagons."

"Heading for Antioch?"

"They'll be here within the hour."

I thought on that for a moment. "Guards?"

He shrugged. "A few lightly armored mercenaries. I could've taken them with my scouts, though we might have lost a man or two," he added, gesturing to the six men on horseback with him. "It didn't seem a prudent risk. What do you suggest?"

"Within an hour?" He nodded, and I frowned. "Tancred won't be here by then," I replied, more thinking aloud than speaking directly to him. Elric and I shared a glance, though neither of us felt capable of making a decision. I looked across the courtyard and met Ásvaldr's gaze. He saw me and trotted over.

"*Hils*," he said by way of greeting, then asked, "Vat do your scout see?"

"Merchants," I answered.

"Coming here?" he asked, though it sounded like *combing here.*

I nodded. "And lightly guarded."

"Horses?"

John Mark answered. "A few," he said. "Mostly donkeys and oxen."

Ásvaldr pursed his lips and stroked his beard, then turned to look north, likely pondering the same thing I did: should we act before Tancred arrived?

"Vill they fight?"

John Mark shrugged. "Hard to say. I imagine not, if we show with enough force."

"How much is enough, I vonder?" Ásvaldr asked, though he clearly didn't expect an answer. He looked at John Mark, his scouts, then at me and Elric. "This vill do."

"Just us?" I asked. "Is that enough men?"

"*Det er ingen ko på isen,*" he said with a smirk.

John Mark and Elric exchanged a confused glance, but even in my short time with Ásvaldr, I knew he'd explain himself.

"There is no cow on the ice," he said, though that did little to explain it. "Is no problem," he added once he saw that we didn't know what he meant. When he still received no response, he frowned. "Come," he said. "Come. I vill show you."

I sat on *Ankída* atop a small rise a mile south of our soon to be fort. White, wispy clouds skated across the blue canvas of a mostly clear sky above. A dense forest of pine and oak covered the land on both sides of the road—if the dirt path I waited upon could be called a road. Worn cobblestone and the occasional cracked gray brick rose from the dirt like half-buried gravestones, and low wooden fence posts lined long stretches of the road, showing that sometime not too long ago this way had been heavily trafficked. The constant back and forth battles between the rising and falling Saracen nations—fighting among themselves and with Constantinople —had likely led to the disrepair. Our presence had helped little.

I waited alone and watched as a caravan of merchants approached, no hurry to their step nor anxiety in their gaits at the sight of me. A trio of overly confident guards rode at the front. They wore clean mail armor underneath leather jerkins, flowing cloaks hemmed with ermine, and sneering, smug scowls. One had a short bow stowed on his saddle at his leg, along with a quiver of goose-feathered arrows on the opposite side. The other two gripped long, freshly polished spears that looked too pristine to have seen any battle in recent memory. Wagons stretched along the dirt behind them, sturdy contraptions rolling along the road and pulled by the most robust oxen I'd seen in months.

For myself, my left hand rested on a sheathed *Vindicta*, and I'd slung my shield to my saddle and let it rest against *Ankída's* rump. Heavy mail hung from my shoulders and wrapped my legs, iron shod my boots, and my horse-headed helmet rested upon my lap with my right arm draped over it. Bohemond's colors—faded and perhaps a touch dirty—lay over my mail, and my worn and heavily used cloak draped down my back, clasped at my neck by an iron brooch. Amina's blood-stained blue cloth still clung to my right bicep.

The caravan rumbled to a stop at the base of the low hill I sat upon, and the two spear-wielding guards trotted up to meet me. The man left behind made no move to string and ready his bow. Their skin tone matched my own, and the swords I could now see upon their belts were straight rather than curved, though they wore high-pointed helmets common among Saracen soldiers. Likely, most of their gear had been scraped together through thievery and deceit or been pulled from the hands of dead men, which made me wonder at the high quality of their cloaks, the clean polish of their spears, and the smugness of their smirks.

"*Size yardım edebilir miyim?*" one of them asked as they stopped a handful of paces out. "Can I help you," he'd asked in Turkish, though his leering smile implied he hadn't expected me to understand.

"*Hayır,*" I responded. No. His eyebrow raised a fraction in surprise as I continued in Turkish. "You can turn around and head back to wherever you came from. And leave the merchants and wagons."

He chuckled and shared a grin with the other mercenary. "How about no," he offered, still speaking in Turkish.

"You can have a wagon," I said. "The rest stays."

"I'm afraid I have to take them all the way to Antioch."

I nodded in understanding. "They only paid you half up front?"

"Less than half," he said, turning and spitting into the grass. "Nervous little rats, they are."

"Likely not without reason."

He shrugged. "I might have had plans to leave them at Tripoli."

"Shame."

"We'll see. Antioch's not far that way," he added, pointing north with his chin. "And it's just you in my way."

I frowned. "Fine. You can have two wagons."

He looked over his shoulder and counted the wagons. "That leaves almost fifteen for you."

"I've got thousands of men to feed."

"Any reason I can't just run you through?"

I smirked, then brought my left hand from my sword and crossed it over my right atop my helmet. "No reason you can't try."

This drew a laugh. "I like you," he said. "Too bad I've got to kill you. After I—"

SHADOWS OF ANTIOCH | 259

The sudden shriek of the third guard cut him off. They both spun to watch their fellow mercenary tumble from the saddle with a pair of arrows rising from his back. Ásvaldr and Elric—along with John Mark and his scouts, three of whom held bows they'd stolen from fallen Saracens—came rushing forward from the dense woods and quickly surrounded the merchants.

I gripped *Vindicta*, ripping it free of its scabbard just as the two men looked back at me. The end of my blade clipped the jaw of the man who'd spoken, throwing blood, bone, and teeth into the face of the other. The first stumbled from the saddle, clutching his wounded face and howling in pain.

The last guard cautiously met my gaze. He glanced at *Vindicta's* bloodied tip, then down at his friend still squirming in the grass.

"Two wagons, you say?" he asked, bringing his eyes back up to me.

"That deals off the table now, lad," I said with a pleasant smile. "But if you start riding, we might not chase you."

He seemed to think for a moment, then guided his horse off the path and cantered back the way they'd come, giving Ásvaldr, Elric, and the rest of the caravan a wide berth as he did. I leaned forward and took the reins of the now-riderless horse, then guided both it and *Ankída* around the man still writhing in pain on the ground.

The merchants had by now drawn in tight to their wagons, and I realized that not all of them actually appeared to be merchants. Most were dressed in simple tunics, faded cloaks, and gray or brown cloth mantles. These men cowered behind two others—the only ones on horseback—who seemed unfazed by our sudden appearance. These two wore elaborate yellow robes over similarly decorated silk shirts of green and red and brown. Their wide belts were fitted with square metal plaques and bars, and curved swords hung from silver chains in ornamented scabbards at their sides.

The older of the two sat confidently atop his horse, making no attempt to either draw or surrender his weapon even as Ásvaldr approached him. John Mark, Elric, and the scouts moved in to peruse the wagons, and I trotted over to Ásvaldr, silently guiding *Ankída* beside him. Together we stopped in front of the man who clearly led this caravan.

The merchant exchanged a quick look between Ásvaldr and me, then, deciding correctly that Ásvaldr was in charge, directed his attention to the Dane.

"*Benim adım Firuz,*" he said, and Ásvaldr glanced at me.

"His name is Firuz," I translated.

Firuz cracked a small, sideways smile, though he didn't look away from Ásvaldr. "*Antakya'dan,*" he added.

"He's from Antioch," I said, though I doubted Ásvaldr needed that translated.

"Sir Ásvaldr of the Danes," Ásvaldr said.

Firuz nodded in understanding, then finally turned his attention to me. I belatedly realized that as a knight I was expected to make an introduction, as well. "Sir Daniel tou Pouthená."

Firuz narrowed his eyes, and I suspected he understood at least rudimentary Greek. His next words confirmed my suspicion.

"You risk much killing me or my son," he said, switching to Greek as he nodded to the younger man sitting on horseback behind him. "Powerful we are in Antakya."

Ásvaldr chuckled. Having been a Varangian guard, he understood Greek quite well. "I vould say that your power matters little as you travel these roads."

"We had no choice. You starve Antakya." He gestured back toward his wagons. "We were sent in search of food."

"And we thank you for it," I said with a smirk. "This will feed us for quite some time."

Firuz clenched and unclenched his jaw. "You are smug, Christian. Confident when you should not be."

"Aye," I agreed. "That sounds like me. Brave and foolish, they say. But surely someone less *powerful* could have been sent for supplies. Why risk the journey when we control your city. There's no way in or out aside from the Iron Gate."

He raised an eyebrow at that. "You block the southern gate now?"

"As of this morning," Ásvaldr answered.

"It was not so when we set out for Tyre." He let out a long sigh and stared at the ground for some time. "Antakya is truly lost now," he finally said, then jerked his head up and glared at us. "You come here to take what is not yours. You pillage and steal and—"

"I don't care," I said, cutting him off. He scowled and opened his mouth to continue, but I kept going. "I've heard it before. We're ruthless invaders, brutal Christians, and you're the innocent victims. It's all nonsense. You know it as well as I do. Yes, our men beheaded your people, but yours burned ours alive." I nudged *Ankída* forward until I was uncomfortably close. Close enough that he could reach out and touch me. His hand twitched toward his sword. I ignored it. "Your people are as heartless as mine, and your city will fall whether we're right-eous or not. Pointing out our misdeeds will do nothing, especially when you're so full of your own."

His scowl deepened enough that he bared his teeth, and for a moment I expected him to finally draw his sword. I confidently laid my hand on *Vindicta's* hilt, daring him to pull his weapon free. I wanted nothing more than to have an excuse for more blood. But his face relaxed, and he seemed to realize that drawing his sword would end in his death and likely that of his son.

"You speak true enough, Christian," he finally said, though he spat that final word. "*Kahretsin!* Siyan will see us all killed." He sighed, deep and long, then glanced back at his supplies. "You'll be taking my caravan, I suppose."

"Looks that vay," Ásvaldr answered.

"And my son and I?"

"That is up to Lord Tancred."

26

The late afternoon sun threw elongated shadows across our monastery when we returned. Tancred stood waiting in the courtyard of the complex, watching our approach with mild interest. The young lord stood among neatly stacked lumber, piles of stones and bricks, and enough tools and hardware to equip a small army. Likely he'd have his fort—whatever shape that took—built within a few days.

Firuz and his son—Mundzuk—rode between Ásvaldr and me. We'd relieved them of their swords and a pair of curved daggers that Firuz carried at the small of his back.

"This is your lord?" Firuz asked, eyes on Tancred and contempt lacing his voice.

Tancred indeed looked to be younger even the Mundzuk, who himself might be barely a year old than me. Yet I'd seen Tancred in battle, seen him command thousands through some of the harshest fighting imaginable. His youth did nothing to deter my willingness to follow him. The man was a warrior and a leader.

"He is our lord," Ásvaldr confirmed, though his voice held a warning. Apparently he held the same level of respect for

264 | BRYAN R SAYE

Tancred I did. "And you should vatch your tone when you speak with him."

Firuz scoffed, but said nothing further. He knew he was in no position to argue. Behind us, Elric led John Mark and the rest of the scouts in something of a cordon around Firuz's caravan of supplies. The servants plodded along on foot among the wagons and oxen, giving the occasional furtive glance toward us as they likely expected to be killed even if their master lived. Given the ruthlessness I'd witnessed—and had taken part in—I suspected they may be right.

"What have you found?" Tancred asked once we led Firuz and his son into the courtyard. He glanced at our captives then turned toward the caravan waiting behind us in the grass.

"A merchant, Lord," Ásvaldr answered. "Returning to Antioch."

"Returning with supplies, I see," Tancred said with an arrogant smile. He looked Firuz up and down, noted his costly garments and confident demeanor. "Am I to guess you are a man of import in Antioch?"

"I am," Firuz replied. "I command several towers along the southern walls."

"It doesn't seem like you will be commanding them much longer."

The threat did nothing to unnerve Firuz. "I think it is in your best interest if those towers remain under my command."

"And why is that?"

"Because I want to live, and I've seen what you do with Saracen prisoners."

Tancred's snorted a laugh. "It's no different than what you do with Christian prisoners."

"What *Yaghi Siyan* does," he said, nearly spitting out the name. "And he is a fool. The fight is lost! We should be negotiating, and what does he do? He takes in mercenaries, brigands, gives command to one-armed men. His pride will see our mighty city fall, and there will be—"

He'd said it so fast, so indifferently, that I almost missed it. "One-armed men?" I asked, cutting him off.

"Yes," Firuz shouted, still venting his anger. "What can a one-armed man do in battle? Nothing!"

"Did he have white hair?"

He narrowed his eyes. "He did."

I said nothing as I felt my heart race and my blood boil.

"You know this man, Pouthená?" Tancred asked.

"I do," I said. "He killed Amina."

"Yes…your woman," Tancred said, then nodded in understanding. He turned to Firuz. "You know where this man is?"

"He laid claim to one of your Christian churches," he said. "He and his bandits."

"Which church?" I asked. "Which one?!"

Firuz glanced at Tancred, as if seeking permission to continue. Tancred gave a small nod. "It is a church dug into the mountain," he said. "The main church of those Christians still dwelling in the city. It lies to the north. They call it *Sen Piyer Kilisesi*."

"Saint Peter's Church," I translated. I knew where he was, knew how to find him. Now I only needed to make it inside the city and survive long enough to reach him.

"That's enough of that," Tancred said. "I hope you find your man if we ever make it inside the city. For now," went on, turning his attention back to Firuz, "you still need to explain to me why you should live."

"Because I would help end the siege," Firuz said. "In whatever manner benefits me most."

Tancred narrowed his eyes. "You would betray your lord?"

"I would safeguard my position."

Tancred said nothing, only continued to study Firuz. The seconds dragged on, and no one spoke.

"Elric, Ásvaldr," Tancred finally said. "Take our guests into the church."

The sun set, an uneventful night passed, and harsh morning light peeked over the tip of Mount Silpius and glared down on our monastery complex. Thick clouds the color of dirty mail armor hung in the western sky, lumbering toward us with the promise of a downpour. Men-at-arms rose from their slumber, eyed the menacing clouds, then silently ate eggs and scraps of hard cheese, washed in a nearby creek that was a runoff from the Orontes, and finally began construction of the fort knowing they would be working in the rain before long. Bruno called out commands and directed the men and supplies, and soon midday came and went and the makings of our fort began to take shape as those baleful clouds moved ever closer.

And still Firuz remained inside the church with Bohemond and Tancred. Mundzuk stood between Ásvaldr and me at the entrance to the church as the three of us watched our men-at-arms and Firuz's servants work together to build up our fort, the latter continuously looking in our direction with the wide eyes of fear.

Mundzuk stood like a silent statue, his face restrained and expressionless as stone. I'd yet to hear him utter a single word, and I wondered if he spoke Greek like his father or only Turkish. Despite his silence, he didn't look nervous or apprehensive. Either he trusted in his father to negotiate their freedom, or he cared little whether he lived or died. I sympathized with this latter mindset. Only my craving for Temür's blood kept me going.

My hand drifted down to *Vindicta's* scabbard and fingered the small, frayed length of rope. William's rope. I'd not been without it since his death, and now more than ever I felt his loss. I'd killed him. I hadn't wielded the blade, yet I'd been the reason for it. My pride had ended his life, and I knew it played no small part in Amina's death, as well.

"*Bu nedir?*"

I glanced to Mundzuk, whose eyes rested on William's rope. "What's this?" he'd asked.

"*Bir halat?*"

I released the rope. "*Evet,*" I said, then added—still speaking Turkish—"It was my brother's. He's dead."

"Good," Mundzuk said unapologetically. He continued to speak in Turkish, as well, and Ásvaldr only looked on. "Another Christian in the dirt."

My blood ran instantly hot. I turned to face him, gripped *Vindicta's* hilt with my left hand, and met his eyes. "You're brave for a dead man," I said.

Before he could respond, Firuz stepped from the church followed closely by Bohemond and Tancred. Bohemond looked at Mundzuk, then at me.

"Are you threatening my prisoner, Pouthená?" Bohemond asked.

"Only a little, Lord."

He chuckled at that. "I'm afraid it must be empty threats," Bohemond said. "At least for now. They're to be unharmed."

Mundzuk smirked at me, and I felt my heart sink. I wanted to see him cut open and dying in the mud, not released back into Antioch. "Why?" I asked.

A flash of anger passed over Bohemond's face, and I knew I'd overstepped. "Because I am your lord," he snapped. "And because having a man inside Antioch will prove useful. Firuz is as tired of this siege as we are. He seeks an end, the same as us, and he no longer cares whether Yaghi Siyan rules or we do."

Even Ásvaldr frowned. "So ve just…let them go?"

Bohemond nodded. "He and his caravan, though we'll

have to bloody him up a little and perhaps slaughter an ox or two to make it believable."

At this, Firuz drew himself up. "Bloody me? I think not!"

Rather than reply, Bohemond jabbed a fist out and punched him in the mouth. Firuz's head snapped back, and blood spurted down his shirt. His son lurched forward, but—following my lord's lead—I took a step and headbutted him in the nose. He stumbled down at his father's feet, hands cupping the warm blood running from his ruined face.

"Hayvan!" Mundzuk growled. He glared up at me, and I couldn't stop the smile on my face. He'd called me an animal. I didn't think it an insult at the time.

Firuz scowled at Bohemond. His hand held his bleeding jaw, and he didn't seem to care that his son knelt on the ground with a bloodied and broken nose. "That was unnecessary," he mumbled, his voice muffled from his already swelling lip.

"We'll also be keeping a few of your servants," Bohemond went on, ignoring him. "And your son."

Firuz's nostrils flared, and Mundzuk's anger quickly became fear.

"You'll do no such thing!" Firuz shouted. "My son will be—"

"Staying here," Bohemond cut him off, "or I'll behead the both of you at the foot of the walls, then drag your lifeless corpses behind my horse."

Firuz's face reddened behind his hand, which still clutched at his jaw. It seemed they hadn't discussed this within the church, which made me wonder what they had discussed given how long they'd been inside. Like always, I assumed Bohemond had a plan and would reveal it only when he was forced to or when the circumstances finally presented themselves to be fully in his favor. Everyone suspected he sought sole control of Antioch, and now it seemed he might have a way to achieve it.

"I do not like this," Firuz said, finally bending down to help his son stand. "I do not like this at all."

"Hold up your end of the deal, and your son will be fine," Bohemond said. "Betray me, and I'll send you his head."

Mundzuk's gaze shifted from Bohemond to his father. He pleaded with his eyes, begging Firuz not to leave him in our less than amenable care.

Firuz ignored his son's gaze. "Nothing happens to my son," he said, though his tone implied it was a question.

"Nothing will happen to your son."

He drew a breath, then finally looked to Mundzuk—who shook his head in disbelief.

"We have a deal."

We kept a pair of Firuz's wagons and scarred the rest of them. I personally hacked a chunk of wood away from several wagons using Skull Splitter, and Tancred cut loose three of the oxen, forcing those wagons to stumble forward with only a single ox pulling the heavy load.

In addition to keeping wagons, Bohemond forced over half of Firuz's servants to stay behind, and these men continued their efforts at building our fort. The remaining servants were bloodied as Firuz had been, though we inflicted only minor wounds to ensure their continued loyalty to their master. Maiming them would have done nothing but give them a reason to betray Firuz to Yaghi Siyan.

Once our ruse was complete, the Saracen merchant took what remained of his caravan and finished his march toward Antioch. He planned to deliver news to Siyan that Tancred had taken up residence south of the Saint George Gate. A trio of our men-at-arms—along with Elric—followed from a distance, and once close enough to Antioch's walls, would resume their "attack" on Firuz's caravan, falling back only once they entered the range of the city's archers. Firuz could then recount to Siyan how he'd miraculously escaped with his life, though his son—along with all his guards and several of his servants—had been callously murdered by us barbaric crusaders.

I watched Firuz's caravan amble away with Elric and three others leaving shortly thereafter. As they faded into the distance, evening settled over us and those ever-looming clouds fully engulfed Antioch along with the plains and hills surrounding it. The air grew thick and humid, and a light rain fell as distant forks of lightning stabbed at the western horizon.

Once I could no longer see Elric, I turned back to the monastery. Tancred's fort was coming along, though *fort* may have been too strong a word to describe the cobbled together wood and stone structures that the men-at-arms were building atop the remnants of the monastery.

Tancred—along with Ásvaldr, myself, and the remaining knights—took up residence in the chapel, and we stashed Firuz's son inside with us. He was given better accommodations than I would have liked. I was the only one among us who spoke Turkish, and since Mundzuk and I had little to say to one another, he remained essentially silent. Bohemond returned to Malregard—his fort in the north—and the days dragged sluggishly on as the rain and clouds lingered.

During this time, I had little to do but sit and stare at the city's high walls through the thin veil of rain. Most of the crusader army had spread out to the north and west of the city, with only Tancred leading our small band of several hundred here in the south. We felt isolated, alone, separated. Not in danger, since Siyan seemed to understand that any sorties sent against us would ultimately fail. Additionally, after his losses at the Bridge Gate battle, he likely only had a thousand or fewer men still garrisoned in the city, whereas we still boasted numbers that approached twenty thousand.

The tedium led to long stretches of silence, especially when it was my turn to guard Mundzuk. He'd eye me suspiciously as

I brought him food and wine—a gift from Tancred—and said nothing for the several hours I'd been assigned to sit with him. Yet a week after Firuz had returned to Antioch and Mundzuk still remained in our care, he finally broke his silence.

It happened on a trip to the nearby creek to wash. We walked down at midday with the sun peeking through a break in the clouds and the gentle yet irritating rain finally coming to an end. Once there, he removed most of his clothing and waded waist deep into the slow-moving water to wash. I knelt further up the shore and cleaned some of my own gear. I wrapped my worn and faded cloak around a fallen branch and dipped it into the creek, letting the water run over it to rinse it clean. As it slowly washed itself, I removed Amina's blue cloth from my arm and dipped it into the clear water, squeezing it until small rivulets of dirt and grime ran away with the current, though the dark stains of Amina's blood remained. I held it in an open palm, letting the gentle breeze dry it.

"Another trinket," Mundzuk said in Turkish.

I glanced at him. He stood, still half-naked, and watched as I held Amina's cloth. I didn't bother answering him, though I held his gaze.

"Why do you carry a scrap of cloth?" he asked. The scorn had left his voice, and he spoke with sincerity I hadn't expected. Perhaps his days of silent captivity had changed his mindset.

I still didn't respond, despite his change in tone. I wanted him to try and escape, to find a weapon and come after me. I wanted to kill him, and no amount of amicable conversation would change that. He studied me, eyes narrowing as if he understood my thoughts.

"You have such hate in your eyes," he said. "And such pain." He frowned and sighed. "I…I'm sorry for what I said of your brother. I, too, want this war to end."

Finally looking away, I tied Amina's cloth back on my arm.

He knew nothing of my pain, nothing of my suffering. It revisited me every night as I was forced to watch her death over and over again. I saw the shock on her face as the sword pierced her, felt her bleeding out in my arms as the rest of her body went cold. Every morning I awoke in a hot sweat and with a thumping, aching heart. Her death left a hole inside me, an empty pit that I filled with hate and bitterness. Even now, as Mundzuk tried to make amends for his callous words, I felt only anger.

When I didn't respond, he continued. "It seems we both have suffered much in this needless war," he went on. I stood and began to walk down the shoreline toward him as he continued. "My own cousins have died in battle. I have seen friends fall, and I do not think—"

I stepped out into the water and ripped Thief's Prick from its sheath. His face shifted, eyes wide and mouth open as if he wanted to cry for help. He tried to backpedal, but he remained waist-deep in the water and could only stumble a step before I reached him. I grabbed him by his hair and bent him over backward until only his face bobbed above the surface of the creek. I jammed the flat of the blade against his throat.

"Say another word," I growled, pressing Thief's Prick hard enough into him to break skin and draw a small trickle of blood that ran away with the flowing water. "Say another word, and I'll bleed you here in this creek. I'll tell Tancred you tried to flee and forced my hand." I paused as he studied my expression. "Say. Another. Word."

His nostrils flared in anger, and I watched him grind his teeth. Any remaining civil discourse he may have had in him quickly faded. I gave him another few moments, hoping he would speak, hoping he would give me a reason to kill him. Instead, he nodded almost imperceptibly and remained silent.

"Good," I said. "I don't—"

"Are you threatening my prisoner again?"

I glanced over my shoulder, saw Bohemond sitting atop his horse surrounded by several of his knights.

"Only a little, Lord," I said again. I released my grip on his hair, and he fell underwater. "He has a big mouth."

Bohemond grinned as Mundzuk came up sputtering and spitting. "Save your strength," he said. "You will need it."

I sheathed Thief's Prick. "For what, Lord?"

"For better or worse, this siege will be over within a week. Battle approaches."

"Battle, Lord?"

He glanced north. "Yes, Pouthená. Battle." He paused, met my eyes. "Kerbogha is coming."

27

A ntioch's plight had echoed across the Muslim world. Last fall, as we'd neared the city, Yaghi Siyan sent his son—Muhammed—to negotiate support from Baghdad. Six months of pleading to the sultan had finally shown results, and a Mosul general named Kerbogha was put in charge of gathering forces.

At first, we believed Kerbogha to be a general in the service of the sultan of Baghdad, though we would later learn that his loyalty to that singular ruler did not run deep. He'd made a name for himself as a shrewd and calculating man. He may have been the sultan of Baghdad's ally—and so a somewhat distant friend of Antioch—but it seemed he served no one man. As he spent months gathering his army, he likely saw himself as Antioch's future ruler rather than Yaghi Siyan's liberator.

Godfrey of Bouillon was first to receive word that his forces approached Antioch. Baldwin of Boulogne, Godfrey's brother, had long ago abandoned the crusade and instead struck out east, eventually seizing control of the city of Edessa through a mixture of force and political intrigue. From Baldwin, Godfrey learned of Kerbogha's army, for it seemed that the Mosul general had paused on his trek to Antioch in order to attempt to seize Edessa. With this information, Godfrey had called for a council of the princes. He'd chosen La Mahomerie—Raymond of Toulouse and the French Provençal's fort near the Bridge Gate—as the meeting place, perhaps due to its centrality among the crusaders or perhaps as a sign of respect to Raymond himself.

La Mahomerie, built atop the corpse of a dead mosque, resembled our own fort in the south, though having been built with more manpower and supplies, it was double the size of ours and substantially more fortified. Stone and wood towers rose at the fort's corners, one of which had been built using the remnants of the mosque's high minaret. A shallow moat surrounded the fort, along with a low palisade punctuated with sharpened stakes. Stands had been built inside the palisade to provide a position from which our limited archers could fire from cover. Overall, it would not withstand a lengthy assault, but it had already survived several raids long enough for reinforcements to arrive from other sections of our camp.

A circle of stools, chairs, and overturned logs had been set into the dirt and cobblestone road that ran from Antioch to Saint Simeon, passing by the front of La Mahomerie. Already a crowd of Saracen guards had gathered atop the Bridge Gate to watch our council, which the lords made no attempt to hide.

Most of the lords and princes were present, many of whom I'd become accustomed to seeing. The elderly Raymond of Toulouse held a place of prominence, though whether that was because he deserved it or simply because he "hosted" the council, I didn't know. As always, he held a small rag in one hand, and I could see that it was already stained pink with blood from his constant coughing.

On one side of him sat Robert of Flanders, and Stephen of Blois, who might have matched Raymond in age though not in frailty, sat on the other side. Stephen and Robert had ridden into battle with us against Ridwan of Aleppo. Their bravery, vigor, and leadership had been as instrumental in that victory as Bohemond's. Though I knew them little, I respected them, if only for that. Godfrey sat with Hugh of Vermandois. The former led his men with integrity and honor, while I'd yet to see the latter join in a single battle, this despite his arrogance and unearned hubris. Likely it came from being the brother to King Philip of France.

Tancred, Bohemond, and several other lords and princes whose names I didn't know completed the circle, each of them with a knight standing guard behind them. Ásvaldr stood behind Bohemond, his massive axe planted in the dirt at his feet and the axe-head resting in his hands at his waist. Tancred had chosen me as his escort. Like all the other escorts, I'd spent the afternoon polishing my mail and armor and cleaning my cloak and surcoat so as to properly represent my lord. Finally, once everyone had settled onto their makeshift chairs, Godfrey began the council, choosing the same blunt speech that was normally reserved for Bohemond.

"My brother sends word of Kerbogha's approach," Godfrey said. "His Muslim army laid siege to Edessa in the east."

Only a few of the lords reacted, telling me that Bohemond had not been the only one aware of Kerbogha's army and the siege of Edessa.

"Does Baldwin send any useful information? The size of Kerbogha's forces or their makeup?" Stephen asked.

"There are a mixture of mounted archers and infantry, taken from across the Muslim world." Godfrey paused, then added, "And there are at least thirty thousand of them."

My heart leaped to my throat for the span of several beats. It seemed the lords of the crusade shared my shock as a collective gasp went through the council. Even Hugh sat up straight on his stool.

"Thirty thousand," Robert repeated. "How can we be sure?"

"I sent my own scouts to confirm," Raymond put in. "Baldwin's estimations are correct."

Murmurs went through the men. "But…thirty thousand," Robert repeated. "Is that even possible?"

"*At least* thirty thousand," Godfrey clarified. "And there are probably more. While we have scrapped to stay alive here at Antioch, Kerbogha has been collecting an immense force of Muslims. This is not just the army of a single ruler, such as we faced with Duqaq or Ridwan. Baldwin's messengers report a force of Turks, Arabs, Kurds, Persians, and many other peoples who could almost not be counted. There is no doubt of its size."

"It seems all the Muslim world has come against us," Stephen said. He sighed, shook his head. "I suppose we should not be surprised."

"When will he arrive?" Robert asked.

"My brother's messengers claim Kerbogha began breaking off his siege a week ago," he said. "My guess is that they have been marching toward us ever since."

"So we have another week," Stephen said. "Perhaps less, if he pushes his men."

Hushed conversations rippled among the lords. A few of the knights standing guard exchanged nervous glances, and I found myself looking for Hendry. Instead, my eyes found Ásvaldr, and he gave a quick shrug, though his face revealed the same apprehension my own likely did.

"My lords," Raymond said, raising a fist that still clutched his bloodied rag as he tried to silence the conversations. "My lords! We must discuss strategy."

Hugh scoffed. "Strategy? What strategy can there be against such numbers?"

"We have faced worse odds," Robert said, though the words lacked conviction. Likely he referred to our miraculous victory over Ridwan, but even I knew this was not the same. We could not rout an army of thirty thousand men with a coordinated cavalry charge of seven hundred.

"This is not Ridwan," Stephen said, echoing my own thoughts. "We cannot ride out to meet him. It would require the entirety of our forces to face such an army. Every man, woman, and child would need to be armed and saddled. Even if I thought it would work, we don't have the horses for that, nor the weapons and armor."

"Arming woman and children was never an option," Godfrey said. "But we cannot simply sit here and let Kerbogha crush us under Antioch's walls."

"What do you propose?" Hugh asked, though his tone suggested he didn't think there was an answer.

I looked to Bohemond but found him stoic and controlled. As ever, he betrayed nothing with his demeanor. I wondered if he'd shared with the other princes that he now controlled a man inside the city.

"A battle is in our future," Godfrey said, bringing my attention back to the council. "In our *immediate* future. Whether we would seek it out or not, we must be prepared to face it."

"How can we face it?" Hugh insisted. "How? We have struggled here for eight months. Eight! The men are tired, hungry, and weary. Kerbogha comes with fresh forces. He outnumbers us. And we still face Antioch. How can we fight this, Godfrey?"

The lord of Bouillon unflinchingly met Hugh's accusatory gaze. "Do we have a choice?"

More murmuring among the lords as Raymond coughed into his rag. Never had I seen them so distressed, so pushed to their edge. Even Hugh, who normally scoffed at the enemy—likely because he never had to face them—seemed terrified of Kerbogha's coming army. The men moaned and complained, five or six independent conversations rising at once. They talked over each other, scolded and accused one another, some yelling at no one in particular as they vented their frustration.

"We can flee," Stephen shouted. The grumbling ceased with shocking abruptness. All eyes turned toward him as he paused and seemed to think on his next words. "I do not say this lightly, brothers," he went on, "nor do I wish it so. But our men need not die for our ambitions. They need not die for our pride. I do not see a way to defeat such a force. Thirty thousand? Perhaps if we'd faced them at Nicaea, when our own numbers could match them. Or even before this winter, before the incessant cold and constant battles whittled down our army to what it is now. Hugh is right: the men are tired; they are weary. We cannot defeat thirty thousand men. We simply cannot. Staying to fight is madness. It is death assured."

Silence descended on the council, thick and heavy like a morning fog on a harsh winter's day. The lords exchanged tense glances. No one wanted to second Stephen's words despite everyone sharing his doubts. For myself, I couldn't fathom the thought of retreating. I knew vengeance drove my thoughts, but I saw no path forward that involved abandoning Antioch and letting Temür remain safely inside. I'd not lost everyone I cared about to simply let him live. Whether they stayed or not, I'd not leave Antioch.

Thankfully, despite our differing motivations, Bohemond shared my view.

"When did such timidity enter into our ranks?" Bohemond asked, and everyone shifted their attention to him. "Such faint-heartedness? Such cravenness? You say the men are tired. *I* say they are hardened warriors, purified through the fire of battle and struggle. My men are elite, ferocious, and well-armed.

Weak? Tired?" He scoffed. "My men will not run from a challenge."

Stephen frowned, shook his head, and said nothing for the remainder of the council.

"What you say is true," Godfrey said. "The chaff have been burned away, and we are left with some of the best knights I have ever fought beside, but it still does not help us defeat his army. We cannot match his numbers."

"What if there was a wall between us and Kerbogha when he arrived?" Bohemond asked. "Would that enable your men to find the courage to fight?"

Godfrey said nothing and only narrowed his eyes in distrust.

"What are you saying?" Robert asked.

"I can open the gates," Bohemond said.

Silence once more fell over them, this time brought on by unbelief rather than fear. Hugh snorted a laugh, though when no one else joined him, he, too, fell silent.

"How?" Godfrey asked.

"I have a man inside and his son as my prisoner. He controls several southern defensive towers."

"And he will give them up?"

"He is as tired of Yaghi Siyan as we are, as everyone is. Antioch no longer supports its ruler. I can get us inside."

"Several towers?" Hugh asked. "What will several towers do when Antioch is guarded by hundreds of them? Can your man open *all* the gates? Can he let our entire army inside?"

He shrugged. "At least one. I can get to the Gate of Saint George in the south."

"And you will seize Antioch yourself? Are you so strong, Lord Bohemond?"

Bohemond only smirked, then glanced over his shoulder to Ásvaldr. "Can we, Bad Crown?"

Ásvaldr met his lord's gaze, patted the axe-head in his hands. "Of course, my lord. The Saracens vill fall before us."

Bohemond looked at me. "What about you, Pouthená?"

I forced a smirk of my own and laid a hand on my sword. "*Vindicta* is anxious to shed Saracen blood, Lord," I said, channeling my bitterness and anger into false confidence.

"You see?" Bohemond turned back to the circle of lords. "My men will not cower before a challenge. They will not recoil from fear or doubt. They do not shiver or tremble at the thought of the enemy but rather welcome battle. They know martyrdom awaits them should they fail and glory if they succeed. *When* they succeed." He looked beyond the princes and lords and instead gazed at the knights standing behind them. "Do you wish to flee? Do you wish for Kerbogha to arrive and find your backs to him? Or do you wish to fight?"

The knights said nothing, though many tightened their expressions and clenched their jaws in determination. They wanted to fight as much as I did; it was obvious. They'd not come this far to run.

"In two days, as dawn breaks on the third of June, you will look up and see my men atop the city walls and my banner waving atop Mount Silpius. Join me if you will."

After a long pause, it was Godfrey who finally spoke. "You ask much, Bohemond."

"To whom much is given, much is demanded."

It always shocked me how well Bohemond knew his Scripture, especially given how unscrupulous the man was.

Godfrey sighed, and even I could tell it was a sigh of resignation. "Can you open any of the other gates? We cannot all storm the city through a single gate."

"Your men have ladders, do they not?"

"You'd have us storm the city with ladders?"

"How many fighting men remain inside the city?" Bohemond asked. "A thousand? Perhaps more? I shall have that many of my own knights inside the walls before the sun rises. You will find little resistance along the walls, should you find the courage to attack them."

It was a fair point, but he was also essentially saying that he expected us to take the city alone. Bohemond wanted to rule Antioch, and this was his chance.

Godfrey exchanged a glance with Robert. "Fine," he said. "My men will fight. But if we must storm Antioch with ladders, we shall storm the citadel."

At this, Bohemond tensed. The citadel lay along the eastern wall of Antioch, near the summit of Mount Silpius. Since this section of wall traced the peaks of the twin mountains—and because it had no gate other than the inaccessible Iron Gate—we'd been unable to blockade it. Bringing siege ladders up the slope—likely under cover of night—in order to attack the citadel was as dangerous as it was stupid. More than likely, Godfrey and his men would perish, but that wasn't what worried Bohemond. Indeed, Godfrey's safety mattered little; if anything, he admired Godfrey's spirit. The problem would arise if Godfrey actually found success. If his flag flew from within the citadel, he would likely be given first rights to the city, and that was something Bohemond feared.

"I will accompany you," said Robert, giving a nod to Godfrey. "Perhaps together we can end this siege once and for all. That is," he added, turning back to Bohemond, "as long as your men are capable of taking the Gate of Saint George."

Bohemond gave a mirthless smile. "My men will be fine," he said, and I felt myself stand up that much straighter despite the pounding of my heart.

28

The following afternoon, I sat a stone's throw from
Tancred's fort—the Tower of Tancred, as we began to
call it, though "tower" was a generous description—with *Ankída*
as my only company. I watched a pot of cabbage soup boil
over a low fire as *Ankída* munched happily at a patch of green
grass behind me. I'd tried to mimic Luke's recipe, though
judging from the smell, it seemed my version would be even
less appetizing. It looked like dirty bath water, milky and gray
with bits of inedible debris bobbing at the surface. Nevertheless, I muscled it down with a knob of hard and moldy bread
and a block of crusted cheese. It tasted worse than it looked. I
kicked out the fire and upended the remainder of the soup
over the dying embers. Chunks of cabbage and a single radish
landed among ashes that hissed and steamed and threw up
wisps of gray smoke.

I sat alone in sight of Antioch on the eve of what would
likely be my most significant battle to date, and somehow it felt
fitting. I'd seen nearly everyone who mattered to me die. All I
had left were remnants, trinkets left behind by the deceased:
Hendry's sword, William's rope, Amina's scrap of blue cloth.

Even my life before the crusade had been filled with hardship and struggle. I'd thought to begin a new life under the tutelage of Hendry, had even found love with Amina, but then my pride struck again and now only Novella remained, though she'd yet to speak with me since Amina's death. She was in the care of Piccolo now, and she was better for it. I'd started out to prove my worth as a crusader and, instead, found nothing but death and loss. Had my life as a poor thief been so much worse than this?

A distant horn sounded. I was being summoned, along with the rest of the men who would lead the assault into Antioch in the darkness of the night. With a deep sigh, I began to don my armor, beginning first by fastening my aketon over my shirt. My hands lingered over the many scars in the fabric, patches Amina had sewn back together, repairing my armor and healing the wounds underneath. I almost felt her touch on my skin, her delicate fingers stitching me back together as I returned from each battle bloodied and broken. Those had been the moments that sustained me through the fighting. I knew it was—at least in part—the knowledge that my *peristéri* waited for me that kept me alive in the chaos of battle. I'd needed to get back to her, so I lived, even when the odds said I shouldn't have.

What would happen now that I had no one to return to?

I pushed aside my own morbid thoughts, pulled on my chausses, and slipped on my mail, the latter made by Amina's father. We'd buried him in the fields of Dorylaeum along with thousands of others. It had been his death that had forced Amina's hand in accompanying me on this crusade. Now she lay beneath her own mound of dirt. Everything I touched turned to ash. I began longing for this final battle, one last chance to avenge my loved ones. A chance to slay Temür, then die in a field of Saracen blood.

It hadn't taken long for the morbid thoughts to return.

Iron-shod boots came next, then a mail coif that was diffi-cult to fasten to my hauberk by myself, and finally Bohemond's surcoat and my helmet. I hefted my sword belt and fastened it tight about my waist. Skull Splitter and *Vindicta* rested comfort-ably at my sides; Thief's Prick had been moved to a makeshift sheath at my right boot. I held my roughly made throwing axe and could nearly hear Hendry's admonishments about the weapon.

"Why're ye carrying that again? Only an idiot throws his weapon."

I stuffed the axe into my belt. Despite my ruminating, it was not a time for mourning my losses; it was a time for avenging them.

The horn sounded again. I slung my shield and turned to check *Ankída*'s gear. She stood tall—tall as she could—as I tugged at her saddle and pulled tight the straps that held it to her back.

"It's just us now, girl," I muttered, running a hand through her scraggly mane. "Just us. At least for one more night."

Another horn blew, and I mounted up and joined the growing formation of crusaders just beyond the monastery. Seven hundred of us met in sight of the Gate of Saint George as evening continued to settle over us underneath an overcast summer sky. A fierce western wind snapped our banners and sent undulating waves of grass across the rolling hills. Ásvaldr and Bohemond sat mounted at our head, the checkered blue and red standard high as Ásvaldr struggled to keep it upright in the gusting wind.

Once in the formation's front row, I gripped *Vindicta*'s hilt and thought about saying a prayer before the coming battle, yet I would be praying for death and destruction, for as much bloodshed as was possible, and I doubted God would answer such a request. I looked at Amina's blue cloth fluttering in the furious wind, felt a wave of raw anger, and decided to say the prayer anyway, even if would fall on deaf ears.

Hundreds of Saracens stood atop Antioch's walls and watched our formation, likely quaking in fear as they suspected an incoming assault. They were right, though it would not come this evening. We were facing the wrong way. Our formation looked south, away from Antioch, and with another blast of the horn, we set out.

The plan was as simple as it was audacious. We would fake a retreat from the city, hopefully lulling Antioch into a false sense of security. Once darkness fell, we would return, coming so close as to touch the stone of the city's walls, and Firuz would lower a rope. We would attach an oxhide ladder to the rope, then Firuz would pull up the ladder and fasten it on top of the wall. Quickly and silently, we would scale the wall and take as many towers as possible. With luck—and God, according to Bohemond—on our side, we should be able to open the Gate of Saint George before the garrison even knew we were there.

When a final blast of the horn sounded, we marched south until the walls of Antioch faded into the distance, disappearing over the hills and leaving behind a likely bewildered garrison. Godfrey, Robert, and their own band of crusaders awaited us three miles from the city. They would attempt to take the citadel positioned near the summit of Mount Silpius as we simultaneously attacked from the south. At dawn—or whenever we were discovered—the remaining lords would attack the rest of the city.

And hopefully Antioch would fall.

We dismounted, and Bohemond greeted Godfrey and Robert as we passed our horses off to more waiting men, men who would see no battle and instead spend the next morning caring for our steeds and praying for our success. The three lords spoke in hushed tones while the rest of us fidgeted in our armor, waiting uncomfortably in the grassy plains until night came in full and the overcast sky turned to a blanket of shadow.

Ásvaldr and Elric found their way to me, and together we sat in the grass and silently stared up at the night sky. We were to be the first three men up the ladder and onto Antioch's walls, the ones who must hold the top as the rest climbed. If Firuz kept his end of the deal, then there would be no fighting until our full force was atop the walls. If he did not, then we'd be slain before another man could scale the wall.

"Do you fear tonight, Pouthená?" Ásvaldr asked.

"Fear?" I shrugged. Of course, I was afraid. "No more than you, I suppose."

He nodded. "Ve may die today," he said, then copied my shrug. "But ve may not. And though good men must die, not even death can kill their names."

Elric scoffed. "I'm glad Bohemond will have our names to remember us as he rules Antioch."

We all laughed at this, an odd sound as we waited in the depths of night. "If ve only fight for Bohemond's pride, then ve vill surely die."

"Then what do you fight for?" I asked.

"Glory," he answered without a pause. "Glory and honor and a chance for my name to ring in the halls of eternity." He looked at Elric. "And you? Vat do you fight for?"

He shrugged. "I've got nowhere else to go," he said, and I could almost hear my own voice in his. I'd given that same answer in the past. The two now turned to me. "Daniel?" Elric asked. "What about you?"

I sighed, said nothing, then looked down at the grass in hopes they would simply let the question go unanswered. I hated that question, yet now a fire had grown in my belly, a blazing storm of anger and bitterness and vengeance, and I clearly saw what I fought for. At least what I would fight for that night.

290 | BRYAN R SAYE

"*Lex talionis,*" I said, speaking.

Ásvaldr nodded in understanding. "The law of retribution."

"Aye," I said. "I fight for revenge."

"The one-armed man."

"Temür," Elric added.

"That's him," I said.

"He killed your woman?" Ásvaldr asked.

"He did."

He thought on that for a moment. "Ambition and revenge are alvays hungry," he finally said.

"What does that mean?"

"It means killing the one-armed man might not be as satisfying as you hope."

I said nothing. He was right; I very much doubted killing Temür would bring any kind of satisfaction.

That wasn't going to stop me from doing it.

The night stretched on, and we waited another two hours before finally backtracking toward the city, accompanied now by Godfrey, Robert, and their own knights and men-at-arms. We numbered near two thousand now, and together we fumbled through the inky-black darkness until we reached the dense forest three hundred yards from the city's walls.

Here we stopped. Bohemond bid godspeed and good luck to Godfrey and Robert—though I knew he didn't mean it— and we watched in silence as their slightly larger group of shadows disappeared deeper into the forest for their long trek through dense foliage and up the slopes of Mount Silpius. Moving slowly and stealthily, they would most likely need the rest of the night to reach the citadel, especially burdened as they were with ladders.

They faded into the trees, nothing but ghosts in the night. Then it was our turn, and seven hundred of us crept through the forest and closer to the city. Bohemond knelt at the forest's edge, and sixty of us pulled tight to him. We were to be the ones who would scale the wall, the ones who would climb the oxhide ladder and open the city's gates.

At least, we were the ones who would try.

The walls of Antioch loomed in the darkness only a dozen paces away. Points of light bobbed atop those high walls like stars that had lost their grip on the night sky and dropped below the cloud cover. These were the guards patrolling the parapets with lanterns. Bohemond turned to us, to his sixty picked men, and even in the darkness I saw the eagerness on his face. He longed for battle as much as any of us.

I also felt the fervor of the men around me, yet I could almost hear the shaking of their bones. Men's hearts raced, their teeth clattered, sweat beaded brows in the windy summer night. This was like nothing any of us had ever faced. Charging headlong into battle when you can see your enemy is one thing; climbing a ladder in utter darkness, unsure what awaits you at the top was another entirely.

"Tonight," Bohemond whispered harshly, his voice nearly silent as the wind continued to whip through the trees and echo in my ears. "Tonight we take Antioch. Take heart, trust in your fellow crusaders. Do not fear, for God wills our victory. He wills that we should wrench control of Antioch from the filthy grip of the Saracens and turn it over to His elect, to His righteous ones."

I frowned at that, knowing full well that few of us were righteous. Most were as bloodthirsty as I, though likely for different reasons. Gold and glory and women awaited them over the walls; vengeance and the hopes of unrestrained blood-shed awaited me.

"I shall accompany you to the walls," he went on, then turned his gaze to me. "Bad Crown and Pouthená shall be the first up the ladder."

The others eyed us, and I felt the massive Dane pound me on the back.

"Daniel and I vill try to leave some men for you," he said, and the knights around us grinned.

"Speak for yourself," I added. "If they take too long, I'll seize Antioch myself."

Chuckles sounded in the silent night.

"Your bravery will be remembered long after our crusade has faded to memory," Bohemond said, and mumbled agreements went through the men.

Brave but foolish, they called me. Tonight, I was vengeful and foolish.

"*Deus vult,*" I muttered.

"*Deus vult,*" they echoed.

"Come," Bohemond said. "It is time."

We set out across the final stretch of open field between the trees and Antioch's walls. Our boots squelched on dewy grass, and armor and weapons clinked together despite every effort to hold them still. Every sound echoed through the night like a crack of thunder, and every breath left a puff of misty air that the still-gusting wind snatched and blew away.

I knew they would see us. How could they not? Sixty of us loping through open fields like madmen. Despite our dark cloaks and coal-blackened faces, I *knew* they would see us.

Yet we reached the walls and pressed ourselves against the cool stone, and no alarm sounded. No Saracens called into the night; no arrows ended our silent charge. We waited there in the shadows of Antioch, all eyes locked on the parapets above and the bobbing lanterns that patrolled it.

Silence.

Now what?

The lanterns passed us by, disappeared into the nearest tower, and the walls above fell into the same blackness that engulfed us below. The seconds passed, our hearts thumping loudly in our chests, and once more I knew the garrison would hear us.

Instead, I heard the thin scratch of feet on stone, the scuff of something rubbing against the walls—all barely audible over the mad wind—then a frayed rope fell almost perfectly in front of me.

"God bless you, Firuz," Bohemond whispered as he snatched the rope. Seven men came forward carrying a cloak. Inside lay the bundled oxhide ladder, and Bohemond tied the rope to one end and gave a quick tug. A moment later the rope went up, and the ladder unfurled as it ascended to the top of the wall in quick, jerking motions. Bohemond watched it go, his face nearly glowing in excitement despite the darkness. "God bless you," he said again.

It took almost a full minute for the ladder to stop moving. Bohemond gripped it and tugged hard. When it didn't move, he looked to me and Ásvaldr, smiled, then held it out toward us.

I took the ladder, the rough oxhide scratching against my own leather gloves.

"*Deus vult*," Bohemond mouthed.

I nodded in response, then turned and looked up the wall as the ladder disappeared into darkness above me. I drew a breath, gave a quick exhale.

Then I started to climb.

29

The oxhide ladder swayed in the wind, my added weight doing nothing to steady it. Ásvaldr and Elric held the bottom in an effort to stop the movement, but even this did little to stop it. The rungs sagged under my boots as the weight of my armor, shield, and weapons made each step a battle.

Several rungs up, a vicious gust nearly lifted me from the ladder, pushing me far enough off the wall that my helmet clanged against the stone wall like a struck bell when I finally jerked back into place. I froze, head ringing and jaw clenched shut, and waited for the arrows to come. This was why Bohemond had asked me to be the first up the latter: if I died, he would lose nothing of value.

Yet no arrows came, only the wind thrashing through the trees and my own rapid breathing echoing inside my helmet.

I climbed another few rungs, then the ladder sagged suddenly, pulled down by some added weight. I glanced below, saw Ásvaldr taking his first steps as Bohemond took his place holding it steady beside Elric. With the weight of both of us, the oxhide creaked and moaned, and for a moment I thought of telling him to wait until I reached the top. Yet the ladder held, and up we went, one rung at a time until I could see the parapets above, nothing more than dim outlines in the shadows.

I was greeted by a hand stretched over the stone when I finally reached the top. I clasped it—thankfully it was Firuz and not someone looking to kill me—and climbed over the low rise of the parapet and onto Antioch's walls. From my new vantage point, I gazed down over the sleeping city for the first time, peering into the darkness as I tried to find *Sen Piyer Kilisesi*, Saint Peter's Church. Antioch's eastern wall rode the summit of the twin mountains, and thin pinpoints of flickering light bobbed along the parapets like fireflies in the night. I could just make out the citadel that Godfrey and Robert would be assaulting come sunrise. It spread inward from the eastern wall near Mount Silpius's summit, another partition of high stone encircling the citadel. A heavy concentration of guards— obvious by the extra torches and lanterns—walked along the walls of the citadel. Godfrey and Robert would face a much harder challenge in their assault than we had thus far.

After the citadel, the wall followed the downward slope of Mount Silpius until it became the Iron Gate, little more than a high stone arch wedged into the narrow valley between the two mountains. Antioch's wall continued up Mount Staurin and faded into the darkness.

Sen Piyer Kilisesi should be there, just beyond the Iron Gate, built into the rocky slopes at the base of Mount Staurin. Though I saw nothing in the darkness, I knew I was close. Vengeance was within reach. My fingers twitched at my side, eager to pull my weapons free and run wild through the city as I carved my way north to the church.

"*Selam.*"

I turned and acknowledged Firuz for the first time. Sweat beaded his forehead, and his tightly clenched face had a clear sheen in the darkness.

"Hello," I said back, then gave a smile that was probably more than a bit smug. "Good to see you again, Firuz."

He grunted a reply.

Watch towers rose in either direction along our section of the wall, each at least fifty feet away, and open doorways threw squares of dancing firelight onto the stone at each one. Though I knew that Firuz's own guards manned both of these towers, I still felt as if I stood in the center of the lion's den. Unlike Daniel from the Scriptures, I yearned for these lions to bare their teeth.

The oxhide ladder had been secured to a pair of empty sconces. It shook and stretched, groaning loudly as Ásvaldr joined me atop the wall with a heavy grunt.

"That vas not fun," he huffed.

"No," I agreed.

Ásvaldr glanced at Firuz, looked as if he was about to speak, then we both heard the rustling of the ladder and together we leaned back over to help Elric up. As we did, another roaring gust of wind cut across the parapet, this one powerful enough to send us both tumbling to our hands and knees. A terrible rip sounded in the night, like a gambeson being torn asunder, and the ladder came free from its hold on the sconces. Elric cried into the night, then came the tumbling crash of more than one crusader falling down the face of Antioch's stone walls.

I leaped to my feet and peered over the edge, yet darkness shrouded the ground below. My heart thudded in my chest, sweat drenched my face and soaked through my aketon under my mail. Ásvaldr joined me, and I knew he thought the same thing: surely someone heard that. Even if the nearest towers were manned by Firuz's guards, others *must* have heard the noise. Surely guards would come. The two of us could do nothing but die.

"Get the rope," I hissed, glaring at Firuz as if he'd been to blame for the gusting wind. He didn't move, only stood wide-eyed and stared at the two sconces that no longer secured the ladder. "The rope! Firuz!"

He shook his head clear and grabbed the rope, then tossed it back over the edge. I pulled Skull Splitter free—*Vindicta* would wait for Temür—and turned to face one of the towers. Ásvaldr did the same, though he clutched his large axe and looked in the opposite direction.

The seconds dragged on, and I heard the scrape of the ladder being dragged back up along with Firuz's own struggling grunts. Several minutes passed before he bent over and pulled the ladder over the parapet and lashed it once more to the sconces. This time he knelt nearby and held the ladder tight himself.

The same howling wind that had dislodged the ladder must have been loud enough to drown out the commotion, for after another handful of tense heartbeats Elric tumbled over the parapet, collapsing onto the stone like a dead lamb. He looked up, his face aglow with sweat and a trickle of blood from a cut on his forehead, and frowned.

"Was anyone hurt?" I asked.

He pushed himself to standing. "I don't feel great," he said, wiping at the blood, "but I think Pate broke his head."

"Broke his head?"

Elric winced. "Saw his brains and all."

The ladder scraped against the stone and up came another crusader, then another, and soon we stood cramped together on our small section of wall. The light continued to flicker through the doorways of each tower, and occasional words or bouts of laughter carried on the wind, yet no one but us stood on the walls. We waited until the tenth man joined us, then Ásvaldr tapped his axe to indicate it was time to fight.

"What about Bohemond?" Elric asked.

"Ve go vest," Ásvaldr said, "and he vill go east to place his flag atop the vall."

"Wait," Firuz hissed, and we turned as one to look at him. He pointed west, to the tower we were about to assault. "Remember, that tower is mine," he said. "They know you're coming. They will not sound an alarm." He paused, glanced from me to Ásvaldr. "Don't harm them."

"If they lay down their arms," Ásvaldr said, "then ve vill let them live."

And with that, we left. Only two towers stood between us and the Gate of Saint George, though the gate itself was flanked by its own towers that we would have to take. Our boots scuffed on the stone as we approached the first one, and the wind continued to scream over Antioch, taking with it any sound we made. We reached the tower's doorway unnoticed. Weapons and shields were already drawn, and our hearts continued to race.

Ásvaldr waved me forward. "You go," he whispered.

"Me?"

"You speak their tongue."

"So?"

He frowned. "I don't vant to kill Firuz's men. Go."

"I don't like it," I said, despite knowing he was right. As I took my first step toward the tower's door, he grabbed my surcoat and jerked me back.

"Put that avay," he said, nodding to my axe. "Do not start a fight."

"And if they start one?" I asked, slipping Skull Splitter back into its carriage on my belt.

He smirked. "Then ve vill avenge you."

"Thanks," I grunted, then stepped into the tower with hands held up and empty palms forward. The right wall—the wall facing Antioch—was flat and without feature, while the outward-facing side bulged in a semicircle of stone. Four narrow slits allowed the archers to fire into the plains below, and a pair of torches hung in sconces, the smoke drifting up and disappearing through thin cutouts in the flat ceiling. The rest of the interior of the tower was empty.

Except for the five guards standing ready, weapons in hands, eyes locked on me.

"*Ben Daniel*," I said, and even I heard the trepidation in my voice. "*Beni Firuz gönderdi.*"

Firuz sent me.

At first they said nothing, only kept glaring at me with angry eyes.

"*Firuz'a hizmet ediyor musun?*" I asked.

Do you serve Firuz?

Finally one of them stepped forward.

"*Rahatlamak*," he said, his voice low and guttural. "*Güvendesin.*" "Relax," he was telling me. You're safe. Clearly, he could see my nerves.

I leaned back and waved the rest of the men in, and one by one we filled the small space inside the tower. As each crusader entered, the Saracens took a step back, until they crowded against the outward-facing wall and silently stared at us. It felt odd to be so close to the enemy, even if they were not our enemy tonight, and I sensed the same tension in the other knights around me.

"Vill they stay here?" Ásvaldr asked.

I turned to the man who'd spoke. "*Burada kalacak mısın?*"

He nodded. "*Evet. Müttefiklerimizle savaşmayacağız.*"

"They'll stay," I said. "They won't fight us, but they won't fight the rest of the garrison, either."

"Can't say I blame them," Elric muttered.

"What now?" I asked.

Ásvaldr nodded to the opposite side of the tower. "Ve have a gate to take. Ask him if ve have any allies in the next towers."

"*Diğer kuleler dost canlısı mı?*" I asked.

He shook his head and said, *"Hayır."* No one needed me to translate that.

"Looks like ve fight."

"Finally," I said.

Taking cautious steps, we shuffled the rest of the way through the tower, being sure to give our new Saracen friends plenty of space. We slipped out along the top of the wall—which still lay dark and empty—and slowed once we reached the second tower. Ásvaldr held up three fingers. Slowly, he counted down—three...two...one—and together we rushed into the tower.

Only a single guard of the five inside was awake, and Ásvaldr took his head with a swipe of his massive axe. The guard managed a quick yelp before his decapitation silenced him, just enough to awaken the remaining four men. We pounced on them, weapons rising and falling with brutal efficiency. They stood no chance.

Two towers down. Only the gate remained.

Yet that wouldn't be quite as simple.

"There are men on the vall," Ásvaldr whispered after glancing outside. "Two of them. Ve cannot let them sound the alarm."

"Will they see us?" Elric asked.

"Ve don't exactly look like Saracens."

"But it's dark. Maybe they won't notice."

Ásvaldr frowned. "They vill take notice of a dozen men, vether ve look like Saracens or not. Do you vant to fight all of Antioch?"

"Kind of," I muttered, and both men glanced at me. "I certainly don't want to sit here all night."

"Vat do you suggest?"

I scanned the dead Saracens at our feet. "Give me a cloak," I said, pointing to one of the guards. "And a torch."

"A torch? You vant them to see you?"

Elric passed me the cloak of a dead Saracen, and I swept it over my shoulders. "A little," I said, then scooped a torch from the wall and slipped Skull Splitter back into its carriage. I met Ásvaldr's confused gaze and pulled the cloak up over my head. "Trust me."

He frowned. "I don't like this idea."

"You can always avenge me," I said, then stepped out onto the wall.

I clutched the cloak at my neck as the wind snatched it and pulled it back like a banner before battle. I held the torch out in front of me so the glare would block my face, though the wind seemed eager to extinguish it as the flames danced and flickered. The two Saracens looked to be in conversation, though their words were lost to the gusting wind. They held a single lantern between them, and their shadowy figures only glanced my way.

"*Selam*," I called out, shouting to be heard over the wind.

"*Selam*," they said back in unison.

"*Firuz gönderdi beni*," I said as I neared them. "*Firu— kahretsin!*" I shouted, pretending to trip and tossing the torch out in front of me. I aimed it at one of the Saracens, and he put his arms up to block it, shouting in irritation as the flames licked at his bare hands. I ripped Thief's Prick free from its home on my right boot as I continued my fake fall. The other guard made to catch me, but I stood upright and rammed Thief's Prick into his stomach. He grunted quietly, and I jerked the dagger up, splitting him open and letting him fell backward into the low parapet with his innards spilling into his hands.

"*Ne yapıyorsun*," the still-living Saracen said, clearly more irritated than worried. He patted his hands against his chest. "*Seni aptal.*"

I turned away from the dead guard and let the cloak go. The wind immediately snatched it, sending it flying out over Antioch like some kind of massive bird. His eyes widened as he saw my face and his dead comrade behind me, but I was already moving, jabbing Thief's Prick into his chest even as he reached for the sword at his hip, my other hand coming up to cover his mouth as he tried to scream. The narrow seax grated against his ribs, and he let out a low moan against my palm before sliding off the blade. He opened his mouth as if to call for help, but I pressed my hand tighter against his lips. After another few heartbeats, he gave a last exhale as he went limp against the parapet.

The torch had already gone out, and only the small lantern gave light. I lifted it and turned toward Ásvaldr and the others, waving them forward. Once I saw them scrambling along the walls toward me, I extinguished the lantern and set it down beside the bodies.

"Vell done," Ásvaldr said, glancing down at the two dead guards before turning his attention on the towers guarding the Gate of Saint George. "Last one," he said, looking back at the rest of the crusaders atop the wall. Nearly thirty of us had gathered by now. The rest had gone east with Bohemond at their head. "This is the gate tower," he went on. "It vill be guarded more fiercely. Their vill be no sleeping guards, no easy killing. It vill be a fight."

I pulled Skull Splitter back from its carriage, then slung my shield into my left hand. Around me, others did much the same, and soon we all stood ready to continue the battle. Ásvaldr stepped forward, and I trod quietly alongside him. Behind us, the rest of the crusaders moved.

Ásvaldr and I crept into the tower first, both surprised to find it free of guards. Unlike the previous towers, this one had been built with two rooms, and we found ourselves standing in a kind of entryway. A few feet to our right, a stairwell descended toward the ground and disappeared quickly into blackness. A narrow doorway to our left led to what was likely the main section of the tower. A heavy winch lay exposed in the corner, likely the very winch that would open the gate.

More crusaders filed silently in behind us, and Ásvaldr eyed Elric, then pointed with his chin to the stairwell. Elric gave a nod of understanding and led a dozen crusaders quietly down the stairs, their iron-shod boots clicking on the stone steps. Then, with his axe held in both hands, Ásvaldr gave a loud shout that echoed violently in the tight quarters and charged through the narrow doorway.

I gave my own battle cry and followed him into a room where four stone walls, each with narrow slits for archers, rose to a flat ceiling. Torches burned in sconces, smoke swirled up and out through thin slits in the roof, and—more importantly—five Antiochene guards stared dumbfounded back at us.

Ásvaldr was already bringing his massive axe down on the nearest guard, who hadn't had time to draw a weapon. The axe powered through the mail at his shoulder, splitting the man's collarbone and nearly cleaving him in two. A fountain of blood shot up, painting the gray stone crimson in the orange firelight. I attempted to copy Ásvaldr with Skull Splitter, but my own axe glancing off the nearest guard's helmet and embedding itself into his shoulder. He bellowed in pain, but still had the presence of mind to draw his curved sword. I jabbed with my shield and caught him in the jaw, the iron rim throwing teeth and snapping his head back. He stumbled, Skull Splitter ripped free, and he collapsed among the remaining guards.

More crusaders charged into the small room, and all three of the guards raised their hands in surrender. Yet we'd sat beyond the walls of Antioch for eight months, starving and tired and living in our own filth. Disease had devastated us, constant battles and skirmishes and assaults had ravaged us. We'd fought back Duqaq and Ridwan, each nearly spelling the end of our crusade, and each of us knew Kerbogha approached at that very moment with an army nearly twice our size. Impotently we'd stared at Antioch, dreamed of a day when we'd get inside, and so not a single one of the crusaders heeded these men's surrender.

Soon, five guards lay dead in our small tower.

"Open the gate," Ásvaldr growled, wiping the blood from his axe on the cloak of a dead Saracen. "Let the men inside."

30

The winch creaked and clanked as the chain scraped up, pulling with it the portcullis of Antioch. I stepped back out onto the wall and surveyed what had quickly become a dim predawn morning. The sun had already begun to announce its arrival in the east as a faint haze of fiery light peeked over the mountains. I surveyed the silent sleeping city one final time, knowing it was about to descend into chaos and bloodshed.

The outlines of buildings became visible beneath me as black shadows turned to fuzzy gray smudges. A light fog sat between blacksmiths and tailors and markets, obscuring walkways and lingering over an open stable near the base of the wall beneath me. The pinpoints of orange light dancing along the parapets faded into bobbing yellow blurs, and a few of the lanterns and torches went out entirely as the city began to embrace the coming day. I heard water splashing, a dog barking, and one rooster calling an early start. Shapes and silhouettes emerged from homes as people began their daily chores; no one seemed to notice the Gate of Saint George slowly creaking open.

They had no idea we were there.

The battle for Antioch had already begun. The blood of the slain guards stained my surcoat. Skull Splitter sagged lightly in my right hand as more blood dripped from the blade and splattered onto the cold gray stone beside my iron-shod boots. A streak of crimson smeared the rim at the bottom of my shield, and Thief's Prick was crusted with the blood of the two unsuspecting Saracen guards I'd killed minutes before. Only *Vindicta* remained clean, slumbering in its sheath and awaiting the time I could draw it.

Soon I would have vengeance.

I spotted *Sen Piyer Kilisesi* in the new light, little more than a darkened shadow near the Iron Gate. A square frontage had been built around the cave church's entrance, though it was insubstantial and barely visible from the distance. A mile or more stretched between me and the church, a distance I would cover in short order. I only prayed Temür would be inside when I arrived. My blood ran hot at the thought of reaching him.

The blast of a horn cried suddenly from the east, inter-rupting my reverie as its faint and angry call rumbled like distant thunder. It rolled over the city and echoed against the walls and into the stone tower before fading into the dawn. I froze, as did the faraway bobbing torches and lanterns as the guards searched for the noise. A long, eerie silence fell over us, and it seemed that even the mad gusting of the wind paused for just a brief moment. I tightened my grip on Skull Splitter as I waited along with the rest of the city. No one cried out, no one reacted, no one moved.

Then it boomed again, undulating once more out of the east, and this time I recognized it. It belonged to Bohemond, and our lord was calling us to battle. As it rang, I saw his blue and red flag sprout atop the wall near the citadel, its bold colors rising as the raging wind returned. The flag snapped and fluttered as three men held it aloft, and Bohemond's horn continued its sonorous call over the city. Before the final, throaty vestiges of his lone horn faded, a dozen more calls to arms sounded, these rising from the south, the west, the north. They cried out into the dawn, pounding the city with their noise, shouting for battle and blood.

Raymond and Hugh and Tancred and every other lord emptied their camps, sending forth all the men they could to take the city, and a great barrage of screaming crusaders rushed the walls with ladders and ropes and shields, trampling the grass and dirt underneath their feet and throwing great clouds of dust as if a wave rising from the earth itself flowed toward Antioch. Bohemond's horn sounded again, and farther in the east came another, and I knew Godfrey and Robert had begun their assault on the citadel.

The battle for Antioch began in earnest.

"Get the gate open," I shouted, turning back to the knights still in the tower. "Hurry!"

"Vat do you think ve're doing!" Ásvaldr called as he and three others worked the massive winch. Beneath me, I could feel the rumble through the stone as the gate creaked up. I looked once more into the city, saw dozens of hazy silhouettes rushing down the path through the fog and toward the base of the tower.

I sprinted to Ásvaldr's side. "There are men coming below," I told him, but even as I said it more Saracens charged across the wall that spanned the gate on the far side of the tower.

He saw them, too, and began shouting for a shield wall at the entrance to the tower. I moved to join it.

"No!" Ásvaldr said. "Help Elric below. We can handle this!"

The entrance to the tower was thin, and already six of our

own crusaders had piled into that gap. I could do nothing to help.

"Go!" he shouted again.

"Don't die," I told him, and he gave me a quick nod as he continued to work the winch.

I charged down the darkened stairs and onto the stone courtyard sitting at the base of the tower beside the Gate of Saint George. Blood splattered the ground all around me, and Elric and the others stood over a score of dead Saracens. Two crusaders lay among the victims. A cobblestone path led away from the tower and forked, one way winding through the fog-covered city and the other turning back toward the still-rising gate.

"More Saracens are coming," I told him.

He rolled his shoulders and stretched his neck. "How many?"

"I don't know, but we can't let them up the tower." The gate jerked to a stop, barely a few feet off the ground, and the sounds of battle came from above. "Ásvaldr needs more time."

Elric scowled at the gate, then looked into the city just as the Saracens began to stream from the fog and into the court-yard. They wore mail and helmets, held shields and swords. Only a few of them carried their distinctive curved horn bows.

"Ready to fight?" Elric asked.

I still held my axe and shield. "Always."

"Good," he said, then rapped his sword against the iron rim of his shield. "Shield wall!"

The men fell in at his side, and I joined them, eleven of us in total pushing together and linking shields in the smallest shield wall I'd ever been a part of. Climbing the oxhide ladder had forced us to forgo spears, which meant we'd not have the advantage of distance. This would be a close fight, a bloody one. We formed a crescent in front of the tower entrance as the few archers opened fire. Arrows bounced harmlessly from shields as the rest of the Saracens began to build a small formation of their own. More men surged from the fog, growing their number to twenty, then thirty, then fifty.

"Two minutes," I shouted. Somewhere in the very great distance came the sounds of battle as other crusaders found breaches either through the wall or over it. "Two minutes," I said again, ignoring the noise, "and Tancred will lead hundreds of men through the gate behind us. We need only stand for two minutes."

I cracked Skull Splitter against my shield's face, and the men around me echoed it even as the Saracens began their advance. More arrows came, these doing just as little as the first volley. They cracked into shields, skittered on stone, ricocheted into the air. Behind me, the gate began to rise once more. I dropped Skull Splitter back into its carriage—it was large and unwieldy in the close quarters of a shield wall—and pulled out Thief's Prick, wiping the blood-crusted blade as clean as I could against my own surcoat. The Saracens crept forward, not eager to enter battle against our shield wall, yet knowing they must if they stood any chance of securing the gate and safeguarding their city.

The shield wall is a ferocious thing, a deadly thing. Men talk of battle, and they speak of glorious deeds and valor. And they should, for without courage and boldness, no battles could be won. Yet what they do not speak of is the ugliness of it, and there is nothing uglier than the shield wall, nothing uglier than staring down a snarling man only a foot away, both of you knowing that only one of you can live. That one of you must gut the other, then trample him underfoot as you press forward, slipping in blood and guts and piss.

Yet I had come for bloodshed, for battle. I had come for something far uglier than the shield wall.

I had come for vengeance. And these few men would not stand in my way.

As all warriors do, they shouted in a vain effort to build up their courage as they closed the final steps. We lunged forward, as well, and our two sides came together in a crush of bodies, wood, and steel. Their scimitars cracked into our iron-rimmed shields, some lancing underneath or overtop only to glance off mail or iron-shod boots or thick steel helmets. I jabbed Thief's Prick, felt it turn on the edge of a Saracen shield, then twisted and jabbed again, this time hitting mail as the seax caught in the metal links without penetrating them. I kneed my hand holding he seax, forcing Thief's Prick through the armor, and felt hot blood gush onto my hand. The weight against my shield vanished as the man stumbled back, only to be replaced with someone else as a new face pressed forward.

I shuttled Thief's Prick back and forward again and buried it into the new Saracen's thigh. He howled in pain and tried to backpedal, only to be pushed forward by the man behind him, forcing the seax deep enough that it grated on bone and elicited another shriek of pain. A hand gripped the rim of my shield, and I snapped my head forward, the crown of my helmet crushing fingers and breaking bones. The man dropped to a knee, the movement snatching Thief's Prick from my hand as it stayed in his thigh. Yet another Saracen stepped forward, and a curved scimitar skated across the top of my shield and cracked into my helmet, shoving it back and nearly ripping it from my head.

I ducked low and drew Skull Splitter, but already the scimitar crashed down again, this time cracking into edge of my shield, splitting through the iron rim and lodging itself into the wood underneath. I twisted the shield, the Saracen stumbled forward as he kept his grip on his stuck sword, and I brought my axe down in an overhead strike. The heavy blade hammered into his helmet, chopping through the steel and into his skull underneath. His eyes rolled back immediately, and he collapsed at my feet.

Elric roared beside me as a scimitar sliced through the mail at his ribs. Blood sluiced down the blade, and his shield no longer pressed tight against mine as it sagged in his hand. The Saracen stabbed again, but the sword stayed wedged between our two shields. I swung Skull Splitter across my body, the large weapon hampered by the close quarters and awkward angle, and the axe only bounced against the mail at the Saracen's shoulder. Still, the blow was enough to stagger him, and Elric stabbed low, burying his own sword into the Saracen's stomach. They both fell at the same time, Elric's wound finally overcoming his fading strength. A knight unceremoniously shoved him backward, and we tried to close the gap, but we moved too slowly and soon the Saracens pressed forward, splintering our shield wall and sending the small skirmish into chaos.

I backpedaled and heaved a wild swing with Skull Splitter, putting as much space as I could between myself and the sudden rush of Saracen soldiers. My strike met nothing but air, and moments later a trio of blows beat the face of my shield. I swung again, and felt the axe-head ricochet off mail or a shield or maybe even flesh—in the mayhem I couldn't tell. A blow landed on my back, not breaking mail but sending me stumbling forward. I slipped on the blood-slick stone and fell to a knee, raised my shield on reflex and caught another pair of strikes. A blade skirted underneath my guard and stabbed me in the shoulder, thankfully catching on the mail but spinning me backward as someone ripped the shield from my grip. I started to lift Skull Splitter as a scimitar cracked into the haft of the axe and knocked the weapon from my hand.

I reached for Thief's Prick, remembered I'd already lost it, then grabbed *Vindicta* and wrenched it from its scabbard only to find no one to attack. I rose to a knee and saw the Saracens running back through the courtyard toward the city. Then came the roar of hundreds of crusaders streaming through the now-open gate and hacking at the fleeing Saracens, running over them like a wave on sand. Shouts rose in the courtyard, cries of pain and victory, of death and defeat, and moments later the courtyard sat empty once more as the crusaders rampaged through the city, splitting down every street or path or alleyway like water flowing through rocks.

31

The clamor of battle descended onto the city. Skirmishes erupted atop the parapets as crusaders climbed ladders and fought against Saracen guards still recovering from the shock of Christian soldiers inside their walls. Steel on steel echoed from as far away as the citadel as Robert and Godfrey fought for its control. Shouts of pain and effort and death rang out in the early dawn, carried along on the angry wind as the crusaders continued their mad flood through Antioch, pouring through the single open gate and scaling the walls to shed blood with abandon. We outnumbered the garrison at least fifteen to one, and now that we'd pierced their protective shell, it wouldn't be long before Saracen corpses covered the streets of Antioch and we had control of the city.

I heaved myself to my feet. Everything in me hurt, and a light trickle of warm blood ran from the shallow wound in my shoulder. My helmet sat askew atop my throbbing head, knocked that way from a Saracen scimitar. The nose guard pressed into my face, and the cheek guard obscured an eye. I twisted it straight and took in the sight in my immediate vicinity. Crusaders and Saracens lay dead all about, their blood running between the stones of the courtyard in gruesome rivers of gory crimson. Elric sat against the tower not far away. Another knight knelt beside him and pressed the shredded remains of a cloak into his wound before turning to eagerly join in the sacking of Antioch. Elric watched his momentary physician depart, then gave me a weak grin and winced in pain at the slight movement. He was hurt, but he would live.

I found my shield beside a dying Saracen, his eyes on the sky as he gasped and panted, hand clutching around Thief's Prick still embedded into his thigh as a puddle of dark blood steadily grew around him. His mail and tunic were shredded, showing that I'd not been the only one to wound him. I lifted the shield, ripped out the curved sword still lodged in the iron rim, tossed it aside, then knelt and jerked Thief's Prick unceremoniously from the Saracen's leg. He grunted weakly and had only enough energy to glare at me as he silently continued dying.

"You would have done the same," I muttered, bending down and scooping up Skull Splitter, which lay a few feet away. I gave him another glance, then stepped over him and made my own way into the city.

The morning sun had burned away the nighttime fog, and the city lay exposed. The main force of feral and angry crusaders had already passed through, leaving behind a wake of destruction that rivaled even the most gruesome of battle-fields. Men, women, and children lay dead in the gutters of Antioch, in the middle of the stone pathways, and at the entrances to alleys and parks and markets. They lay sprawled atop of one another, killed as they'd tried to flee and left where they'd been slain. Their blood splattered the surrounding buildings and pathways, covering shops and storefronts. Doors had been kicked open or hacked apart, and looting men-at-arms still occupied many of the buildings. Knights dashed across the road, moving from one building to another, some with handfuls of goods and others still searching for their first spoils. Shouts echoed randomly from alleyways as men murdered and pillaged and did worse things that I'll not speak of.

A woman stumbled from a home in front of me, her tunic torn and blood running from a gash on her forehead. She paused and stared at me in fear, likely expecting me to assault her or worse, yet I froze as I saw her. I recalled Temür burning down an Armenian village not far from Dorylaeum, remembered fleeing through the carnage and mayhem as I tried to protect Novella and her mother, both of whom I'd found suddenly in my care thanks to the mercilessness of the Saracens assault. Now I stood on the other side. Though I wasn't looting and burning and murdering, I wasn't stopping it, either. Lost in my reverie, I almost didn't see the knight stomp from the same home the woman had fled from. Her shriek of terror pulled me fully back to the present. She quickly forgot about me and clawed back to her feet, sprinting away with the knight in pursuit. They disappeared behind a blacksmith's shop, and I never saw either of them again.

Dozens of columns of black smoke rose above the buildings all around me, the screams of the dying falling on me like rain. I heard the rumble of the Bridge Gate as it groaned open, the renewed cries of more crusaders pouring into the city as if another dam had been loosed. Men and women ran in panicked zigzags through the streets—none in armor, none with weapons, some even carrying children and yet cut down nonetheless—as a flood of new knights stormed the city. They wore surcoats of Godfrey and Raymond, of Hugh and Robert, and they killed with the same reckless abandon as the rest. I heard one Antiochene man scream "Christian! Christian!" before having his throat gashed open by a crusader who wore the red cross of Christ on his shield.

None of this mattered, I told myself. Not the looting or the killing or the things much worse. Nothing mattered but getting to Temür, reaching *Sen Piyer Kilisesi*.

Nothing mattered but my vengeance.

I ignored the suffering all around me—I'd suffered, why shouldn't they—and shook out tired and aching muscles, then began a light jog northeast toward Mount Staurin and a church built into a cave.

I stopped in front of *Sen Piyer Kilisesi*, my legs aching from the effort, my ears ringing from the endless screams still filling the streets, and my eyes burning from the dark and acrid smoke that had replaced the cool morning fog. Everything that could be burned had been set to flames, and the fire ran unchecked through the city with murderous crusaders at its head shedding blood and pillaging as they released months of pent-up aggression. I shook away the thought of what was happening behind me and instead focused my attention on the church in front of me.

The church was unassuming, little more than a decorated cave in the side of a mountain. I stepped inside, and instantly the din of Antioch fell away. Distant became the shouts of pain and death, the metallic clang of weapons and shields beating together, the horrific cries of innocent men and women. Even the smoke seemed to stop short at the cave's opening. It was as if I'd stepped into another world, one that held only a single goal and purpose: find and kill Temür.

A round window above the door threw a diagonal shaft of orange, dust-filled light onto the floor in front of me, which itself had been decorated with mosaic tiles of red and yellow and green. Four square stone-and-brick pillars rose near the entrance, gentle arcs connecting them to the church's frontage. Six dirty and disheveled bedrolls lay in the center of the church. A low fire burned in their midst, and a dozen or more wooden benches—most of which had been hacked apart to provide the fuel for the fire—surrounded the bedrolls.

Gray stone walls glistened with moisture in the dim light. A stone altar carved with the Greek alpha and omega sat on an elevated dais at the deepest part of the cave. Shadows shrouded a corner to the left of the altar, and it seemed that perhaps the cave led deeper into the mountain through a thin recess there. Beside the altar stood a crumbling wooden pulpit from which the priest would conduct mass. A baptismal font had been cut out of the wall to the altar's right, and two cups and a clamshell sat in a small puddle of surprisingly clear water inside it. Above the altar, in yet another alcove dug into the stone, stood a statue of Saint Peter looking down upon the church that bore his name.

But most importantly, Temür knelt near one of the stone walls and rummaged through an open chest with his single arm. A traveling bag sat beside him, the top open and already overflowing with gear even as he stuffed a handful of dried and crusted bread into the recesses of the bag.

"Temür!"

He jerked upright and spun, fear and panic on his face until he saw that it was me. He wore a mail hauberk and a small skull cap, and his sword hung at his hip.

"*At hırsızı*," he intoned, forcing a smile. "You came. I thought you might, once I saw the beginning of Antioch's end."

"And you wasted no time preparing your retreat."

"Why stay?"

"To fight."

He scoffed. "And be killed defending a burning city? No, thank you." Even as he finished the sentence, the distant scream of a woman in pain echoed dimly through the church. "You hear that? Your Christian thugs are butchering women."

"No worse than you've done."

He smirked. "This is true. Did you at least bury her?"

"Don't talk about Amina," I said through gritted teeth.

"Ahh, Amina. Was that her name?" He frowned in thought, then grinned wide in unrestrained glee. "That's a Turkish name. Your woman was a Turk! It seems you have fine taste. A shame she had to die."

I said nothing, though my heart pounded, thudding in my head like a thunderstorm. I could see her face, feel her touch, and anger bubbled under my skin because I would never again experience either beyond these thin flickers of memory.

Temür read my emotions. "Am I offending you? Do you not like having your loved ones slain?" He looked at my helmet —at *his* helmet—and saw the horse head built into the nose guard. His grin vanished, replaced instead with a crazed scowl. "You wear Safanad on your face, and you *dare* to mourn in my presence?" He shouted this last part, leaning forward and spitting as he yelled, his words bouncing off the hard stone walls of the church and assaulting me from all sides.

I still said nothing.

"I would kill *Amina*," he sneered, "a hundred times over if it would bring back Safanad." He stood tall, brushed a hand down the front of his mail as if to knock off dust. "Shall we do this, *at hırsızı*? You did come all this way for a fight, after all." He scoffed. "And alone, at that."

"I don't need help."

"You've had help in the past."

"I have all the help I need here," I said, resting one hand on *Vindicta*.

"And that?" he asked, nodding toward my shield. "Would you fight a one-arm man with a shield?"

I let it fall from my grip, the iron rim striking the tiled floor and echoing through the stone church like a crack of thunder.

Temür smirked. "And your axe?"

"I don't need it, either."

"Oh, I think you do. I've faced you with a sword before. You do not instill confidence."

I jerked Skull Splitter free and tossed it aside. It clattered against the tile and struck the base of one of the pillars. "Any more requests?"

"Only that we make this quick. It seems I'm running out of time to make good on my escape."

I pulled *Vindicta* free and stepped toward him. "Your death will be anything but quick."

He grinned at that, then slowly drew his sword, the blade scraping along the metal throat of his scabbard and hissing at me as I approached. He took a step over the nearby bedrolls and lowered his sword. I readied a block, but he dragged his blade instead through the fire and flung a cloud of ash and coals at me. I lifted an arm and caught a handful of hot coals in my leather glove. Burning ash rained onto my face and helmet, sending me stumbling backward and momentarily blinded. His sword followed, lancing forward like a striking snake and biting at my left wrist. I yelped, continued to stumble back, and whipped *Vindicta* in a desperate defensive loop in front of me. My blow met only air, and my vision cleared to show Temür standing back and smiling.

"You're slow," Temür said. "Slower than I remember."

Blood ran from a shallow cut at my wrist, wetting the shredded rings of my mail and the fringes of my still-steaming glove. I had little time to examine the wound as he lunged forward once more. Our blades came together like a hammer striking an anvil. I backpedaled, *Vindicta* barely turning aside his scimitar as he struck low and high, stepping into my guard and driving me into a defensive retreat.

"I have but one arm, *at hırsızı*," he taunted, stooping low and swiping at my legs. His blade glanced off the mail at my shin without breaking through, but the impact forced me to a knee. He stepped back and looked at me, still grinning. "You're so slow."

"I thought you wanted this to be quick," I muttered, pushing myself back to my feet. Thick, black smoke rose suddenly beside me as one of the bedrolls caught in the now-scattered fire. Temür spotted it, too, and kicked at another bedroll, sending it tumbling into the growing flames and smoke. I sidestepped the fire and lunged at him, yet he was already moving, turning aside *Vindicta* with relative ease and sending me stumbling forward and up the raised dais. *Vindicta's* tip stabbed the altar with enough force to send a shock of pain up my arm and carve away a chunk of the altar's ancient stone.

Temür followed me up the dais, and I swung a horizontal strike to meet him. He swatted it aside and drove *Vindicta* once more into the altar. The blade clanged against the stone like a dull bell, this time hacking a chip into the sword's edge. I jerked forward and headbutt him with the crown of my helmet, striking him in the nose and sending him falling back from the dais onto the filthy bedrolls, more of which had already begun to catch fire.

He spat blood onto the tile floor before pushing himself back to his feet. I charged down the dais, and our blades clashed together once more. He parried my first attack, back-stepped from my second, then flicked his wrist, and his sword rushed up at my face, where it struck the side of my helmet and knocked it from my head. My ears rang as the helmet clattered to the floor. He lunged forward and struck, and his scimitar skated down my chest, throwing a dozen broken steel rings into the smoky air although the mail held. I stabbed wildly with *Vindicta*, felt the point dig into the armor at his shoulder and shove him backward.

We parted once more, and he glanced at the helmet on the tiled floor. "You do not deserve to wear Safanad," he said, bending and scooping it up. He knocked aside his own steel cap and slipped the helmet on. "You're home, my dear," he muttered.

The fire had leapt to one of the benches, and the flames spread and danced, throwing scattered shadows against the glistening stone walls. Smoke choked the church, growing at the roof like a blackened thundercloud. The once-orange shaft of morning light dulled to gray and dimmed until it was almost imperceptible. Outside, beyond our small world of smoke and fire and anger, came the distant crying of more battle and bloodshed as the raging crusaders continued their slaughter.

"I'm afraid it's time to end this," Temür said. "I'll miss you, *at hırsızı.*"

I drew a raspy breath in the smoky church as he came at me. Our blades clashed together, binding and scraping as he shoved me backward until I stumbled against the pulpit, bending over the decaying wood as our swords ground together between us. His scimitar scraped down my blade and caught on the upswept hilt. I ripped Thief's Prick from the sheath at my boot and threw a desperate slash. The tip of the seax grated against the face of his helmet and slipped between the cheek and nose guards. He howled in pain and staggered back, flinging a ribbon of bright red blood across the front of the stone altar. I wasted no time and lunged forward, stabbing savagely with *Vindicta*. He threw out a hasty parry that somehow caught my sword. The impact sent his scimitar spiraling away, though it drove *Vindicta* tip-first into the floor. The sword punched between the mosaic tile and buried itself halfway into the ground, nothing but a few inches of blade and the hilt sticking up above the tiles.

I froze in surprise. Clearly the floor wasn't stone under the tile. Tightening my grip on the hilt, I tried to rip it free, but Temür was too fast. With his only hand covering his bleeding face, he kicked me in the chest and sent me stumbling backward. I refused to release my grip on my weapon, and with a crack like thunder, *Vindicta* snapped, the hilt and two inches of blade remaining in my hand while the rest of the sword stayed where it was between the tiles. I tumbled through a pair of fire-riddled benches, sending up a plume of ash and cinder that rained down throughout the church like a winter's snowfall.

Amina's blue cloth caught on the burning edges of the bench I'd tumbled through and ripped free of my arm. It caught fire instantly, then a waft of smoke sent it fluttering into the air and slowly burning away until it faded into nothing like a wisp of vapor. I numbly watched it vanish, then stared at the shattered sword in my hand. Hot ash fell all around me, singeing my exposed skin and even setting the pulpit alight, yet I ignored it, too stunned to even move.

"We must continue this another time," Temür shouted over the rising crackle of the flames. I looked up but saw little more than a dim silhouette on the other side of the now-roaring fire. "I'll see you at Jerusalem, *at hırsızı.*"

With that, he was gone, disappearing into the deeper recesses of the cave at the back corner of the church.

And I was left with nothing but a broken sword and a failed attempt at vengeance.

32

The fire raged throughout the small cave church for the rest of the morning, eating through the benches, bedrolls, and pulpit until it finally starved itself out, leaving behind small pockets of simmering orange heat and the lingering vestiges of gray smoke that slowly filtered through the church's entrance and joined the fires still burning throughout the city. I sat in silence and held my broken sword until even the smoke had fully dissipated and the echoing sounds of battle beyond the church dimmed to almost silence. Long shadows slowly stretched over the tiles as the sun began its slow descent to the west and the battle for Antioch waned.

Everything hurt when I finally stood, a combination of the day's fighting and stiffness from sitting on the hard tiles for hours. Gray ash caked my face as I slipped the corpse of *Vindicta* into its scabbard where the last few inches of blade held it in place, and gazed at the rest of the sword still sticking up from the tiled floor.

In the end, Luke's command had won the day; *Vindicta* would never be drawn in battle again.

The axe head of Skull Splitter sat in a pile of ash not far

off, the shaft having burned away with the rest of the furniture turned firewood. I still clutched Thief's Prick in my left hand. I looked at it, saw Temür's crusted blood on the blade, then tossed it into the ash beside Skull Splitter's ruined cadaver before stepping out into the early afternoon sun.

I stood on the slopes of Mount Staurin, and Antioch lay open before me just as it had the night before as I'd waited atop the walls and dreamed of my vengeance. Yet today showed a different view. Though the battle seemed to have ended, small fires still burned unchecked, and thick black smoke clung to the streets and alleyways between blackened husks of buildings. The parts of the city untouched by fire or smoke instead ran red with blood. It stained the walls, formed puddles in parks and courtyards, and flowed through streets that were clogged with great mounds of freshly killed men, women, and children, now piled unceremoniously beside the roads. I recognized the unbearable stench of blood and crap and piss that accompanied the end of every battle, though my senses seemed to have numbed, and I felt nothing.

I staggered down the stone steps of the church and into the mayhem. Posts already lined some streets, the heads of Saracens adorning them. Light whimpering came from an alleyway, and I turned to see a small girl cradling a wooden doll and weeping. Blood smeared her face. She didn't look up at me, only kept crying and clutching the doll, and I turned and continued my slow trek through the ruined city.

Raymond's flag fluttered to the west near a knot of buildings that still stood at the foot of the Bridge Gate, and Bohemond's continued to wave from its place on the eastern wall. The two would fight over the city, but I didn't care. I didn't care about anything in that moment and let my feet take me where they would. I ambled by charred homes, looted shops, and bloated corpses. I shuffled across the path of weeping widows, sobbing parents, and all other manner of mourning souls. Like the girl in the alley, they didn't acknowledge me. Everyone had lived through their own tragedy today except for the exuberant crusaders who continued to pillage what little Antioch had left to give.

I found myself underneath the Saint Paul Gate in the north. Malregard rose dominantly in the east, and the rest of Bohemond's camp spread through the trampled plains before me. I followed the cobblestone road out of the city, dragged my feet as I passed men and women carrying their goods toward Antioch, fleeing Kerbogha's approaching army. Many pulled carts laden with tents and food and supplies, and precious few had wagons pulled by oxen or donkey.

I walked in silence through Bohemond's now-deserted camp, passed tents, extinguished fires, and low fences that once held our horses, all left behind as the people fled to the city. The camp lay barren, empty, abandoned, and it took no time for me to pass completely through it, following the road once more as it led north and away from Antioch.

I came to the church as evening approached, its shadow stretching long and pale over the cemetery beside it. It took no time to find Amina's grave site, and I sat down in the moist grass and rested my aching back against the low tombstone that Father Luke had erected days after we'd buried her. I read its inscription for the first time.

Amina,
Daughter of Asbat
Wife of Daniel
Mother of Novella
Ubi caritas et amor, Deus ibi est.

The tears finally came, running silently down my cheeks as I knelt beside my dead wife. I cried until I could cry no more, releasing weeks of pent-up grief that had been masquerading as anger and vengeance and bitterness. Eventually I slept, curled up like a child beside her gravestone, and in the clear dawn of the next morning I awoke to the beating of drums and a gentle rumbling in the ground beneath me. I looked north and saw the first glimpses of Saracen banners.

Kerbogha had come.

EPILOGUE

EPILOGUE

AD 1115
Jerusalem

Roland sat once more on the stone bench in the Church of the Paralytic. Orange light filtered through the narrow window near the roof, and Sir Daniel once again rested a hand on the hilt of his sword, though he held it calmly now rather than with an iron grip as before.

"What does it mean?" Roland asked.

Sir Daniel drew a long breath before slowly letting it out. "What does what mean?"

"The words on Amina's tombstone."

"Where charity and love are, there God is." He gave a distant smile. "It was her favorite hymn."

Roland swallowed and glanced again at the sword. "I...I thought you said that was Hendry's sword?"

"It is," he said. "Mostly."

Roland squinted at the upswept hilt in the fading light, at the disk pommel with its bronze center. "Mostly?"

"Aye," he said, sweeping the scabbard once more onto his lap. "Mostly."

He drew the sword, and Roland's eyes widened as he saw the mottled steel of the blade, the two grays mingling together like poorly mixed wine.

"Is that…"

"Aye," he said again. "I had Hendry's hilt fastened to Bohemond's blade, though that's a tale for tomorrow." He slammed the sword back into its home, the thud of the cross guard hitting the steel throat of the scabbard echoing through the narrow corridor.

They stepped from the church and into the fading light of dusk where Roland spotted three knights coming down the path and clearly walking toward them. They wore blood-red surcoats, and their pivoting heads told Roland they searched for something. Or someone.

He glanced at Sir Daniel, who seemed to also be studying the three knights.

"Do you know them?" Roland asked.

Sir Daniel gave a curt nod. "Aye," he answered. "And I know their colors."

"Should we be worried?"

He drew a breath and didn't answer right away, instead waiting until the three knights spotted them and their gait took on a new purpose. "Maybe." A pause. "You still want to be me squire, lad?"

"Of course," Roland said. He suddenly wished he'd brought his shield with him, though he didn't know what he would do against three knights with only a shield and no training. Thankfully, they stopped short of Sir Daniel without any sign of aggression. One of the knights stepped forward, and he and Sir Daniel met one another's gaze. Neither reacted; neither moved. They stared at one another with steely determination, with stoic resolve. After the span of several minutes, the knight broke first, smiling and stepping forward as the two men embraced.

"God's bones," the knight said once they finally separated. "How long has it been?"

"Too long, lad," Sir Daniel with a rare smile. "Far, far too long, though I fear you don't bring good news."

The knight frowned. "I don't. Roger requests your presence."

"When?"

"As soon as possible. Muslims are marching as we speak."

"Muslims are always marching, just as we seem to always be."

The knight tensed. "Lord Bohemond knighted you," he said. "Knighted *us*."

"Bohemond's dead," Sir Daniel pointed out.

"His son isn't. Fleeing to Jerusalem hasn't freed you from his service."

Sir Daniel scoffed. "I didn't flee to Jerusalem," he said. "I followed the crusade. It isn't my fault Bohemond didn't."

"I—"

"Simmer down, Elric," Sir Daniel said. "You know I'll go."

Elric? Roland looked once more at the knight, then at Sir Daniel. "Elric?" he blurted out. "Is this—"

"Aye, lad," Sir Daniel cut him off. "The one and only."

Elric smirked, the tension gone as quickly as it had come. "You've been talking about me?" He looked at Roland. "To who?"

"Me squire."

Roland stood taller at the title, but that only drew a laugh from Elric. "Your squire? I thought you hated squires."

"I do," Sir Daniel said, and Roland felt some of the air go out of him. "Lad's an exception."

"Since when?"

He looked down at Roland. "Been, what, three days now?"

Roland nodded, and Elric barked a laugh. "Three days?! And you're bringing the boy with you?"

"I'm not a boy," Roland muttered.

"Yes, you are," Sir Daniel said. "And aye, I'm bringing the lad."

He laughed again. "Very well. Your squire, your choice. I'm going to find me a good tavern."

And with that, Elric and the other two knights left, leaving Sir Daniel and Roland standing at the entrance to the church.

"Who's Roger?" Roland asked.

"Regent of the Principality of Antioch."

"Are we going to Antioch?"

"Unless you got somewhere else to be."

Roland swallowed. "No."

"Good," Sir Daniel said. "I suppose we should find you a weapon."

HISTORICAL NOTE

When writing historical fiction, there is a balance that must be struck between telling an original story and fitting that story into the framework of existing historical events. As always, I have tried very hard to remain true to history, yet this is a work a fiction and I had a story to tell.

One example of an attempt at accuracy involved the battle with Duqaq during the crusaders' December 1097 foraging run. Duqaq indeed caught them unawares, killed much of the infantry, and most of the mounted knights were able to escape. Due to an exceptionally rainy season that winter, Duqaq then elected to count his losses—small as they were—and return home.

Another striking case of history being more interesting than fiction was Bohemond's charge against Ridwan of Aleppo. While sources vary as to the exact numbers, the crusaders used an army of mounted knights numbering under a thousand with seven hundred being the most common mentioned. Ridwan's army was also accurately represented in this book. The cavalry charge is indeed a terrible thing.

Firuz was an interesting character. For someone who

played so important a role in the crusaders' sacking of Antioch, there is precious little information about him. Aside from his name and the fact that he controlled several southern towers, much of him was made up for this book. Bruno is another historical figure for which I could find only sparse information, so much of his behavior and actions are a product of my own imagination.

An interesting note, however, was the falling of the oxhide ladder just after Daniel finished his ascent during the assault of Antioch. The ladder indeed fell, and the strong winds that night blocked much of the sound so that the assault could continue undetected.

Additionally, some of the dates have been stretched or embellished to make my story fit, though these changes were typically of an insignificant amount. Finally, it is up for debate as to whether the crusaders commissioned the ships that arrived at Saint Simeon for the construction of Raymond's fort in front of the Bridge Gate. I chose to lean toward the crusaders' foresight, though the ships' arrival could very well have been chance.

In the end, this is a fictional novel based on real events. Some stretching of the truth was necessary, but, as always, I made every attempt to stick with history where able.

ACKNOWLEDGMENTS

There are far too many names to mention in order to acknowledge the many people who have helped me get to this point. First thanks should always go to God, whose Word and presence have gotten me through more than I care to admit. He also brought me my wife, Jessica, who has spent endless hours allowing me to talk at her about my imaginary characters and plots and worlds. She suffers much in being my wife, and I am better for it.

Though it pained me to end his life, Sir Hendry of Scotia is still a Scottish version of my own father, who is thankfully still kicking around (and hopefully for quite a long time still). Thanks, old man. I hope you still liked Hendry.

A special thank you to my editor, Alison Imbriaco, and my cover designer, Betty Martinez. As always, Alison's critical eye and amazing attention to detail make me appear better than I am. I have to say, Betty, this is easily my favorite cover.

As a work of Historical Fiction, there was a great deal of research that went into the creation of this book. Just as with Storm of War and Dorylaeum, the two most helpful resources were *The First Crusade: A New History*, by Dr. Thomas Asbridge; and *The Medieval Warrior: Weapons, Technology, and Fighting Techniques, AD 1000-1500*, by Martin Dougherty. Dr. Asbridge's vivid and detailed recounting of the events of the first crusade were not only an excellent outline, but his many references to first-hand accounts were a constant inspiration for my own work. Dougherty's book was filled with helpful illustrations and detailed descriptions of the weapons and fighting techniques pertinent to my timeframe, which ensured I remained as close to accurate as possible. Additionally, translations of ancient Greek and Latin works such as *The Alexiad*, *The Gesta Tancredi*, and *The Gesta Francorum* have provided some exciting first- and second-hand accounts.

Being a self-published work, I feel a need to express gratitude to the many services made available that helped bring you the product you currently hold. While I will not list them by name, I hope fellow writers looking to self-publish their work will find encouragement to pursue their dream.

EXCERPT FROM THE
SHEPHERD AND THE KING

DAVID

Forty-two, forty-three, forty-four...

David frowned when he didn't see the forty-fifth sheep and began counting over, hoping he'd made a mistake the first three times. Another minute proved the only mistake he'd made was losing a sheep. His eyes drifted to his father's house on the low hill at the edge of the sheep pastures. The late-afternoon sun was close to the horizon behind it, bathing the small home and green grass in soft, orange light. He felt a looming sense of dread. He had little desire to be around his family in the first place—it was why he had practically begged to be a shepherd, to be out in the fields and away from them. Now he had to tell his father that he'd failed his first day alone with the sheep.

He's going to kill me...

He gave a low sigh of defeat and walked across the fields toward the house, dragging his feet as he went. His father— Jesse—and two of his seven older brothers were behind the house. Eliab and Abinadab were sparring while his father stood to the side, arms crossed as he watched their every move with critical eyes. Already these two had been to war with the new king, fighting against the Amalekites. While he was jealous of their success—and more importantly, the attention they received from their father—battle wasn't something he was built for. He was smaller than his brothers, almost laughably so. Rather than interrupt their training, he stood and absentmindedly played with the sling on his belt, the only weapon he was permitted to use.

"It is all you will need to protect the sheep," his father had said.

And a fine job he'd done.

He knew how his father would look at him, with that mixture of shame and disappointment he'd become accustomed to. He leaned against the side of the home, hiding in the shadow and keeping his eyes on the ground as he listened to his brothers' sparring. As the mock battle wore on, he found himself fidgeting, rubbing his now-sweaty hands together as he waited for his father to notice him.

"What do you want, runt?"

David's head jerked up. Eliab was standing over a fallen Abinadab. "I'm not a runt," he said, though the words sounded weak even to his ears. *Better to have said nothing.*

His brother laughed and stepped up to him. David stood barely to Eliab's barrel of a chest, and he had to crane his neck to keep eye contact. "Is that so?"

Jesse stepped between them. "That's enough." Eliab smirked and turned away. His broad frame knocked David back a step. "What do you want, David?"

The annoyance in his father's voice was thick. Jesse didn't even know he had lost the sheep, and already he was unwelcome. "I"—he swallowed hard—"One of the sheep has wandered off."

Eliab laughed and looked at their father. "I told you he couldn't do it."

He met his brother's judging eyes, searching for and failing to find something to respond with. David had never been quick with words.

His father sighed, the annoyance mixed now with disappointment as he made the face David had known would come. "You said you could do it. You begged."

He couldn't take his father's expression and returned his gaze to the ground. "I'm sorry."

"Do you know when?"

"I last counted them at midday. They were all there."

"Midday?! It's nearly sundown." His father let out a long sigh and seemed to think. "I told you to count them on the hours. I should have left Ozem with you."

David flinched at the words. *He is barely a year older than me.* "Let me go and find it."

"It's nearly sundown," Jesse repeated. "It's too late to go wandering into the woods."

Eliab scoffed. "If the runt is afraid of the dark, it is."

David glared at him, though he said nothing. He turned back to his father. "Let me go. I'll find it."

His father looked down at him with one part pity and three parts doubt. "I don't know. The forest is——"

"I can do it."

"Let him," Eliab said. "He may prove himself a good shepherd if nothing else. And besides," he added with a grin, "you've got seven more sons."

His father gave Eliab an unhappy look but said nothing to him. He thought for another moment and then looked at David. "Be safe. Your mother will kill me if something happens to you."

Wouldn't want mother mad at you. David turned and left, not wanting to be among his family any longer than he had to. He stomped down the hill, by the sheep, and to the small stable at the opposite end of the fields where he kept his shepherding supplies. After packing a quick meal—it could take all night to find the lost sheep—he grabbed his shepherd's staff and made one final stop at the small creek that edged the fields. Here he ducked down and splashed some of the cool water on his face to try to clear his mind. For a moment, all was silent.

As the ripples faded, he saw the creek bed and the smooth stones he'd come for. The still water reflected a sky turning black above him. A few stars had already twinkled to life. Yet all he saw was a young shepherd, a scared boy.

Nothing more.

He sighed and dug through the creek for the stones. He found some about the size of his palm and stuffed them into the small pouch at his side, counting to be sure he had five. He hoisted his pack and set off into the woods, searching for a trail to follow.

David crested the small hill and stepped from the edge of the trees. Below him were rolling pastures that dipped into a low valley. The sky burned with the breaking dawn, fiery yellows and reds lighting the green grass. He saw the forest of cypress and oak resume in the distance. Even the brilliant morning sun could not penetrate the thick canopy of branches, leaving the forest covered in shadow.

He was beginning to have his doubts. It hadn't taken him long to find the sheep's rambling trail as it crushed its way through the dense foliage and underbrush of the forest. Here, however, at the relatively brush-free valley, it seemed to end. His eyes searched the valley—though now with little hope.

For a moment, he thought of turning back, of forsaking the sheep, of letting it wander lost in the forest. Yet he knew he could not. It was alone in the woods because of him, in danger because of him. He'd been entrusted with his father's sheep. Regardless of how he felt about his father—or how his father felt about him—David was a shepherd. It was his job to protect the sheep.

And it is not my sheep to lose.

David hefted his pack more securely onto his shoulder. He put his hand into the small pouch on his belt and felt the five smooth stones he'd gathered for his sling. Taking a quick drink from his skin, he gripped his staff and began the walk down into the valley.

It was still early morning when he finished his search of the valley. He'd found seven rabbits, three of which he'd killed with his sling and now hung from his pack, the used stones safely back in his pouch. He'd found an anthill that rose to his knees. He'd found the dung of a lion, an antelope that fled at the sight of him, and a flock of ibis, yet he'd found no signs of his father's sheep. No recently trampled grass, no feeding grounds, no prints.

David looked at the forest on the far side of the valley and the line of trees marking the pasture's end. He let out a low sigh and walked toward them. Perhaps the animal had wandered back into the forest. He stooped and began his search once he reached the trees. He dragged his hands through the dirt, spread the low shrubbery aside to examine the ground beneath, searched through the tall grass for signs the sheep had stopped to eat.

At least I am in the shade.

There.

He stopped and touched the blade of grass that had caught his eye. It was broken, split into two ends. Rough.

Chewed.

After another cursory search, he found a handful of blades that looked the same. The sheep was heading east, farther into the forest and farther from his father's home.

Of course it is.

He rechecked his pack, then set off into the woods,

following the now obvious trail left behind. The sheep seemed to be wandering without direction into the forest. It had trampled the foliage with such carelessness that it must have finally decided it wanted David to find it.

And then he saw it, standing and chewing absently at a small patch of grass. It paused and looked up at David, almost as if it had been expecting him.

"You've been a headache," he said. "You know that?"

The sheep bleated and then went back to its meal.

"Go ahead and eat," he said, walking toward the animal. "I'll make sure you're our next sacrifice."

There was movement in the trees behind the sheep and then a flash of brown and yellow and red fur. The sheep disappeared under the weight of a lion, its nonchalant bleating becoming a desperate scream of pain. David's sling was in his hand before he had time to think. He had a stone loaded and flying—*load, swing, aim, throw*—before he'd taken his first step. It bounced off the lion's back with enough force to push the beast off its new meal. It paused, seemed to evaluate the new threat, then rose and faced David.

He froze as the beast stared at him with evil eyes, the sheep's blood dripping staining its matted mane. For a moment, they stared at one another, a challenge hanging in the air.

Turn around…go home…it is only a sheep.

Yet, again, he knew he could not.

It is not my sheep to lose.

David moved slowly, reaching to his sack for another stone. The lion sprang forward at the movement, and David snapped into motion, his muscles working from memory: *load, swing, aim*—must be perfect this time—*throw*. The stone hurtled through the air and bounced off the lion's skull, ricocheting into the woods. The beast barely faltered. For a moment that lasted forever, David knew he was going to die. Then the lion's feet went limp, its momentum carrying it another few paces. In a flurry of fur and dirt and grass, the beast skidded to a halt a step from David.

I just killed a lion.

He let out a breath he hadn't realized he was holding. His white-knuckled hand slowly opened, and he put the sling back on his belt. He stepped around the fallen lion on shaking legs—giving the dead animal plenty of space—and then ran to the sheep.

There was a large gash in the sheep's leg, but the wound didn't look mortal. It was still bleating for its life, a healthy leg kicking at nothing as it lay on the dirt.

"You'll live."

David slipped his pack from his shoulders, dug through it for something to use as a bandage, and found the cloth he'd wrapped his own food in. Setting his pack aside, he went to work bandaging the sheep's wounded leg.

"You've ruined my day; you know that."

The sheep bleated as if in response.

"I suppose that—"

There was a roar, and David felt a mass slam into him. He tumbled away from the bleating sheep and found himself on his back, face to face with a bloodied and angry lion. He froze, his muscles refusing to move. The beast stood over him and let out a roar so concussive it knocked David back, and his head slammed into the dirt hard enough to leave a divot in the ground. Blood and saliva rained down on him. The lion went quiet, teeth bared, a low rumbling growl still rolling from its throat like thunder. Hot, sticky breath filled his face. David could see the open wound just above the lion's left eye from his previous shot and the blood running down into the beast's face.

Its jaw opened a moment before it struck; David felt paralyzed. For the second time within the span of a few minutes, he was sure he was going to die. Then he felt his arm move. It shot up of its own accord and seized the animal by the mane, halting its teeth only a finger's width from his face. He felt his muscles tense all the way down to his shoulder, an otherworldly strength filling his arm and holding the lion in place.

The movement unfroze David, and he reached into the pouch at his side with his free hand. He scooped up the three remaining stones and bashed the lion along the head, aiming for the existing wound. The beast roared in pain and lurched back, its mane ripping and tearing. Yet David's hand held firm. He struck it again and again, blood splattering his face and chest as the lion roared and jerked. Finally, the animal went silent and collapsed on top of him. Foamy blood leaked from his open jaws as the animal exhaled for the final time.

David wiggled free of the beast and stood.

I just killed a lion…again.

He looked at his hand; a lock of the lion's mane was still clutched in his throbbing fingers. His entire arm buzzed with strength not his own. He felt it aching, throbbing with unseen power and energy. Then it was gone. He felt faint and swayed on his feet before he steadied himself.

What was that?

The beast lay defeated and bleeding in the grass. David's entire torso and the side of his face were covered in the animal's blood. His gaze drifted to the sheep, bleating and still kicking its good leg out at nothing.

And then he heard a voice in his head. It was as clear as his own thoughts, and though he would at times ignore it, it was a voice he would hear for the rest of his days.

It was not your sheep to lose. But it was yours to save.

ALSO BY BRYAN R SAYE

THE KINGS OF ISRAEL

The Shepherd and the King
The Rise of David

THE CRUSADERS CHRONICLES

Storm of War
Dorylaeum
Shadows of Antioch

DID YOU ENJOY THIS BOOK?

Your feedback helps me provide the best quality books and helps other readers like you discover great books.

It would mean the world to me if you took 2 minutes to share your thoughts about this book. You can leave a review with amazon at the link below. Also, if you like, you can send me an email with your honest feedback.

https://www.amazon.com/review/create-review?&asin=B096FYKS2B

ABOUT THE AUTHOR

Who is this guy?

Bryan currently lives in Idaho with his wonderful wife and two amazing children. He's a happy follower of Jesus, a proud member of the United States Air Force, and an often disappointed but always dedicated fan of the Jacksonville Jaguars (This is our year!).

He started his writing career late in life (if you consider almost 40 late), mostly because his little buggers wanted to eat everyday and have health insurance. His daughter says he can't talk without teaching (and no, he's not a teacher). According to his son, if you want to know anything else then you'll just have to meet him (come to Idaho, it's not that cold).

What does he write?

By drawing on real events and stories from history, Bryan writes quality fiction with powerful character arcs that display and encourage real change. Though always reflecting a Catholic worldview, he strives to write fiction that is accessible and relatable to people from all faiths and cultures that excludes no one.

For further information and updates, visit www.bryanr saye.com, or follow the social media links below.

f facebook.com/BryanRSaye

a amazon.com/~/e/B08Z3QHJWG

Made in the USA
Columbia, SC
29 June 2025